HAMMER OF DAEMONS

WHEN THE FORCES of the Imperium suffer a crushing defeat by Chaos, Grey Knight Alaric is captured and taken back to Sarthis Majoris, a daemon world in the Eye of Terror. Stripped of his armour and weapons, he is forced to fight as a gladiator for his daemonic masters, who worship their god Khorne with endless slaughter. His only chance of escape is to find the Hammer of Daemons, a legendary weapon with the power to destroy the forces of Chaos. As Alaric is forced to fight more and more dangerous opponents, he must not only triumph in combat, but work out a way to escape, for even a Grey Knight cannot resist the dark powers of corruption forever.

The third novel in the best-selling Grey Knights series, by Ben Counter.

A WARHAMMER 40,000 NOVEL

HAMMER OF DAEMONS

Ben Counter

A BLACK LIBRARY PUBLICATION

First published in Great Britain in 2008 by
BL Publishing,
Games Workshop Ltd.,
Willow Road, Nottingham,
NG7 2WS, UK.

10 9 8 7 6 5 4 3 2 1

Cover illustration by Clint Langley.

A CIP record for this book is available from the British Library.

ISBN 13: 978 1 84416 511 7
ISBN 10: 1 84416 511 6

Distributed in the US by Simon & Schuster
1230 Avenue of the Americas, New York, NY 10020, US.

See the Black Library on the Internet at
www.blacklibrary.com

Find out more about Games Workshop
and the world of Warhammer 40,000 at
www.games-workshop.com

IT IS THE 41st millennium. For more than a hundred centuries the Emperor has sat immobile on the Golden Throne of Earth. He is the master of mankind by the will of the gods, and master of a million worlds by the might of his inexhaustible armies. He is a rotting carcass writhing invisibly with power from the Dark Age of Technology. He is the Carrion Lord of the Imperium for whom a thousand souls are sacrificed every day, so that he may never truly die.

YET EVEN IN his deathless state, the Emperor continues his eternal vigilance. Mighty battlefleets cross the daemon-infested miasma of the warp, the only route between distant stars, their way lit by the Astronomican, the psychic manifestation of the Emperor's will. Vast armies give battle in His name on uncounted worlds. Greatest amongst his soldiers are the Adeptus Astartes, the Space Marines, bio-engineered super-warriors. Their comrades in arms are legion: the Imperial Guard and countless planetary defence forces, the ever-vigilant Inquisition and the tech-priests of the Adeptus Mechanicus to name only a few. But for all their multitudes, they are barely enough to hold off the ever-present threat from aliens, heretics, mutants – and worse.

TO BE A man in such times is to be one amongst untold billions. It is to live in the cruellest and most bloody regime imaginable. These are the tales of those times. Forget the power of technology and science, for so much has been forgotten, never to be re-learned. Forget the promise of progress and understanding, for in the grim dark future there is only war. There is no peace amongst the stars, only an eternity of carnage and slaughter, and the laughter of thirsting gods.

ONE

THE FLOOR AND walls of the medicae bunker were painted dark green, so the blood just looked like dark water pooling under the beds.

'He's at the back,' said the medicae orderly. Her face was grey with fatigue, but her eyes were alert.

'Then let's hurry,' said Colonel Dal'Tharken.

The medicae led the colonel between the rows of beds, each with its wounded man lolling semi-conscious with sedation, or grimacing as an orderly bent over his wounds. Some of them managed to nod or even salute to the colonel as he walked by, and he returned their greetings with a moment of eye contact. Most of the conscious ones, though, were focused on the man who followed the colonel. He was huge, and armoured in gunmetal, something the Hathrans had never seen before they had come to this world. Indeed, he was someone very few of them had ever seen up close. He seemed to take up what little room remained in the bunker.

'Three came in,' the medicae continued, casting a curious glance at the armoured figure behind the colonel. 'One made it. We had to burn the others.' Her manner was short and efficient, as if all her compassion had been drained away.

Colonel Dal'Tharken didn't have to ask how the survivor was doing. At the back of the bunker there was a row of beds with mesh insect nets, useless in the arctic climate of Sarthis Majoris, but enough to create a barrier between the recovering and the most severely wounded men, the ones who hadn't realised they were dead, and the sights of suffering around them. The patrol's survivor was going to die, and soon.

'If it matters, he's in no condition to talk,' continued the medicae.

'Is he conscious?'

'In and out.'

'That'll do.'

The medicae pulled back the netting from a bed at the back of the bunker. The smell of burnt meat and hair welled up from the bed.

'Arse on the Golden Throne,' swore the trooper who lay there. 'I must really be in trouble.'

'Trooper Slohane?'

'Yes, sir.'

'Officer present.'

'Sorry, sir. Can't salute.'

Trooper Slohane was missing most of his lower jaw. It had been replaced with a temporary prosthetic that was just mobile enough to allow him to talk. The face on the damaged side was raw meat. A wad of bandage was taped over the ruins of one eye. The jacket of his fatigues had been cut away and a wound swallowed up most of his chest. A transparent slab of gel-skin lay over the wound to staunch the bleeding, but the injury was far too severe for Slohane to be saved. There was so much blood on the floor and soaked into the bed that blood loss would get him even if his organs held out.

Slohane's eye focused on the shape towering over the colonel. For a moment, he didn't seem to focus, as if the figure was too big to fit within the confines of the bunker.

Slohane smiled with what remained of his mouth. 'You. Heh, I never thought I'd actually get to be face to face with one of you: a Space Marine. When… when I was a child I thought you were just a story.'

Justicar Alaric stepped forward. In full power armour he was almost twice the height of a man. His armour was ornate steel adorned with devotional texts picked out in gold, and one massive shoulder pad bore the heraldry of a black and red field with a single starburst. The symbol of a book pierced by a silver sword adorned the other shoulder. Alaric wore no helmet, and his face seemed too human for the size and ornamentation of his armour, even with his scars and the service stud in his forehead. He had a halberd in his hand, long enough to scrape the bunker ceiling, and on the back of his other hand was mounted a double-barrelled storm bolter.

'No stories,' said Alaric simply. 'We are here for the same reason you are. This is a world worth saving.'

'What did you see, trooper?' asked the colonel.

Slohane arched back and coughed. The wet mass of his lungs was visible through the ruin of his chest. 'Six of us went out. The captain said we were heading… heading through the southern route to get to the foothills before nightfall. Avalanche must've come down the day before, because the route was blocked, so we skirted up along Pale Ridge.' Slohane looked at the colonel. 'We should've turned back.'

The medicae picked up a handful of the printout that had spooled out of a monitoring cogitator. She gave the colonel a meaningful glance. The irregular life signs on the printout meant Slohane didn't have long.

'Go on, trooper,' said the colonel.

'Things started… coming out of the ground,' said Slohane. He was looking up at the ceiling. There was too much in his mind's eye to let him focus on anything real. 'Hands, and faces. They started screaming. And there was fire. The captain died. We had to let him go. He was melting into the ground. Tollen went crazy and started shooting. I just ran, sir. I ran away.'

'And then?'

'I was heading up the ridge. I was on fire, I think. These dark things were coming up through the snow. I got to the top of the ridge and kept firing. The damn lasgun was red-hot. I ran back along the ridge away from it all. I just looked back once.'

Alaric knelt down beside the colonel, so he was the height of a normal man. 'What did you see?'

Slohane's eye rolled around. Tears welled up. 'There were millions of them,' he said, 'millions, all standing on the other side of Pale Ridge.'

'Men?' asked Alaric.

'Men,' said Slohane, 'and things. Huge things. Monsters, waiting there like animals on the slaughterman's ramp. Then the clouds blew by and stars came out, and the whole valley was covered in blood. The mountain streams had thawed and they were blood, too. I could hear them chanting. It wasn't no language like a man might speak. It was words straight from the warp.'

'What about artillery?' asked the colonel. 'Armour?'

'I don't know,' replied Slohane, 'but there were monsters in the air, too, with wings. And a tower... lit up in red... and him up on the battlements, like a king.'

'Who?' asked Alaric urgently, leaning down so his face was close to Slohane's. 'Who did you see?'

Slohane tried to reply but his words came out as a painful gasp. A tear of blood ran from his remaining eye. The medicae dropped the printout and fiddled with the controls on the monitor.

'He's unconscious,' she said. 'He's losing blood faster than we can pump it in. You won't get any more from him.'

'Pale Ridge,' said Colonel Dal'Tharken. 'Right under our bloody noses.'

'We knew it would come to this,' said Alaric.'

'That we did.' The colonel turned to the medicae and pointed to Slohane's convulsing body. 'Burn him, too.'

'Of course,' she replied.

ALARIC MET UP with his squad on the fortifications above the medical bunker. The night had been even colder than usual, and cloaks of ice clung to the rockcrete battlements. Wisps of vapour rose from the pillboxes and weapon points, from the breath of the Hathran Guardsmen huddled beneath their greatcoats. The Grey Knights were standing watch at the right of the line, where the medical bunker met the ice wall of the mountainside. The rest of the line stretched across the pass, manned by the Hathran soldiers who still stole half-fearful glances at the Grey Knights. None of them knew what a Grey Knight was, but they had all heard of the Space Marines, humanity's saviours, the greatest soldiers in the galaxy. A Space Marine was a symbol of the Imperium, a reminder of what they fought for.

'What news, Justicar?' asked Brother Haulvarn as Alaric trudged through the slush of the night's ice-fall.

'It's coming to an end,' replied Alaric.

'Good,' grunted Brother Dvorn. Dvorn, along with Haulvarn, had fought with Alaric since he had first been elevated to the rank of justicar. Where Haulvarn was a born leader, Dvorn was a pure warrior. His nemesis weapon was in the form of a hammer, a rare weapon that perfectly suited Dvorn's brutality. Alaric was glad to have both of them at his side on Sarthis Majoris. If Trooper Slohane's testimony had any truth in it, he would need them soon.

'Do we know what we're facing?' asked Brother Visical.

'Not yet,' said Alaric.

'Looking forward to finding out,' said Dvorn.

'Don't be too eager,' replied Alaric. 'It's bad. The enemy must have been gathering strength since we made landfall. They're massing past Pale Ridge right now. The colonel is mobilising every able-bodied man as we speak. And it'll happen soon. The enemy can't keep a force like that in check for long.'

'Will the line hold?' asked Brother Thane. Thane and Visical had been drafted into Alaric's squad after the losses it had suffered on Chaeroneia.

'That's not for me to say,' said Alaric gravely. 'The Hathrans will decide that. We must show them how the enemy must be resisted, and help lead them in their prayers. After that the battle will fall on them.'

'Not if we get there first,' said Visical with a smirk. While Thane had only recently earned the armour of a Grey Knight, Visical was a veteran. The gauntlets of his power armour were permanently blackened by the flame from his incinerator, in spite of the wargear rites supposed to keep them spotless. 'We'll show them how it's done.'

Dvorn nodded in agreement. Some men just fought like that, Alaric had decided; they simply threw aside all concept of failure and trusted in their training and determination to carry them through. They were, after all, Grey Knights, some of the Imperium's best soldiers, but Alaric could not think that way.

'Thane, lead the prayers,' said Alaric. 'Our bodies are prepared, so ensure that our souls are the same.'

A sound reached Alaric's ears. The voices of the Imperial Guard, low and mournful, rose as one in the death song of Hathran.

FATE HAD SEEN fit to place Sarthis Majoris in the path of the most terrible Chaos incursion since the ancient days of the Horus Heresy. The Thirteenth Black Crusade had erupted from the warp storm known as the Eye of Terror, led by the greatest champions of the Chaos Gods. The initial campaigns had seen Cadia besieged and whole Imperial armies annihilated as they tried to stem the tide. Only the sacrifices of the Imperial Navy had kept the Black Crusade from reaching the Segmentum Solar itself. The Inquisition had made appalling decisions that not even a hard-bitten Guard general would stomach: bombing Guard regiments into dust for witnessing the predations of the Enemy, sacrificing whole worlds to slow down the Chaos hordes, betraying Emperor-fearing citizens at every turn to buy tiny slivers of hope. The whole galactic north was mobilised to barricade the Imperial heartland against the Black Crusade.

Chaos brought with it daemons. The Ordo Malleus, the most secretive and warlike branch of the Inquisition, had sent unprecedented resources to the Eye of Terror. Whole companies of Grey Knights had been thrown into the cauldron of the Eye. The Eye of Terror drew in the Imperium's daemon hunters, and more often than not it spat them out mutilated, mad or dead. Yet still they fought, because that was what it meant to be human: to fight when any sane man would say the fight could not be won.

Sarthis Majoris supplied fuel to the Imperial Navy. Its refineries turned the radioactive sludge in the planet's mantle into the lifeblood of the Segmentum battlefleet. Maybe that was why a fleet of Chaos ships, ancient things shaped like filth encrusted daggers, was diverted to invade Sarthis Majoris. Or perhaps the millions of colonists huddled in the refinery cities were simply too tempting a sacrifice to the Dark Gods. Either way, if Chaos took Sarthis Majoris, the engines of Imperial battleships would fall silent, and dozens more Chaos ships would break through the Imperial blockades.

The Hathran Armoured Cavalry were close enough to be landed on Sarthis Majoris shortly after the Chaos forces made landfall on the southern polar cap. The hurried strategic meetings confirmed that the Chaos army's northwards march would have to take them through the ice-bound pass in the towering Reliqus Mountains. Once through the mountains, there was no telling which refinery city would be sacrificed first. So the pass had to hold, and the Hathran Armoured Cavalry had to hold it.

Imperial commanders requested assistance from any quarter to help deliver Sarthis Majoris from the enemy. The Ordo Malleus heard these requests and performed astropathic divinations that confirmed the presence of daemons among the hordes landing on the planet. In a perfect galaxy they would have sent armies of Space Marines and storm troopers led by daemon hunters to crush the Chaos forces on the polar cap, but the galaxy was far from perfect, and those legions and inquisitors were spread across a thousand worlds threatened by the Black Crusade.

The Inquisition's contribution to the defence of Sarthis Majoris consisted of Justicar Alaric and four Grey Knights.

TWO

'Movement!' cried one of the sentries. 'Two kilometres! West face!'

The Hathrans stationed on the wall hurried to their posts, peering into the breaking dawn light. It was running down the sides of the valleys in a thin, greasy film, turning the ice of the peaks far above an angry gold. The depths of the valley stretching southwards were still veiled in the dying night's darkness.

'I see them,' said one of the officers commanding the watch. He pulled magnoculars from his greatcoat and looked through them down the valley. Shapes were moving in the darkness, scrabbling along the side of the mountain. A human couldn't climb like that, especially one almost naked, clad only in its own flayed skin.

'Is it the big one?' asked another Guardsman, a support gunner, leaning forward on the barrel of his fixed autocannon.

'Might be just another sacrifice,' said yet another. Most of the Guardsmen believed that the Chaos attacks, up to that point, had been deliberately mounted to sacrifice cultists and mutants beneath the Imperial guns, to seed the valley with blood and please the Chaos Gods. A few, more prosaically, thought the enemy was just trying to use up the Hathrans' ammunition, but everyone was certain that an attack was coming, after the rumours had spread that a vast Chaos horde, millions strong, was pooling behind Pale Ridge.

'Guns up! Men to your stations!' cried the officer. Sirens sounded as Guardsmen swarmed up onto the battlements. The few who were sleeping jumped from their beds and were still pulling their scarves around their faces as they emerged into the freezing dawn. Their breath formed heavy clouds rolling between the battlements.

The attacks had come nightly. The enemy had thrown handfuls of men at them. It was simpler to call them men. The officers called them 'cultists', a useful catch-all for the mutated, heretic and insane that made up the bulk of the Chaos army. Their bodies, frozen solid, were dark red smudges below the latest snowfalls. Some of them had been robed madmen who chanted in inhuman tongues. Others were scrabbling things that had presumably been human before their skins were removed and nailed back onto their wet, red bodies in scraps. Some of those had made it onto the walls, and most of the Hathran wounded in the medicae bunker, or in the grim frozen heap of bodies on the fortification's northern side, were the result of those leaping, screaming creatures.

Sometimes red lightning had struck from the heavens, searing men to charred meat. Sometimes soldiers had gone mad and killed their brother soldiers, and no one could tell if it was some sorcery of the enemy or old-fashioned battle psychosis. Many of the patrols sent out to locate the enemy had not returned, or had crawled back burned, mutilated or mad. The enemy wanted the Hathran line bruised and tender, its teeth ground down, its men exhausted and its guns well-worn.

There had been enough petty death. The gods wanted a spectacle.

'You there!' yelled Colonel Dal'Tharken at the closest officer, as he stormed out of the command bunker. 'Get some men into that firepoint! And get the engineers up on the battle cannon. The damn things jam every three rounds.' Guardsmen were scrambling to their posts, including the tanks iced in at the ends of the line. The Hathrans were an armoured regiment, but the fuel had frozen in the engines of their Leman Russ battle tanks and those that still worked were dug into the ice to be used as fixed gun points.

'Colonel,' said Alaric as he pushed his way through the soldiers now thronging up onto the battlements. 'Where do you need us?'

'Hold the right,' said the colonel. In truth he had no right to give orders to the Grey Knights, attached as they were to the Inquisition, but protocol was less important here than the battle plan. 'If they get explosives between the medical bunker and the valley wall they can blast a breach. That's what you have to stop.' The colonel's features softened for a second. The man underneath the soldier showed through for a moment. 'Good luck, Justicar,' he said. Colonel Dal'Tharken, alone among the Hathrans, had some understanding of what the Grey Knights really were and why they had been sent to Sarthis Majoris.

'The Emperor is with us,' replied Alaric, and turned to join his men.

The Grey Knights were already in position. The medical bunker on the extreme right of the line was crowned with battlements like the jawbone of a stone-toothed dragon, but it was still the line's weak point. The enemy would pool here, forced wide by the crossfires of Hathran guns, and sooner or later a cultist would throw a demo charge or a bundle of grenades into just the right place to shatter the ice and blast a gap wide enough for men to pour through. Then the line would be surrounded and everyone defending it would die.

Except, the Grey Knights were there. As far as the Hathrans were concerned, nothing could destroy them as long as there were Space Marines still alive to fight.

'It's not another sacrifice,' said Brother Visical. 'They're holding back.'

'Not for long,' said Alaric. 'The enemy isn't that patient. They'll hit us here and now.'

'Justicar,' said Thane, 'it's the Blood God, isn't it?'

Alaric glanced around at the youngest Grey Knight. Thane was right. The symbols, the chanting, the crazed desperation to die, the blood: the Blood God's hand was on Sarthis Majoris. However, enough Grey Knights had died in battle through thinking that they understood the enemy, and Alaric was not going to be one of them. 'Chaos has infinite faces,' said Alaric. 'We won't know which one it has here until we look it in the eye.'

'Armour,' said Haulvarn, pointing into the darkness at the southern end of the valley. The ice-cold sunlight was picking out ridges of snow and rock amid the shadows, and as Alaric followed Haulvarn's gaze, he could see vehicle hulls, corroded and barnacled like ancient creatures from the sea bed, lumbering through the seething darkness.

'Then this is it,' said Alaric. 'Thane?'

'I am the Hammer,' began Brother Thane, because in Alaric's squad, the newest recruit led the others in their prayers. 'I am the point of His spear, I am the gauntlet about His fist…'

The drone of prayer joined the faint hiss of the wind along the Imperial lines. The Hathrans were praying too, old war songs from their home world of endless plains and violet skies.

In reply, the sky overhead turned purple, then black, and then red. Clouds heavy with blood rolled across, and the valley was bathed in deep rust-red, the colour of dried blood. The ridges of the mountains were picked out in scarlet. A sudden flash of red lightning burst overhead and, for a split second, Alaric took in the scene revealed at the southern end of the valley: tangles of limbs, heaving masses of robed bodies, lumbering contraptions like ancient metal spiders, and a tower carved from frozen blood with an armoured figure leaning from the battlements. Even that briefest glimpse somehow conveyed an infinity of arrogance and evil.

Even the wind changed. It was drumming against the battlements in a terrible rhythm, carrying with it voices speaking a language that burned the ear.

'They're praying,' said Haulvarn.

'It's not a prayer,' replied Dvorn bleakly. 'They're begging. They want their god to be watching when they die.'

The Hathran prayers rose in competition with the heretic drone. Thane's voice rose as the wind battered more blasphemies against the Imperial lines. The wind was hot now, stinking of old blood and sweat, and slowly the darkness was creeping forwards.

The horde was hundreds of thousands strong. Deformed and insane, robed or stripped naked even of their skins, some carried guns or knives, while others wielded the bloodstained bones of their fingers as sharp as blades. Alaric saw a war machine anchoring the horde. Its pitted hull was held up by four mechanical legs, and it waddled through the melting snow like a fat metal spider. Banners held over the horde bore symbols of stylised skulls and parchments of flayed skin carved with bloody prayers. Mutants twice the height of a man were whipped ahead of the horde. Their torsos were pierced by iron spikes on which were mounted the heads and hands of fallen Hathran soldiers, and these walking trophy racks lowed like cattle as the cultists drove them forward.

The blood from thousands of self-inflicted cuts stained the snow and the valley sides before them. It was as if the valley was a bleeding wound, the Chaos army a welling up of gore rising to drown the Hathrans in its madness. The sun of Sarthis Majoris struggled to shine down through the gathering clouds, fighting its own battle in a sky dirtied by the sight of flapping creatures circling overhead.

'Let us be His shield as He is our armour,' Thane continued. 'Let us speak His word as He fuels the fire of our devotion. Let us fight His battles, as He fights the battle at the end of time, and let us join Him there, for duty ends not in death.'

All along the line, the Hathrans were taking up their firing positions. The battle cannon swivelled to point at the centre of the horde, icicles scattering from its massive barrel as it moved.

'Flares up!' yelled an officer, and several bright flares were fired to land on the snow between the line and the advancing army. Thick plumes of green and red smoke curled up. They marked the furthest accurate range of a lasgun, the line beyond which an enemy could not be permitted to advance without having to wade through las-fire as thick as rain.

The battle cannon fired, rocking back in its mounting above the line. The battlements shook. Shards of ice fell from the mountainsides. Even after weeks on the line, Hathran soldiers flinched at the appalling sound. A grey tongue of snow and pulverised rock lashed up in front of the horde, carrying body parts with it, sending out a shockwave through packed bodies as cultists were thrown to the ground by the impact. Yet the horde advanced all the faster, the front ranks breaking into a run.

Alaric took his position behind the battlements. Brother Haulvarn was beside him. If Alaric fell, Haulvarn who would take command of the squad, and Alaric could think of no one he would rather have next to him in a fight.

'They'll get in close,' said Alaric. 'They won't run. We'll have to take them on face to face. Visical, that means plenty of fire.'

'It would be an honour,' said Visical. The pilot flame of his incinerator flickered, ready to ignite the blessed promethium in the weapon's tanks. The fuel had been prayed over that very night, and the Emperor implored to manifest His will through the holy flame. Fire burned the enemy's flesh, but faith burned its soul, and faith was the weapon of choice for a Grey Knight.

The horde reached closer. The stench of it was choking. The tower of frozen blood was visible to all, and it was warping, its front folding down like an opening jaw to form a flight of steps. A man in black armour, lacquered in red, descended from the battlements to the ground. He carried a two-handed sword with a blade as long as he was tall. He was noble and arrogant, his face so pale and angularly handsome that it looked like it had been cut from the ice. The warrior was as tall as a Space Marine and carried with him an air of such cruelty and authority that it took a conscious effort not to kneel before him. The horde parted as he descended, hulking warriors in rust-red plate armour gathering in a cordon around him. The tower was still well beyond lasgun range, but the lord of the Chaos host was obvious, like a beacon in the horde.

'See him?' asked Haulvarn.

'Yes,' said Alaric.

'The Guard can't take him,' said Brother Dvorn. 'It's up to us.'

'For now, Dvorn, we help to hold the line.'

The horde reached the first of the marker flares. At this range Alaric could see their faces, buried under scars or masks of blood, or just so twisted with hatred that there was nothing human left.

'Open fire!' yelled the colonel, and the air in front of the fortifications was streaked with las-fire. The front ranks of cultists were riddled, fat crescents of laser lashing off arms and slicing bodies open.

Billows of steam rose up where the snow and ice were vaporised. The sound was immense, like reality itself ripping under the fury. The battle cannon fired again, but its roar was almost lost among the gunfire, the explosion of smoke and gore just a punctuation mark amid the slaughter.

Alaric took aim and fired. The Grey Knights around him did the same. A Space Marine's aim was excellent, and he picked out the individual shapes of heads and torsos among the confusion, and spat explosive bolts into them. Where the bolts detonated, puffs of blood and bone showered. Alaric fired in bursts, picking out a cultist and blasting him apart. The Grey Knights chewed a hole into the end of the Chaos line like a bloody bite mark, and within moments cultists were clambering over the ruined bodies of their dead.

However, the front ranks were just weak-willed fodder for the guns. The true power of the army followed them, ensuring the Hathrans used up ammunition and time killing the scum herded into the firing line.

The tide drew closer. The rhythm became frantic, trigger fingers spasming as the Hathrans sprayed rapid fire into the mass of men swarming towards them. A war machine rose through the fire, its guns opening up even as las-fire rained off it in showers of sparks.

'Visical! They're in range!' shouted Alaric, relying on the squad's vox-link to carry his voice over the din.

Brother Visical leaned between the battlements, his incinerator aimed down the steep slope of the fortifications.

The horde swarmed faster, chewed up and riddled with las-burns and bolter fire, but still numbering countless thousands. Their hands and feet were bloody from tearing on the ice. Pale, frost-bitten limbs reached from tattered red robes as they scrabbled to get a purchase on the fortification wall. The skinless ones leapt over the cultists in front, agile as insects.

Alaric looked into the eyes of one of them. They were rolled back and blank. There was nothing human left there.

All along the Imperial line, with a million voices raised in a scream, the Blood God's army hit the wall.

THREE

'FOR THE EMPEROR!' yelled young Brother Thane as he sliced a screaming robed killer in two with his halberd. The cultist's twin blades clattered to the rockcrete of the fortification as Thane kicked out and knocked another from the parapet. Autogun fire spanged off the Grey Knight's armour as he swept the battlement clear, the arc of his halberd blade taking off a hand, and then a head.

Another blast of sacred flame washed the battlements clear. A once-human shape, now hunchbacked and many-armed, reared up and screamed, cloaked in flame. It collapsed, skin and muscles boiling away.

'The dead,' said Brother Haulvarn, 'they're climbing their dead.'

Haulvarn was right, The Grey Knights' guns and Visical's incinerator had killed so many, so quickly, that cultists were piled up at the bottom of the wall, high enough for the killers behind them to clamber up. They were on the wall now, fighting each other to die by the Grey Knights' hands.

Along the walls, huge mutants had clambered up onto the battlements and were fighting with the Hathrans. Alaric saw one Guardsman thrown from the wall by a deformed giant, and another having his brains dashed out by a foul creature with weeping skin and giant crab claws. A mutant fell from the wall, chest flaming from las-fire, and crushed the cultists below him. The battle cannon fired again, almost point-blank, throwing Hathrans from their feet, and showering them with earth and body parts, but it was not enough. Cultists were making it onto the walls to lay into the Hathrans with guns and blades.

Haulvarn's halberd took the arm off a feral warrior with woad painted skin, before he ducked back below the battlements to shelter from the fire of the closest war machine.

'Too many?' he asked.

'Too many,' agreed Alaric.

'Then it's ours to win.'

Alaric looked around at his oldest comrade. 'The line cannot hold, not against this. Be ready to take command.'

'Why?'

'Because I might not come back.'

'Justicar, your brothers need–'

'My brothers need what the Emperor needs. They need victory. Standing back and letting the enemy kill us will not win us that victory. It is up to us, which means it is up to me. That is a justicar's responsibility. Can I count on you?'

'Of course, Justicar, always.'

'Then we need to get to the centre of the walls. Open up a path for me through this rabble.'

Haulvarn paused, just for half a second. He stood to his full superhuman height, holding his halberd up so the squad could see. 'Brothers!' he yelled above the din of battle. 'Forward! Down the line!'

Visical was first up, spraying the blessed flame along the battlements stretching westwards. Cultists screamed in the fire. Thane cut them down with his sword, his power armour protecting him as he strode through the burning fuel. They loomed from every side through the fire and smoke, and each scarred face was met by a sword or halberd crackling with the harnessed power of a Grey Knight's mind. Alaric felt bones fracturing under his halberd, and saw wet ruins opened up in enemy torsos from his storm bolter.

He barely had to think. He was a Space Marine, a Grey Knight, created almost whole to be a killing machine. Every fatal movement was hard-wired into him, as if a machine-spirit guided him, as if the Emperor himself was controlling his actions.

However, a Space Marine was not a machine. He was driven by passions that a normal man could not understand. The obscenity leading this horde had to be destroyed. That was the thought that drove Alaric on.

Thane wrestled a giant mutant as they went, something so foully warped there was barely any human left in it at all. A leathery winged creature swooped down to snatch Alaric off the wall. Alaric snatched it instead, crushing its throat in his fist while he tore its wings off and threw it into the fire still slathered over the battlements behind him.

'Here!' shouted Alaric. 'Break through them!'

Hathrans were dying all around. The Chaos horde had forced the walls in a dozen places, and knots of combat were erupting everywhere. An explosion tore a massive chunk out of the battlements on the left of the line, and the horde surged forwards, a war machine walking relentlessly over the slope of the rubble, impaling Guardsmen on its mechanical talons.

And there were daemons. They were redskinned and hideous, leaping amid the carnage, wielding swords of black iron that glowed and smouldered.

'Damn you!' shouted a voice that Alaric recognised as that of Colonel Dal'Tharken. 'Hold to your post, Grey Knights! The flank will fall! Get back to your post!' Alaric caught sight of the colonel, covered in burning daemon's blood, wielding his sword and plasma pistol, surrounded by the bodies of friend and foe.

He was a tough and unrelenting servant of the Emperor. The Imperium would miss him. Alaric ignored his words and pressed on.

The champion of Chaos was the key. Chaos adored its champions as much as it despised everything else. It granted particularly foul-hearted men and women with the power to command their forces, and the authority to speak with their gods' own voices. The Imperial line could not hold the enemy. It would barely make a dent in the vast force that had landed to claim Sarthis Majoris. It had, however, achieved a goal that, though the Guardsmen did not know it, was every bit as valuable to the Imperium.

It had brought Alaric and his Grey Knights face to face with the champion who represented the dark gods on this world.

'USE THE THIRTEENTH Hand,' said Duke Venalitor. His voice was loaded with disdain, for the Thirteenth Hand were the lowest dregs of his army.

One of Venalitor's heralds, black armour welded to its weeping skin, blew a long note from its war horn. The Thirteenth Hand, hunched subhuman creatures dressed in rags, hurried forward for the honour of dying at the wall.

The battle was going as planned. If any truly human emotion could be ascribed to Duke Venalitor, it could be said that he was happy with it. By the time the regiments of proper soldiers reached the front, the battle would be over and the refinery cities of Sarthis Majoris would be Venalitor's.

A messenger descended on tattered wings of bloody skin.

'My lord,' it slurred, 'their flank has fallen. The defenders have abandoned their posts.'

'Cowards,' sneered Venalitor. 'Their skulls are not fit for the Brass Throne.'

'They were from the corpse-emperor's legions,' said the messenger.

'Astartes?' Venalitor's perfect, pale brow furrowed. 'They would not run.'

The pit of Venalitor's mind dredged up memories from a time when he had been a man. It was a weak and shameful part of his existence, before the Blood God had found him. That man recalled that Space Marines were the guardians of the Imperium, the last line against all horrors, soldiers who would never flee, never, not even with Venalitor himself bearing down on them.

'Close order!' yelled Venalitor. His sword was in his hand, its huge blade shining in the red-tinged dawn. 'Now! Shields up! Give no quarter!'

He saw them among the carnage, silver-armoured figures picked out in scarlet flame. They had not abandoned the right of the line out of fear. They had left their posts to effect the only victory they could gain from Sarthis Majoris.

They thought they were going to kill him.

Duke Venalitor laughed. They had absolutely no idea what the Blood God had made from that man. He had looked upon the throne of flaming brass and knelt at the foot of the skull mountain. He had tasted the blood of Khorne Himself. No Space Marine was fit to die beneath his blade, which was a shame, because they would die very soon.

Venalitor saw one of the Space Marines run at the edge of the wall, behead a cultist without breaking stride, and leap off the wall heading directly for Venalitor.

Venalitor felt every muscle in his warp-blessed body tense, and hoped that this one would at least give him a worthwhile fight.

THE BATTLEFIELD WHIRLED around Alaric as he fell. He could hear the voices of his battle-brothers, and feel the heat rippling off the chains of bolter fire that followed him down.

He hit hard enough to crush a cultist beneath him. Alaric plunged a foot down through the mess to get his footing, and the stinking, subhuman creatures were on him. Filthy nails raked at his armour, trying to prise between his armour plates or drive claws into his eyes.

Alaric swept his halberd around in a brutal arc. He forged forwards, every sweep of his halberd battering back the deformed bodies pressing in on every side. A huge mutant reared up over him carrying a rock in its paws to crush him. A stream of bolter fire battered its head into pulp and it collapsed. Alaric glanced back to see Haulvarn aiming, the muzzle of his storm bolter still flaming.

The cultists gave way before him. Alaric kicked the last one aside. In front of him, now, stood a warrior in black armour as tall as Alaric himself, a wall of steel. Its shield bore the symbol of an eight-pointed star and its spear was tipped with a huge sharpened fang. The warrior lunged, but Alaric turned its spear away, spun around and shattered its shield with the butt of his halberd. He squared his feet and drove the blade of the halberd into the warrior's face, dropping the tip at the last moment so it plunged into the hollow between neck and chest.

Hot blood sprayed, and the warrior fell to its knees. There were other warriors on either side, forming a circle around Alaric's target.

Alaric half-stumbled into the circle. This was his only chance. This planet would not get another shot at survival. If the Chaos horde continued to march under its leader, Sarthis Majoris would fall.

The gods had seen fit to send to Sarthis Majoris a champion of such presence that Alaric felt it forcing him back. His armour was impossibly intricate, covered in images of heaps of skulls around a burning throne. The champion's face was the very image of arrogance, pale and perfect, with eyes like black diamonds.

'Leave us,' said the champion. The armoured warriors around him took a step back to leave an open duelling ground around Alaric and the champion.

Alaric was in a low guard, eyes fixed on the champion's blade.

'A Grey Knight,' said the champion with a smile. 'Khorne's gaze is upon us. I shall give thanks to the warp that the corpse-emperor sent one of his very own daemon hunters to die beneath my blade.'

'Let me help you return the favour, then,' said Alaric, his words sounding like those of a stranger, 'for you will be looking upon your god soon enough.'

The champion smiled. His teeth were ebony black fangs. He lunged forward, and his sword was like chained lightning striking down at Alaric.

Alaric turned the sword aside and suddenly the duel was on. The champion didn't just want blood. Blood alone was enough for the scum who threw themselves at the walls, but not for their leader. He wanted to prove his superiority. It was why he existed. It was in proving his superiority that the champion offered up his prowess to Khorne the Blood God.

It was also Alaric's only chance of survival. If the champion wanted a duel, then that was what Alaric would give him.

Alaric's halberd spun around faster than any normal man could move, its head carving down at the champion. In response the champion's intricate armour opened up like a bloody flower and tendrils of gore reached out to snare Alaric and drag him down. Alaric cut through them and dived clear as the champion's sword sliced down through the frozen earth beside him. More tendrils snaked around Alaric's arms and lifted him up in the air. Alaric ripped one arm free and aimed his storm bolter down at the champion, fixing his aim on the champion's face, still impassive with the certainty of victory.

The champion threw him down. Alaric hit as hard as a comet, cultist's bodies splintering under him, and then the rock-hard earth shattered. He planted a hand on the ground and forced himself up from the mess of bodies, his other hand groping for his halberd.

He forced the clouds from his eyes. He was battered but alive. It took a lot to fell a Grey Knight. As long as there was life in him and a weapon in his hand, victory was in his sights.

The corpses were moving. The one closest to Alaric burst open like a seed pod, crimson blood flooding out. More bodies were erupting all around him and beneath him, sinking him in a swamp of gore.

The champion laughed. The blood flowed up from the bodies, forming shapes like blocks of melting crimson ice. The champion stepped up onto them as they created a bleeding stairway up into the air. He stooped to pick Alaric up by the collar of his armour and held him up like a scolded animal, like a sacrifice. The sword in his other hand was ready to slice Alaric open and let his innards spill out onto the battlefield in a sacrifice to Khorne.

Alaric kicked out and caught the champion on the side of the face. The champion reeled, and Alaric grabbed the wrist at his throat, wrenching it around so that the champion let go. Alaric landed on the platform of blood that had formed below them, and was still rising up over the valley. Below him, he caught sight of the dark mass of cultists flowing around the right end of the line, which the Grey Knights had abandoned. The line was collapsing, the Hathrans surrounded and besieged. Alaric had sacrificed them for this chance at victory. He owed them the champion's death as surely as he owed it to the Emperor.

Alaric rolled to his feet, halberd still in hand. The champion wiped a smear of blood from the cut Alaric had opened on his face, and confronted him.

'Duke Venalitor avenges his insults,' spat the champion.

'A Grey Knight avenges his Imperium,' said Alaric.

The sword and the halberd flashed. High above the battlefield on a platform of animated blood, Duke Venalitor and Justicar Alaric fought a duel so rapid and intense that the few eyes that looked up from the battlements below could not make any sense of the blur of strikes and parries. Tentacles of blood lashed around Alaric's ankle and threw him to the bloody floor. Alaric's leg kicked out and knocked Venalitor reeling towards the edge. Gashes and scars opened up in Alaric's armour, some of them scored deep enough to draw blood. Alaric's halberd blade rang off Venalitor's armour as the champion of Chaos turned it aside at the last moment time and again.

Alaric lunged for Venalitor's heart. Venalitor grabbed the haft of Alaric's halberd with one hand, dragged Alaric forwards and brought an elbow down on the back of Alaric's head hard enough to send the world black for a moment. When Alaric forced vision back into his eyes he was being held in the air over Venalitor's head.

Alaric groped down trying to force a finger into the swordsman's eyes. His hand passed through writhing wetness, a nest of squirming bloody worms that opened up in place of Venalitor's face. Somehow it retained enough features to smile as it threw Alaric down.

Alaric plummeted down towards the frozen ground behind the line. He realised a split second before he landed that below him was not solid earth, but the pile of frozen Hathran dead.

Weeks' worth of casualties shattered beneath him. His armoured bulk blasted a crater in the red-black ice.

Pain slammed up through his body. His head cracked against the rock-hard chunk of a soldier's frozen corpse. The world of Sarthis Majoris seemed very far away. The voices he heard were from a different planet entirely, a different plane, which meant that he had sunk down through the earth into one of the hells to which the Imperial Creed maintained every sinner went.

Reality was slipping away. The pain of his battered body, so familiar to a Space Marine, was ebbing away, and he wished it would return to prove he was alive. The world, to his eyes, was dim and distant. The dawn was bleeding away to leave the valley dark. Something inside Alaric reminded him that he was not supposed to simply die like this, that there was something else he had to achieve, but it slipped away even as his mind reached to grasp it.

He assumed that the cry of despair was the last sound he heard. It was raised from a hundred throats at once and it was so deep that it cut through the gunfire and the screams of the battle.

It was the sound of Hathran. It was a funeral song. Alaric had heard it sung over the same pile of dead in which he was lying.

They were singing their own funeral dirge. The Hathrans knew they were going to die. They knew it because they had seen a Space Marine, the Emperor's warrior, defeated and thrown down from the heavens by the champion of the Blood God.

'No,' gasped Alaric, 'not here. Not now.'

Sarthis Majoris swam back into focus. Alaric was lying on his face in a pile of shattered, frozen corpses. He looked around for his halberd and saw that it had landed point-down, impaled in the earth a short crawl away. Alaric got to his knees. He would retrieve his weapon and fight on, because that was the only way to victory, however slim the chance might be.

A weight slammed down on his back, forcing him back onto his face. He fought to turn over, and for a moment the pressure was lifted. Alaric rolled onto his back and the foot came back down on him.

Duke Venalitor had one foot on Alaric's chest like a hunter standing over his prey. The magnitude of his arrogance was such that even the corpses recoiled at it, the blood in them heating up and melting at Venalitor's presence. Fingers of blood reached up from the corpses to lick at the boots of Venalitor's armour like the tongues of sycophants. Venalitor commanded all blood, even that of his enemies, such was the esteem in which the Blood God held him.

'My lord Khorne has a use for you,' said Venalitor with a smile. He gestured at the Hathrans dying on the walls behind him. 'Most of them are only good for fodder. Mankind provides little more than distractions for me now. However, there is much more you can do for the Blood God than merely die, Grey Knight.'

Venalitor held out a hand, and Alaric felt the blood seeping from the cracks in his armour. He kicked out, trying to throw Venalitor off him, but his strength was gone. Ribbons of blood spiralled out of him and his vision began to grey out.

As Duke Venalitor drew Alaric's lifeblood out of him chill pain filled him up in its place. Darkness fell all around him, and Alaric was not too proud to scream.

FOUR

ALARIC SAT FOR a long time in the Cloister of Sorrows before Chaplain Durendin approached.

'Justicar,' said Durendin. 'The Grand Masters have spoken with me of Chaeroneia. Your faith was sorely tested.'

'It was,' Alaric said. He was sitting on the drum of a collapsed column, typical of the cloister's fallen grandeur.

'The day is fine,' said Durendin, indicating the magnificent sky of Titan, the vast ringed disc of Saturn hovering over the void. 'I shall sit with you a while, if I may.'

The Cloister of Sorrows was open to Titan's sky, its atmosphere contained within invisible electromagnetic fields, and for Alaric to sit there among its age-worn tableaux was to allow the great eye of the galaxy to look down on him. The Emperor was a part of that gaze, always examining the soul of every one of His servants. Alaric felt naked and raw beneath it.

'I feel that there is more on my mind,' said Alaric, 'than Chaeroneia.'

'And that is why you have come here,' replied Durendin simply, 'to be alone with your thoughts, away from the war gear rites and battle songs, and if a Chaplain were to happen along with whom you could share your thoughts, then so be it.'

Alaric smiled. 'You are very perceptive, Chaplain.'

'It is merely the Emperor's way of using me,' replied Durendin. To be a Space Marine required an extraordinary man, but to be a Chaplain required more. A Chaplain of the Grey Knights was a rare specimen indeed, and the Chapter had precious few like him. He had to minister to the spiritual needs of soldiers destined to fight the most horrible of foes. The men of his flock had looked upon the warp and heard the whispers of daemons, and yet, thanks to him and those who had preceded him, not one Grey Knight had ever become corrupted by the enemy.

'Chaeroneia is a part of it, certainly, but I was troubled before that, ever since Ligeia.'

Inquisitor Ligeia was the bravest person Alaric had ever met. The sunburst on his personal heraldry was in memory of her. She had lost her mind to the machinations of the daemon prince

Ghargatuloth, but enough of her had remained pure to give Alaric the knowledge he had needed to defeat the daemon. She had been executed by the Ordo Malleus for her madness.

'Men and women like Inquisitor Ligeia will always die,' said Durendin. 'That is the way it was even before the Great Crusade, and it will continue to be so long after both of us are gone. What matters is that we know those sacrifices work towards the goal of safeguarding the human race. Do you believe she died in vain?'

'No, Chaplain, far from it.'

'Then this galaxy seems too cruel for you?'

'If I could not stomach the things I must see then you know full well I would not have been selected for training at all,' said Alaric, perhaps a little too harshly. 'I just feel there is… there is so much for us to do, and I do not mean the battle. I have always accepted that the battle will not end, but there is much more to our fight than meeting the daemon with swords and guns. I have glimpsed the… the realities behind it all. The words of the Castigator come into my mind unbidden. Ghargatuloth wove space and time to create the events that summoned him back, and we were a part of it. I will fight to the end of my days, for sure, but the enemy is not just bodies to be put into the ground. It is a concept, perhaps it is even a part of us. I wish I could understand it, but I know no one can ever understand Chaos without becoming corrupt.'

'So, you do not believe our fight is futile?'

'No, Chaplain. How could I, when I have seen the results of the daemon's depravity? But our fight is only half the battle, and I wonder if the other half can ever be won.'

Durendin looked down at his gauntleted hands. He was no stranger to the battlefield, and his Terminator armour, ornate gunmetal trimmed in a Chaplain's black, was not just for show. 'These hands,' he said, 'have fought that same fight for longer than you have been alive, Justicar, and not for one moment have I ever believed it was anything but the true and righteous purpose of any human being. What you say is true, however. The daemon is but one manifestation of the enemy and its violence is but one weapon of the warp. The Inquisition battles the plans of Chaos just as we battle its soldiers. Do you not agree?'

'How many inquisitors have we lost?' replied Alaric. 'Though we should not speak of it, Valinov was far from the only rogue in the Holy Orders, and he hid from us for so long. How many other heretics are wearing the Inquisitorial Seal? How many in Encaladus Fortress? How many directing the Grey Knights? I know it is our place to leave the thinking to the inquisitors, but how can we trust them if they delve so deeply into the corruption?'

Durendin sighed. He was an old man and sometimes, as then, Alaric had seen a reflection of those years in him. 'I have led Grey Knights through every trial of the mind that Chaos can inflict upon them.

You are not the first to doubt, Alaric, and certainly not the first to glimpse the futility in the Inquisition's task.'

'It is not futile,' said Alaric, 'but I feel I am failing if I do not do more. The daemon is a symptom, not the disease. I want to be a part of the cure.'

'I had these thoughts, myself,' continued Durendin. 'I spoke with my battle-brothers and the Grand Masters, and with the most knowledgeable inquisitors. None of them had the answer. In the end, I found the answer myself.'

'And what was it?'

'You will find it yourself. You are going to the Eye of Terror, I hear.'

'Yes, when my squad is reinforced.'

'Good. Then that is your answer. The Enemy's atrocities at the Eye know no bounds, and only men like us can stop him. Think about it. In your moment of doubt, the Emperor has sent you to the bloodiest battlefields of the Imperium. That is no coincidence. Throw yourself into those battles. See the daemon and butcher him. See the forces of Chaos broken and fleeing. Take those victories and immerse yourself in them. Let victory blot out everything else. Glory in it. Then the doubt will be gone.'

'That is what worked for you?'

'It did, Justicar. The enemy has made a grave mistake in bringing the fight to us. Men like you will punish that mistake. This I promise you, Alaric. You will become whole at the Eye of Terror.'

'Thank you, Chaplain,' said Alaric. 'I must see to my squad. I have two new men and we must pray together before we go.'

'That is good,' replied Durendin. 'Your men's spirits need counsel before they witness the Eye.' The Chaplain looked up at Saturn, deep blue and streaked with storms. Below the planet was Titan's skyline, an irregular toothed band of darkness. The whole of Titan had been turned into an ornate fortress, the moon's surface carved deep with canyons and vaults, and many parts of it such as the Cloister of Sorrows had become ruined and near-forgotten. 'I shall think here for a while. Saturn will set in an hour or so. It helps one think.'

'Then I shall speak with you soon, Chaplain.'

'Until then, Justicar.'

Alaric stood up to leave. The way down through the half-ruined fortress beneath the cloister was long, and it would give him plenty of time to consider Durendin's counsel.

'And Justicar?' said Durendin.

'Yes?'

'You are not dead.'

'That is good to know.'

'Although it may be an idea to wake up soon.'

'This isn't how this conversation ended.'

Durendin smiled. 'No, it is not, but then, I am not really here. I am probably elsewhere at the Eye. Perhaps I am even dead. What matters is that you are alive, and you can still do something about the situation in which you find yourself.'

'Then, what next?' asked Alaric.

'I cannot answer that, Alaric. I am not even here, after all. However, I think it is very likely that your situation is not a good one.'

The Cloister of Sorrows exploded in pain.

ALARIC SCREAMED.

The pain was howling from one of his shoulders. He was hanging from his wrists, which were chained above him. There was nothing else to bear his weight, and one of his shoulders had come out of its socket.

Alaric fought back the pain. He had been vulnerable for a moment and the pain had got to him, as it would to a man without the mental conditioning of a Grey Knight. His armour would normally be dispensing painkillers into his bloodstream, but he did not have his armour. He was naked. His war gear had been stripped from him.

As he fought back the pain, he began to hear again. A deep noise like an angry ocean boiled beneath him, and he could hear the clanking of vast machinery, mixed in with sobs and screams from broken throats. The smell hit him: blood and smoke, sweat and machine oil. His mouth tasted as if it was full of iron. He could not see, but that was a problem he would deal with in due time.

He forced his feet up, pulling up on his screaming shoulder. Slowly, he pulled himself up so that his body was almost upside-down. His feet found the roof of the cage he was in. He pushed down with everything he had, and he heard the bars buckling.

The chain holding his hands came loose from the ceiling of the cage and Alaric crashed down onto the cage floor. He lay there for a few moments, catching his breath, gingerly testing the tendons of his shoulder. It was hurt, but it was nothing permanent. A Space Marine healed quickly. He lay on his side and let the joint slide back into place. The gunshot of pain that accompanied it was profound, but there was something triumphant in the fact that he could feel at all.

Alaric reached up and found a blindfold tied around his face. He pulled it away and blinked a couple of times as his augmented eyes reacted to the sudden light.

His cage was one of several hundred suspended from a great iron column down which poured dozens of waterfalls of blood. These fed the sea of blood below him, in which writhed thousands of bodies, slick with gore. It was impossible to tell if they were in agony, or in some ecstasy of worship. Daemons waded among them, hulking things with red-black skin, lashing the bleeding bodies with their whips. Corpses and parts of corpses bobbed everywhere, fished out and carried away by scuttling alien creatures with lopsided, tumoured forms.

Slowly, the column rotated on gears that ground like thunder. The other cages had their own occupants: human prisoners, naked and weeping, old corpses, half-glimpsed freaks either alien or mutated, all of them suspended above the titanic blood cauldron. Alaric could hear droning alien prayers, pleading with the Emperor, and the ragged breaths of dying men. Tears and blood fell in a thin drizzle.

Walls of black stone rose around the column and the cauldron. Alaric looked harder and saw that it was not stone at all but flesh, rotted black. High above, the cliff edge was festooned with barrel-sized cages, each holding a body in an advanced state of decay. Flocks of flying creatures, like over-sized crows, but with ribbons of flayed skin instead of feathers, feasted on them. The decaying cliffs were riddled with tunnels and caves, and the beetle-like alien creatures scurried through them, chewing at the flesh with insect-like mandibles. The sky above was indigo, almost black, shot through with red, as if the sky itself was bleeding.

He was in hell. Alaric had died at the hands of Duke Venalitor and woken up in hell. He had failed. Everything he had ever done, ever thought or said, and everything he might ever have done had he lived, was meaningless. He had failed as completely as it was possible to fail.

Alaric slumped down onto the floor of his cage. He had never felt such despair. It was made complete by the fact that if he was already dead. He could not die again, and so it would never end.

However, Durendin had told him he was not dead: Durendin, a Chaplain of the Grey Knights, a man he could surely trust completely.

Alaric looked up. Through the bars he could see the cage above. Inside it was a huge humanoid form, one that Alaric recognised. The huge size and surgical scars matched Alaric's own.

'Haulvarn!' called Alaric. 'Brother Haulvarn, can you hear me? Do we yet live?'

Haulvarn did not answer. He was presumably unconscious, or dead, and like Alaric had been stripped of his war gear. Alaric tried to force the bars of his cage apart, and then to rock it from side to side in the hope of grabbing the gnarled metal of the column and climbing up to Haulvarn, but the cage was too strong and suspended too far out.

'Haulvarn! Brother, speak to me!' shouted Alaric.

As if in response, Alaric's cage fell.

Alaric kicked out in desperation as the cage plummeted towards the blood cauldron. He was slammed against the side of the cage as it hit the surface of the blood. Blood closed in around him, and hands reached in, the skin sloughing off them. Alaric kicked at the hands of the revellers, but there were too many of them. The sound of them was horrible, blasphemous prayers spilling from bloodied lips in a hundred different tongues.

Something roared, and a whip cracked. A daemon threw the worshippers aside and stood over Alaric, leering. Alaric recognised its kind from countless battlefields. It was a foot soldier of Khorne, a 'bloodletter' in the jargon of the Inquisition. Alaric remembered they carried two-handed swords as weapons of choice, but this one's whip was just as cruel.

The daemon recoiled as soon as the bodies were clear of the cage. The mere presence of a Grey Knight was anathema to the daemon. Even without the pentagrammic wards built into his armour, the psychic shield around Alaric's mind pushed back against the daemon's presence with enough violence to make its skin smoulder. The bloodletter snarled and lashed at the revellers around it, slicing off a hand here, a leg there, in its rage. Then it grabbed the bars of the cage with one hand and dragged it through the gore towards the chasm wall.

The daemon hauled the cage out of the blood and into a cave opening. The smell was appalling, putrescence so heavy in the air that Alaric could see it trickling down the walls in foul condensation. Dark, twisted creatures scuttled towards him. These were not daemons, but some alien species, and their skin carried the brands and manacle scars of a slave race.

The aliens dragged Alaric through the stinking tunnels into a cavern that glowed with a close red heat. It was a forge, where human and alien slaves pulled glowing weapons from vats of molten metal. Other slaves were chained to anvils, their spines twisted by years of servitude, where they beat an edge into the swords and spear tips. The din was appalling.

Alaric saw Haulvarn's cage being dragged through another opening, a gaggle of aliens following it.

Haulvarn had awoken and was raging inside, trying to kick his way out of the cage.

'Haulvarn!' shouted Alaric over the ringing of the anvils. 'We are not dead! We are not dead!'

A crowd of alien slaves pressed around Alaric's cage as he was dragged towards one of the anvils. They were misshapen, asymmetrical creatures with a dozen eyes each, arranged without pattern around their faces, and complex mandibles that dribbled slime as they gibbered to each other in their language. A bolt was drawn back somewhere and the top of the cage swung open.

Alaric tried to force his way out, but shock prods were jabbed down at him. His own strength was turned back on him as he spasmed. A single shock prod with a semicircular head was pressed down against his torso, and he was pinned in place. His muscles were paralysed, save for involuntary convulsions, and though he fought against it with everything he had left he couldn't break free. At full strength, he would have thrown the aliens out of his way, grabbed a weapon fresh from the anvil and killed everything he saw, but he was wounded and exhausted. He did not give in, he could not, but in the back of his mind a voice told him that it was futile.

One of the aliens, larger and darker-skinned than the rest, and evidently in charge, reached a pair of tongs into the closest forge. It withdrew a circle of glowing metal that was hinged on one side so it hung open. It was a collar.

The alien leaned over Alaric. Its caustic spittle dribbled onto his chest.

'Rejoice,' said the alien forge master, its Imperial Gothic thick and slurred through its mandibles, 'for this shall make you holy.'

The alien plunged the collar down onto Alaric's throat. It snickered shut around the back of his neck. His skin hissed as it cooked under the hot metal.

Alaric could struggle no more. His mind felt as if it was suddenly frozen.

He realised what had been done to him.

He knew, for perhaps the first time, what fear was.

THE HUMAN SPECIES was evolving.

This was a truth the Inquisition went to great pains to suppress, but it could not be denied by the inquisitors themselves. Some even held the heretical belief that the Emperor planned to shepherd this evolution onwards and help the human race achieve its potential. The emergence of psychic humans created one of the critical tasks of the Inquisition: the identification, imprisonment and liquidation of emerging psykers. Every planetary governor was under pain of death to hand over all the psykers collected by his forces, whenever the Inquisition and its Black Ships came calling. What happened to the great majority of psykers herded into those Black Ships, only those sworn to secrecy knew for sure.

A few of the psykers, perhaps one in ten or less, were strong and adaptable enough to be properly trained. An untrained psyker was a dangerous thing, an unguarded mind through which all manner of horrors could gain entry to the worlds of the Imperium. However, a properly trained psyker could guard his mind against such threats, and sometimes even make his mind far stronger than those of his fellow men.

It was an irony, often a cruel one, that such trained psykers were essential to the functioning of the Imperium. They were the astropaths whose arcane long-range telepathy made interstellar communications possible, the soothsayers whose skill with the Emperor's Tarot enabled them to advise on the vagaries of the future. Many Imperial citizens viewed even these sanctioned psykers with fear. Yet, in spite of the fear that followed the psyker everywhere, without him the Imperium could not function.

To most citizens a psyker was a witch, a rogue prowling the shadows of the Imperium's worlds to corrupt Emperor-fearing minds or bring forth foul things from the warp. A child foolish enough to display an unusual talent for magic tricks could expect his friends or family to turn him over to the local clergy. Wise women and fortune-tellers were burned at the stake on backwater worlds where Imperial servants rarely visited. Spaceship crews swapped tall tales of night-skinned humans who could rip a man's mind out of his skull, shapechangers, firebreathers and stranger things besides. Once, long ago, a time before he could remember anything at all, Alaric had been one of those witches.

Alaric was a psyker. All Grey Knights were. While most Space Marine Chapters made use of some psykers, only the Grey Knights required psychic potential from all their recruits. It was what made the Grey Knights capable of fighting the daemon, for a daemon's most potent weapons threatened the soul itself.

Daemons brought with them corruption, and fighting them exposed a Grey Knight to that corruption. They were trained to resist it, taught prayers of will-power so potent that they drove some recruits mad. Their armour was impregnated with sigils against the powers of the warp, the same symbols tattooed on their skins so that their bodies were shielded against corruption, but the most powerful defence was a Grey Knight's psychic shield. Alaric had been taught in the very earliest stages of his training to imprison his soul in a cage of faith and contempt where no daemon could reach it.

It was the only weapon a daemon truly feared: an incorruptible mind, anathema to the warp. The mere existence of the Grey Knights was a victory of sorts against Chaos.

The collar fixed around Alaric's neck was a dead, heavy thing that weighed down Alaric's soul. It was an artefact of Khorne, the Blood God. The Blood God despised sorcery, and it despised the righteous, holy mind of a Grey Knight.

The Collar of Khorne suppressed psychic abilities. Alaric's shield was gone. He was still a Grey Knight, he had still trained his mind and his body beyond a normal man's tolerances against corruption and possession, but without that psychic shield, he was ultimately defenceless.

FIVE

It was a long time before Alaric could feel anything. He was somewhere infernally hot.

Alaric was standing, and he was chained to the wall. The chamber was lit by ruddy furnaces taking up the opposite wall. Unfinished swords and sections of armour were heaped up either side of a well-scored anvil.

'You're not supposed to wake for a good while,' said a voice behind Alaric. Alaric tried to turn, but he was chained in place. He was dimly aware that he was still in the forge where his collar had been attached, and the iron weight of it around his neck seemed to drag him down towards the floor.

'Where is my battle-brother?' asked Alaric through split and bloody lips.

'I heard there were two of you,' said the voice. It was deep and gravelly, from a throat scorched by years amid the forges. 'He's somewhere in this hole, probably having the collar fixed. They had you down as witches as soon as they brought you in. Not many get the collar, you know. It's quite an honour.'

The speaker walked to the anvil, his back to Alaric. He was a massive man with brawny shoulders and dark skin that gleamed like bronze. Tools hung from his waist. He bent over the anvil and picked up a sword, a magnificent blade, but rough and half-finished. 'I have been down here a long time,' he continued, 'heard a lot of things, but it has been a long time since an Astartes graced this world. A long time indeed.'

'Who are you?'

The speaker did not look round. 'A smith by trade. Too useful a man to kill. I guess I should thank the Emperor for that. If there's one thing this planet needs, Astartes, it's blades, good blades, and lots of them. So this is where I shall stay until I die, and probably well beyond, making their blades. Perhaps you'll end up with one of mine. Believe me, you'll know it. There are no blades like mine on this world.'

'Where am I to be taken? What will happen to me?'

The smith still did not turn to face Alaric. The muscles on his back snaked beneath his dark skin as he laid the sword on the anvil and took up a hammer. 'Not for me to say, Astartes. Not for me to say. If I had anything worthwhile to my name, though, I'd wager it on you fighting for your life sooner rather than later. So, I'll make you a deal.'

Alaric laughed, and it sounded as bitter as the taste of blood in his mouth. 'A deal, of course.'

'Ah, hear me out, Astartes, unless you have somewhere better to be.'

Involuntarily, Alaric fought against his chains.

'I'll make you a suit of armour,' said the smith, 'the best you've ever held.'

'I have armour.'

'Not any more, and you've never had armour such as I can craft. Fits like a steel skin. Bends like silk. Toughened by fires as fierce as the heart of a star, strong enough to turn Khorne's own axe aside. How does that sound? Tempting?'

'But it will not be for free. I know your kind. Any promise from the corrupted is as good as a betrayal.'

'Oh no, you do not understand. In return, I ask that you seek something out for me. I dare say you will have more luck finding it out in the world than I will down here.'

'End this,' said Alaric. 'No servant of the Emperor would bargain with one such as you.'

'Such as me? And what am I?' The smith turned just enough for Alaric to see his face in profile. His face was as beaten as one of his blades, his nose broken many times, his eyes almost hidden in scar tissue. 'Find the Hammer, Astartes: the Hammer of

Daemons. They say it lies somewhere on this world, and with it a hero will rise up and topple the lords of the Blood God. What would be dearer to a slave like me than to see that?'

'Lies.'

'The Hammer of Daemons is very real. Nothing more is known of it, but it most definitely lies somewhere on this planet. If I didn't know better I might even say that it is right before me, chained to a wall in my forge. For you are the Hammer. Is that not so, Grey Knight?'

The weight of the collar was too much for Alaric to bear. His head bowed as it dragged him down. Black spots flickered before the forge fires, and he smelled burning iron and bolter smoke.

He drifted back out of consciousness, lulled into oblivion by the ringing of the smith's hammer on the anvil.

KARNIKHAL!

That self-devouring beast! That tumour city, that cancerous glory! A great parasite oozed from the black of the earth!

Some say Karnikhal plummeted to Drakaasi from some distant star, and grew mindless and vast over the aeons. Others claim it as some native thing, some fungus or parasite, mutated to immense dimensions by the ever-present power of Chaos. What fools are they, to seek logic in its form! The caverns of its entrails, the blood rivers oozing from its wounds, the groaning of its eternal pain, these are a face of Chaos, a face of Khorne!

The city built across Karnikhal is a parasite upon a
parasite, shanties crammed between the fatty folds of its
back, spires tumbling at the whim of the beast, temples
and slaughterhouses heaving with its titanic breath. All
this at the whim of the mindless thing, the idiot mon-
strosity, the city monster that is Karnikhal!

– 'Mind Journeys of a Heretic Saint,' *by Inquisitor*
Helmandar Oswain
(Suppressed by order of the Ordo Hereticus)

'GOOD CROP THIS year,' said Lord Ebondrake.

'Indeed, my lord,' replied Duke Venalitor.

'Khorne will be pleased to see them die.'

The torture garden gave Venalitor and Ebondrake an
excellent view of Karnikhal's slave market. The market
was one of the largest on Drakaasi. It was built into
the site of a dried-out cyst like a meteor crater. Hundreds of slavers' blocks were embedded in the tough
skin of the ground, each one with several new slaves
chained to it. The shouting of slavers rang out, punctuated by the sounds of whips and cracking bones.

Lord Ebondrake flexed a claw idly, like a stretching cat. 'The warp speaks of you, Venalitor.'

'Then I am blessed, my lord.'

'It says you have brought the Blood God a very
particular prize.'

Venalitor bowed. 'It is true. The Imperials fought
us at Sarthis Majoris. They were swept aside, and
many were taken alive.'

'More than just Guardsmen, though, so the seers
say.'

'You shall see, my lord.'

Lord Ebondrake padded to the edge of the torture garden's balcony. The garden was a place of reflection for Karnikhal's elite, where they could consider the dismembered bodies displayed where they had died on the intricate torture devices arranged on the obsidian. A rebel might be granted a final honour in death, to be slowly tormented on a frame of silver, to serve as inspiration for the garden's visitors.

Lord Ebondrake was a huge reptilian creature. He bore a resemblance to dragons of various human myths, and perhaps this was not a coincidence, since Ebondrake had presumably chosen his form at some point in his distant past. He had scales of jet-black, yellow feline eyes and countless bony spines, on which were sometimes mounted the heads and hands of those who had displeased him.

His long, sinuous body and enormous wings moved with a speed and grace alien to his size, and he brought with him a majesty that marked him out instantly as the de facto ruler of Drakaasi. For the occasion, Lord Ebondrake wore armour of obsidian and brass, cladding his massive scaly body in a way that echoed the stern armour of his personal troops, the Ophidian Guard. He was accompanied by a detachment of these elite armoured warriors, who followed their master at a respectful distance. They were the most powerful fighting force on Drakaasi, with their black envenomed blades and eyeless helms, and their presence was a constant reminder that strength at arms was the ultimate decider in Drakaasi's power struggles.

'I have no doubt there are rumours,' said Ebon-drake, 'of where my rule shall take us next.'

Venalitor weighed his words carefully for a moment. 'One hears things. I am aware of a great undertaking.'

'We have stayed on this world too long,' said Ebondrake. He stretched out his wings as if indicating the expanse of Drakaasi's bloodshot sky. 'This filthy rock, this lump of bloody dirt, it is too small a place to contain the worship due to our god. Do you not agree?'

'This is a fine world,' said Venalitor simply, 'but there is always room for more blood.'

'Ha! Have some imagination, duke. Think what we could do. We leave Drakaasi only to enslave, and return our captives to this world to watch them die. On Sarthis Majoris you did just that. However, if all Drakaasi's lords made a common cause and took our best followers out into the stars, whole worlds could fall to us. Drakaasi will be a monument to our bloodshed.'

'You speak,' said Venalitor, 'of a crusade.'

'Of course. Even now the one they call the Despoiler leads his armies out of the Eye. Countless other champions of the warp are doing the same all across the galaxy. There are rich pickings in the wake of such bloodshed. The Blood God's own crusade can only grow as more fall to our cause. By the time we return to Drakaasi the Blood God will have his own empire in the Eye. Would that not stand as a greater monument than all our games put together?'

'I can see it, my lord,' said Venalitor, letting an edge of wonder into his voice.

'No, duke,' said Ebondrake, 'you are young. You have not fought long under Khorne's banner. What you see is just the beginning. It takes this ancient creature to understand what Drakaasi could truly be. Soon, all the lords will know of my crusade, and they will be united under me. For now, there are more pressing matters. You say you made a fine haul at Sarthis Majoris?'

Venalitor followed Ebondrake's gaze down over the market. Thousands of captives were for sale, some of them from Venalitor's recent victory, others handed over in tribute to Khorne by pirate raiders, or captured in battles across the Eye of Terror. Most of them were human, for the human forces of the Imperium were battling the servants of Chaos throughout the Eye. Some others were aliens: slender eldar, orks, a few strange creatures plucked from the far corners of space.

'Come,' said Venalitor, 'I have wares to show.'

Together, Lord Ebondrake and Venalitor descended the winding stairway down to the cyst floor. Everywhere they went the slavers, all servants of one of Drakaasi's lords, bowed or saluted at Ebondrake's presence. The wretches who inhabited Karnikhal scurried away in fear, or prostrated themselves on the ground, whimpering and pathetic.

Most of Drakaasi's population was human, or at least originally human, and some said Ebondrake had taken on his draconic form solely to mark himself apart from the scum of the planet's cities. The sounds and smells of the slave market crowded all around, sweat and misery, mingling with the heavy rotting blood stench of Karnikhal itself.

Many of Drakaasi's other lords were there examining the slaves on offer. Tiresia, tall and ebony skinned with a great longbow carried at her side, was picking out new quarries for her court of feral killers, and cultured assassins to chase down in their next great hunt. Golgur the Pack Master was purchasing the weakest, most pathetic slaves to throw to his flesh hounds, two of which he led around the market by chains.

Scathach was making a rare foray from his fortress, probably to buy combat slaves to train his soldiers, and turned one of his heads to follow Ebondrake and Venalitor making their way between the slaving blocks. Scathach had long forsaken the Traitor Legions, but he still wore the power armour of a Chaos Space Marine, and the soldiers who followed him formed a neatly drilled regiment quite at odds with the bloodthirsty rabble many lords gathered around themselves.

'Lord Ebondrake, my kind are honoured,' said a booming voice. Up ahead of Venalitor there was a great cauldron of steaming blood, containing the toad-like form of a giant daemon. The cauldron was carried by blinded slaves, their spines horribly bent by the daemon's weight. Two slaves poured ladles of blood over the daemon's pasty skin as it addressed Ebondrake. On the daemon's chest there was a weeping scab in the shape of a stylised six-fingered hand. The same symbol was branded on the chests of the slaves who carried the daemon.

'Arguthrax, what manner of sacrifices have you brought for the altars and arenas of our world?' said Ebondrake.

Arguthrax waved a dripping hand towards the slaving block beside him. Dozens of bronzed, muscular men and women were chained there, many still shouting curses at the slavers watching over them. 'An entire tribe, my lord,' said Arguthrax, 'a most violent and savage people, yes! Their rage echoed long in the warp. They spoke unto their most ancient god, our god, and brought my servants forth! And so they were enslaved, and soon they will learn to bow before the will of their god. Ha! See how they still rage! Imagine such anger turned for the Blood God's glory!'

'More savages, Arguthrax?' said Ebondrake. 'There is always need of their kind for the arenas. The Blood God ever demands his fodder.'

Arguthrax could not keep the anger from passing over his revolting face. 'Then it is a blessing that the Blood God will hold this offering in such high esteem.' Arguthrax turned his burning black eyes on Venalitor. 'What have you brought, upstart youth, that permits you to walk alongside our lord as an equal?'

Venalitor smiled. Arguthrax hated him. Most of Drakaasi's lords hated him, since compared to most of them he was young and brilliant. They hated each other too, of course, and tolerated one another only because Lord Ebondrake had forged from Drakaasi an immense temple to Khorne that required all their attentions to maintain. Arguthrax, however, an ancient and evil thing spawned within the warp, harboured a particular dislike of usurpers like Venalitor.

'Observe, honoured daemon,' replied Venalitor simply.

Venalitor's servants tended a grand pavilion of crimson silk that dominated one side of the slave market. Many of his servants were Scaephylyds, creatures native to Drakaasi, who had inhabited its mountains and canyons before the first lords of Chaos had set foot on the planet. They were scuttling insect things who, though despised by everything else on Drakaasi, were devoted to Chaos and to Venalitor himself. Dozens of them scurried over the pavilion, and the largest of the number, the slave masters, swarmed around the opening to the pavilion as the silks were pulled back.

Lashes drove human slaves out of the pavilion into the market. They were streaked with blood, chained together at the wrists and ankles. They were all men, and almost all of them had the same tattoo on their shoulders: Imperial Guard, soldiers of the weakling Imperium, finally reduced to the slavery that was their lot in life.

'This is it?' said Arguthrax. 'These wretches are barely fit to feed the flesh hounds. For this you waste our time? The Blood God will spit upon such an offering, Venalitor. Such failure is heresy!'

'Patience, daemon,' said Venalitor smoothly.

A quartet of scaephylyd slave masters emerged, hauling thick brass chains. They dragged a hulking human form out of the pavilion, half again as tall as any of the Imperial Guardsmen. Another followed it, similarly huge. Slabs of muscle rippled beneath their skin, which was streaked with grime and dried blood. Beneath the filth were scars, old battle wounds and the marks of extensive surgery. The dark shape of the black carapace was just visible under the skin, with metallic ports in the chest and biceps where power armour could read off vital signs.

One of the men had broad, expressive features and a service stud in his forehead, while the other had a face as solid and unflappable as a slab of granite. They both strained at their chains, but the metal had been forged in the hottest volcano of Drakaasi's mountain ranges, and they held fast. Each man had a Collar of Khorne around his neck, a fact that was evidently not lost on Lord Ebondrake.

'Space Marines,' said Ebondrake, 'and alive. You have outdone yourself, Venalitor. It has been many years since a living Astartes was brought to Drakaasi.'

'Not just a Space Marine, my lord,' said Venalitor proudly.

'No: psykers, sorcerers. It will please the Blood God to see them die.'

'More than that.' Venalitor snapped his fingers and a scaephylyd slave master scurried up, cradling the shoulder pad from a suit of Space Marine power armour in its front legs. Venalitor took the shoulder pad and held it up for Lord Ebondrake to see the device emblazoned across it. The ceramite was deeply carved with devotional prayers in High Gothic, and it bore the symbol of a sword thrust through an open book.

'A Grey Knight,' said Ebondrake.

'Two Grey Knights,' replied Venalitor. He looked purposefully at Arguthrax. 'Daemon hunters.'

Arguthrax sneered. He would never show obvious weakness in front of Ebondrake and especially Venalitor, but he was leaning back in his cauldron to put as much distance as he could between himself and the Grey Knights. Their very presence was anathema to the daemon. It gave Venalitor savage joy to think that something like fear might be blossoming in Arguthrax's corrupted mind.

'I take it that these specimens will not be for sale,' continued Ebondrake.

'Indeed not. I myself shall see that they reap the greatest glory for Khorne. It is not something I can trust to another. I shall take them back to the *Hecatomb* and make them ready for the next games.' Venalitor waved a dismissive hand at the Imperial Guard prisoners. 'As for the rest of them, they are for sale. It is not for me to hoard the Blood God's sacrifices for myself. There is one further thing.'

Slaves hauled forwards a sled, on which was displayed the rest of the Grey Knights' armour. It was still stained with the blood of the battle on Sarthis Majoris.

'A tribute, my lord,' said Venalitor. Arguthrax snorted derisively.

'Gratefully received, duke,' said Ebondrake, 'rare trophies indeed. Have your slaves take them to my palace.'

'It will be done.'

'So,' said Ebondrake, eyeing the Grey Knights, 'Karnikhal's games will see the hunters of daemons slaying their own for the Blood God's glory. Let it not be said that Khorne does not appreciate such humour.'

Ebondrake turned and began to pad through the rest of the market to inspect the other prisoners being traded between Drakaasi's lords. None of them would come close to the rare prize of a pair of Grey Knights, and no lord could boast such warriors in their arena stables. Venalitor cast Arguthrax a final look before heading for the pavilion. His slave masters had much to do, for Karnikhal's games marked the beginning of a great season of worship in Drakaasi's arenas, and the quality of Venalitor's slaves would determine how quickly he could rise to prominence among the planet's lords. With Grey Knights fighting under his banner, the games would be very good indeed for him.

From his palace in the warp, Khorne would be roaring his approval as the hunters of daemons were sacrificed in combat for his glory. The warp would not soon forget Duke Venalitor of Drakaasi.

SIX

'This is the *Hecatomb*,' said Haulvarn. 'I heard one of them saying its name.'

'One of them?'

'The slaves: the insect-things.'

'Then what is it? A prison?'

'A ship.'

Alaric strained against his chains, but he knew it would be useless. He was chained to the wall of a tiny dark cell, barely big enough for him to stand hunched. The floor was crusted with old blood and covered in a layer of filthy straw. Everything stank. Men had died in these cells.

Alaric could just make out Haulvarn's outline through an iron grille in the wall. Alaric had passed out some time after being presented at the slave market. It took a lot to rob a Space Marine of consciousness; it was surely the collar that was weakening his mind.

'Did you see it?' asked Haulvarn.

'What?'

'The dragon.'

'Yes.' Alaric recalled it, looming over him as if in a nightmare. It was not a dragon at all, of course. A dragon was a mythological creature, a symbol, or the name given by primitive humans to large lizards indigenous to countless inhospitable planets. 'I saw it, and the bloated one: the daemon. Even with my mind blunted it could not hide its nature. The knight, the one in red armour, was the one who took us at Sarthis Majoris.'

'I saw you fight him. It was valiant, Justicar. For a few moments there was hope. Many more vermin died because of your example.'

Alaric sighed. 'He bested me and took me alive. Our example has not finished yet.' He was just able to make out his fellow Grey Knight's features through the grille. 'What of the others? The squad?'

'Thane died,' replied Haulvarn. 'I saw him go. As for Dvorn and Visical, I do not know. We were swamped and separated. Perhaps they were taken prisoner, too, but I have not seen them. Emperor forgive me, but I do not think Sarthis Majoris ever had a chance.'

'Probably not,' said Alaric. He could feel the cell floor tilting, and hear distant rumbling through the body of the *Hecatomb*. It was a ship, after all, creaking as it sailed.

'Where do you think they are taking us?' asked Haulvarn. 'Are we to be sacrifices?'

Alaric held up his hands, chained at the wrists. 'I think they have greater plans for us,' said Alaric. 'A simple knife across the throat is rarely enough to sate the Blood God. They will have something more elaborate in store for us, I feel.'

'And who do you think "they" are, Justicar?'

Alaric paused for a long time. Who indeed? The very nature of Chaos meant it could not be classified. In spite of the volumes of forbidden lore in the libraries of Encaladus, in spite of the learning filling the minds of inquisitors, Chaos could not be divided into categories or dissected like a specimen. Chaos was change, it was entropy and decay, but it was also an abundance of life and emotion, warped birth as well as death. Every time someone like Alaric thought they understood an enemy born of Chaos, that enemy changed, not just to confound the hunter, but because change was a part of its essence.

'Wherever we are, Haulvarn, and whoever has us, we cannot ever answer that question. We will never understand this place or these creatures. If we were to ever understand them then our corruption would be complete.'

'They can corrupt us.'

'Yes.'

'The collar leaves us defenceless.'

'Not completely, we have our training, but yes, we are vulnerable.'

'Then it could happen.'

Alaric knew exactly what Haulvarn meant. No Grey Knight had ever fallen. They had died, or been crippled, or had their minds flayed away by the fury of the warp, thousands of them, entombed in the chill vaults beneath Titan, but none had ever fallen. Alaric and Haulvarn could be the first.

'It will not,' said Alaric. 'It does not matter what trinkets they use to strip away our defences. We are Grey Knights. Everything else is details.'

'I shall share in your faith, then, Justicar,' said Haulvarn. Alaric couldn't tell how convinced Haulvarn was. Alaric wasn't even sure if he believed it.

'We will escape,' continued Haulvarn.

'Of course,' said Alaric.

The cell door banged open and one of the insect slaves threw in an armful of armour and weaponry, which clattered on the floor, chainmail and a few pieces of plate, a sword, and a helmet.

'Prepare,' said the slave in its thick drooling accent. It slammed the door shut and performed the same routine at Haulvarn's cell.

'For what?' demanded Haulvarn. 'For our executions?'

The slave ignored him and slammed his cell door shut. Alaric could hear its talons clacking on the floor as it scuttled away.

The chains around Alaric's wrists snickered away. Alaric looked down at the armour heaped at his feet. He was still feeling the wounds of his defeat by Venalitor. A Space Marine healed with inhuman speed, but even so it had only been a few days since he had nearly died on Sarthis Majoris. Now he would have to fight again.

'What do they think they can take from us?' asked Haulvarn.

The cell doors banged open. Other prisoners were emerging, too, their manacles rattling.

Alaric pulled the chainmail shirt over his head and picked up the rusted sword at his feet.

'They want our blood,' he replied.

ALARIC'S FIRST SIGHT of some of the other slave gladiators came as he was herded down a narrow, dark tunnel towards doors of bone studded with fangs. The tunnel wound through the entrails of Karnikhal, and through holes in the fleshy wall the city's inhabitants hooted and jeered at the men about to die.

Some slaves were no more than fodder. They were dressed in rags, their heads bowed and white with fear. Others looked like they could take care of themselves, like the muscular man with the prison tattoos. They were almost all human, save for a gaggle of grunting aliens separated by a cordon of the insectoid aliens. Alaric recognised the sound and smell of orks, brutal greenskins who lived to fight.

The tattooed man looked Alaric up and down. 'You're not mutants,' he said.

'No,' snarled Alaric.

The prisoner smiled. 'Then they're going to love killing you.'

Alaric reached the doors. He could feel the anticipation among the other slaves. Some were terrified to the point of paralysis. Others were ready for the fight. The orks were chanting, working themselves up for slaughter.

The doors opened. Light and the roar of an immense crowd hit Alaric. The orks shouldered their way past the guards and ran past Alaric into the arena, waving their cleavers and clubs.

Alaric emerged onto the arena floor. There must have been hundreds of thousands of spectators cramming the cages and pens in the stands.

Sunk into the flesh of the city, the arena was a stinking pit, walled with rotting flesh, from which flowed waterfalls of gore and pus. The spectators were kept in huge cages to prevent them from tearing at one another, and they brayed like animals as they hurled filth and insults down at the arena floor. Karnikhal's citizens were as rotten and foul as their city. Flesh and skin hung off them, and their decomposed faces had lost all humanity. Here and there were grand galleries of marble and silk for dignitaries. Venalitor would surely be there, and perhaps other lords that Alaric had glimpsed at the slave market. Ranks of armoured warriors separated the dignitaries from the scum.

'In the name of the Throne,' said Haulvarn.

Another roar went up from the crowd. Gates of bone had opened on the opposite side of the arena,

across the expanse of bloodstained sand. A huge
shape emerged from the darkness beyond it. It had
the upper torso of a massive humanoid and the
lower body of a snake. It had four arms, and in two
of them it held a pair of enormous meat cleavers.
The crowd bayed and screamed as it slithered out
into the sunlight. Alaric's augmented eyesight
picked out its roughly human-like face and forked
tongue tasting the blood on the air, the garland of
severed hands around its neck, and the kill tallies
branded into its leathery skin.

'Throne of Skulls,' cursed the prison slave.
'Skarhaddoth.'

Alaric looked at him.

'The champion,' continued the slave. 'Ebondrake's own.'

'What's your name?' asked Alaric.

'Gearth.'

'Gearth, stay close. We'll surround it. Haulvarn
and I will keep it at bay, the rest of you get behind
it and...'

Gearth smiled. 'It doesn't work that way.'

Rows of spikes twice as tall as Alaric sprung up
from the sand, dividing the arena into pens and
corridors. Alaric was separated from the other
slaves, including Haulvarn.

'Brother!' shouted Haulvarn as the din from the
crowd grew. 'It is bloodshed they want. If we kill
anything, it will be for the glory of Chaos.'

'True, but whatever we do, we must survive first.
Fight as if the Emperor willed it. As if—'

A row of spears snickered back into the arena floor. There was now no obstacle between Haulvarn and Skarhaddoth, the champion of Lord Ebondrake.

Skarhaddoth's eyes fixed on Haulvarn. Haulvarn held up his sword in a guard. It wasn't anything like as potent as the nemesis weapon he had carried as a Grey Knight, but anything could be lethal in a Space Marine's hand.

The crowd was chanting Skarhaddoth's name.

Skarhaddoth slithered towards Haulvarn. Skarhaddoth was huge, much taller than Haulvarn, and its two empty hands pulled a pair of shields from its back. The shields were black with the device of a white serpent, presumably the crest of Lord Ebondrake. It was fitting that Venalitor should give one of the prized Grey Knights in combat to Ebondrake's champion.

'Brother!' shouted Alaric. 'We stand together!' Alaric leapt up and tried to haul himself over the dense barrier of spears. They were slick with the blood of previous combatants, and the gnarled metal bit into his hands.

A great eruption of bloody sand fell over Alaric. He dropped to the ground and turned to see a cage erupting from the arena floor. Inside was a hulking mutant, doubled over in the confines of the cage. The cage door sprang open, and to another roar the mutant stomped out, bellowing in rage.

Alaric's opponent was an abnormal construction of overlong, multi-jointed limbs that writhed like snakes, with a long equine head and a single yellow eye that bled pus as it glared at Alaric. In its hands was a weapon that resembled an industrial circular saw. The crowd screeched their approval as the saw tore into life, flicking shavings of steel and flecks of dried blood everywhere.

Alaric dropped to one knee as the mutant charged and the saw rang off the line of spears behind him. Alaric rolled away as the saw came down and gouged a choking spray of sand from the arena floor. He risked a glance behind him, Haulvarn and Skarhaddoth were fighting, Skarhaddoth rearing up and striking down like a cobra, Haulvarn fending off everything the champion threw at him with desperate swings of his sword.

Alaric turned back to the mutant. It ripped its saw out of the ground and swung it. Alaric turned it aside with his sword, snapping the blade in the process. The crowd loved that, and the mutant did too, its deformed face splitting into a grin as it charged.

Alaric dropped to one knee, the saw passing just over the top of his head, and stabbed the broken sword up into the mutant's ribs. The shattered stump of the blade tore through muscle and bone, and lodged there, torn from Alaric's grip as the mutant reared up in pain. It whipped its unnaturally long arms around and nearly cut Alaric in two with the saw.

Alaric couldn't stay on the back foot. He was unarmed, and the mutant's reach was huge. It would kill him if he let it. He ducked under its arms and leapt onto it, hands reaching up to gouge at its eye and force its head around to snap its neck.

The mutant was forced back onto its haunches. It wrapped an arm around Alaric's torso to lever him off, and its other hand tried to drive the saw through Alaric's back. Alaric's hand was round its throat while his other arm held off the saw. The mutant's eye bulged and turned red with frustration. Its long tongue spooled out, and lashed at Alaric's face and neck like a tiny whip. Alaric held on and tried to crush the bones of its neck in his fist. Whatever strange mutations it had on the inside, it probably still needed to breathe.

The mutant howled and threw Alaric off it with unnatural strength. Alaric tried to scrabble to his feet, but the mutant was on him too quickly. The saw was over his face, the blade shrieking at him, and the mutant was trying to force it down to cut his head in two. For a long, awful moment the two wrestled, the mutant's unnatural strength against the enhanced muscle of a Space Marine, and Alaric did not know which of them would win.

Alaric forced everything into pushing the saw to one side. The mutant's weight drove it past his head into the arena floor, and the circular blade bit deep into the ground. The mutant tried to tear it out, but it was stuck too deep, and the saw's motor screeched, and belched a plume of smoke and flame. The saw exploded in the mutant's hands, and the blade skipped away, ringing off the wall of spears and ricocheting away to bury itself in the meat of Alaric's shoulder.

Alaric forced a knee under the mutant's chest and kicked it off him. The mutant scurried back across the bloody sand, one ruined hand spraying black-green gore. Alaric got up onto his knees, back arched against the pain of the blade lodged in his shoulder. It was the same shoulder he had dislocated in the cage, and the pain was bad enough to grey out his vision.

The crowd loved to see such gore. The other fights were similarly horrible. The ork had defeated its opponent, a crimson-skinned bestial thing, and was waving its enemy's severed leg in victory. Gearth was kneeling over his opponent, a shaggy beast-man with a goat's head, and was in the process of sawing its head off with a jagged knife.

Alaric was on his feet. The mutant was struggling to get up, blood flowing out of the stump of its missing hand. Alaric reached agonisingly around and pulled the saw blade out of his shoulder. The mutant would still kill him. It had one good hand and a foul temper, and that was all it would need, but now, Alaric had a weapon.

The mutant charged. Alaric wound his arm back and threw the saw blade like a discus as hard as he could, ignoring the pain screaming from his shoulder.

The blade sheared the mutant's head clean off. Alaric sidestepped its headless body as it slammed into the spears behind it. The crowd jeered the dead

mutant that had been despatched at the hand of a
newcomer.

Alaric turned and looked for Haulvarn. The Grey
Knight's fight with Skarhaddoth had moved all the
way back across the expanse of the arena floor leaving a trail of bloody footprints. Haulvarn was
covered in blood from dozens of cuts. One side of
his face was cut open from brow to chin. He was
losing.

Skarhaddoth loomed over Haulvarn. Haulvarn
was striking at it with blurring speed, but Skarhaddoth was just as quick, and he batted each sword
blow aside with his shields. The distraction of
Alaric's battle was over, and every eye in the arena
was fixed on Lord Ebondrake's champion as he
forced the Grey Knight back step by step.

Alaric tried to climb the spears again. Many
hands had tried to do the same, and clumps of
ragged flesh still clung to the spears. Alaric reached
the top and tried to haul himself over the rusted
points.

Skarhaddoth backhanded Haulvarn with one of
his shields. Haulvarn sprawled onto his back.
Skarhaddoth dropped one of his cleavers and
picked Haulvarn up, kicking the sword out of the
Grey Knight's hand.

'Brother!' yelled Alaric. 'I am with you! You are
not alone!' He pulled himself over the spear fence
and dropped down the other side, the spear tips
gouging long lines out of his chest. He kicked to his
feet and ran towards Skarhaddoth and Haulvarn.

Skarhaddoth held Haulvarn over his head like a trophy. The crowd screamed. They wanted gore. They wanted cruelty. Alaric had whetted their appetite, and Skarhaddoth knew how to give them what they wanted.

Skarhaddoth had one hand around Haulvarn's throat and another around his leg. He pushed Haulvarn up above his head and pulled. Haulvarn screamed.

Alaric yelled in wordless desperation. His hearts felt like they had stopped in his chest. He watched Haulvarn's body come apart, torn in two by Skarhaddoth.

Haulvarn's blood poured down over Skarhaddoth, who basked in it, open-mouthed. Skarhaddoth slithered over to the arena wall and threw the two halves of Haulvarn's body into the crowd. Spectators fought to tear chunks of flesh from the body. Skarhaddoth brandished his bloodied hands to every corner of the arena, a grin across his blood slicked face. His eyes fixed on Alaric, and he smiled through the blood of Alaric's friend.

Alaric ran. Skarhaddoth was more than halfway across the arena, and Alaric sprinted to close the gap.

Haulvarn was dead. The Enemy had claimed a Grey Knight, and Alaric had lost a friend. The hollow opening up in him could only be filled with revenge. It was not a choice he made. It was a simple, unbreakable rule that had to be obeyed. Haulvarn had to be avenged.

A wall of spears burst up from the arena floor right in front of Alaric. Alaric slammed into it, bending the spears. He grabbed them and shook them, trying to tear them out or bend them, but they held fast. Skarhaddoth flourished his bloodied hands one last time to the crowd and headed out through the arena doors. Slave creatures hauled them shut behind the champion.

Slavers and armoured warriors were entering the arena, hauling away bodies and manacling the surviving slaves. Several of them converged on Alaric. Alaric wanted to tear them apart, rip out the spears and kick his way through the doors. He wanted to hunt down Skarhaddoth and tear him apart, just as Skarhaddoth had torn apart Haulvarn, but the sight of the closing doors had drained all the strength out of him. His rage was like a great weight on him, like a curse laid on him for failing to avenge his friend.

Lashes cut down into the flesh of his back. He fell to his knees. He wanted all of this to be gone. He wanted oblivion, so he didn't have to remember seeing Haulvarn die. He had never felt so broken.

The pain reached a crescendo, and then Alaric didn't feel anything at all.

'ARE YOU SUPPOSED to have two hearts in there?'

'What?'

'You've got two hearts, and three lungs, but one of them's a bionic.'

Alaric's eyes opened. He was staring at a rusted ceiling, filthy with years of dirt. He ached all over, the pain accented by the faint swaying that told Alaric he was back on the *Hecatomb*. The light was poor, but it still pounded against Alaric's eyes.

'I'm a Space Marine,' said Alaric.

'What,' said the voice, 'on Drakaasi? Throne be praised or damned, I don't know which. How did your kind get here?'

'Venalitor,' said Alaric. He sat up, ignoring the pain in his shoulder. He had suffered worse injuries before. He could live with it.

He was at one end of a huge chamber inside the *Hecatomb*. Banks of cells rose on either side, connected by walkways. The floor was filthy, scattered with straw or piles of rags that might have been prone bodies. Prisoners were everywhere, arguing over gambling games, snatching sleep in corners, whispering conspiratorially. Most of them were human, with a few xenos mixed in. Alaric recognised Gearth idly sharpening a knife in a corner. At the far end was a heap of filth and trash that was evidently home to a group of orks, separated from the other slaves by bars hung with gory orkish trophies. One of the greenskins was the same one-eared ork that Alaric had seen in the arena. About half a dozen more of the creatures squabbled and fought in the shadows. Alaric realised that the isolation cells were probably below this deck. The majority of the slaves lived here, kept isolated by fear of one another more effectively than by the bars of individual cells.

Alaric was sitting on a large, stained iron slab. Standing over him was a pudgy middle-aged man with a beard, wearing an old apron stained almost black with blood. A few blunt medical implements were laid out beside Alaric.

'Haggard,' said the surgeon, 'medical officer second class.'

'Justicar Alaric,' replied Alaric. 'You were Imperial Guard?'

Haggard shook his head. 'Agrippina Planetary Defence Forces, the Ancient and Honourable Fifty-First Governor's Own Rifles. A whole lot of us surrendered at Mount Dagger. Turns out we should have fought to the death, but the Eye had only just opened. We didn't know what we were facing.'

Alaric tested his shoulder. It would hold, he decided.

'I pulled a handful of metal out of you,' continued Haggard. 'You weren't supposed to survive out there, you know. You were sacrifices to celebrate the last slave revolt.'

'There was a revolt?'

'For about half a day: the arena slaves in Aelazadne got organised and broke out. The Ophidian Guard were waiting for them, Lord Ebondrake's personal army. You've seen him?'

'The lizard?'

'The lizard. The games are celebrating the revolt being crushed. That's why Ebondrake's champion was there. You were sent there to die.'

'My battle-brother did,' said Alaric. 'Skarhaddoth killed him.'

'I heard, and I know you'll want revenge. It's what I wanted, too. When Venalitor's army hit Agrippina I lost everyone and everything. But this is Drakaasi, Justicar. Khorne owns this world. Surviving here is victory enough. You either fight, which is exactly what Venalitor wants you to do, or you die: simple as that. I'm only alive because I'm more useful patching up gladiators than acting as one more piece of arena fodder.'

'Then that's what we are,' said Alaric bleakly. 'We are tools of the Blood God.'

'A lot of us chose death instead,' said Haggard. 'The rest think they'll be saved, or think they can break out on their own. Some of us, like me, are too cowardly to do anything else, and some enjoy the bloodshed, of course.'

'Like Gearth.'

Haggard smiled. 'Gearth's pure psychopath, and he's not the only one. The first thing that happens when Chaos takes a world is that the prisons get emptied. For men like Gearth, Drakaasi's not that different to their old life. There are a few who have plans, of course. See up there, on the third deck?'

Haggard pointed up to a bank of cells suspended high above. Alaric followed his gaze and picked out a pale figure in one of the cells, patiently polishing a suit of dark green armour. A sword was propped up against the wall beside him.

'Eldar,' said Alaric, 'more xenos.'

'That's Kelhedros,' said Haggard. 'Believe me, my mother taught me to hate the alien just like the preachers said, but Kelhedros is one of the best fighters in Venalitor's stable, and I'll be damned if he doesn't have a plan to get himself out of here.'

'How long do we last?' asked Alaric.

'Depends. A few were here long before me. Most don't make it through their first fight. If you're here at all it means you're tougher than most. Venalitor keeps the best slaves, and carts them around Drakaasi on the *Hecatomb* to send them out against the other lords' gladiators. This damn planet is one giant temple to blood, and the arenas are the altars. It's a sacred business, you know, all this death.'

Alaric slid off the slab and got to his feet. He was still wearing the piecemeal armour he had been given by the alien slave prior to the arena fight. He would have dearly loved to have his own war gear back.

'In here, you do as you will,' said Haggard. 'The weak are weeded out quick enough. But try to get anywhere else on the ship and the scaephylyds will know. Venalitor will have you hung from the prow or fed to the greenskins.

Haulvarn, the best soldier Alaric had ever fought alongside. Haulvarn would have been appointed a justicar with his own squad, and sooner rather than later. He could have risen higher than Alaric, to the ranks of the brother-captains, perhaps even a Grand Master in charge of whole armies and privy to the highest circles of the Ordo Malleus. Haulvarn was gone, and Khorne had taken his share of the death.

'Make sure you stake your claim soon,' said Haggard. 'Plenty of slaves didn't come back today, and there'll be a rush for their cells. Good ones are rare.'

'I'll do that,' said Alaric. He a saw a group of slaves clustered around one cell. They were on their knees. They were praying.

Alaric went to join them.

SEVEN

Lieutenant Erkhar raised his hands slowly, his eyes turned towards the cell floor. The horrors of this world would be matched by the splendours they would one day witness. They had to remember that, no matter how hard it got.

Erkhar placed his hands palms down on the altar. It was a huge stone head, which had originally belonged to a statue of an idealised human, its face noble, with a long aristocratic nose and its hair in dense marble curls. It was presumably of some Champion of Chaos or aspect of Khorne, but it had long ceased to serve that purpose. It was beautiful, while so much on Drakaasi was ugly, and forgotten by the planet's overlords. The believers had placed their faith in it. It was the face of the Emperor on

Drakaasi, an icon of sin transformed by their faith into something beautiful.

'That we must be tested,' began Erkhar, 'is a measure of our faith. For such faith would mean nothing if we lived lives free of suffering. For every moment of pain, our Emperor, we thank you. For every brother and sister taken from us, we rejoice. For every victory of the enemy and the Blood God's brood, we celebrate, for the true victory is the steeling of the faith in our hearts.'

Around him, the faithful listened patiently. Most of them wore the same threadbare dark blue uniforms as Erkhar, and a few still had the insignia of the Imperial Navy. Some of them had joined the faithful later on, but the core of the congregation were the men and women who had been captured when their spacecraft, the *Pax Deinotatos*, was boarded and its crew handed to Venalitor as tribute.

'They have celebrated the destruction of our brothers in the revolt,' said Hoygens, once a gunnery master on board the *Pax*. 'We lost many faithful in those days, and games have taken place to mark the black lizard's triumph over them. How can we take comfort from this? I feel my faith is shaken, lieutenant. I feel that something at my core is missing.'

Erkhar stood up. In spite of the darkness and the grizzled face Drakaasi had given him, he still exuded the presence of an officer. 'The Emperor takes away those crutches you use to hold yourself up, Hoygens! Rejoice in that emptiness. Think how much the sight of the Promised Land will fill you up, now that you have lost so much! Would that we all could feel such despair!'

Erkhar was about to continue when he noticed the huge shape on the walkway outside the cell door.

It was not a scaephylyd slave master, or even one of the *Hecatomb's* more violent and spiteful prisoners. It was an enormous man, a clear head taller than the tallest man there, dressed in scrappy piecemeal armour that couldn't hide his exaggerated musculature.

Many backed away from him in fear.

'Have you come to share in the Promised Land, stranger?' asked Erkhar.

'It's the Space Marine,' said Hoygens in a voice little more than a whisper. Hoygens had been the chief of a gun crew back on the *Pax*, and he was a big man, but he shied away from the newcomer. 'They said Venalitor had got one alive. I didn't believe it.'

'I think there is much need for prayer,' said Alaric. 'I would like to join you, father.'

'I am Lieutenant Erkhar of the Emperor's spaceship the *Pax Deinotatos*,' replied Erkhar. 'I am not the father of anything, and may I ask your name?'

'Justicar Alaric.'

Erkhar smiled. 'There is always room for a newcomer, as long as he has the capacity to believe. We were sent here to be tested, after all. Drakaasi is a torment for us all, through which the Emperor will know His own.'

'You must have given some thought to escape, lieutenant.'

'Many have tried before, lord Marine,' said Hoygens. 'Believe me, I was nearly one of them in the old days, but every time anyone tries, they die. They either get cut down in the attempt, or they're hunted down and thrown out to die in the arena. It's just another kind of sport for them.'

'Brother Hoygens is correct,' said Erkhar. 'The closest anyone got was very recently, not more than a month ago. Hundreds of slaves made a break for it at the arena in Aelazadne. Some of the faithful were with them, but the Ophidian Guard were waiting for them, Ebondrake's own, and they died to a man. They had spent many months in preparation, so it is said, but it all ended in a few hours.'

'This planet is ruled by Khorne,' said Alaric. 'Of course it would not be easy to escape, but I take it that fact has done little to dull your determination.'

Erkhar shook his head. 'Escape is a dream, Justicar, physical escape, anyway. You see, everything I have seen on Drakaasi has led me to conclude that we are here for a reason. The Emperor delivered us here, because this is the first step on the path to the Promised Land. If we stay faithful, we shall be delivered to that Promised Land. For every sin that is committed against us, one more glory shall be ours when the Emperor leads us there. It is the only way Drakaasi can be made to make sense.'

'The Emperor created Drakaasi?' said Alaric warily.

'No, Justicar. Drakaasi was created by evil men. The Emperor brought us here because we are His faithful, and it is only through suffering the works of these evil men that we can be made pure enough to ascend to the Promised Land. If you join us in our faith then you will be led there, too.'

'Back in the Imperium, lieutenant, what you have just told me would be considered heresy.'

'But we are not in the Imperium.'

'No, we are not, and where is the Promised Land?'

'I have preached that it is a place to which we will be delivered, a land of peace and plenty where there is no pain. As to whether it really is a place, or is somewhere inside us, is a matter for a man's conscience. You, however, I feel, will not be content to seek this solace inside yourself. You want to escape, and get revenge.'

'Perhaps,' replied Alaric.

'You need allies. Not even a Space Marine can get off Drakaasi on his own. You thought that these poor religious fanatics would think you were some kind of icon sent by the Emperor, and that they would sacrifice their lives for your benefit. We are all equal on Drakaasi, Justicar, even Space Marines. If you want to get away from here, the Promised Land is the only way. Faith will conquer Drakaasi, not you, and if you want to bring Duke Venalitor to task, perhaps you do not know enough about him.'

'He bested me and took me prisoner,' replied Alaric sharply. 'I am under no illusions as to his capabilities.'

'Then you know why he is held in esteem by Lord Ebondrake in the first place?'

'I take it you do.'

Erkhar shrugged. 'One hears things. Some of the slaves who were here when we were first captured, long dead by now of course, were there when Venalitor first raised the *Hecatomb* and took his place among Drakaasi's lords. He bested a daemon, they said. The tale was passed down by generations of slaves before us. Its name was Raezazel. It was some magical thing the other lords despised. Venalitor hunted it down and defeated it. The other lords hated it, and that hate won him power. Hatred and power are the same thing on Drakaasi. That is the world we all have to endure.'

'It sounds like you are willing to sit here and take whatever Chaos throws at you, lieutenant,' retorted Alaric.

'When the Promised Land is in sight, Justicar, you will realise that nothing could be further from the truth. If you want to understand that truth, then join us. We will welcome you. Otherwise, fight and die, for without hope of the Promised Land that is all there is for anyone on Drakaasi.'

Erkhar turned away from Alaric, placed a hand on the broken stone head that represented their Emperor, and continued to pray. By the time the congregation had finished entreating the Emperor for deliverance, Justicar Alaric had gone.

* * *

Aelazadne!

It is the song that brings the city into being, not the other way around. A million voices raised in song! A million more in pain! The chorus of Chaos, an endless tune to which dance the very nethermost daemons of the warp!

The spires of the crystal city are a crown anointing the Blood God's world, raised from the sands to resonate with the song by a divine hand! The masters of its choirs direct the Blood God's song from the throats of its slaves, torturing the finest howls of terror and caressing the most beautiful of paeans to suffering. Was there any hideous thing so beautiful as Aelazadne? Were ever glory and horror such close soulmates as in that great crystal cathedral? Was any god exalted as Aelazadne exalts the Skull Lord of Drakaasi?

– 'Mind Journeys of a Heretic Saint,' *by Inquisitor Helmandar Oswain (Suppressed by order of the Ordo Hereticus)*

'This damn song,' said Gearth, 'it gets inside your soul.'

'Stay strong,' said Alaric.

'It's all right for you. Your kind get your minds rebuilt to cope with crap like this. Some of us are just mortals.' Gearth was sitting in the corner of his tiny cage, which was suspended from the ceiling over an open sewer of gore and effluent. Alaric was in the cage next to him, and through the darkness countless cells hung, each holding one of Venalitor's slaves. The slaves had been separated on the

Hecatomb and locked into these tiny cages, which then rattled along chains and rails in the dark crystal depths of the city. The song had begun as the *Hecatomb* approached the city and had never stopped, but only got slowly louder, until it was as much a part of the place as the walls around them.

The arena of Aelazadne was above them, and even here, deep inside the honeycomb of corrupted crystal on which Aelazadne was built, the song keened from every direction. The orks were singing their own song, a horrible sound, worse than Aelazadne's music. The idea that any living thing could relish life on Drakaasi was obscene.

'Do you know what we will be fighting?'

'Heh? No one ever knows. I bet they've got something special for you, though.'

'You must have thought of getting out of here,' said Alaric.

'Yeah, thought about it plenty. Thought about being skinned and eaten by the flesh hounds, too, 'cause that's the best I could hope for if they caught me. The way I figure, there's no way off this planet. The best I can do is make them suffer. Every now and again we get to face something in the arenas that they don't want us to kill. When I come up against something like that, I'm gonna kill it. That'll hurt them more than anything I could do if I broke out.'

'But all the killing is for the glory of Khorne. Every time you kill out there, you are doing the will of Chaos.'

'Then, when they send you out there, just curl up and die. I don't care, Marine.' Gearth sneered. 'I hear they killed your friend.'

'That is true.'

'The Imperium killed mine. The arbitrators dragged them around the back of the precinct fortress and shot them in the back of the head. There's nothing good in the universe to fight for. It's all going to hell. If you want to die out there then be my guest, but make sure you take a good look around first, Marine, 'cause soon that's what the entire galaxy is gonna look like.'

'Then Venalitor didn't have to do much to break you,' said Alaric levelly. 'You were Khorne's servant long before he ever found you.'

Gearth spat at Alaric. Alaric ignored it. Men like Gearth were a natural by-product of the Imperium. The Imperium was a cruel place because the galaxy was cruel. Its people had to be oppressed, because if they were free to do and think as they wished, they would do horrible things that would lead the human race to destruction. Gearth was one of the many who didn't fit into the mould the Imperium had prepared for its people.

Sometimes Alaric wondered if the Emperor could one day awaken and show the Imperium a way to survive that did not require such relentless cruelty towards its citizens.

'Do you really believe,' Alaric found himself saying, 'that Drakaasi could exist without people like you?'

Gearth gave Alaric a look full of hate. Before he could retort, Alaric's cell was cranked suddenly upwards. It was hauled up a stinking narrow shaft, and a thin veil of reddish light picked out the claw marks along the sides. The sound of the arena crowd mingled perfectly with Aelazadne's song in a terrible harmony that could have broken a lesser man than a Grey Knight.

The light broke around him. The cage fell apart, and Alaric was standing in the centre of Aelazadne's arena.

THE LIGHT WAS coming from a single opening in the stone sky above Alaric. Around him a labyrinth spiralled off in all directions. It was a buried part of the city, its buildings rotting bastions of stone, with empty windows like blinded eyes and broken doorways like teeth in shattered mouths. Aelazadne had always been grand, but now the excessive decoration had decayed into a parody of beauty, sculpted pediments sagging and faceless statues lying in severed chunks on the pitted ground.

Alaric spotted tiny glistening eyes winking on the walls, swivelling to follow him. Through them, Aelazadne was watching. He heard the cheer as they focused on him, a new player entering their game.

He spotted the first body lying close by, slumped against a collapsed wall in a pool of glistening blood. It had originally been human, but more than that Alaric couldn't tell, for it had been torn clean in two. Alaric picked up the rusted blade lying by the corpse's outstretched hand.

Something lowed in the distance, deep and angry. Someone screamed. A cheer rose at the sound.

Aelazadne's song wove a different pattern here. Filtered through the layers of the city, its individual threads were clearer, and Alaric could pick out the voices, strangle sounds and gurgling, opened up to the glory of Khorne. He could pick out some of their words, too.

They were telling him to be grateful, for very few were given the honour of such a death.

Alaric flinched at a movement nearby. Another slave skulked from the shadows. He was armed with a club with an iron spike through it. Alaric realised the man was a mutant, his scrawny body disfigured with ruffs of waving cilia that wove up his neck and down his arms. He was dressed in ragged remnants of armour.

'Where is it?' the mutant demanded.

'Where is what?'

'What they sent us here to hunt.'

'I don't know. I haven't even seen it.'

'Of course you ain't. What, you fresh out of the sky?'

'Yes.'

The mutant looked Alaric up and down. 'What are you?'

'I was going to ask you the same.'

'Touched,' said the mutant with pride, 'in the blood.' Blood oozed from the fronds wriggling all over his skin. 'Bleeding for His glory, weeping Khorne's own tribute for…'

A sound close by cut off the mutant's voice. A second later a body crashed through a wall behind Alaric, bringing decayed chunks of marble crunching to the ground.

Alaric rolled away from the destruction and just caught sight of the corpse out of the corner of his eye: another mutant, a multi-armed creature, its chest an open red ruin and its face locked in an expression of surprise.

The club-armed mutant roared and charged into the seething darkness. A muscly hand grabbed him and dragged him through the ruin of the wall. The mutant screamed, and it was a scream that went on far too long for the enemy to be killing him quickly.

Alaric ran around a corner, away from the enemy's line of sight. He still had not seen it, save for its hand. He heard it lumbering away, issuing a deep rumbling growl, followed by a wet crunch that Alaric guessed was the mutant's body being mashed against the ground.

Alaric caught his breath. The monster was definitely huge, and judging by the mutant's scream it had more in its arsenal than mere strength. He could smell it, too, a mixture of sweat and heady chemicals.

Alaric had emerged into a ruined town square built around a grand fountain. The fountain's statues had lost their heads and hands and the water, if it had been water that flowed through it, had long since dried up. A sagging basilica stood along one side of the square, gutted by fire. The creature's smell told Alaric that it had retreated in that direction. The sounds of its footsteps were all but hidden by the droning bass of Aelazadne's song, but they were there, and audible enough for Alaric to know that the beast was still close.

A stone head on the ground looked up at him. Its eyes were the same as the ones studding the walls of the labyrinth. Alaric stamped on it, shattering the head and crushing the eyes. Somewhere in Aelazadne, he hoped, two members of the audience were blinded.

The basilica's interior was twisted by heat and decay. Columns bowed under the weight of a half-fallen roof. Skeletons were embedded in the stone of the columns and walls, petrified like fossils, reaching from the rock as if they had been alive when they turned to stone.

Alaric backed up against a pillar. He looked down at the sword in his hand. It was pathetic, little more than scrap metal beaten into shape. It was worse than nothing. He put it on the ground at his feet.

He listened to the song. It was telling him to welcome death, and let it speed him towards a blessed release from life's pain. He ignored it. The song might have wormed its way into a broken man's mind, but Alaric was better than that. He listened harder.

He could hear drops of water spattering down through the hole in the roof, and the sound of the city groaning as it settled. A Space Marine's senses were all greatly enhanced, but rarely had so much hinged on Alaric being able to make the most of them.

It had come through the basilica, through the rubble at the far end, and had headed upwards.

Alaric slipped from behind the column, and began the hunt.

He crept through a collapsed colonnade that had once fronted a mighty palace, now collapsed into a sprawl of rubble. He followed the trail through its cellars, between mouldering works of art and altars to the perverse faces of Khorne.

The trail led through a garden of petrified trees and a stream bed half-filled with flaking dried blood. He moved past a pyramid of bones, and a complex of slaughterhouses, where hooks still hung from rails on the ceiling and the occasional skull still dangled.

Alaric knew that the beast he had trailed was close by. It was instinct as much as the signs: the fresh, six-toed hoof prints on the wet floor, the newly killed hunters whose blood had yet to start drying, the smell of the chemicals, and the glints of blood where the beast had torn itself on a sharp piece of rubble. Alaric slowed down, making every step an exercise in discipline, as he passed over the threshold of the slaughterhouse and onto the grand processional bridge.

Once, a great palace of Aelazadne had risen over the rest of the city. It had long since collapsed, but the way up to it remained, a mighty bridge over a deep canal. Alaric walked carefully onto the bridge, keeping a statue between him and the hulking shape he just glimpsed among the stonework. The statues rose on either side of the bridge, a stern parade of Aelazadne's kings, all of them dressed in obscene majesty that only accentuated their deformities. Eyes covered them, blinking excitedly as Aelazadne watched.

Alaric got a better look at the prey he had been sent to hunt. It was a hunched giant wrapped in swathes of scabbed skin, covered in wounds and brands. Its back was to Alaric, and he saw that it sported a crest of bony spikes along its spine.

Alaric recognised some of the beast's tattoos: an eye, a compass, a star. He had seen them many times before, and that gave him an advantage that the keenest of Drakaasi's hunters lacked.

'I know,' said Alaric aloud, 'what you are.'

The beast looked up from its meal, a hunter it had chased down and killed on the bridge. Alaric stepped out from behind the statue. The beast's face was humanoid, but no longer human, severely lopsided with a single fang reaching down past its chin. Its hands were fused into crab-like claws of muscle and talon.

Its eyes were sunk so deeply into the scarred folds of its face that it had to be blind. A larger third eye in its forehead was closed.

'When did they find you?' asked Alaric. 'How long have you been down here?'

The beast did not attack. Something like recognition came across its face.

'Remember what you once were, Navigator.'

Navigators were a paradox of the Imperium. They were members of a bloodline that sported a stable mutation in its genes. A Navigator had a third eye through which he could look upon the warp and not be driven mad, as most men would be. As a result of the mutation, only they could guide a ship on long warp jumps, and without them all ships would be limited to the stilted, short jump journeys that meant civilian craft took decades to get between star systems. Without Navigators the Imperium's armed forces would reach war zones centuries late, rapid forces like the Space Marines would never be able to launch their lightning operations, and the Imperium, bloated and sluggish at the best of times, would fall apart.

Their third eye, spacefarers said, could kill a man with a look.

It stood to reason that this creature, which had once been a Navigator, would make for very challenging quarry indeed.

Alaric slowly approached the mutant Navigator. Perhaps exposure to Drakaasi's brand of Chaos had mutated it, or perhaps it had been born that way. Although their mutation was relatively stable, Alaric had heard tales from inquisitors of the monstrous aberrations every Navigator family kept imprisoned beneath their estates on Terra.

It did not attack. Alaric was probably the first person the Navigator had encountered on Drakaasi who had not tried to kill it.

'I know why they sent me here,' said Alaric, as much to himself as to the Navigator. 'You are supposed to kill me.'

The song of Aelazadne rose to a sudden, brutal crescendo. The whole city shook, chunks of masonry and statues clattering down into the deep canal beneath the bridge. The Navigator roared and reared up, clamping its paws over its ears. Alaric, too, was shaken by the ferocity of the atonal chord that hammered down from the city above.

The Navigator thudded down onto all fours and roared at Alaric. Its third eye snapped open.

Alaric threw himself to the ground. A black ribbon of ragged power leapt from the Navigator's eye, and scored a deep furrow across the bodies of the statues around him. A stone arm clattered to the ground, the sound almost lost amid the din.

Alaric ran out of cover as the Navigator's third eye spat dark power over the bridge. He sprinted for the Navigator, head down at full tilt, and slammed into its side, vaulting over the line of dark power and up onto its back.

The Navigator bucked to throw him off and reached up to grab him. Alaric caught its hand and forced its forefinger back, feeling ligaments snapping. The Navigator's scream of pain mingled with the song, and Alaric was so dazed by the painful harmonics that he lost his grip and fell off the Navigator's back.

He reached around instinctively. His hand found the warm sticky mass of the last hunter to stalk the

Navigator. He looked up and saw something metallic there: the broken haft of a spear ending in a jagged steel blade. The Navigator's shadow fell over him as he grabbed it.

The Navigator's bulk fell down on top of Alaric's legs. The mutant's face was centimetres away from his. The third eye opened again, the brow above it furrowed in anger and pain.

The song had driven it wild. Aelazadne was not about to cheat its audience of another death.

Alaric rammed the spear up at the Navigator's face. The tip splintered against the stone hard cornea of its third eye. The shaft followed it, shattering and filling its eye socket with splinters.

The Navigator barked angrily and jumped backwards, clawing at its face.

Alaric jumped to his feet. The Navigator was not a creature of Drakaasi, but it had been warped and rendered mindless by this world, turned into a weapon. Drakaasi took good people and turned them into monsters. It wanted to do the same to Alaric, if it did not kill him first.

The Navigator charged half-blinded. Alaric jumped, not into the creature's wounded face but over it, his back smacking against the creature's hide as he rolled over it.

The Navigator continued, its massive momentum too great for it to stop.

It smashed into the stone rail of the bridge, and ploughed through it. Its forelimbs found nothing as it powered forwards. The Navigator howled as it fell from the bridge, the sound followed by a terrible wet thump as it smacked gorily into the bed of the dry canal.

Alaric picked himself up off the bridge, breathing heavily. A thousand eyes were looking at him.

He had killed their Navigator. That had not been in the script.

Soldiers from Aelazadne's battlements were despatched to round him up, for the hunt was over and the audience had got their blood. Alaric knew that to fight against the armoured gauntlets holding him down would only give the city more bloodshed to gloat over, and so he let them wrap him in chains and drag him back towards the *Hecatomb*.

They had got their blood, but Alaric had got something, too. Amongst the Navigator's tattoos had been the familiar brand of a six-fingered hand.

The Navigator could kill with a look from its third eye. It was a quarry intended to kill its hunter. That was why Alaric had been thrown into the labyrinth with it. The daemon Arguthrax had made sure that Alaric was pitted against his best slave killer, in the hope that Venalitor would lose his best new slave.

The lords of Drakaasi had a weakness, a weakness that masqueraded among their number as a strength.

They hated one another. Their weakness was that hate.

EIGHT

'I HEAR MANY things,' said the eldar carefully, 'and I wish to know if any of them are true.'

'Get away from me,' said Alaric. 'I feel unclean enough as it is.'

Kelhedros tilted his head and looked at Alaric with utterly alien eyes.

Alaric was in an isolation cell. Evidently Venalitor had been angered at Arguthrax's attempt to kill Alaric with the Navigator and had taken out a measure of that anger on Alaric. Alaric was chained to the wall on a lower deck, and he was glad of it. Until Kelhedros's shadow had fallen across him he had been alone.

'I have tried to understand you,' continued Kelhedros, 'your kind, I mean, your species. It is like facing an animal, with its baffling instincts.'

Alaric had not had a good look at the alien before. Eldar were familiar to many Imperial citizens, since they were often depicted as weakling aliens crushed beneath the feet of conquering humans in stained glass windows or in the margins of illuminated prayer books. The truth was that no human artist could ever realise one properly. An eldar looked almost human from a distance: two arms, two legs, two eyes, a nose, a mouth, but everything else was different. An eldar radiated wrongness, from its huge, liquid eyes to the many jointed, worm-like waving of its fingers. They were disgusting and unnerving, and Alaric hated them. Kelhedros was as filthy and scarred as the rest of the slaves, but he still carried that typical alien arrogance with him. His armour still incorporated the jade green plates of the eldar armour he must have been captured in.

'This animal will not heel to an alien,' replied Alaric.

'Of course. You want to be free. They all do when they arrive here.'

'I have nothing to say to you.'

'You want to get out. I want to get out, too. I find you as vile as you find me, human, but it cannot be denied that we have the same goal in mind. I think neither of us has much of a chance on his own, but we are both far superior to the rest of Venalitor's rabble, and our skills would complement each other.'

Alaric laughed, and it hurt since he was still battered from the fight with the Navigator. 'Yes, I have seen what happens when a human enters into a pact with the alien. I was there at Thorganel Quintus. The Inquisition brokered an alliance between the Imperium and the eldar there. I saw you xenos fall on our troops as soon as the Daggerfall Mountains were secured. I saw you butcher us like cattle because you did not want anyone to know you needed our help to destroy what we found there. I will never trust your kind. You would see all of us exterminated just to save one of your own. You would kill us all for your convenience.'

Kelhedros drew his weapon from his back – a slender chainsword, its teeth meticulously cleaned and gleaming in the shadows of the isolation deck. 'The eldar you fought alongside. Were they of the Scorpion temple?'

Alaric sneered. 'They all looked the same.'

'You would have remembered. No eldar is stronger or more resolute than a follower on the path of the Scorpion. The Scorpion is relentless. It cannot fail, because it will die before its claws let go, and once it has its enemy in position, its sting always kills. I walked the path of the Scorpion before fate brought me here, human. They say that you are a hunter of daemons, something remarkable by the standards of your species. The eldar think the same of me. The Aspect of the Scorpion does not come easily to us. I am not just another alien, Grey Knight, even to you. I am a Striking Scorpion, and of every living thing on this planet I am by far the most likely to escape it. Without me, you will die here, probably a broken and willing slave. Together we might return to the galaxies we know. Think upon it. You have no other choice.'

'I am very picky about who gets to betray me,' said Alaric, knowing insults would be lost on the alien, but unable to help himself when confronted with such arrogance, 'and you don't make the grade.'

'You will change your mind, Grey Knight,' replied Kelhedros. It was unlikely he even understood human hatred when he saw it. If he did, he did not respond to it. 'I am out here, and you are in there. If you are so content to stay then little I can say will sway you.'

Kelhedros gave Alaric one last glance with those huge black eyes, and ducked back into the shadows. He was gone, with not even the sound of footsteps to suggest he was on the isolation deck. Alaric let himself wonder how Kelhedros had got down there at all. The alien had free run of the *Hecatomb*, and was certainly as tough as he suggested to have survived on Drakaasi for so long, not least against the human slaves, whose most ingrained instincts included hatred of the alien. However, Alaric knew what the eldar could do. An oath from an eldar meant less than nothing. It was a promise of betrayal.

Alaric had a long time to think in the darkness beneath the *Hecatomb*. Mostly, he thought about the Hammer of Daemons.

* * *

GHAAL!

That seething pit of vermin! That filth brimming sink-hole of despair! In such degradation there is purity. In such ugliness there is wonder. In such death and suffering, there is life, so holy to Drakaasi for it is life that must be ended!

The endless slums of Ghaal breed misery as they breed vermin. Its people are no more than vermin, writhing in an endless murderous mass, struggling to the surface to snatch a few moments of exultation! Was there ever such a city as Ghaal, where the trappings of wealth and culture are stripped away to reveal the raw, bleeding organs of poverty and exploitation? There is the truth of the human condition, that a human mind so easily sinks into animal violence and killing. It is a city of death where murder is the only way out, and where even the most relentless killers find but another layer of Ghaal's anti-society to slaughter their way through.

This cauldron of hate, this pit of ugliness, this aeon's worth of murder forced into the crumbling shell of a city! From the blood that runs in its streets are writ the names of Khorne!

– *'Mind Journeys of a Heretic Saint,' by Inquisitor Helmandar Oswain*
(Suppressed by order of the Ordo Hereticus)

ALARIC'S FIRST EXPERIENCE of Ghaal was the stench. Down on the rowing decks, it rolled in like a foul mist. It was decay and misery, sweat and effluent, the stink of endless poverty.

'We're in the Narrows,' said Haggard, chained to the bench just behind Alaric. Though the slaves were discouraged from speaking on the oar decks, the slavers seemed used to ignoring Haggard. 'This is Ghaal. It's a damned orifice.'

'Literally?' asked Alaric, for whom the images of the living city Karnikhal were still vivid.

'Not quite. It's worse.'

Alaric peered through the oar-hole in the hull. It was night, and by the light of Drakaasi's evil greenish moon he could see piles of ramshackle buildings heaped up by the side of the blood canal. The canal was part of a spider web of bloodways that divided up this part of the city, presumably the narrows after which the place was named, and the *Hecatomb* moved slowly as its hull scraped along the side of the canal. Occasionally, a reedy scream filtered through the night air from the city, followed by a dull splash as a body fell into the blood.

'A city of murderers,' said Haggard. 'Every madman and piece of filth on Drakaasi ends up here. They say it's like a beacon that drags scum.'

'What purpose does it serve?'

'Purpose? There's no purpose here, Justicar. It's just a city.'

'Everywhere on Drakaasi has a reason to exist. Karnikhal is a predator. Aelazadne was an altar to the Blood God. What does Drakaasi gain from Ghaal?'

Alaric looked out on the city again. Here and there the inhabitants of Ghaal, like primitives

forced into ragged clothes and let loose in the
streets, skulked among the shadows hiding from
the moonlight. A rooftop fight sent a skinny body
falling to the streets far below. Freshly slain bodies
lay like heaps of rags in the street, and the sense of
fear emanating from behind the black windows of
the hovels was enough to suggest the thousands of
people huddled there in their nightly terror. Even
those few glimpses of Ghaal showed that killers
walked every street and murder was the sport of
choice.

'It's a farm,' said Alaric grimly. 'This is where they
breed their vermin.'

'Loose the anchors!' yelled one of the scaephylyds
in its strange accent. The oars were drawn in and
the heavy anchor chains rattled against the sides of
the Hecatomb. The ship came to a slow halt along
a massive dock of black stone, where crowds of
Ghaal's vermin hurried to and fro at the barked
orders of mutant gang masters.

'To arming!' yelled the scaephylyd over the grind-
ing of the hull against the dockside. The ship
groaned as ramps were lowered, and the anchors
reeled fast.

Alaric knew the drill. He was starting to lose count
of the number of times he and the other slaves had
filed past the arming cages to pull on tattered armour,
still bloodstained from its previous owner, and pick
up a weapon or two. This time, however, it was different. In one arming cage was a scaephylyd guarding an
oversized suit of half-plate armour.

'You,' said the scaephylyd at Alaric's approach. 'Here.'

The armour was many times more lavish than anything the slaves had been given before. The breastplate looked like a pair of bat's wings folded over the chest, and the shoulder guards were wrought into snarling faces. Scale mail protected the joints. Beside the armour was a two-handed sword that looked like it had been carved out of an enormous fang.

'You're famous now,' said Gearth, who was choosing from a selection of rusted knives in the next cage, 'gotta look the part. They'll be betting on you an' all sorts. Reckon you've got a fan club? Kids who know your name?' Gearth smiled through his blackened teeth. 'Eh? Maybe sign something for 'em, tell 'em to listen to their mums and stay off the stimms?'

Alaric cast him a glance, and then looked back at the armour. It would certainly provide more protection than the disintegrating chainmail he usually wore, and which he had chosen purely because it was big enough to fit him. The sword looked useful, too.

Alaric pulled the armour on as the other slaves prayed or psyched themselves up. At the other end of the cages were the orks led by One-ear, kept separate from the rest of the slaves as they eagerly grabbed cleavers and swords. One-ear banged heads together and barked orders to keep them in line.

Alaric wondered how long it would take before he was like them, before he lived for the fight.

The balance of the sword was good. Nothing compared to a Nemesis weapon, but it would do. The ports swung open and the slaves were herded out to kill and die for Khorne.

GHAAL'S ARENA, THE Void Eye, was a squat cylinder of black rock honeycombed with caves where thousands of Ghaal's subhumans lived. Heaps of skulls lay at the bottom of the wall like snowdrifts, and the open corpse pits around it bubbled evilly in the darkness.

Alaric could hear the sound of the crowds in the arena, hordes of scum eager to get their fix of bloodshed. He could hear clubs and whips hitting flesh, and knew that ranks of arena warriors would be funnelling the crowds through the entrances into the arena. Many of the vermin would die, but then that was why they were on Drakaasi in the first place, to live short lives whose pain and bloody endings brought pleasure to the Blood God.

The slaves passed through an archway into darkness, hot and close. The scaephylyds hauled the doors shut behind the slaves, and they were trapped inside, packed close. Alaric could see through the darkness, and he registered the familiar mix of confusion and apprehension on the faces of Venalitor's slaves. Even the orks did not like it, and the human slaves kept as much distance as possible between them and the aliens. Kelhedros, on the other hand, looked focused. Nothing seemed to rattle the eldar.

Alaric looked around and picked out a small knot of faithful, clustered around Erkhar and praying. Alaric pushed his way through the crowd and pulled Erkhar aside.

'Lieutenant,' said Alaric, 'whatever lies inside the arena, there is a chance that you will not survive it.'

'A good chance,' replied Erkhar, 'if the Emperor so wills.'

'Then I may not get another chance to ask you.' Alaric dropped his voice to a whisper, and Erkhar had to strain to hear him above the nervous breathing and muttered prayers. 'What do you know of the Hammer of Daemons?'

Erkhar stiffened as if in shock, and his eyes darted as if to see if any faithful were nearby, even in the darkness. 'The Hammer? Where did you hear of it?'

'A rumour,' replied Alaric. 'A legend of the land, a weapon that lies somewhere on Drakaasi.'

'You seek it?'

'Perhaps.'

'You cannot find it, Justicar.'

'Why?'

'Because it is an idea.'

From beyond the skull-studded inner doors of the chamber came a deep rushing, rumbling sound, like an earthquake. The Void Eye shook, dislodging some of the skulls nailed to the black walls. Some of the slaves quivered in fear, others grinned and whooped with anticipation. The orks began a low, chanting death song, something ancient and primitive, and Alaric would not have been surprised if some of the killers like Gearth had joined in.

'Tell me, Erkhar,' whispered Alaric in the lieutenant's ear.

'One day we will all be taken to the Promised Land,' said Erkhar. 'We do not know where it is or how we will get there, only that we will be delivered, but there is more to what I know. Only I and a few of the faithful understand. Some of the more... weak-minded would reject us if they understood. Their minds will be ready one day, but not yet.'

'The Hammer?'

'The Hammer shows us that we were not placed on Drakaasi just to run away. It is a weapon to be used against the enemy. The Hammer of Daemons will be wielded by the faithful to punish the servants of Chaos. Do you see, Justicar? Do you see why it is so dangerous, why so many would despair to hear of it?'

Alaric couldn't answer for a moment. There was genuine fear in Erkhar's face. The Hammer represented something unexpected and powerful in the faithful's patchwork religion.

'The faithful just want to get off this planet,' said Alaric, 'but you know it's not that simple.'

The doors opened a crack and a thin line of purplish, polluted light slid into the chamber. Blood rushed through the gap, covering the floor in a shallow red pool. One of the orks howled like a wolf, and the others joined in. Some of the humans raised their voices, too, echoing the frenzied applause from the vermin packing the Void Eye.

'Correct, Justicar,' said Erkhar. 'One day the Hammer of Daemons will be delivered to us and we will raise it against the enemy. Only then will we in turn be delivered to the Promised Land. Do you see what that means, Justicar?'

'It means that the Emperor isn't going to save you for free.'

'It means that survival is not enough.'

The doors boomed open. A thigh-high tide of blood flooded the chamber, knocking some men off their feet. Alaric saw Gearth dipping his hand into the blood and branding a bloody hand print across his face. Kelhedros drew his chainsword.

Erkhar turned back to his faithful. 'Take heart! These doors take us one step closer to the Emperor's halls!'

'One step closer to death, boys!' shouted Gearth in reply, and the other killers laughed raucously. 'Human blood doesn't come cheap! Let's show them the price!'

There was an ocean of blood beyond the doors. The canals must have been diverted to fill the whole Void Eye with it, and it churned beneath the hulls of a dozen ships of black timber, their sails daubed with bleeding runes. Already the blood bobbed with bodies and severed limbs. Fortified compounds separated the vermin in the stands from the dignitaries, and Alaric was sure he saw the bloated whitish form of Arguthrax squatting in its cauldron of gore.

The closest ship drew nearer. Arena slaves on board threw ropes through the door, and the orks grabbed them eagerly, hauling the ship in. Orks and killers were leaping onto its deck.

Across the arena, the scene was being repeated, but this time daemons were leaping onto the decks and scrabbling up the rigging, glowing-skinned creatures with shifting forms composed of teeth, claws, eyes and shimmering muscle.

It was a sea battle. The lords of Drakaasi had given the subhuman filth of Ghaal a different kind of murder to cheer.

The first ship was full and the next one drew near. Alaric followed Kelhedros onto it, along with several of Gearth's murderers and Erkhar's faithful. The blood churned beneath it and drew it away from the dock chamber, towards the centre of the arena where it would meet the daemon crewed warships. The crowds howled in anticipation.

At least, thought Alaric grimly as he crouched down on the deck of the ship, the good people of Ghaal will not be disappointed.

NINE

THE UNHOLY PITCHED wildly in the howling winds that suddenly sheared across the Void Eye. Alaric gripped the rail on the prow as the ship tilted. A couple of slaves fell from the rigging into the blood.

The battle had begun as soon as the slaves were on board. The wind had thrown the ships across the blood sea. The blood churned with predators who dragged down the slaves who fell in, and Alaric saw chewed corpses being thrown out of the blood into the stands where Ghaal's spectators tore them apart. It had happened so quickly there had been no time to organise the slaves on the ship. They had time only to hold on and hope that the blood did not claim them. The opposing ships, crewed by daemons, were launched from the far side of the arena to an enormous cheer from the crowds.

'We're gonna hit port side!' yelled Gearth, who was armed with a pair of rusty daggers, and holding on to the fore mast to keep from being flung across the deck.

'Which way's port?' asked one of Gearth's killers.

'There!' replied Gearth, pointing. 'Didn't your dad never tell you nothing?'

The *Unholy* was drawn around towards the opposing ship. The name etched below its prow proclaimed it as the *Meathook*. Red-skinned daemons danced on its pitching deck.

'Grapples ready!' shouted Gearth.

'We're going aboard?' asked Erkhar, who was holding on to the deck rail close to Gearth.

'We go to them,' said Gearth. 'If you wanna die, you just sit back and let them come to us.'

'He's right,' shouted Alaric. 'If we let them pounce we're dead. Erkhar, get the faithful to draw in the *Meathook*. Gearth, get your men ready to board.'

'Just try and stop 'em,' said Gearth. With a grin on his blood-spattered face he looked completely at home.

The slaves had found a number of ropes with grappling hooks below decks. Erkhar's faithful, muttering desperate prayers to the Emperor, got ready to fling them across to the enemy ship as the *Meathook* closed in.

Elsewhere, the sea battle was close and extremely bloody. The orks were having the time of their lives as their ship, dubbed the *Soulbleed*, had rammed the daemon-crewed *Wrack*. It was impossible to tell who was winning, since both the greenskins and daemons were whooping with joy as they cut one another to pieces. The daemons on the *Soulbleed* were led by a huge creature: a dog-faced, muscular horror armed with a huge axe, who stood on the stern slicing up anything that came close. Alaric spotted the brand of a six-fingered hand seared into the daemon's chest.

The third slave ship, the *Malice*, was in the process of sinking, its slaves scrabbling up the tilting hull. The daemons on the ship that had rammed it, the *Gorehallow*, were diving into the blood to circle the sinking *Malice* like sharks and drag down any slaves who fell in.

It was the clash of the *Unholy* and the *Meathook* that would decide whether the slaves or the daemons triumphed for the delight of Ghaal's hordes.

A handful of hooks found purchase on the *Meathook*. A volley of arrows whistled across from the *Meathook* in reply. Alaric took cover as an arrow thunked into the deck beside him, and he saw that it was not an arrow at all but a dart shaped insectoid creature, mandibles working as it bored into the wood. One of Erkhar's faithful screamed and stumbled backwards with one of the creatures embedded in his chest. He had dropped one of the ropes attaching the *Unholy* to the *Meathook* and Alaric grabbed it, putting all his weight into dragging the two ships together. Alaric's enhanced muscles burned as the prows of the ships swung together, and with a screech of breaking wood the two ships collided.

Gearth stood up, brandished his blades, and howled. The murderers followed him as he ran for the prow and leapt across. More arrows streaked into the *Unholy*, but the assault had already begun. The daemons were dropping their bows of bone and leaping with teeth and claws into the fray. Gearth cut off a tentacled arm, and slit open a belly, charging on through the slick of glowing, burning entrails. The daemons on the *Meathook* were sinewy and cruel faced, with tiny burning eyes and axe-like faces full of teeth. They grew new limbs and re-formed to sprint spider-like through the rigging or along the side of the *Unholy's* hull.

Alaric jumped the gap between the ships. A daemon leapt down from the rigging onto him. Alaric didn't even draw his sword, simply grabbing the daemon by a wrist and an ankle, tearing it in two, and throwing it into the blood churning below.

Gearth skidded into place beside him. One of his knives was gone, probably buried in the skull of a daemon. He was covered in smouldering gore, for these daemons bled scalding embers as well as blood.

'About damn time!' cackled Gearth. 'Just like home!'

Alaric drew his sword and took stock of the situation. Gearth's charge had taken half the deck, but there were daemons everywhere. More were emerging from below decks, but these were not warriors, they were shrieking creatures of skin and bone, flapping like startled birds.

'There's something below decks,' shouted Alaric above the din. 'These were just keeping it down there.'

'Good!' replied Gearth.

Daemon corpses rained down. Kelhedros was somewhere up in the rigging, and Alaric could hear the scream of his chainblade through daemonic flesh.

The *Meathook* was a trap. The *Unholy* had run into it, but Alaric could not have stopped it. The only way to deal with it was to fight on through.

The deck heaved. Men and daemons were thrown into the blood. The stern of the *Meathook* splintered and burst into the air, shards of blood-soaked timbers flying everywhere. A scaled shape ripped up out of the ship: a sea serpent far longer than the *Meathook*, dredged up from some Emperor-forsaken trench in Drakaasi's oceans and coiled up inside the ship, goaded until it was angry and ravenous.

The serpent looped up into the air above the ship, crashing through the rigging. Its head, a fanged horror fringed with tentacles, plunged back into the deck amidships, and the *Meathook* split in two. The rear half tipped to stern and filled with blood. The prow did not begin to sink straight away, buoyed up as it was by the *Unholy* alongside it.

Alaric stood on the prow of the shattered *Meathook*, sword out, trying to follow the snake-like movements of the sea monster. It snapped at the rigging, picking up a daemon in its mandibles and tossing it down its throat. A slave, one of Gearth's killers, followed, stabbing haplessly at the thing's vast jaws as he disappeared down its gullet.

Oozing green eyes ringed its head. One of them settled on Alaric.

The serpent reared up and arrowed back down at Alaric. The Grey Knight dived to one side as its neck slammed down onto the prow of the *Meathook*. The remains of the ship sagged under the impact, and the *Unholy* listed with the weight. A tentacle whipped around Alaric's leg and dragged him towards the yawning jaws of the serpent.

Alaric kicked out, shattering a tooth. Foul blood sprayed everywhere. In desperation, he braced with his arms as the jaws closed around him and held the sea serpent's mouth open, bathed in its stinking, rotting breath, writhing flagellae in its throat trying to snag his feet and drag him down.

Alaric yelled as he fought to keep his elbows straight. He could hear screaming below him as the slaves and daemons already swallowed were forced through the serpent's corrosive guts. His sword was still in his hand, but to use it he would have to stop bracing the serpent's jaws and its teeth would come crunching down on him.

The whine of a chainblade cut through the serpent's roar. Blood sprayed over Alaric as the tip of a chainsword bored down through the top of the serpent's jaw. The serpent convulsed, and Alaric

planted a foot against a huge fang and kicked himself free.

Alaric skidded onto the deck of the shattered
Meathook as the serpent reared up in pain. A figure
was flung off the top of its head and landed near
Alaric, just keeping its footing on the blood-slick
wood.

It was Kelhedros, the alien.

'Xenos,' said Alaric, 'you saved me.'

'It benefits none of us if you are dead.'

'We can't beat that thing,' said Alaric, looking over
at the serpent, which was demolishing what
remained of the *Meathook's* stern.

'No, we cannot, but this battle is over. The winds
have changed. If we cut the *Unholy* free we can get it
back to the dock. It was the serpent they wanted to
see.'

Alaric followed Kelhedros's gaze towards the
crowd. They were frenzied with delight to see the
serpent swallowing slaves and daemons alike. They
were shrieking their approval of the orks and daemons butchering one another on the *Wrack*, too,
which was being driven closer to the wreck of the
Meathook. Alaric could see Arguthrax in the crowd,
wallowing in his cauldron of gore, and surrounded
by slaves close to the wall that encompassed the
mock ocean of blood. He could see Duke Venalitor,
too, pale and dignified among the crowd, as he
watched his slaves providing entertainment for
Khorne's faithful.

'Cut the *Unholy* free,' said Alaric. 'Get them to safety.'

'And you?' asked the alien.

'Survival is not enough,' replied Alaric.

The *Wrack* drifted closer. Alaric could see the dog-faced daemon champion flinging an ork down from the stern. On the prow, the ork leader One-ear was building up a pile of broken daemons with a two-handed hammer.

Kelhedros didn't hang around to see what Alaric was planning to do. The eldar leapt from the prow of the *Meathook* onto the deck of the *Unholy* and immediately set about cutting the ropes attaching the two ships together.

The front mast of the *Meathook* was almost horizontal as the prow half sunk further. It was pointing towards the approaching *Wrack*. Alaric ran up it, struggling to keep his balance as his considerable weight tipped the mast down.

The *Wrack* closed further. The daemon champion bit into an ork, bright blood running down its scarred chest. The crowd in the stands was in a bloody frenzy, and Arguthrax bellowed his approval.

Alaric broke into a run. He reached the end of the mast and jumped.

The deck of the *Wrack* swirled below him. He was strong, but he barely made it. His chest thumped into the deck rail of the ship's prow, and he grabbed with one hand, his other still holding his sword. With a final effort he hauled himself onto the deck of the *Wrack*.

One-ear looked down at him and grinned. The alien looked like it was having the time of its life.

Several other orks were still alive, enthusiastically wrestling daemons onto the deck or hacking them up with cleavers.

The daemon champion fixed its eyes on Alaric. It was half again as tall as the Grey Knight, packed with muscle and drooling from its dog-like muzzle. It fought with claws and a barbed tail. Dismembered greenskins were piled up around its feet. A pair of ragged, leathery wings sprouted from its back as it snarled a war cry in its daemonic tongue and leapt up into the air.

The crowd cheered as the daemon charged, swooping down towards the prow on its wings. Its weight alone could crush Alaric onto the deck. Alaric moved faster than he had ever done. He dropped his sword and grabbed the mast that jutted from the prow of the *Wrack*. With a massive effort, he broke it free, and turned it around so that the wooden point was aimed at the daemon's chest.

Too late, the daemon tried to correct its charge. It beat its wings once to carry it over Alaric, but Alaric lunged, and the point of the mast hit the daemon in the stomach. The daemon's weight forced the mast into it and it slid, dead weight, down the mast until its feet hit the deck. Impaled on the mast, stuck like an insect pinned to a board, it screamed.

Alaric pushed down on the broken mast and forced the daemon to its knees. The crowd adored it, and the orks cheered too. In the stand, Arguthrax scowled. The six-fingered hand branded on the daemon's chest indicated that it belonged to

Arguthrax. No doubt he had sent it to the Void Eye to help humiliate Venalitor's slaves. As far as Arguthrax was concerned, the battle had not worked out as planned.

Alaric picked up his sword again. With a single bloody strike he struck the daemon champion's head from its shoulders. Burning multi-coloured blood sprayed from the stump of its neck. Alaric let go of the mast and the daemon's body keeled over to one side onto the deck. Alaric bent down and picked up its head.

One-ear saluted Alaric for a job well done. The other daemons on the *Wrack* keened, and the remaining orks plunged into them, tearing malformed limbs from bodies, and cutting torsos open. The sea battle in the Void Eye was emphatically over.

There was one more victory to win. Alaric stood up on the deck rail and drew his arm back. He had only just enough strength left, and he would have to be accurate. He didn't know if he could do it. The crowd cheered him, thinking this was a victory pose, and Alaric let their howls of delight give him strength.

He threw the head as far as he could. It was still snarling and glaring at him as it tumbled towards the stands. With a wet thump, it landed at Duke Venalitor's feet.

Every eye in the arena followed it as it fell. Every eye turned to see the look of pure hatred on Arguthrax's face.

The *Wrack* drifted back towards the arena entrance, where the slaves on the *Unholy* were already disembarking. The orks around Alaric were celebrating their victory, following his lead by hurling chunks of dead daemon towards the stands. One-ear bellowed a war cry and the other greenskins joined in.

For all Alaric knew, they were chanting his praises.

TEN

THE DESPOILER OF Kolchadon, the Bloody Hand of
Skerentis Minor, the End of Empires, Arguthrax the
Magnificent slid from his cauldron into the entrail
pool that dominated his sanctum beneath Ghaal.

Human emotions did not trouble the mind of a
daemon. No mortal could truly understand what
went on in a daemon's head without going insane,
for the rules of logic had no hold over them. No
human emotion could therefore be properly
ascribed to a daemon. Nevertheless, Arguthrax was
definitely angry.

'Filth!' the daemon bellowed as his bloated body
sank into the tangle of entrails. 'Whelp! Weakling
dog! He will pay. He and his slaves, and his... his
natives! That filth will suffer!'

'My lord,' said Khuferan, the majordomo of Arguthrax's sanctum, 'something has vexed you.'

Arguthrax glared at him. Khuferan had been completely human before he had died and been drawn, in the form of a bone-dry mummified corpse, into Arguthrax's army as it marched across the ruins of his home world. Khuferan had been some kind of king or high priest thousands of years ago, but he had forsaken whatever he had in life to serve Chaos in death. 'The upstart, Venalitor. That near-human thing who calls himself a duke. He has sought to humiliate me... me!'

'It is the way of Drakaasi.'

'So is revenge,' snarled Arguthrax. 'Who do we have on the streets and on the plains? Who heeds the words of Arguthrax?'

Khuferan snapped his bony fingers, and lesser daemons, scurrying things like animated blobs of flesh with vestigial limbs, hurried away from him into the dark corners of the sanctum. The sanctum was a spherical cyst in the earth, half-filled with the entrails of thousands of sacrifices. A spur of rock held the sacrificial altar, black with generations of blood, as well as giving Arguthrax's mortal followers like Khuferan somewhere to stand when they addressed their master.

One of the daemons brought Khuferan a heavy book bound in strips of beaten brass. Khuferan leafed through its pages, on which were written the names of thousands of organisations and individuals loyal to Arguthrax. Every lord of Drakaasi had followers he could call upon, many of them hidden deep in the underbelly of Khorne's cities, waiting for the call to action.

'Lord Ebondrake's pronouncement of the crusade has led to a great mobilisation,' said Khuferan. 'We have called upon the Legion of the Unhallowed to bring themselves forth from the jungles and march under your banner, Lord Arguthrax.'

'Savages,' said Arguthrax, 'primitives, but useful. Who else?'

'The Thirteenth Hand are still off-world, but they are returning at your command. The warp shall deliver them to us in a few days. They are battle-hardened, my lord, and have acquired many new members.'

'Hmm. That is good.' The Thirteenth Hand were a fanatical murder cult whose leaders had been ordained in the will of Khorne by Arguthrax himself. 'What of the warp?'

'Relations are... strained,' said Khuferan. 'Many have been lost. The warp dislikes so many losses. Profligacy in the arenas has left us–'

'I am the Despoiler of Kolchadon!' spat Arguthrax. 'How many billions of gallons of blood have rained into the warp at my behest? The daemon lords will heed one of their own, one such as I. I want hunter daemons on the streets, black as the void, and with Venalitor's scent. I want furies in the sky following every movement of his underlings. I want the *Hecatomb* under siege!'

'It will be done. The losses at the Void Eye will require greater recompense for the warp.'

'Tell them they are having revenge. Venalitor had his pet Astartes kill my daemon champion to insult me. He even took its head for himself! It was an insult to all daemonkind, and the warp will have its due if Venalitor suffers. We will bring him low, and then we will kill him. Tell that to the warp. It will listen.'

'Very well, my lord.'

'And the rest of them: the Haunters of the Nethermost Shadow, the mutant cults beneath Vel'Skan. Bring them all in.'

'And the watchers?'

Arguthrax paused. The lords of Drakaasi spied on one another. It was like a game, played with agents who went into deep cover among the coteries of the lords. No doubt other lords had eyes and ears among Arguthrax's followers. Arguthrax had uncovered and eaten more than a few of them. They were mortals and daemons with some talent to obscure their true selves, and they were pariahs. It was not the way of Khorne to skulk in the shadows, and so Drakaasi's spies were a sort of underclass present at the very highest layers of the planet's society. Arguthrax had his own shape shifting daemons and old-fashioned human informers bound to him by contracts of blood.

'If they can fight,' said Arguthrax. 'Punishing Venalitor is a higher priority than anything else. The games, Ebondrake's crusade, everything can wait until he has been brought low.'

'If it is your wish, Lord Arguthrax,' said Khuferan. He bowed his ancient death shrouded body before his master, and turned to walk back down the spur of rock and begin organising his lord's slaves.

The light in the sanctum dimmed. Arguthrax sank into the great cauldron of entrails, deep in thought.

'I REMEMBER,' SAID Kelhedros, 'when I learned of the Fall.'

Kelhedros's cell was relatively clean. The other slaves on the *Hecatomb* knew better than to invade the place. Kelhedros had painted complex rune patterns on the walls in paint mixed from blood and sand. His green metallic armour lay against the wall. The eldar was picking the blood from between the teeth of his chainsword. The sea serpent's blood had been particularly viscous and it was a job to work it out of the mechanism.

'The Fall?' asked Alaric.

'I forget, human, that you are not well versed in our ways. Some of you have studied us, I understand: the biologists of your Inquisition. The better to kill us, of course. But not you.'

'I know that you are aliens.'

'Strange. That is all I once knew of you.'

The journey back from the Void Eye had been deeply strained. Venalitor had stood glowering at them from the helm of the *Hecatomb*, the head of Arguthrax's daemon champion in his hand. Many slaves had been lost, and Haggard had been unable to keep up with the wounded. The orks, forced to wait until last for treatment since they healed so well, were squabbling with each other in their barred enclave. Alaric had sought out Kelhedros. It had become apparent to him early in his career as a Grey Knight that having his life saved at least deserved a few words of thanks, and the possibility of an ally on Drakaasi, even an alien, could not be ignored.

'Long ago, my kind ruled the galaxy,' continued Kelhedros, 'much as your kind claim to rule it now. We were artists and aesthetes, while you are soldiers. We took worlds and made them beautiful instead of merely inhabiting them like insects in a nest.'

'None taken,' said Alaric.

Kelhedros gave him a quizzical look. 'Quite, but we were arrogant, prideful. Some of what I see in your kind, my kind must have seen in themselves. They indulged their base delights. The warp took heed. From the sinful pride of my people was born… one of the great powers of the warp. I cannot speak of it. It plagues us still and reaps its toll among humankind, too.'

'I imagine this is not something an alien would normally speak of to a human.'

'Indeed it is not. Many would think me a traitor for saying it, but then I am a traitor for surviving here amongst such… pollution.'

'Then why tell me?'

'Because I see it on this world, too, and in your Imperium.' Kelhedros looked up from his chainblade. 'The Fall killed the better part of my species. Only those who saw it coming escaped it in their world ships. My kind, so far advanced compared to yours, was almost wiped out. Think what another Fall would do to you. Do not think that you will see it coming, or that it has not already begun. You are living through the death of your species at this very moment and you do not realise it.'

'I cannot believe that,' said Alaric. 'There must be hope.'

Kelhedros arched an eyebrow. 'Why?'

'Because without it we are lost.'

'You are lost anyway. Whether you truly believe in salvation or not is irrelevant. Death is death.'

'Perhaps everything you say is true and these are the death throes of the human race, but even if that was true, I would not lose faith. There must be hope, and I must fight for my Emperor against Chaos and its servants. That is just the way it is.'

'That is insanity.'

'Wrong, it's being human.'

'That's it? That is why you have managed to spread to the stars and found this Imperium, in spite of all the obvious primitivism of your minds?'

'That's right,' said Alaric. 'We believe. I suppose that's it.'

'There are such strange things in the galaxy,' said Kelhedros.

'Now there we can agree.'

Kelhedros put his chainsword to one side and began on his armour. Like the weapon, it was old and battered but well-maintained. Beneath the armour, Kelhedros's body was slim but muscular, quite the opposite of Alaric's own oversized frame. He was scarred, too, and like Alaric not all of them were war wounds. Runes were scored into the eldar's torso. They were symbols with half-glimpsed meaning: half a face without a mouth, a hand, a stylised blade, all twining together in thorny knot work.

'I do not think, Grey Knight, that you are here to discuss the state of the universe,' said Kelhedros.

'I came here to thank you.'

'It is not necessary. It does not benefit any of us to lose our best fighter.'

'You took a risk.'

'One can hardly survive on Drakaasi without taking risks. If we flee death, we only run into its waiting arms. My own chances of survival are increased if you are there by my side, so I took risks to prevent your death. Anyone understanding the reality of our situation would do the same thing. Likewise, you are taking a considerable risk by speaking willingly to an alien that your kind despises to the point of genocide, and so you have a reason to be here, too.'

Alaric leaned across the rail and looked down on the floor of the main chamber. Kelhedros's cell was one floor up, and gave him an excellent view of what was going on among the *Hecatomb's* slaves. 'Look down there,' he said.

Kelhedros stood by his side. 'At what?'

'The greenskins.'

'The animals? I sully my eyes with them as little as possible.'

'Then for the first time, try watching them.'

The orks, those who had survived the Void Eye relatively unscathed, were scrapping with each other amid the filth of their enclosure. One-ear was standing aside, barking insults and grunting appreciation.

'They are just turning on each other,' said Kelhedros, 'for they know that the humans will mass against them if they do not. They are cowards.'

'Wrong,' said Alaric. 'Watch.'

One-ear dragged two fighting greenskins apart. He cuffed the loser around the back of the head, shoving him away. The winner he clapped on the back, much as he had congratulated Alaric for cutting the head off the daemon, and turned back to watch the other greenskins scrapping.

'That one,' said Kelhedros, 'he's in charge.'

'Exactly.'

'But it is the way of the animal. The strongest rules.'

'And he is using that. He's training them, toughening them up.'

'He simply wants to survive.'

'We all want to survive, eldar. One-ear has a plan, which is more than most of the humans here. Think about it, the best way for the orks to survive on Drakaasi is to make themselves essential. That way they can be sure that Venalitor won't throw their lives away. The better they fight, the better a show they put on for the crowds, the longer they will live.'

'So the creature has a plan?'

'A plan, to survive.'

Kelhedros smiled, which was disconcerting to see since his alien face produced only expressions that looked fundamentally wrong to human eyes. 'I was under the impression that you humans and these greenskins once encountered each other in the early stages of exploring the galaxy, and took an instant dislike to one another that has never dimmed. It sounds as if you admire One-ear.'

'I hate the ork just like any other Emperor fearing citizen, but the fact remains that One-ear has a better grasp of the situation, and a sounder plan for surviving it, than most of the slaves here. I thought the same as you, Kelhedros, and assumed that an ork was just a fighting machine that couldn't even think. Then I took the time to watch, and I found I was wrong.'

'What is your plan?' asked Kelhedros bluntly.

'I haven't quite decided yet,' said Alaric, 'but I am not willing to wait in this damned ship to die, or to serve their god by fighting until someone kills me in the arenas. I'm getting out.'

'And you need me.'

This time Alaric smiled. 'Forgive my bluntness, eldar, but I did not seek you out in the name of inter-species relations. You are one of the *Hecatomb's* best fighters, and you have the run of the ship. I may well have a use for you. Be ready for that, Kelhedros, and try not to die in the meantime.'

'How do you know I will agree to your plan, human, whatever it is? That I do not have a way of my own to escape?'

'Because you are still here,' said Alaric, and walked away.

ELEVEN

Duke Venalitor stood at the helm of the *Hecatomb*, watching as the war city of Gorgath rolled up onto the horizon.

The *Hecatomb* was a bulbous hulk, fat and groaning. Venalitor appreciated the impression the ship gave: it looked full to bursting with slaves or riches, or perhaps blood like a sated parasite. Its black timbers creaked as it sailed slowly along the blood canal that wound towards Gorgath. Above, the masts and rigging were like a ribcage of dark wood, its sails like funeral shrouds. Drakaasi's dawn was fighting to clamber above the horizon, but the night was putting up a stern resistance.

As Venalitor had known it would, the first of the shadows peeled off from the rigging and slid down the mast near the stern. It pooled on the deck, twin eyes flickering in its dark body. Another slid over the deck rail. Venalitor often had his scaephylyds stand to attention on the deck as an honour guard, but not tonight. He wanted to do this alone.

The first shadow skittered along the edge of the deck, heading for the raised helm where Venalitor stood. It wanted to sneak up behind him. No doubt it had his scent, and had tracked him all the way from the warp. It was probably aeons old, congealed from a nightmare in the warp, and finally let loose in real space to hunt. It was strange that it should die here after all that.

More shadows gathered. They formed fanged maws and keen silver eyes. They thought that Venalitor could not see them.

Venalitor's sword was in his hand even as the first daemon slunk towards him. He had drawn it so quickly that not even a daemon's eyes could have followed the movement.

'The toad daemon will not have his fill of blood from me tonight,' he snarled.

He spun, and sliced the daemon behind him in two. The shadow-stuff of its body sprayed like black blood. The other hunter daemons howled and bounded towards him. They were up in the rigging, charging across the deck. Venalitor met them head-on, slicing through the first and spearing the next through the eye.

It was a display of swordsmanship so precise and flowing that it was not combat at all, but the carving of a work of art into the flesh of the hunter daemons. Venalitor bayed them into charging, and then cut them apart as they ran at him. One dived down from the rigging, maw distended to swallow him whole. Venalitor let its substance flow over him, and then slit it open and stepped out of its body like a man free of a straitjacket. He flicked the black gore off his blade and finished killing the hunter daemons. It was not even a contest, just a matter of course, a final flourish.

Venalitor returned to the helm for a while, as the blood of the hunter daemons soaked into the planks of the deck.

Eventually, his slave master shambled from inside the ship. 'It has come to pass?' the scaephylyd asked.

'Of course it has,' said Venalitor. 'Arguthrax is a creature of habit. He felt he was insulted at Ghaal and he wanted me dead, so he sent his hunters after me. No doubt their trail will lead back to Arguthrax's court in the warp.'

'A war with Arguthrax is something we can well do without.'

'Those are the words of an animal of real space, not a creature of the warp,' replied Venalitor sternly. 'War is war. It comes upon us not as a plague to be feared, but as an opportunity to be grasped. Arguthrax has decided to make war upon me. Every lord of Drakaasi must war with his peers, it is as sure a law as any on this planet. I shall make war upon him in return and I shall win, and his share of Drakaasi shall be mine.'

'And Ebondrake?'

'The dragon will not know. He focuses too much on his crusade to bother with us. Arguthrax will fall before Ebondrake knows of any feud. Make ready my briefing chambers, I wish to review the disposition of our followers. This war must have a general.'

'Very well.'

'What of the slaves?'

'They plot, as they might. The religious ones pray and the killers plan to murder us all.'

'Good, good. And the Grey Knight?'

'He is quiet. He spoke with the eldar, but otherwise he has done little to elicit suspicion.'

'The Space Marine and the eldar? The universe brings something new with every moment. You may be about your duties, slave master.'

The slave master bowed to the bloodstained deck and scuttled back inside the ship.

Dawn was breaking over Gorgath. It broke, as it always did, over war.

Venalitor watched the sun rise and vowed, as he did every morning, that it would set on a world where Duke Venalitor held a little more of Drakaasi in his fist.

GORGATH!

A city only in name, for none would claim to dwell there. A battlefield in form and function, into which endless columns of damned men are fed to oil the war machine!

None can say when the battle began, and many are those that say it had no beginning. It is an echo of a battle yet to come, or the shadow of a war fought out of time, or a reflection of all the bloodshed in the galaxy sprung up in all its hideous forms to blood the plains of Drakaasi.

The battlefield of Gorgath is ever-changing, filled with the ruins of fortresses and of cities raised only so they can fall again to siege. Here is a weapon of fiendish design, brought low by spears and flint arrowheads! There are cavalry in their finery, cut apart by bullets, and scorched by mechanical flame. There can be no tactic for victory, for Gorgath despises victory, and its battlefields deform to deny any ruse, no matter how brilliant. Only blood lust and hatred can win the day at Gorgath, and then only until the next day, when a new war blooms among the corpse strewn plains.

What can Gorgath be? A creature with a sentience of its own, with violence for lifeblood and warfare for breath? A machine for the blooding of Drakaasi's armies, whose lords feed their underlings through Gorgath to take command of the bloody veterans that emerge? Or some conglomeration of Chaos, some function of the ever-changing warp, bled through into flesh and blood?

Not one of these questions troubles the mind of Gorgath's killers, for they are truly its children, devoted to it and yet despising it, trapped in the war machine, the age of slaughter, the one true battlefield that is Gorgath!

– 'Mind Journeys of a Heretic Saint,' *by Inquisitor Helmandar Oswain (Suppressed by order of the Ordo Hereticus)*

* * *

THE STRONGEST SLAVES were up on the deck, forcing the *Hecatomb* along with poles, as gangs of scae-phylyds slogged their way along the shore hauling ropes tied to the ship's prow. Alaric, the strongest of all the slaves, was up near the stern. It was the first time he had got a good look at the *Hecatomb* from outside. By the Emperor, it was ugly.

'Justicar,' said a voice behind Alaric.

Alaric turned to see Hoygens, the member of Erkhar's faithful who had spoken to him at the prayer meeting. 'I heard you speak with Erkhar.'

'Before Ghaal?' asked Alaric.

'Yes, though it was not for my ears.'

'I merely seek to understand what is happening on this world. I intend to survive it.'

'The lieutenant does not think my faith is strong enough to be indoctrinated in the truth he sees,' continued Hoygens. 'He would not have told me about the Hammer of Daemons. I am just the kind of weak-willed man who would lose his faith if he understood it.'

'But your faith is not gone?'

Hoygens shrugged. 'I don't have that much else. I lose my faith and what am I?'

'Not much.'

'Less than that. I'd be one of Gearth's men. I'd have given up being human. Listen, Justicar. I know more than Erkhar thinks I do. I was there on the *Pax*, and I know where this religion comes from. Erkhar gives us readings from a religious text he has. I have been unable to follow their meaning many times. I don't see this place in the same colours as Erkhar does.'

'Have you seen this text?'

'I haven't read it, but it exists. I don't think Erkhar wrote it, either, and I don't believe he had it before we were brought to Drakaasi.'

'He found it here?'

'Perhaps, I don't know, but Justicar, if the Hammer of Daemons is more than just an idea, maybe it's here, and we can grasp and use it.'

'Perhaps it can get us off this planet.'

'If it can, if there's even a chance, then you have to find it. Emperor knows a sinner like me can't do much, but you're a Space Marine, you can do anything.'

'Not quite, Brother Hoygens,' said Alaric. 'Can you get this book?'

'Not without killing Erkhar,' said Hoygens, 'and I won't do that. I believe in him, Justicar. Whether he's right about the Hammer or anything else, he's the only thing that's kept any of the crew of the *Pax* alive.'

'The Hammer is real,' said Alaric, 'and if it can be found, I will find it.'

'If it's a weapon, Justicar, you're the one who's going to have to wield it.'

'I would look forward to it,' said Alaric, 'if it can help us fight back.'

One of the scaephylyds lashed a whip at Hoygens. Hoygens scowled at it and went back to his post.

Only Chaos could create a place like Gorgath, thought Alaric, and only the followers of Khorne would do it with such blunt, literal brutality. Columns of robed cultists and wild mutants marched on either shore of the blood river, following armoured champions towards Gorgath's endless battle. Alaric could hear the sound of its devastation, and could even make out the outline of a feral Titan as it lumbered around firing indiscriminately. Everywhere were the scars of war: bones poking from the barren soil, the foundations of long-fallen fortresses, monuments and mass graves. This was where the army that had taken Sarthis Majoris was first blooded. It was a factory for war, a machine for churning out armies, where the dregs of Drakaasi were fed into the battlefield and transformed into instruments of Chaos.

Alaric could see hundreds of thousands of them. Gorgath was an obscenity. It was a celebration of war for its own sake, death without purpose, a dreadful hollow slaughter that offended Alaric to the core.

The *Hecatomb* ground its way through the ruins of a barricade still draped with the blackened skeletons of those who had fought over it decades before. The great dark stain of the battle emerged on the horizon, shot through with plumes of fire, the feral Titans stalking through the carnage, and ragged banners streaming everywhere. At the heart of it stood Gorgath's arena.

* * *

CENTURIES BEFORE, ONE of Gorgath's most creative
and brutal warlords had decided to create slaughter
on such a scale that it would forever be remembered by Drakaasi. He enslaved an army and put it
to work mining deep beneath Gorgath's tortured
earth, tunnelling around charnel pits and buried
war machines until they reached the site of some of
the fiercest fighting.

Then the warlord's slaves carted huge amounts of
explosives into the tunnels and laid them there,
waiting for the battle above to reach a peak. They
prayed for destruction, and wound the explosive
caches with prayers of fire and horror. When the
time came they detonated them and let Khorne's
holy fire wipe them off the surface of Drakaasi.

The explosion was heard all across Drakaasi. The
towers of Aelazadne shook, and Ghaal's shanties
collapsed. Hundreds of thousands died in
moments. Ash and shattered stone rained down
over Gorgath for a week afterwards. The debris and
the dead formed a dark cloud that some said had
never fully cleared away.

No one remembered the name of the warlord,
but the crater remained, and on Lord Ebondrake's
orders it had been cleared out and made ready as
Gorgath's grand arena.

IT WAS THE smell of Gorgath, and the taste of it on the
air, that really got to Alaric. It hit him as Venalitor's
slaves were driven between two huge blocks of
ruined fortifications towards the arena. It tasted like

fear, blood and voided bowels, gun smoke and fragments of steel. It smelt of smouldering bodies and dust from collapsed buildings. The engine smoke from the feral Titans completed it. Alaric had been at a thousand battles, and Gorgath felt like every one of them distilled and mixed into one experience.

The fortifications crawled with spectators. They had been taken off the front lines to celebrate Lord Ebondrake's impending crusade. They threw rocks and filth down at the slaves as they marched, heads bowed, under the eyes of Venalitor's slavers.

'What are we facing?' asked Gearth. The man had sought out Alaric and made sure he marched alongside the Grey Knight.

'I don't know,' said Alaric.

'Come on,' said Gearth. 'You've got your plan. You think no one saw what you pulled at Ghaal? You know enough, Space Marine, and some of us would like to be in on it.'

'What did you do?' asked Alaric.

'Do? When?'

'Those are prison tattoos. You asked me a question, now I'm asking you. What did you do to get thrown in prison before Venalitor captured you?'

'Rule one,' said Gearth, 'you never ask that, not of any man.'

'Then you don't need to be a part of whatever plan I might have in mind.'

'Hey, I didn't say that.'

A huge pair of doors stood in front of the slaves, made of sheets of salvaged metal welded together.

Two smoke-belching tanks stood ready to pull them apart on lengths of chain. Alaric recognised the tanks as Leman Russ battle tank variants, no doubt captured and brought to Drakaasi in one of the lords' slave raids.

'Murder,' said Gearth. 'Alright? Happy?'

'Who did you kill?'

Gearth swallowed. Alaric had never seen him anything less than completely confident, but that was a question Gearth obviously feared.

'Women,' he said.

'Why?'

'What do you mean "why"? Why does anyone do anything?' Gearth scowled. 'I don't have to give you a reason.'

'So you don't know why,' said Alaric. 'I will call on you when the time comes.' Gearth stepped out of line, dropping back through the slaves to get away from Alaric.

A slave that Alaric did not recognise shuffled through the rain of filth. 'Astartes,' it hissed through a harelip.

Alaric peered beneath the slave's hooded rags. Its face was disfigured with some skin disease, so the only recognisable features were two watery eyes. 'You know me?'

'Your fame grows.'

'Who are you?'

'I saw you at Ghaal. I fled from there to follow you.'

Alaric sneered. On every Imperial world there was some diversion for the citizens, and adoring followers accompanied the most famous fighters or sportsmen everywhere. Drakaasi's arenas held the same position on Drakaasi, on a far larger scale. The idea that Alaric could have devotees seemed as pathetic as the slave looked.

'Go home to Ghaal.'

'There is no home there now. I bring you a gift.' The slave produced an axe from beneath his robes. It was clearly made for a fighter of a Space Marine's size, the haft far too broad and weighty to fit in a normal man's hand. It was bright and gleaming with a head the shape of a crescent moon, so sharp that the edge was transparent and glowing.

'From the forge,' said the slave.

Alaric took the axe. It was weighted perfectly. Alaric had rarely held a weapon of such craftsmanship, even in the artificer's halls on Titan.

'Who made this?' demanded Alaric.

'The city's forge lies at the crossroads,' said the slave, 'two fortresses and the siege works between them. That is all he told me to say.'

'Who? Who told you?'

A whip lashed around the throat of the slave, yanking him back. The slave was dragged back into a knot of Gorgath's soldiers, and Alaric knew that in a few moments the man would be dead beneath their boots and blades. The slaves around Alaric surged on beneath the soldiers' whips, and Alaric lost sight of the slave.

He looked down at his axe. It was perhaps the first beautiful thing he had seen on Drakaasi.

In front of him, the tanks gunned their engines and the doors were pulled apart.

Two massive armies were revealed on the arena floor, lined up in ranks, banners streaming. The ground between them was patrolled by bloodletters, snarling at the front ranks to keep them back. A pack of the daemons stomped up to Venalitor's slaves and began directing the gladiators into the ranks, splitting them between the two sides.

A battle, of course. It was the only way that Khorne could be celebrated in Gorgath.

'QUITE MAGNIFICENT,' SAID Venalitor, taking up his position beside Lord Ebondrake at the top of the stands. Every arena had a place for Drakaasi's lords to spectate, away from the crowds, and in Gorgath it took the form of a covered section of seating with chained daemons broken and bound to serve the planet's rulers. They skulked and cowered like beaten dogs around Ebondrake's feet. Ebondrake and Venalitor ignored them. They were here to witness the games, not to be fawned over.

'Indeed it is,' said Lord Ebondrake, settling his enormous reptilian body on the throne erected for him in the stands. 'The lords have outdone themselves. Khorne anticipates greatly.'

'And not just bloodshed,' said Venalitor. 'I would have thought that the most appropriate celebration was slaughter, but of course this is much more appealing to the Lord of Battles.'

Ebondrake turned his great head towards Venalitor and narrowed his eyes. 'Your flatteries are disappointing, duke,' he said, flickering a forked tongue dangerously over his teeth. 'I had thought more of you than this. I had thought you had some imagination.'

'You misunderstand me, lord,' said Venalitor. 'Do not think I have been modest. My very best are down there.'

'Including your Grey Knight?'

'Of course.'

'You would risk him here?'

'The Blood God would not hold me in high regard if I could not risk everything to worship him,' replied Venalitor slickly. 'My Grey Knight would do none of us any good back on the *Hecatomb*.'

'You have great plans for him, I feel.'

'So do you, Lord Ebondrake.'

Ebondrake smiled, baring his spectacular array of teeth. 'He will try to get out. He will want revenge.'

'That would be a spectacle worth seeing.'

Ebondrake's enclosure was ringed with Ophidian Guard warriors. The audience was little danger at that moment, since all eyes were fixed in anticipation on the battle lines below. The slaves were divided into two armies, and kept separate by a host of bloodletters. Huge banners hung above the front ranks, dripping power from the runes painted on them. Each army had tens of thousands of men, from frenzied cultists from the slums of Ghaal to tribesmen from beyond Drakaasi's cities, and even elite gladiators from the personal stables of lords like Venalitor. More than a few of the spectators recognised the Venalitor's most prized possession, the captive Grey Knight, known to many of them as Alaric the Betrayed, who was destined to die competing for the mantle of Drakaasi's champion at Vel'Skan a few weeks hence. That was, of course, if he made it out of Gorgath.

There were brute mutants three times the height of a man, tentacled subhumans, and hated psykers, chained up and herded before the armies to make sure they died first. Whole cults of the Blood God stood in their robed finery, desperate to die beneath the eyes of their god.

At a signal from Lord Ebondrake, one of his Ophidian Guard raised a war horn and blew a single discordant note. The banners dipped, and the bloodletters dissolved into the floor of the crater. The armies swarmed forwards.

The spectators erupted in celebration. They had been a part of the hellish machinery of Gorgath for so long. Now they were on the outside looking down at others fighting for their pleasure, as if they were Khorne, soaking up the adulation of their bloodshed. It was the most glorious thing they had ever seen.

The front lines collided with a thunderclap. Bodies were thrown into the air. Heads parted from bodies. Torsos split open. Men swarmed over a brute mutant, dragging it down to cut it to pieces. A tide of bodies heaved up as the dead piled on top of one another, and soon the armies were battling atop a rampart of the dead.

Alaric the Betrayed was at the heart of it all. With his bright silver axe and ornate armour, he cut a more dramatic figure than any other gladiator. He kicked enemies and friends aside as he drove his way through the battle. Other slaves of Venalitor's followed in his wake: an eldar swordsman cutting enemies apart with his chainblade, a host of human butchers who despatched wounded foes on the ground. It seemed that Alaric had finally lost his mind, and had become one with the Blood God's will. Here was a hunter of daemons, the Emperor's finest, out-slaughtering Drakaasi's most brutal for the glory of Khorne.

Alaric drove for the closest edge of the arena. A tentacled monster tried to snare him and drag him down, but Alaric stamped down on its torso, crushing its ribcage before slicing through its tentacles with a sweep of his axe. One of the captive witches lurched towards him, lightning crashing from its eyes. Alaric took the first bolt, letting it discharge through his armour and arc into the earth. A single step brought him face to face with the witch, and he slammed the blade of the axe through its skull. There was nothing the spectators of Gorgath loved more than seeing the weak-bodied psykers put to death. Some of them began chanting Alaric's name.

One of his side's standard bearers was fighting near Alaric. It was an armoured warrior from the bodyguard of one of Drakaasi's lords. The warrior was badly hurt, blood pouring from the shoulder joint of his armour, his helm split and gory. Alaric pushed him to the ground and took up the banner. He held it up so the whole stadium could see the image of the stylised skulls emblazoned on it. Alaric ran up to the edge of the arena's seating, which sloped up above him along the curve of the crater's edge.

He hurled the banner into the stands. Dozens of soldiers leapt up to catch it.

'What are you waiting for?' yelled Alaric.

The crowd responded by chanting his name ever louder as they poured down past him, off the stands and into the arena.

This was war, and suddenly watching wasn't enough.

'CLEVER BOY,' SAID Ebondrake as he watched the crowd around Alaric break ranks and pour down into the arena.

'My lord,' said Venalitor, 'this is… this blasphemy is…'

'You have said enough, duke,' said Ebondrake. 'Commander?'

One of the Ophidian Guard, hulking and sinister behind the visor of his black armour, turned to Ebondrake. 'My lord?'

'Kill the Grey Knight,' said Ebondrake.

TWELVE

ALARIC FOUGHT AGAINST the tide. His head was forced under the sea of bodies, and he fought to breathe. His own name, chanted over and over again, was like the dim crashing of the ocean.

His was not a complicated plan. Khorne probably would have approved. The bloodlust of Gorgath's soldiers, ingrained by generations of carnage, only needed the right kind of impetus to send them swarming into the arena to join in.

All Alaric had to do was get out. He had been sent a message, and to discover its meaning he had to break out of the arena and into Gorgath.

Alaric kicked his way out of the crowd, clambering over them until he found the top of the arena floor wall. He hauled himself up onto the seating that had been erected around the sides of the arena crater. The battle swarmed beneath him, all battle lines now lost in a swirl of violence.

The lords would be angry. There was plenty of blood, of course, and Khorne would have his due, but a free-for-all wasn't what the lords of Drakaasi had wanted. Alaric's riot was an insult to the planet's ruling order.

Lord Ebondrake was ahead of Alaric, advancing behind a line of Ophidian Guard.

Alaric's hearts sank. All he had to do was get out. Ebondrake was not part of his plan.

'Grey Knight!' roared Ebondrake. 'Betrayed of the Corpse God! Puppet of Khorne! Is this the vengeance you seek? To face me, and slay me, in my own domain?'

The Ophidian Guard were moving towards him, black swords drawn.

Alaric wouldn't get his vengeance. Ebondrake wouldn't roll over and die for him, but he was human, and that meant fighting on.

Ebondrake inhaled, his wings spreading behind him.

Alaric hit the floor. Ebondrake breathed a sheet of black flame that flowed over Alaric like water. It scorched him down one side, and he rolled away from it, trying to smother the flames before they caught on his flesh. The sound was like a hurricane of fire roaring in his ears. The Ophidian Guard kept advancing straight through the flame, their armour proof against it.

Alaric couldn't fight Ebondrake, not without being immolated by black fire again.

He was going to die.

He jumped to his feet. The Ophidian Guard were upon him, and he lashed out at them, smashing one black, eyeless helm apart with his axe. Another forced forward, trying to bull him to the ground, but Alaric slammed a knee into his face and threw him aside.

'What victory do you believe you will win, little creature?' growled Ebondrake, black fire coiling from between his fangs. He loomed up over the line of Ophidian Guard protecting him, and cast off his cloak as his wings unfurled fully. 'What can you take from me?'

The Ophidian Guard around Alaric closed ranks and raised their swords like executioners waiting for the word so they could take his head.

'Kill me, and you kill Drakaasi. Is that correct?' Ebondrake grinned horribly through his anger, his eyes, slits of yellow fire. 'Is that the sum of your imagination?'

Ebondrake looked past Alaric suddenly. The roar behind Alaric grew like a wave crashing through the arena. He risked a look behind him.

Tens of thousands of Gorgath's soldiers swarmed up the seating behind him. At their head was the banner Alaric had thrown them. They wanted to fight, and perhaps to die, and for that they needed the best opponents in the arena. All the finest gladiators were tied up in the melee on the arena floor, and that left the Ophidian Guard.

'Kill him!' shouted Ebondrake as the spontaneous army charged. 'Close ranks!'

A sword came down.

Alaric was faster.

He brought his axe up through the visor of the helmet looming over him, and rammed an elbow into the throat of the Ophidian Guard behind him. His would-be executioner fell, head split apart, and the second guard tumbled as Alaric cut a leg out from under him.

Ebondrake breathed. The flame rippled over Alaric's head into the army charging the Ophidian Guard. Men disappeared in swathes of black fire.

Alaric was only half aware of being carried up onto the shoulders of the army, even as they burned and vanished beneath Ophidian swords. He saw the banner still held high, and realised that he, like the banner, was a symbol of rebellion and war for these people. The broken creatures wanted nothing more than to follow Alaric to their deaths, because they knew that no one on Drakaasi could die as well as a Space Marine.

Somewhere amid the carnage, Ebondrake wolfed a clawful of Gorgath's soldiers down his gullet to quench his anger. The lords had lost control of Gorgath's arena completely. He turned from the carnage in disgust. The rioting soldiers were too lowly a prey for him. Alaric had disappeared into the rioting mass, and there was nothing worthwhile for him to kill any more.

Alaric watched the fire starting to burn, and the drifts of dead building up at the edges of the arena, until the tide of soldiers carried him through the dimness of an archway and out into the war city of Gorgath.

GORGATH'S NIGHTS WERE cold. They killed off the day's wounded, so that only the worthy and fit could fight in the morning.

Alaric did not feel the cold as men did. He knew that this night could kill a weak man, but it meant nothing to him. He wished that he could feel it and fear it, because that would be something he could understand, something he could grasp. It was an enemy he could defeat: find shelter, build a fire. Drakaasi was an enemy he could not face like that. There was no simple solution to it. If he could feel the cold, at least he could take some pride from the fact that he was still alive.

If Ebondrake had died, what would have been achieved? Ebondrake himself had seen through that. If the dragon was gone, something else would take its place, perhaps Venalitor, perhaps Arguthrax, or perhaps some ancient horror of Drakaasi that Alaric hadn't even heard of.

Alaric had reached the siege works a few hours after the army escaped from Gorgath's arena and took the carnage out into the city. He had left the army behind as he made for the twin fortresses. He didn't care what happened to the rioters. They were probably being put down to avenge the insult of the failed Gorgath games.

Alaric walked carefully along the trench. It had been dug decades ago when the two fortresses had evidently been at war, and their lords had ordered the trenches dug to approach the opposite fortress and take it. The siege lines had passed one another in a web of tunnels and criss-crossing trenches, and there were still signs of the struggle: old broken bones poking from the dark earth, heaps of spent cartridges rusted into lumps of red-brown corrosion.

Each fortress was a war-scarred cylinder bristling with rusted guns and gouged by the siege engines that lay in ruins around them. Alaric could almost hear the din of their guns, and the screams of the dying. He wondered for a moment how many had died there, fighting a miniature war in the midst of Gorgath's grand battle, but there did not seem to be room in the city for any more death.

There was a temple ahead, lying at the place where the siege lines had first met. It was built from shell casings, from massive artillery shells carved into fluted columns, the individual bullets forming the teeth of the gargoyles squatting on its roof.

Through the shattered windows, Alaric could see the abandoned forges and anvils, piles of flawed swords and rusted ingots. A forge door swung open, exposing the dark and cold inside. The temple's altar had been used as an anvil, and was covered in deep scores. Alaric walked carefully inside. He could smell the smoke and molten metal, and almost hear the ringing of the hammer on a newly forged blade.

The place was abandoned. It had been for some time. Since he had received the axe at the gates to the arena, Alaric had believed, somewhere inside him, that the smith who had spoken to him at Karnikhal was trying to give him a message. He didn't even know if the smith had been an ally or an enemy, or even a figment of his own imagination. However, he was a potential ally, and Alaric knew that he needed one outside the *Hecatomb*.

Had he really thought he would find something here? Certainly no more than he thought he could kill Lord Ebondrake alone.

Something glinted in the dimness of the abandoned temple. Alaric pulled aside a few unfinished blades, and saw a hammer propped up against the altar anvil. Its head was bright silver, and carved with images of a comet streaking down to shatter a planet, an armoured fist clutching a lightning bolt, and a dragon with a sword through its heart. Alaric picked up the weapon and felt its weight. It was as finely made as the axe. He recalled how Brother Dvorn would have dearly loved to wield such a brutal looking weapon, and wondered whether Dvorn and his other battle-brothers had made it off Sarthis Majoris alive and free.

On one face of the hammer, the face that would strike the enemy when the hammer was swung, was the image of a skull. One eye was blanked out, the other burned with an intricately carved flame. Alaric stared at the image for a long moment, trying to guess what message it held.

It had to be a message. For him to seek this place out, to risk his life escaping the arena, there had to be a point. A half-blinded skull, it had to mean something, even if the meaning came from within him.

Perhaps the skull represented Alaric. With the Collar of Khorne around his neck, he was half-blind.

'There is no Hammer of Daemons,' said Alaric aloud. 'There is no sacred weapon waiting to be wielded. It's me. I am supposed to bring this planet down. I am the Hammer.'

What if the Hammer of Daemons was another Chaos trick? It would be typical of the followers of Chaos to perpetrate such a hoax, if only to give desperate humans a shadow of hope that could be snatched away.

Alaric wanted to have faith in something, even if it was only a decent way to die on Drakaasi, but there was nothing left for him to believe in.

A sound snapped Alaric out of his thoughts. Something was moving outside: a footstep through loose rubble, weight shifting on debris. Alaric took his axe in one hand and the hammer in the other, sure, by their balance, that they had been forged by the same master smith.

He hear more footsteps, voices, and swords unsheathed.

Alaric tensed. He faced the door, his back to the altar, sure that he could cover the distance in a few huge strides, shatter the first visored face he saw with the hammer, and cut the legs out from under the next warrior with the axe. He was ready.

One side of the temple collapsed with a roar of torn metal and stone, and a Rhino APC rode up through the rubble into the temple. Alaric had to vault over the altar to avoid been dragged beneath its tracks. The side hatch swung open, and a pair of Ophidian Guard emerged, not in the hulking armour of Ebondrake's bodyguard, but wearing chainmail and leather, faces obscured by leather masks, wielding whips that shone like bright silver. They lashed out at Alaric. He let one whip twine around the haft of his axe, and yanked it out of the warrior's hands, but the other caught him across the shoulder, and hot white pain lanced through him. He convulsed onto his knees, swinging blindly with the hammer, feeling it crunch into bone, but unable to see what he had hit.

Ophidian Guard stormed in through the doors and windows of the temple. There were dozens of them. More emerged from the Rhino, slashing with their whips. Alaric stood and fought back, pulling them into striking range, and battering them down to the floor, but there were too many of them.

He was on all fours, pain streaking down through him like lightning bolts. He caught a whip-wielding soldier with the hammer, shattering his knee, and then cut off his head as he lay writhing on the floor.

He cut up into the torso of another, and forced himself to his feet, but the Ophidian Guard surrounding him carried tower shields emblazoned with white dragons, which they used to slam him back, as he tried to break free of them.

He was on his back. His body fought on, but something in the back of his mind told him to give in. It was a part of him that had been given free rein by the Collar of Khorne, a hidden coward that had finally surfaced to tell him he was going to fail.

He reared up, one last time, silencing the coward. He roared like an animal.

A great cold weight pressed down on his back, mirrored by heat blossoming in his chest. He looked down to see the tip of a black sword emerging from his breastbone. He tried to look up, and glimpsed the Ophidian Guard, who had just impaled him, towering over him. Alaric tried to slide off the blade, but it would not move. The shock of it finally caught up with his mind, and the world greyed out.

The blade snapped, and Alaric slumped to the floor, the tip of the blade still sticking out of his chest.

It didn't matter whether he gave in or not. The pain won, and Alaric passed out.

'I SEE YOU have thought about what I said.' Durendin's voice was low and quiet, very different from the strident tones he used on the pulpit while reminding the Grey Knights of their duties towards their Emperor.

'I have,' said Alaric. Around him was the subdued majesty of the Chapel of Mandulis. It was built of sombre stone, the columns holding up the ceiling carved into representations of past Grand Masters, who had fallen in battle against the daemon. However, instead of having granite walls inscribed with the names of fallen Grey Knights, the chapel was open to the outside, and through its columns could be glimpsed an endless golden desert under a dark blue twilight. Strange stars winked in the sky, the same shifting constellations that bled from the Eye of Terror.

Alaric was sitting on one of the stone pews. Durendin was a couple of rows in front of him, evidently at prayer, since he was not wearing the black trimmed power armour that was the badge of a Chaplain's office. Alaric realised that he was without armour, too. He was wearing the remains of a badly battered breastplate in the shape of folded wings, and the point of a black sword stuck out of his chest.

'And?' said Durendin.

'You were wrong.'

'Really?'

'Some things, you can't fight.'

'Interesting. Do you believe that these Grand Masters would have thought that? That Mandulis could have come up against a foe and said, "This I cannot fight"?'

Alaric looked at the column that represented Mandulis. The Grand Master had carried a sword with the hilt worked to resemble a lightning bolt. Alaric had held that sword, and tried to echo the deeds of Mandulis in vanquishing the daemon prince Ghargatuloth, but those events felt like they belonged in another man's lifetime.

'I am not one of those Grand Masters,' replied Alaric.

'No, you are not, not if you are going to simply give up.'

'I am not giving up, Chaplain.'

'Then what, Alaric? What quality do you possess that can win you victory if not a Grey Knight's willingness to fight?'

'Imagination.'

Durendin laughed. It was a strange thing to see the old man doing. 'Really? How so?'

'It is the understanding that there is more than one way to fight.'

'I see. So, you think that bringing the bolter and the blade to them is not enough, and you seek another way.'

'Yes, I learned that against Ebondrake. I cannot fight them as I would any other enemy, not this whole planet. Even if I win, every drop of blood I spill is a victory for them. It has to be something else.'

'Then what?'

'I do not know.' Alaric sat back, feeling the strength bleed out of him.

'And you think that I can give you answers?'

'I don't know what I think.'

Durendin stood up and smoothed down his devotional robes. He walked up to the chapel's altar and took a brazier from its stone slab. An icon of the Emperor looked down on the Chaplain, as one by one he lit the candles and incense lanterns arranged around the altar. It was an ancient ritual, reflecting the lights that had gone out in the souls of so many Grey Knights since the Chapter's foundation, and reminding the Grey Knights who still lived that their battle-brothers' souls were gathering to fight alongside the Emperor at the end of time.

Alaric imagined those souls gathering like fireflies around a pyre, eager to fight, and he felt sorry for them. For the first time, it occurred to him that their sacrifice might not be worth anything after all.

'I cannot give you answers to this, Alaric,' said Durendin. 'I think you come to me more in hope than in expectation, and I must disappoint you. I was given the Chaplain's burden because I am exactly the opposite of you. I see only the Grey Knights' way, the endless battle against Chaos. Everything else must be seen through that lens. There can be no doubt and no compromise in the eyes of a Chaplain. You are alone, Justicar, as are we all.'

'Then I do not think I can do this,' said Alaric. 'My duties on Drakaasi are clear. Chaos must be punished. The Emperor's justice must be done, but I am just one man, and the lords of Drakaasi are so many and so strong. It is just as Venalitor said, I can either die here accomplishing nothing, or fight on and win renown for their Blood God. I cannot win.'

'Then that is your fate, Alaric. A Grand Master would never accept that, of course, but as you said you are not a Grand Master. Please, it is best that you leave now. You are bleeding on the floor of my chapel, and it is an ill omen.'

Alaric looked down at his chest. The wound was bleeding, blood flowing in time with the pumping of his hearts. The blood was trickling down the pew and pooling around his feet.

'Am I going to die?'

Durendin looked around at him, but Alaric could not read his expression. 'If I was to say yes, what would you feel?'

'Relieved,' said Alaric. 'The choice would have been made for me.'

'But Drakaasi would carry on as before, so I suggest you live.'

'I'll see what I can do.'

'Good luck, Justicar. Perhaps I can meet with you again, the real me, I mean, back on Titan. I imagine I would be very interested to learn of these conversations.'

'Goodbye, Chaplain.'

Durendin looked away, and as he turned, his features melted away and left him without a face. The features of the Grand Masters dissolved away, too, leaving columns of smooth, unmarked stone. One by one the stars outside began to go out, and the Chapel of Mandulis withered away into the desert.

Alaric took a long, painful breath, and the darkness lifted.

THIRTEEN

ALARIC AWOKE TO light. He lay on his back, staring up. He blinked a few times as his eyes adjusted. He wondered, not for the first time on Drakaasi, whether he was dead.

The light was coming from a chandelier, hanging from a ceiling frescoed with images of battle. Victims were painted lying in heaps beneath the feet of armoured warriors, all of them with the sigils of Khorne glowing on their armour. The sky above writhed with blood-laden clouds, and carrion daemons swept in to tear apart the living and the dead. Titanic armies clashed in the distance.

It was a work of genius. The artist would have been one of the greatest of his generation on any Imperial world, perhaps good enough to gain

187

sector-wide recognition. Instead, the mind behind the work had been enslaved by Chaos, withered away by madness until unholy masterpieces were all that was left.

Alaric wondered who that person had been. Had he been insane to begin with, tortured and brilliant, listening to the whispers of the warp for solace? Or had he been just one of those millions of citizens preyed upon by Drakaasi's forces? Alaric imagined the nameless artist huddled among a great crowd of other terrified citizens, waiting for death, perhaps praying for deliverance or trying to offer some comfort to his loved ones. Then the death had come, but not for him. Drakaasi's servants had found out about his skill and chosen him to live on, enslaved, and had rotted his mind away until visions of bloodshed and war were all that he could create. He must have wished he were dead. Perhaps he was still alive somewhere on Drakaasi, still creating horrors for Khorne.

Alaric lay still for a long time. It was only by the Emperor's grace that he was not dead or insane, too. He wondered how easily he would break. It would take longer to break Alaric than to corrupt the painter who had created the image above him, but how much longer? As the galaxy reckoned things, probably not a great deal.

Alaric tried to sit up, but the pain inside him was a hot, red spike piercing his torso. He gasped and fell back. Beneath him was an unyielding surface, and Alaric wondered if it was a mortuary slab in a cathedral of the Blood God, and if he was finally dead.

He turned his head. He was lying on a huge hardwood table laid out as if for a feast. Bronze plates and chalices had been pushed to one side so that he could be laid there. The table was one of several in a grand feasting chamber as dark and lavish as anything Alaric had seen on Drakaasi. The walls were hung with silken drapes of crimson and black, held up by false columns of black marble. The floor looked, at first, like marble, but at a closer look revealed that it was paved with gravestones in so many different styles that they must have been brought from many different worlds. Devotional inscriptions of Imperial Gothic marched past Alaric's eyes, the names of the desecrated dead.

An altar to Khorne stood at one end of the room. It was a great, irregular chunk of stone, stained black, and covered in ancient gouges: an executioner's block. Behind it was the symbol of Khorne, wrought in brass, and inlaid with red lacquer. It was the symbol of a skull, so stylised that it was little more than a triangle topped with a cross, nevertheless, it radiated such malice that it hurt to look at it. The floor in front of the block had drains to carry away the blood. The executioner's block was still used for its original purpose.

Alaric tested his body for injuries. It felt comforting, because it was part of his training. There was still enough Grey Knight left in him for him to act like a soldier. He had the familiar cacophony of pain from hundreds of minor injuries. His chest was the worst. His breathing was hampered, and one of his hearts was wounded. He could still move, and fight if need be, but it was a major injury, even for a Space Marine, and back on Titan he would have been sent to the apothecarion to recover. On Drakaasi, he would just have to fight through it.

One of the drapes was pulled aside. Beyond it, Alaric glimpsed more finery, a magnificent chamber surrounding a grand staircase lined with brass statues.

Haggard entered the feasting chamber. He looked so completely out of place, unkempt and grimy like all the slaves, wearing his stained surgeon's apron, that Alaric wondered for a moment if he was really there at all.

'You're awake,' said Haggard.

'So it seems.'

'How are you?'

'I'll live.'

'It was a real mess in there,' continued Haggard. 'One of the lungs won't work. One of the hearts is looking shaky, too. Your spine made it, that's the main thing. There were splinters of metal in there as long as my finger. It was only by the Emperor's will that none of them severed your spinal cord.'

'Thank you, Haggard,' said Alaric. 'I don't know if I could have survived without your help.'

'Don't thank me,' said Haggard. 'Please, don't thank me. I don't know what will happen next.'

Alaric tried sitting up again. This time he bit down the pain. A few of Haggard's crude stitches burst, and fresh blood ran down his chest. He saw that he was wearing the armour in which he had been fighting at Gorgath, with the breastplate removed. The wound on his chest was huge and ugly. No one but a Space Marine could have survived it.

'Whatever happens, Haggard, I'm better facing it alive,' said Alaric.

'I pulled this out of you,' said Haggard. He held up the shard of the Ophidian Guard's sword. In his hand, it was the size of a short sword, the broken haft like a hilt, the edge and point still sharp enough to glow in the candlelight. 'You didn't really think you could kill Ebondrake, did you?'

'Our meeting was unplanned,' replied Alaric. 'I wonder if anyone on this planet could kill that.' He looked down at the shard in Haggard's hand. 'Can you hide that among your medical gear?'

'It certainly looks painful enough,' said Haggard, slipping it into one of the pockets of his stained apron where he kept his makeshift surgical tools.

'Keep it for when I return to the *Hecatomb*. Speaking of which, where am I?'

'Still on board,' said Haggard. 'These are Venalitor's chambers.'

'Here? The ship isn't big enough.'

Haggard shrugged. 'Physics only works here out of habit. If Venalitor wants to bend it to give himself a place fit for a duke, then he can. Listen,

Justicar, it was Venalitor who brought me up here to keep you alive. Whatever he's going to do, he needs you alive and conscious to do it. He's going to punish you.'

'But he doesn't know I'm awake.'

Haggard looked down at the floor. 'Yes, he does, Justicar.'

The sound of scaephylyd claws on the gravestone tiles was unmistakeable, so were the armoured footsteps descending the marble staircase. An honour guard of scaephylyds clattered into the room, pulling Haggard away. Haggard didn't resist.

Duke Venalitor followed them in. He was surrounded by scaephylyd slavers carrying shock prods. He dismissed them with a wave of his hand, and they scuttled away. Behind him, Alaric could just see Haggard being herded up the staircase.

'So, Justicar,' said Venalitor. He suited his surroundings perfectly. The dark magnificence of his chambers matched his own, with his splendid red and black armour and the multitude of swords at his back. The place was a reflection, like Venalitor himself, of pure arrogance.

Alaric didn't reply. Venalitor had deliberately made himself vulnerable without his attendant slavers, but Alaric was wounded and unarmed. Venalitor would kill him if he and Alaric fought, and Venalitor wanted to remind Alaric of that fact.

Venalitor walked past him and knelt in front of the altar to Khorne, whispering a few words of prayer.

'The Blood God,' he said, turning back to Alaric, 'listens. When you have earned his respect as I have, he hears you. I ask him for strength to conquer, and I am granted it. I ask for armies, and they march under my banner. They call you Alaric the Betrayed, you know, because you were betrayed by your Emperor. You asked him to deliver you from Chaos, from Drakaasi, and he ignored you. He is just a corpse, who cannot hear your prayers, Grey Knight. That is the ultimate betrayal. My lord will grant you everything you want if you only get his attention.'

Alaric climbed down off the table and stood. He was unsteady on his feet, but he did everything he could not to show it.

He could fight here, and die. At least it would be over. At least he wouldn't have to listen to Venalitor's blasphemous words any more.

'You have that chance, Alaric,' continued Venalitor.

'You are asking me to join you?' Alaric smiled. 'Only in desperation would anyone think such a thing was possible.'

'You have seen the scum of Drakaasi's cities,' said Venalitor unshaken. 'You have mingled with the even lower vermin of the *Hecatomb*: those killers, those broken men, the violent dregs of your Imperium. That is the lot of the great majority of those who come here. Khorne despises them, and they are left to rot or be killed as fodder for His bloodlust. The lucky ones become sacrifices, but you, you are different. You do not belong with those scum. You have yet to even glimpse what you could become on Drakaasi. The Blood God is willing to listen to you if you will only let him.' Venalitor indicated the altar. 'It is so easy, Grey Knight, and it is the only choice you have. No matter what you do, or how hard you try, you will die in the Blood God's name. The only way out is to bow before a real god for once.'

'Then I will die,' said Alaric.

'A few drops of blood,' said Venalitor, 'that is all he requires.'

'He will have to wring them out of me.'

Venalitor shook his head. 'You try to humiliate me. You even try to cross swords with Lord Ebondrake. The Blood God looks upon such audacity, and smiles. That you honestly believe you can win some victory over me is indication of the mental strength a champion of Chaos requires. The fact that you are still alive shows you have the strength of arms. You could rule this planet, Alaric. Then you could do with Ebondrake as you please. You could even put me on this altar, and have me slit from neck to belly, if only you do it for Khorne.'

'Never,' said Alaric, 'not as long as I live, never. You will just have to sacrifice me like all the rest of your vermin.'

Venalitor smiled. 'There is something noble in you, I think. The Emperor's lackeys taught you well, I will give them that. Victory means so much to you, and you see it in the bleakest of situations. For you, dying here is a victory.'

'My duty allows for no failings,' said Alaric, 'and it does not end in death. You cannot defeat that, Duke Venalitor.'

'You had a duty towards Sarthis Majoris too, did you not?'

Alaric could not answer.

'Do you know what we did to that planet?'

Alaric fought for something to say, something that would silence Venalitor, something devastating, but there was nothing.

'We separated the men from the women,' continued Venalitor with a smirk, 'and we killed the women in front of the men. We killed them badly, in all the ways you can think of and a few you cannot. Then we let the men fight back. Half of them wanted revenge and the other half just wanted to die. The grief in their eyes was like a hymn to the Blood God. The madness was joyous. So many of them were begging the Blood God to take them in, to turn them mindless, that I made a new army from them and marched them on to the next city. Your duty was to prevent that, Justicar. I think it is fair to say that you failed.'

'Your atrocities are nothing new,' said Alaric, trying to keep his voice level. 'We cannot save every world. We can only fight.'

'Until death?'

'Until death.'

'But you did not die. You are here. Sarthis Majoris died, but you survived. What manner of duty did you fulfil, exactly?'

'Your words cannot sway me, Venalitor. I am a Grey Knight.'

'Not any more. You became something else, something less, the moment I was able to take you alive. At least your friend had the good grace to die at the first opportunity. You cling on like a disease, pretending there is some victory in your failure to the Corpse-Emperor, and ignoring the only chance for redemption you have, the chance given to you by Khorne.'

Alaric looked around him for a weapon. There was nothing of use. It would have to be bare hands. 'I shall be redeemed, Venalitor. Here and now, I shall be redeemed.'

Alaric charged Venalitor. The duke had been at ease, speaking idly as he stood before the altar, but he was still ready.

His hand caught Alaric by the throat. His other arm knocked away Alaric's fist. Venalitor lifted Alaric off his feet, and threw him back down into the table. His body splintered through the table, throwing gilded plates and chalices everywhere. The wound in his chest tore open, and for a moment he was blinded with pain.

'So you really do want to die?' asked Venalitor.

Alaric sprang to his feet. The wound in his chest was bleeding freely. Venalitor waved a hand, and the blood formed tendrils that lashed around his neck. He tore them aside, but by the time he had his bearings again, Venalitor had got behind him. Venalitor caught him by the shoulder and the neck, and kicked his legs out from under him. Alaric fell forwards, and Venalitor thrust him into the executioner's block of the altar. Alaric's head smacked into the stone, and the smell of old dried blood hit him.

Venalitor drew a sword from his back, a short, curved blade, like a shining razor in the candlelight. He stabbed it into Alaric's back.

Venalitor knew the ways in which a human body could be made to feel pain. The tip of the blade hit just the right point, and nerve endings caught fire in agony. Alaric could not move, only spasm on the altar as pain washed through him.

He fought it. Venalitor pulled the blade out, and let Alaric slide to the floor. Venalitor flicked the blood from the tip of his sword onto the altar, and it smouldered there, the brass icon of Khorne glowing in gratitude.

'I will not kill you, Justicar,' said Venalitor. 'You are too valuable to me in the arenas, and there is still some use the Blood God can get from you. Just because you refuse His will now does not mean that He will be denied. I will just have to break you first. In the long run, it makes no difference.'

The slavers entered the room. Alaric fought them for a while, throwing them aside, dashing them against the floor, and snapping their insect limbs, but, slowly, their shock prods found their mark, and he was forced down onto his knees, still fighting.

Venalitor watched. There were always more scaephylyds to be enslaved, and there was no need to risk damaging his valuable gladiator. Alaric fell onto his hands and knees, and a shock prod was forced down on his neck above his iron collar, so that his face was pressed against the gravestone floor.

'I know what you are, Grey Knight. I know about Ghargatuloth and Chaeroneia, about Valinov and Thorganel Quintus. I know what you can do. None of it will help you now.'

The scaephylyds swarmed over him like ants over a corpse. They manacled his hands and feet and turned him over to carry him up on their shoulders.

'Take him below decks,' said Venalitor.

One of the scaephylyds, a particularly old and gnarled creature, had stood aside from the fracas. He turned to Venalitor as Alaric was carried, still struggling, from the feasting chamber.

'Below decks, duke?' asked the creature. It had practised the language of humans for so long that its mandibles pronounced each syllable almost perfectly.

'You heard me, slave master.'

'Do you mean to the–'

'Not to the cell block,' snarled Venalitor. 'Open up the wards, throw him inside, and seal them again. Those are my orders.'

'Of course, my duke. There is another matter.'

'What?'

'That of the war.'

* * *

THE WAR HAD started with the hunter daemons. They had begun with an audacious first strike, a lesson in superiority. They had probably not intended to kill Venalitor at all, but to teach him that he could be reached anywhere, at any time. The *Hecatomb* was not safe, not from an evil as ancient as Arguthrax.

Venalitor had called upon the Wrath of Ages, a warrior cult dedicated to self-mutilation and martial excellence, to descend on the stronghold of the Thirteenth Hand. The Thirteenth Hand, since returning from their failure to disrupt Venalitor's armies on Sarthis Majoris, had taken up residence in a huge and filthy tangle of entrail sewers beneath Karnikhal. The fanatics of the Wrath of Ages had besieged it, working night by night into the tangle of dried-out organs and sumps of decaying filth, while the shambling vermin of the Hand fought back with poisoned arrows and fiendish traps.

Eventually, the Wrath had reached the heart of the fortress, and had enacted a ritual that brought life back to the organs that had hung dead for many centuries of Karnikhal's lifespan. A few of the Wrath made it out, while the Hand was drowned in filth, or dissolved by digestive juices. Their remains were disgorged into the blood canals, silting up the river between Karnikhal and Aelazadne, a fittingly meaningless end for such a lowly cult.

An open battle had broken out on the plains between Ghaal and Gorgath, a dismal and lifeless place. An alliance of cults loyal to Arguthrax had fought an army of scaephylyds, all from clans hoping to ascend to Venalitor's service. Venalitor was a saviour to them, a prophet of Chaos, promising to elevate them above the status of animals.

Arguthrax won. The scaephylyds were slaughtered, and the many cults took their heads and limbs as evidence of their devotion. A parade reached Ghaal, where they presented these body parts to Arguthrax. Arguthrax appeared to look on their offerings, and blessed them with a disdainful wave of his flabby hand.

Drakaasi had seen many such wars. In a way, they were a part of its machinery of worship, for the aggressors were ultimately fighting for Khorne's recognition. However, they took place away from the arenas and altars, far from the eyes of Drakaasi's lords, filthy shadow wars and rolls of assassinations. Most of Drakaasi's lords had reached their positions by eliminating a rival in such a war, and all of them had survived such aggression from rivals jealous of their position. That was how power worked: aggression and annihilation. Khorne's patronage ensured that on Drakaasi it always took the form of naked violence.

Times were different now. Lord Ebondrake's pronouncement had demanded that the lords of Drakaasi work together to create a vast army to conquer worlds for Khorne in the wake of the Thirteenth Black Crusade. That did not allow for open conflict between the lords, and when Ebondrake took his lords to task, the results could be bloodier than any battle they could fight between themselves.

This was the matter of the war.

FOURTEEN

It was so profoundly dark that not even Alaric's augmented eyesight could pick out anything. It was unnatural. Something was drinking the light away.

Alaric groped out in the darkness. His hand found the floor in front of him, polished metal. It was the first clean surface that Alaric had touched below decks on the *Hecatomb*.

In response, there was music.

It was quiet at first, a strange lilting sound, mournful, but beautiful. The last music had Alaric heard was the wailing of Aelazadne. This was something else. It sounded like a thousand distant voices. For a moment, he felt that he had intruded on something ancient and sacred, and felt ashamed to be so wounded and flawed in its presence.

However, this was the *Hecatomb*. This was Drakaasi. There was nothing beautiful here. Alaric tried to tell himself that over and over again as the lights began to rise around him.

He was in a chamber of gold and silver. Constellations of gemstones twinkled everywhere. The chamber was huge. It must have run the whole length of the ship's keel and more, another manipulation of time and space within the ship. Asymmetrical pillars, knurled like twisted ropes, ran up the walls to support a ceiling that bulged down as if a golden sky was falling in. Panels of deep blue set into the golden walls were painted with symbols so elegant that they glowed as Alaric looked at them, bright rivulets of power running through every curve. The whole chamber seemed to shift subtly, rippling in and out, as if in time with some ancient breath.

Alaric stood up. His chest heaved, and he coughed out a clot of blood onto the golden floor. Diamonds and sapphires winked up at him through the blood.

He had never seen anything like it. It was almost organic, the knots of the pillars like ancient tree roots, the biological forms of the walls and ceiling like a great golden throat.

The music was coming from the far end of the chamber. Alaric took a couple of steps towards it. The floor gave almost imperceptibly beneath his feet, and the pillars curved over him, as if he was inside a vast creature reacting to his presence.

The chamber flared out ahead into a wide, roughly spherical space, dominated by a stepped pyramid, crowned with a great shard of glowing white crystal from which the song was emanating. More crystal hung from the walls, resonating in time, and filling the chamber with light. At the top of the pyramid there was a magnificent throne, cut from a stone like deep blue marble, covered in intricate golden script. A figure stood on the pyramid, wearing a gold-threaded, blue robe. Braziers burned with silver fire, and the song rose to acknowledge Alaric's presence, the light reaching a near-blinding crescendo.

Alaric glimpsed galleries leading off from the pyramid chamber. The place was far bigger than the *Hecatomb*. For some reason, this was not the least bit surprising to him.

The figure looked up. Silver flames licked from inside the hood.

'Who are you?' it asked in a voice dry like the hiss of a snake.

'Justicar Alaric of the Grey Knights,' replied Alaric.

'I see. You may kneel.'

Alaric stayed standing.

'No? Very well. Few of them kneel to begin with, all do eventually.'

'All of whom?'

'All of you, of course, the slaves, the lowly, fed to me, as if I should be grateful, as if it is some compensation for the wretchedness of my station.' The figure waved an arm to indicate the blinding glory of the pyramid chamber. 'You see what I have to work with here.'

Alaric dearly wanted to wrench the collar of Khorne from around his neck, and let his soul tell him what he was facing, but he had tried before, and he could not remove it with his bare hands, not without breaking his neck.

'So, what is it that you desire?'

'Desire?' Alaric paused. There were many things he desired. There was so much anger and misery inside him that he could not separate it all out. 'I want to escape.'

'No, that is just a primitive lust, a basic thing, a need for freedom, no more elegant than hunger or thirst. No, what do you truly desire?' The figure rose from the throne and took a couple of steps down the pyramid. 'Revenge? Conquest? Redemption? I used to grant wishes, Justicar Alaric of the Grey Knights. Habits die hard, so they say. They always ask me for something once they realise that, but, of course, no desires can be fulfilled here, not as I am now, unless you desire to have your soul flayed away, which I gather you do not.'

'Many have tried,' said Alaric.

'So I see from the state of you.'

'Then this is how it will end,' said Alaric.

'Oh, yes.'

Alaric flexed his fists. He was in no position to fight. He was still exhausted from his battering at the hands of Venalitor, and struggling against his scaephylyds, but no Grey Knight had ever backed down and given himself to the enemy's mercy. 'I should warn you, I am not an easy man to kill.'

'Kill? Justicar Alaric, I had thought you would have more brains in that scarred head than that. You and I are much alike in that Venalitor has uses for us aside from piling up our skulls on his god's throne. No, he does not want you killed.'

The figure pulled back its hood. Beneath was the face of a man flayed of skin, with silver threads for muscles. Silver flame rippled over it. Its eyes were points of burning blue. Tiny mouths opened up in its flesh, muttering syllables of spells that cast a corona of power over it.

'He wants you possessed,' said Raezazel the Cunning.

DUKE VENALITOR WATCHED the battle from his quarters, the bloody events shimmering on a great sheet of crystal that dominated one wall of his audience chamber.

'Let me see the *Scourge*,' said Venalitor. The image shifted to display Drakaasi's newest city. The *Scourge* was a collection of ships and flotsam roped together in a gigantic conglomeration of wreckage floating on the planet's southern ocean, where millions of outcasts and heretics lived. Rumours persisted that the *Hecatomb* had been cut from the *Scourge*, and that perhaps it was the very first ship to become a part of the *Scourge*, and therefore sailed as the excised heart of a dead city. Venalitor did nothing to deny such rumours.

The *Scourge* was the link between the surface of Drakaasi and the civilisations of its deeps. Creatures evolved from scaephylyds lived there, along with lords of Drakaasi, like Thurrgull the Tentacular, who had forged their domains away from the eyes of the surface.

Ocean-going mutants crawled from the sea to kill and abduct, drowning the inhabitants of a great temple ship that dominated the outskirts of the *Scourge*. The temple was dedicated to Arguthrax, ministered by his daemonic priesthood, and the mutants were creatures with gills and webbed hands, who had answered Venalitor's call for allies from the deeps.

Arguthrax's priests, each with six fingers on their mutated hands, were dragged down and killed. The splendid temple ship was holed below the waterline and began to sink, dragging the dwellings of many outcasts down with it. Icons of the warp toppled into the fouled waters.

The image shifted. This time it showed a staging ground for one of Venalitor's allied cults, the Ebon Hand, a band of pirates corrupted and turned to Khorne by Venalitor's agents. They were assembling high in the mountain roosts where they had docked their skyships and dirigibles, ready to marshal their numbers and join Ebondrake's off-world crusade.

The Ebon Hand's sentries alerted the whole cult, as the sun broke over the mountain. On the flagpole at the centre of their assembly ground, where

once had flown a banner blessed by Venalitor himself, now hung the body of their leader, Garyagan
Redhand. Redhand's face had been removed, and a
huge, bloody maw yawned in the front of his head.
His hands had been cut off, too, no doubt added to
the trophies of whatever assassin Arguthrax had
sent.

'The war continues, then, my lord,' said the slave
master. The ancient scaephylyd waited patiently at
the back of the room. It was a shrewd creature that
had survived as long as it had by aligning itself with
Drakaasi's lords and offering them complete sub-
servience.

'It continues,' said Venalitor. 'It will not end until
one of us is dead.'

'Then how will we be victorious?'

Venalitor looked at him. 'I will sacrifice everything I have to, and nothing more.'

'Lord Ebondrake must be guarded against.'

'A dull mind would think so, slave master, but the
truth is that Ebondrake admires strength as we all
do. When Arguthrax is done with, I will be closer to
Ebondrake's position, not further away.'

'Then what is your will?' The slave master
crouched down on its haunches. It was the equiva-
lent of a deep bow, which a scaephylyd could not
do normally since it was so hunched over.

'Keep it quiet,' said Venalitor, 'for now. Use soldiers we can say were acting on their own, and
that we will not miss. Kill Arguthrax's outer circles first, the allies of allies, the props holding up

his domain. He is a thing of anger and hate. He will try to strike at me as directly as possible. He will elicit Ebondrake's wrath before I do, and when that happens, he will be open for the deathblow.'

'So it shall be, my lord.'

'Keep me updated on the Grey Knight,' added Venalitor. 'Once Raezazel has him, he is destined to kill Arguthrax.'

'Of course.'

The slavemaster left the chamber to pursue his many duties, leaving Venalitor watching the shadow war unfolding.

ALARIC SLAMMED INTO the wall behind him. Shards of gold showered down around him as he slid to the floor. His mind reeled. Images of the daemon's life battered against him like gunfire.

He forced himself to breathe, and to ground his thoughts, to fight the flawed human instinct to run.

Raezazel the Cunning was flying above him. Silver wings unfolded from his robes. Fire rippled up off its body, and hundreds of mouths in its shining flesh sang at once.

'You know that I can give you what you desire,' said Raezazel in its hundred voices. 'You are stronger than the others. You believe that you can see through the lie. Perhaps you are right.'

Alaric got to his feet. He felt weak and small. Never had he been so at the mercy of another creature.

'Do you desire death, Grey Knight?' asked Raezazel. 'I can give you that.'

Alaric forced a breath down. He was a Grey Knight. He had faced the lies of Chaos before, and thrown them back into the darkness with the power of truth. Daemons had tried to possess him before, too, and not one of them had prised open his mind.

However, none of them had ever attacked him while he was so unprotected.

'I desire freedom,' said Alaric.

'Then you can have it.'

'Freedom from you.'

Raezazel cocked its head to the side. Its burning eyes looked at him quizzically, as it might have regarded a particularly unusual kind of lunatic.

'That,' it said, 'is something you will have to take from me.'

A hand coalesced from golden energy, picked Alaric up, and held him against the wall. Power was pouring off Raezazel, burning from the crystals, and turning the golden walls into sheets of molten light. Alaric fought back, feeling the hand closing around his mind. Dull pain throbbed behind his eyes.

'I will wear your flesh and leave this prison, Justicar Alaric. I will escape this world and become one with my god. That is what I desire. That is what Venalitor has offered me by sending you here, for even the Blood God's servants must perpetuate the lie.'

Alaric fought back with everything he had. It took all his remaining strength just to draw breath, but he would not let Raezazel in, never! He would die first. That would be his last service to the Emperor. The enemy would never have a possessed Grey Knight to parade before its armies, never... unless Raezazel was stronger.

Raezazel's burning face floated down low above Alaric's. A silver hand reached out to touch his head.

Alaric was filled with cold pain.

Raezazel was showing him what he could do to him: fill him up with agony a thousand times worse, for a thousand years. He was telling Alaric to give in.

'Not this mind,' hissed Alaric between his teeth. 'There is no pain save the fires of failure. There is no torture save a duty undone. My Emperor claims me, and no other may challenge.'

Raezazel dropped Alaric. 'The condition of your soul matters not,' he said. 'I will flay it alive if I have to.'

Alaric tried to get back to his feet. Raezazel threw horrors at him.

Rotting bodies loomed from the floor and walls. Alaric had seen thousands of corpses. They would not force him to his knees.

They took on the faces of his friends, his battle-brothers and everyone he had ever trusted.

Alaric had lost many friends. The penalty for being trusted by Alaric seemed to be death. He felt his might tighten as it recoiled from the images, but he held firm.

Worlds burned. A galaxy suffered, and the stars went out. Hollow laughter filled the universe.

Alaric fought back.

Victory after victory bloomed into existence. He knew that Chaos could be defeated. Perhaps it would take all the time in the galaxy, but it would happen. For every vision of desolation Raezazel pumped into him, Alaric countered with something glorious: the destruction of the Chaos fleet at the Battle of Gethsemane, Lord Solar Macharius winning a thousand worlds back from the galaxy's dark, the vanquishing of Angron in the First Armageddon War. Alaric pulled victories from every history book and inspiration a sermon he knew.

We are weak flesh and fools, thought Alaric furiously. *We are young and blind. Perhaps one day we will be gone, but we burn so bright, and the galaxy, which has forgotten so much, will remember us.*

Raezazel hissed in frustration. The images of horror dissolved away. Alaric slumped down against the wall of the chamber, grinning like a madman.

'You can't terrify me into submission, daemon. I am a Space Marine. We know no fear.'

'Then it seems you are in need,' spat Raezazel, 'of an education.'

Raezazel's mind picked Alaric up off the floor. Alaric fought back, as Raezazel drifted closer on wings of light, and placed a hand on Alaric's forehead.

Filaments of silver and gold wove around Alaric's head, and wormed into the skin of his scalp. Alaric bellowed, and tried to tear them free, but they were inside him now.

He could feel them writhing through his skull into his brain. Synapses misfired, and extremes of heat and cold rippled over him, nausea, pain, confusion. The world spun around him as his sense of balance went haywire.

He beat at Raezazel's body with his free hand. Silver ribs crunched. It would not be enough.

A thousand mouths were laughing at him.

Alaric's consciousness melted like the gold.

WHEN EVEN ARGUTHRAX was young, Raezazel the Cunning had granted wishes.

The image in Alaric's mind was of a largely formless thing, just a scrawl of psychic matter in the warp. He knew it was a simplified image, distorted by being forced into a human mind. The scale of the warp still battered at Alaric's brain.

The youthful daemon, little more than a tadpole swimming through the mindless infinity of the warp, had suckled on the misery and hatred of the young races populating the universe. From them, he learned deceit and malice, and saw their fleeting joys and moments of affection as the hollow things they really were. The living things of the galaxy were nothing but bundles of lies, woven to keep them from understanding their true hateful natures.

Lies were the fabric of the mind. To the mortal races, lies were reality. The power of a lie could bring empires up from the dirt and cast them back down again. They could drive men, greenskins, eldar and the rest to acts of heroism and devotion... and of hatred, genocide and evil. Lies were power. Deceit was reality.

There was a god of lies in the warp. There could be no greater power. Congealed from the deceit of the universe, older than reality, Raezazel could only become a part of it. It was Tzeentch, and yet it was nothing, for this purest manifestation of Chaos was so infinitely mutable that it could never truly be fixed as anything. Its very existence was a lie, because Tzeentch could not exist. From this paradox flowed such power that the universe could have only one rightful ruler, and it was Tzeentch.

The concept of Tzeentch was an appalling thing, one that filled Alaric with disgust, but Raezazel's devotion to the being mingled with that disgust, the resulting emotion utterly alien to Alaric's mind, a perversion of everything it meant to be human.

Raezazel's understanding grew. Tzeentch desired power, and yet Tzeentch also desired an absence of power, anarchy and confusion, because for Tzeentch to desire any one thing would be to deny its very existence.

There were other gods in the warp. One of them was Khorne, the Blood God, but Raezazel knew that only Tzeentch could draw its power from such a fundamental part of the universe as the lie, and so Raezazel served.

Raezazel found ways through into real space, where the young races dwelled. He found a way through unprotected minds, the naked souls of psykers so bright from the warp that Raezazel could cross the bridge between dimensions and possess their bodies. He did Tzeentch's work, both encouraging others to worship the Liar God and build his power base, but also casting down the structures of power wherever he found them, spreading chaos and anarchy, for only Tzeentch could desire both dominion and chaos at once. Sometimes he even fought other followers of Tzeentch, to ensure that the holy paradox did not falter.

The time roared by, like a hurricane in Alaric's mind. He fought to keep himself from being shredded by the force of Raezazel's memories, because then he would disappear completely and be left nothing but a figment of the daemon's imagination.

Cults of Tzeentch prayed for help. Sometimes Tzeentch really did send them help. Other times, he sent them Raezazel. There were cults who called forth Tzeentch's servants and opened gates through which Raezazel could pass, his own sacred form emerging into real space in all its terrifying silver magnificence. Everyone who worshipped Tzeentch eventually suffered for it, because Tzeentch promised deliverance and succour, and so it was inevitable that this would always be a lie. Raezazel was often the source of that suffering, here an assassin and there a puppet master orchestrating tragic downfalls with an attention to detail that a human mind could not comprehend. Whole empires were shifted and manipulated to bring a single person low, and the lowliest of individuals could be used to topple civilisations with only the slightest touch.

Raezazel lied. He made promises. He became an expert at seeking out the desires of those whose called out to Tzeentch, and fulfilling them in such a way that they became utterly damned. They always came to recognise the lie just before the end, and knew that ultimately it had not been Tzeentch but they, who had damned themselves: yet another paradox. Raezazel was good at what he did.

Aeons passed. Species rose and fell, of which mankind had far from the greatest potential. One species ruled the galaxy, and then another, believers in the lie that true power lay anywhere in real space. The time came when mankind rose to dominate the galaxy in what it called the Dark Age of Technology, and then fell again in the wars of the Age of Strife. It was not the most spectacular collapse, though it provided plenty of fuel for Tzeentch's silver fires, but it was different, because mankind came back. One of them rose on Terra, humanity's birthplace, and began to unite what remained of the species. He very nearly succeeded, this Emperor, but his power, too, was just a hollow lie compared to that of the warp. Forces in the warp played their hand and tried to use this new unification of humanity to seize control of it, and with it the material galaxy.

Tzeentch played his part, too. The Emperor was a lie, and Tzeentch took great pleasure in revealing it to those who rebelled against Him. Raezazel was there, at Prospero and Istvaan V. He was even there on Terra, when the final charades were played out, when in victory the Emperor condemned his species to ten thousand years and more of lightless misery. Raezazel observed much of the Horus Heresy, reporting back to the daemon princes of Tzeentch, or whispering promises of power and deliverance, much as he had always done. When the traitor forces retreated into the Eye of Terror, Raezazel knew that it was just another lie. Chaos was not gone from the galaxy. When they returned and ruled it, the age of the Imperium would seem barely a flicker in the galaxy's history. Then, something went wrong.

The heresy was so pure that it almost filled up Alaric. He had to tell himself over and over again that Raezazel was a daemon and that everything he saw in it was a lie.

Alaric recognised the bloodstained world that Raezazel came to next. An eight-pointed star was carved into its surface, forming canals filled with blood. The star connected its great cities: a crown of crystal spires, a great parasite and an endless slum.

Raezazel came to the world of Drakaasi, where many threads of fate had converged. There titanic daemons had fought in the past, drenching the planet with the blood that still stained it. Khorne had won, and for the first time Raezazel the Cunning was trapped.

Khorne despised the lie, despised fate and magic and everything that made up Tzeentch. Raezazel was cut off from the warp. He lived there for a thousand years, snatching tragedies from the blood-soaked lives of Khorne's servants, promising them yet more bloodshed, and then robbing them of their minds. Khorne's own daemons hunted him, but they were base creatures, and more often than not they consumed each other in their lust for blood, turned against their fellows by Raezazel's brilliance. Raezazel the Cunning was the most hated creature on Drakaasi, that most hateful world.

Then Duke Venalitor arose. An aspiring champion of the Blood God, he was a master swordsman and an ambitious general. He sought out Raezazel the Cunning, as many lords and champions had done before, and, as always, Raezazel asked what Venalitor most desired.

Venalitor said he wanted a worthy opponent. The art of the sword was his personal form of worship and he needed a fitting target to perfect his skills. Raezazel offered him the best of Drakaasi's fighters, knowing that in besting them Venalitor would either kill himself or be driven mad by victory or defeat. However, Venalitor killed everything put in front of him. Finally Raezazel, knowing that the lie had to be believed no matter what, offered himself up as an opponent, knowing that the silver fires of Tzeentch burned brightly in him, and that no mortal could best him.

Venalitor cut Raezazel so deeply that the daemon knew fear for the briefest of moments. Then he glimpsed the warp again, and the many faces of his lord Tzeentch laughing at him. Raezazel had been lied to, as well. Of course he had, it was all part of the divine paradox. Raezazel collapsed, defeated, but Venalitor did not despatch him. Instead he was taken to the *Hecatomb*, imprisoned behind doors marked with the most powerful anti-magical wards, and bound by ancient daemon oaths to accept Venalitor as his conqueror and master.

Then, centuries later, Justicar Alaric of the Grey Knights was thrown into his cell.

All of this information was blasted into Alaric's mind in less than a second.

HE WAS FALLING. A universe of Raezazel's creation stretched around him, endless and black. A weaker man would have lost his mind there and then, overwhelmed by the reality of his insignificance against the universe. Alaric told himself that there was an Emperor out there somewhere, and that Alaric owed Him something. It was just enough.

A world unfolded from the blackness below him. Bare rock, pocked with craters, rolled wider and wider, until a whole planet was looming up below him.

Alaric slammed into it. The planet's surface rippled beneath him like something alive reacting to his presence. The ground folded over him, warm and crushing, and Alaric fought to breathe. Then it spat him out again.

Alaric fought to find something real. He was in a world of Raezazel's making. It had got inside his mind, and it was pulling strings in his imagination and memory to create this place.

It had got in. Such a thing had never happened to a Grey Knight, ever. Raezazel the Cunning had said it would possess him, and it was only a few steps from doing exactly that. With the Collar of Khorne switching off his psychic shield, Alaric was alone with his wits.

Grass was growing beneath him. He got to his feet as it spread away from him like a green stain. The landscape in the distance heaved up into hills and mountains. Deep scars sank into the land and filled with water, heavy fronds of a forest bending over the banks. Tress unrolled from the ground like hands towards the sky, surrounding Alaric in a dense jungle. Vines writhed around tree trunks that blackened with age and moss. The ground underneath became soft with simulated centuries of growth and decay. The first creatures of this world inside his mind winked into life: jewelled flying insects, night-furred predators that skulked among the branches, and birds of brilliant colours. The sound of the place descended around him like a cloak, the wind among the trees, howls, and the distant roars of predators.

The sky was streaked with cloud. Distant mountains were crowned with snow. The sound of a waterfall nearby reached Alaric.

He stood in a clearing of the forest and looked down at himself. He was still wearing the remnants of the armour in which he had fled the arena of Gorgath. He was still the same person. No matter what happened, Alaric existed. It was the only fact of which Alaric could still be certain.

'Raezazel!' yelled Alaric. 'Daemon! A Grey Knight never knelt before witchcraft, and I shall not be the first!'

Only the gentle din of the jungle answered him. Alaric looked around, noting how the forest was darkening as it thickened around him. He could stay there forever, hiding in fear from the daemon inside him. Or he could find it, and fight it.

Alaric tore the branches down that blocked his path in front of it. He wished he had a weapon, but he would worry about that later. For now, he pushed on.

ALARIC CAME ACROSS the waterfall. It was flowing from the shattered skull of a titanic creature that seemed to have lain there for thousands of years, fossilised and claimed by the jungle. The water that poured from the broken cranium was pure, and shot through with leaping silver fish.

The skull was enormous. The dead creature had many, many more, attached to a monstrous spine that formed a thickly forested ridge stretching into the distance. Each skull was different, grimacing in horrible glee or festooned with eyes. The creature, when alive, had been a towering column of insane faces kilometres high.

'Ghargatuloth,' said Alaric. The daemon prince had arisen on the Trail of Saint Evisser, and engineered a sequence of events so complex that Alaric had become a part of it. Those events had been woven to summon Ghargatuloth back from the warp where it had been banished, and only Alaric and Inquisitor Ligeia had been able to bring the daemon low at the instant it emerged into real space.

'Is that the best you can do?' Alaric shouted up at the sky, knowing that Raezazel would hear him. 'Remind me of a past victory? Is that what you are going to offer me, Raezazel? Basking in past glories means nothing to a Grey Knight, not while your kind still exist! That Ghargatuloth existed at all was a failure of my entire Chapter! Is this really supposed to seduce me?'

There was no answer.

Alaric made a spear from a straight tree branch and a chunk of sharp flint. At least now he was armed. He felt more like a Grey Knight, with a weapon in his hand, and less like a man being led through the corners of his own mind at the whim of a daemon. He forged his way up onto Ghargatuloth's spine, and saw mountains in the distance, the glinting ribbon of a river leading towards a dark smudge of ocean on the opposite horizon.

The peak of a snow-capped mountain shuddered, and burst in a plume of dark grey smoke. Minutes later the sound reached Alaric, an angry roar from beneath the earth. The ground quaked. The sky darkened.

'So that's the way it's going to be,' said Alaric. Tidal waves rose up from the ocean and hard rain began to hammer down.

RAEZAZEL BATTERED ALARIC for many hours. Floods ripped through the jungles, slamming Alaric against rocks and tree trunks. Earthquakes ripped the ground open, and he nearly fell into the gaping, burning maw of the earth dozens of times. Predators lurched from the jungle, and Alaric fended them off, skewering a great lizard through the throat with his spear, and wrestling a cat-like monster to the ground, breaking its neck. Birds of prey swooped down, and Alaric grabbed them by the wings, crushing them down against the ground. Poisonous snakes were out-reacted, and had their spines cracked like whips.

Night fell. Burning meteors fell from the sky, casting plumes of scalding ash over the jungle. The jungle, too, changed around him, closing in, reaching thorny limbs. Alaric fought it all off, as he forged on defiantly through Raezazel's world.

He was tiring, however. Presumably his body was not real, and was only a projection of himself, a reflection of his own consciousness, but it still bore its own scars and bruises. The wound in his chest still bled. The burns from the molten gold still flared with pain. He was tired and hurt, and he wondered if he could act with even half the strength and resilience of a fully fit Grey Knight.

He began to see things, faces in the sky. He heard voices speaking to him, half-real sentences pulled at random from his past. Perhaps they were all really there, assembled by Raezazel to torment him.

He stumbled on, half-blind with fatigue. Clawed hands reached from the darkness to tear at his skin. A meteor slammed into the ground close enough to knock him off his feet. He crawled on, writhing through the mud. Scalding rain streaked down on him. He was blind and deaf. Lightning crashed above him, and he didn't even know which way he was heading any more.

His hand found polished stone. He dragged himself out of the mud, and flopped, gasping, onto the cold stone. He could have just lain there, letting the remaining energy bleed out of him until he fell unconscious. Something half-remembered told him to carry on.

He could see stone steps ahead of him. At the top of the steps was the columned front of a temple, with a sculpted pediment depicting battle. In front of the columns, on the top step, was a huge statue of a man in massive ornate armour. His face was wide and noble, his war gear magnificent, and inscribed with devotional texts. He carried a halberd in one hand.

The statue was of Alaric. This was his temple, the one erected in the warp to celebrate all the skulls he had taken on Drakaasi, and perhaps all the creatures and daemons he had ever killed.

He crawled up the steps. Lightning split the night again, and the rain hammered down on him. At least there was shelter here.

Someone was standing between the columns. The dull glow of a brazier emanated from behind the figure, glinting off golden offerings to Alaric the Betrayed. Alaric was just able to make out the details of the figure as he reached the top step.

Justicar Tancred, huge like a standing stone in his Terminator armour, reached down to Alaric. He smiled.

'Take my hand, Alaric,' he said. 'It's over.'

FIFTEEN

Alaric awoke on a pinnacle of rock standing high over a raging ocean. He did not recognise this world. Perhaps it was another part of the same planet that Raezazel had created in his mind.

'Do you see what they do to you?' said Raezazel. The daemon was standing behind Alaric. Alaric stood up, and Raezazel took flight, hovering over him. 'Do you ever put down your implements of death long enough to realise?'

'End this witchcraft!' shouted Alaric. The wind whipped around his ears, sharp with the taste of the sea, and stole his words away.

'What is a man,' said Raezazel, 'if he means nothing to his fellow men? If he is an island, cut off from all others? What kind of an existence is this,

Alaric? Everyone you trust, everyone who trusts you, dies. It is a death sentence. Look at what they made of you.'

Alaric looked down over the edge of the pinnacle. Slick rock receded all the way to the battered shore. This was the tip of a barren peninsula, devoid of life. Alaric was completely alone.

'I offer you a human life,' said Raezazel, 'a real one.'

'I need only to know that my duty is done!'

'When will that be? When all of Chaos is gone and the warp extinguished? Such a thing cannot be, and you know it as well as I do. What is the point of fighting a battle that cannot end, when the sacrifice you make is everything that makes a human what he is? A human life, Alaric, happiness, fulfilment. I show you now what you are. Let me show you what you can be, free of your Imperium, free of the duties you cannot fulfil. Let me show you contentment.'

'Burn, daemon. Pick your hell and stew there.'

'Was there ever a prisoner who so loved the bars that kept him captive? Let go of this, Alaric. All that sets you apart. No man can expect to be more than human. Give up on that dream and live.'

Raezazel was right. Alaric was completely alone, set apart from the human race he was sworn to defend.

He looked once at his reflection and accepted that it was a small price to pay. Every servant of humanity had to make a sacrifice to their duty. This was Alaric's.

Alaric looked up at Raezazel. Then he stepped off the edge of the pinnacle and fell.

HE PLUNGED INTO the ocean, and the ocean became air. It was a void without light or substance, only the wind in his ears.

'Take what you want,' said Raezazel's voice in his head. 'Take it. What is there to existence but that?'

The cold void tore at Alaric. It had fingers like ice, and it would tear him apart. Alaric wanted to land somewhere, to get his bearings, and find Raezazel so that he could work out what the next trick was.

Land appeared under him. Alaric thudded into it. It was dry and sandy, and went on forever. He wanted to see where he was.

A sun bloomed in the eye like a white flower. Alaric looked around, but the featureless plain stretched in all directions. He searched for some landmark to get his bearings by.

He glimpsed a city in the distance. It was a fine Imperial city with the buttresses and granite eagles familiar to him from the fortresses of Titan. Suddenly he was there at his threshold.

'Take what you want,' said Raezazel.

Power, thought Alaric, the power to conquer and do my duty. The power to destroy evil.

He was the city's king. His court surrounded his throne, bowing before him, a hundred Imperial nobles, and representatives of all the Adepta. He had an Inquisitorial seal on his finger and a document in his hand, signed with the initial 'I' and a drop of blood. It gave him the world, and all other worlds upon which his imagination could settle.

'I want you dead,' said Alaric, 'you and all your kind, dead.'

He was at the head of his city's army. Only it was not a city any more, it was a kingdom, one of many on this world that all owed him fealty. He was in armour as magnificent as that of a primarch, and the soldiers around him were Space Marines, legions upon legions of them, millions of them, and they revered him as a king and a brother. There was nothing they could not do.

'You can have what you want,' said Raezazel. 'There are ways. There is nothing within the bounds of human imagination that cannot be granted to you.'

'You offer me power?' snarled Alaric. 'You think I would betray myself to you for this?'

'You cannot deny your desires, Grey Knight. Look around you. Everything you desire, you have. You can have it, and more, forever.'

Alaric wanted lightning in his hand to strike down the daemon. He had it. He wanted Raezazel in front of him, ready to execute. The daemon was kneeling before him. All he had to do was take what he wanted.

'All this I desire, it is true,' said Alaric. 'It comes to my mind unbidden, as you know well, but there is one thing I desire more than anything, one burning need, which you cannot fulfil.'

'Name it,' said Raezazel.'

'I desire a universe where your kind cannot exist,' said Alaric.

Raezazel's mouths opened and closed dumbly.

The force of the paradox was too much even for a servant of Tzeentch.

Alaric's legions disintegrated. His city blew away in a tide of ash, and his world imploded.

ALARIC WAS AT the end of time.

Before him, impossibly, a battlefield stretched on forever, and he perceived every inch of it.

Mankind had gathered, every righteous man and woman who had ever died. Here were the primarchs: Sanguinius, achingly beautiful on wings of silver feathers; Leman Russ, striding titanic at the head of a host of wolves; Jaghatai Khan on a chariot made from stars. The greatest legends of the Imperium had gathered, and behind them the Space Marines and Imperial Guardsmen, the simple citizens and redeemed sinners, who had rallied to face evil at the end.

The Emperor commanded them all. Clad in blazing golden armour, He was the most magnificent sight that Alaric's mind could behold. Majesty streamed off Him. There could be no doubt that He was the master of mankind, a god, humanity's future given form.

Alaric's fallen battle-brothers stood around His golden form. He recognised Thane, who had died on Sarthis Majoris; Lykkos and Cardios, lost on Chaeroneia; Canoness Ludmilla, slain by Valinov

on Volcanis Ultor; Justicar Tancred; Inquisitor
Ligeia.

'Justicar Alaric,' said Tancred with a smile. Tancred
was huge, even by the standards of a Space Marine,
built for the Terminator armour he wore. He
clapped Alaric on the shoulder. 'You have joined us.
We are complete!'

'This is it? This is the final battle?'

'Of course! The sons of Russ call it the Wolftime.
To the Khan's men it is the hunting of the greatest
quarry. To a Grey Knight it is the final battle against
the enemy. See! There they stand, waiting to die!'

Alaric followed Tancred's gaze across the battlefield. The indistinct shadowy mass of the enemy
stood waiting for the Emperor's charge. Four
mighty generals loomed in the background, one
crowned with horns, another a wizard in billowing
robes. One was a writhing snake-bodied thing, and
another was a bloated heap of decay. They were
mighty, and they were terrible, but they would fall.
They could not stand against the Emperor and His
faithful.

'It cannot be,' said Alaric. 'I have not earned this.'

A hand took his, tiny in comparison. It belonged
to Inquisitor Ligeia. She was an ageing, but handsome woman, striking in her deep blue, jewelled
gown. Alaric admired her as much as he admired
the Grand Masters of his own order. She smiled at
him sadly.

'Why do you deny yourself, Alaric?' she asked.
'You have done so much. Who is to say you have

not won your place at the Emperor's side? Look, there is the Castigator, the daemon you destroyed on Chaeroneia.' Alaric could see the daemon titan's form among the shadows of the enemy. 'And there is Ghargatuloth, the Daemon Prince we slew together. Think on all the foes you have sent to this place. Think about those you saved. You redeemed me, Alaric. My death was not in vain, and I owe it to you. There are so many like me. Are they not worth something?' She took hold of his arm and pulled him close. 'You belong here. You deserve this. Your duty is done.'

'Is Raezazel there?' asked Alaric.

'It matters not,' said Tancred. 'He is one amongst many. He is nothing compared to others you vanquished. You are just one man, you cannot hope to banish every daemon from the universe.'

'Those are not the words of a Grey Knight,' said Alaric. 'While even one of them walks in real space, or broods in the warp, our work is not done. I will not stay here unless Raezazel is there, destroyed, among the enemy. Is he there? Can any of you see him?'

'You disappoint me, Justicar,' said Ligeia. 'I thought you would understand your role in the galaxy better than this.'

'Those are not the words of Inquisitor Ligeia,' said Alaric. He looked up at the golden form of the Emperor towering over him. It was like staring into the sun. 'And you, my Emperor! Do you see in me one who deserved his place here? One who lets his conciousness slip away from him while a daemon dances through his mind? One who is brought into the presence of the enemy and cowers away from his duty?'

The Emperor looked down. A hundred mouths opened in his face.

'Is this all you can do, Raezazel? Is this the best you can offer me? A sham victory against the warp? Is this what you will play, over and over again, in my mind as my reward?'

'I am getting closer, Grey Knight,' said Raezazel. 'You cannot deny that. It is only a matter of time.'

Brother Tancred and Inquisitor Ligeia dissolved into molten gold. The battlefield was flooded with it, and it closed, white-hot, over Alaric's head. The primarchs and the Emperor disappeared from view. Alaric fought to breathe.

He would not die, not yet. Raezazel still had to toy with him.

HE DREW A ragged, desperate breath. His hand found something to hold on to, and he dragged himself above the surface of the golden ocean.

A tower of frozen blood rose above him.

Alaric laid a hand on the blood. It melted under his body heat into a handhold. Grimly, forced on by the inevitability of it, Alaric began to climb.

Fallen fortresses rose from the ocean all around. Alaric knew, by some instinct, that each one represented a champion of the warp that Alaric had killed. They were all gone. There was just one left.

Alaric reached the top of the blood tower. The melted blood was smeared all over him, and its smell and taste filled him up. The whole world seemed made of it. He dragged himself over the battlements.

He forced himself to his feet. Duke Venalitor stood in front of him.

A sword had appeared in Alaric's hand. All he had to do was spear Venalitor through the chest, or slice his head off, or open up his abdomen and watch the life ooze out of him as he held his guts in.

Then it would be over. Haulvarn would be avenged.

Venalitor dissolved away. His armour, plate by plate, came away from his body and spiralled up towards the stormy sky. Finally his two-handed blade clattered to the floor and liquefied like mercury.

There was nothing inside the armour. Venalitor, like this whole world, was a lie.

'Did you think you would find him here? Rip him apart, and vanquish him? This is in your mind, Alaric,' said Raezazel. The daemon descended from the sky on silver wings. 'Venalitor is very far away. If you try to hunt him down without me, he will stay just out of reach. You know this, Alaric. He is too strong and too clever for you. I am the only way.'

Alaric knew it was true, and felt that truth dragging him down. He could deny it, but he knew he would be lying to himself. He wanted Venalitor dead, and he would not have what he wanted. He had been bested by Venalitor once before, and on Drakaasi Venalitor was protected by all the followers of a Chaos Lord, by a whole planet beloved of his god. With Raezazel, Alaric could kill Venalitor.

'No,' said that tiny part of Alaric that still remembered what he was. 'None of this is true. You are a daemon. You are a lie, and everything you say is a lie. There is another way.'

'Really?' asked Raezazel. 'Name it.'

Then, Alaric realised his one chance.

'I have read,' he said falteringly, 'from the pages of the Liber Daemonicum. I have looked on the warp and felt madness touching me. I have heard the whispers of the daemon in my mind. I have seen... I have seen a dead world come back to life, a cannibal planet consuming its own to survive. I have seen good men and women murder one another at the behest of a madman. I have fought on a cursed world for the delight of the Dark Gods. I have seen so many things... so much that could not possibly be real.' He looked up at Raezazel. The daemon was beautiful, but its very substance was deceit. 'I am not a Grey Knight. How could one such as I see what I have seen and keep my mind?'

With the last of his mental discipline, Alaric took in everything that he had seen: bodies torn by daemon's hands, glimpses of the warp, the hateful realm of Chaos on the other side of reality, heroes driven to madness and evil, whole planets devoured, and the psychic aftertaste of millions of screaming deaths.

It added up to an absolute certainty that the galaxy of man was doomed, and that Chaos was the inevitable state of all things.

'I am the hammer,' said Alaric. 'I am the mail about His fist! I am the spear in His hand! Though we are lost, I am the shield on His arm, I am the flight of his arrows!'

Too late, Raezazel realised what Alaric was doing. With Alaric's psychic shield still protecting him, there was no way that the horror of such things could affect Alaric as they would a normal man. However, with the Collar of Khorne removing that shield, Alaric's mind was vulnerable, not just to creatures like Raezazel, but to Alaric himself.

He had something to hold on to. He was the Hammer, he was a Grey Knight. He grasped that idea and clutched it to both his hearts. It was all he would have left. It had to count.

'I am the hammer! I am the sword! I am the shield! I am a soldier of the battle at the end of time!'

Alaric let all the horror hit him at once: everything he had seen, everything he had done, the friends he had lost, and the lives he had taken.

'No!' yelled Raezazel with the voices of a hundred mouths.

Alaric lost his mind.

SIXTEEN

Venalitor's strategic chamber on board the *Hecatomb* suited the workings of war. The strategium table dominated the room, a map of Drakaasi picked out in ivory and gold on its surface. The rest of the room was in darkness, so that Venalitor could concentrate on the matter of his campaign against Arguthrax. Venalitor wore the robes of a priest of Khorne, and his sword was propped up against the table. The two-hander never left his side.

'The daemon will be dealt with in due time,' said Venalitor impatiently. 'Just tell me the latest casualties.'

The scaephylyd slave master held a scroll in its forelimbs. It unrolled the scroll with its mandibles. 'The Hand has struck back,' it said.

'The leaders of the Army of Crimson Hate were slain in the night.'

'We didn't get all of the Hand?' asked Venalitor irritably. 'Damnation. They really are vermin.' Markers representing his forces, and those of Arguthrax, were arranged around the map like pieces in some game of strategy. 'Can the Crimson Hate still fight?'

'They are squabbling amongst themselves,' replied the slavemaster. 'To decide who will be their new generals.'

Venalitor reached over and picked up the marker representing the Army of the Crimson Hate. He could ill-afford to lose them, especially considering the sacrifices he had made to acquire their loyalty. He threw the jewelled marker across the room. It bounced off an obsidian column, and skittered behind a shrine to Khorne in his aspect of the Red Knight.

'Others?' asked Venalitor.

'Arguthrax has hit the sleepers,' continued the slavemaster. 'Our agent in the Wild Hunt of Tiresia was murdered but an hour ago.'

'How did Arguthrax find him?' snapped Venalitor, in disbelief. His spy in Tiresia's court was so subtle and cunning that he didn't even have a name, just a face so bland it left no mark in the memory.

'We know not,' said the slavemaster. 'Also the tactician in Scathach's army, who was in our employ, was discovered and denounced. Scathach executed him.'

'Hmm. That is less of a surprise. War Master Thorgellin was less subtle in his methods. At least there was a proper execution. That would have been something to see, Scathach has quite an imagination. What progress have we made?'

'The campaign against the Tribe of the Fifth Eye is a success,' said the slavemaster. 'The Disciples of Murder have pushed them back to the ocean. The final push has commenced.'

'Good, and what of Arguthrax's sleepers?'

'They are well-hidden. My scaephylyds are hunting them down. Many scaephylyds have been found to be suspicious, and have been liquidated, but there are no confirmed spies among us.'

'Your kind were a good choice to serve me,' said Venalitor. 'Without me, you would have been exterminated sooner or later. It is difficult to corrupt those who owe their existence to their master.'

'Indeed, it is so,' said the slavemaster, but there was no indication in its cultured Imperial Gothic of whether it took this as an insult or not.

Venalitor sat back in his throne, a black stone echo of the fabled Skull Throne upon which Khorne sat while observing all the murders committed in his name. Khorne would know how to deal with an enemy like Arguthrax.

Venalitor could not claim to know the mind of his god. Nevertheless, it was certain that, presented with a problem like Arguthrax, Khorne would show no mercy.

'Bring them all out of the woodwork: everything that has ever paid fealty to us, every oath that was sworn. Examine the rolls for every supplication and tribute. How many creatures on this planet have offered their loyalty to me out of convenience, trusting their cunning or power to avoid their obligations? Show them they were wrong.' Venalitor stood up. 'Use the Army of Crimson Hate to enforce this in the open. Use the rest of our sleepers to do so in the shadows. I can always get more followers.'

'It will leave us open, my lord.'

Venalitor looked the slavemaster in its many eyes. 'Victory is given to he who will go further than the next man. Arguthrax is ancient. His connections are thousands of years old. He will not throw them away in war. I am young. I have no allies or followers that I am not ready to expend. If I am the only one who is left, if everyone who has ever knelt before me is dead, then I will still have won if Arguthrax has lost. That is my advantage over him. Make it so, slavemaster, and do not rest until every obligation has been called in.'

The slavemaster, bowed again, rolled up the scroll, and left the chambers.

Venalitor sat back down and looked at the map in front of him. He moved the markers around, each one a finely wrought statue of a daemon, or a warrior of Chaos. Some of them were spies, elite agents hidden in the courts of other lords, who in spite of their immense value were not above being used as foot soldiers in the war. Others were hapless cults created to be sacrificed, drooling madmen competing for the right to die for their master. They all had their uses.

There was one piece that Venalitor could not move around at will. It was a tiny obsidian dragon with eyes of amber. It represented Lord Ebondrake, watching over Drakaasi from his palace in Vel'Skan.

Ebondrake was still the ultimate power on Drakaasi. He had expressly forbidden the war between Venalitor and Arguthrax. The truth was, even if Ebondrake would never admit it, that taking on both Venalitor and Arguthrax could be beyond even Ebondrake and his Ophidian Guard. That was how delicate the balance of power on Drakaasi could be.

Venalitor left the Ebondrake piece where it was. He would deal with the lizard when the time came.

ALARIC WAS STILL there. It was a very small part of him, a fragment of lucidity, and it was trapped. The rest of his mind was a dark ocean, and he was crushed on the bed of its deepest trench. Like deepsea predators, like the feral killers of the warp, venomous things coalesced from the darkness, shards of hatred and misery, regrets and the memories of violence, flitting through his unconscious mind looking for a personality to devour.

He was the Hammer. The prayer kept him intact. He had a duty, encompassed by the prayer, and that duty was his reason for existing. He had to fight on, to act as the hammer in the Emperor's fist, because if he did not, there was no one to take his place. He was a Grey Knight, and without men like him there would be no human race.

Slowly, he tried to drag himself up, piece by piece, memory by memory. He caught glimpses of an almost forgotten man, a giant in armour with a halberd in his hand. Painful flashes of violence assailed him, snapping at him with red teeth. He had unleashed all the horrors of his memory, and they had rampaged around his mind, shattering him until he was just a tiny shard of a human being trapped in the darkness.

SOMETIMES, RAEZAZEL'S MEMORIES flickered past his mind's eye.

There was something in there that Raezazel had wanted to hide from him, something locked away in the madness, some secret, or something shameful, something that even a daemon recoiled from.

Its first sight of Drakaasi bloomed in Alaric's fragmented mind: an eight-pointed star marked out by cities and the blood canals that connected them; emotions, anger, fear and frustration, filtered through an unholy and alien mind.

Alaric fought to understand. There was a key to the Hammer of Daemons and the half-blind skull, but it was wrapped in the mind of a daemon, where even a Grey Knight's mind might never survive.

He fought on. The prayer echoed endlessly as he fell through the void of his mind.

Then slowly, gingerly, clinging to the prayer like a rope, he reached up towards the surface.

ALARIC COUGHED UP a throatful of blood, and spat it out, gasping down a breath. He almost gagged on it. The stench of rotting bodies was so familiar to him that for a moment he wondered what horrible thing he was.

He was Justicar Alaric. He was a Grey Knight. He knew it to be true, but they felt like the thoughts of a stranger, intruding on his mind.

Then there was pain, screaming from his hands and shoulders. It hit him in waves, each stronger than the last, leaving him nauseous and dizzy. He had never felt so physically weak, even during those punishing battles, which surfaced, muted, in his memory.

He took in a couple more heavy breaths. His ribs ached from the force of his lungs sucking the oxygen into him. His head cleared a little, and he remembered that he still had two working lungs.

He risked opening his eyes. The yellow sun burned in a white sky. The scorched desert was strewn with titanic bones, so enormous they must have belonged to truly immense creatures in life. They had succumbed to the desert, their life leached out of them until they fell. Perhaps the bones had been there for thousands of years, protected from decay by the parched desert. He saw a skull rearing up from the sands, and a ribcage, across which had been stretched expanses of canvas to create shade from the sun. Hovels gathered around solar stills and covered wagons. Even here, life existed on Drakaasi. There was not one part of the planet that was not home to some corrupted thing or other.

Alaric tried to turn his head. He must have been hanging there for some time because his muscles had seized up. He tried to look downwards instead.

A ribbon of blood wound its way from beneath him, off between the mountainous dunes of the desert. It was a river of blood down which the *Hecatomb* was sailing, and Alaric was chained to the ship's prow by his wrists and ankles. He had to force himself to breathe when he realised.

He was alive. Raezazel had been real. Now, the suffering would really begin, for he had avoided punishment by possession, and Venalitor would make him pay.

Tiny insects flitted around him. Alaric shook his head to get them off his face. The insects were issuing from the eye socket of a sun-blackened corpse hanging beside him, for they had formed a colony inside the corpse's skull. Executed corpses hung all around Alaric, each in a different state of decay. Many were skeletons picked clean by insects and birds of prey, others were fresh enough to still be in a bloated, discoloured state, blown up by the gases of decay like fleshy balloons.

One of them, well-worn by parasites and the desert sun, was just the upper half of a human body. It was huge and barrel-chested, the ribs fused into a breastplate. The head, when it had still had a face, must have been strong-jawed and forbidding.

It was all that remained of Brother Haulvarn.

The desert turned dark, and Alaric was lost again.

THE NEXT TIME it was the blood that woke him up.

He had no sense of time. It could have been decades since he had looked at Haulvarn's decomposed face, or it could have been an hour. It need only have been enough time for him to become covered in blood.

It was all over him, clotting in the folds of his body, heavy and sticky. He shook it out of his eyes, and tried to understand where he was.

Everything was a whirl. His ears were full of white noise, like the roar of a fire, applause from hundreds of thousands of spectators cramming the seating that towered around him. He was in an arena. He didn't know which one. Arches of granite towered overhead as if the place was built into the skeleton of a vast domed cathedral.

He was standing on a heap of bodies. His arms were thrust up towards the sky in victory. His body ached as if he had been fighting for hours. His hearts were pumping adrenaline through him.

The bodies were beastmen and mutants, mixed in with arena slaves. Alaric looked down at them, seeking some understanding of what he had done. They had been killed with bare hands: skulls cracked, limbs snapped, and necks broken. Among them, Alaric saw men in the ruined uniforms of

Imperial Guard: the men of the Hathran Armoured Cavalry.

Other gladiators were fighting in the arena, finishing off the flood of lowly arena slaves and captive mutants that they had been sent out to fight. Alaric didn't recognise them, but they looked well-armed and trained, chosen slaves from the stables of Drakaasi's lords. One was a mutant with two heads, one tearing flesh from the bones of a slave while the other whooped in victory at the crowd. Another was a giant armoured warrior, pulling its helmet off so that it could shower its face in blood. Alaric's stomach lurched again when he realised that the warrior was a woman.

The female warrior walked over to him and clapped him on the back. Alaric looked up at her. She had a strong, meaty face and a patch over one eye. Her armour was old and scored.

'You shed blood well,' she said with approval.

Alaric tasted blood in his mouth. He prayed that is was his own.

'Is there any here,' yelled the woman to the stands, 'who would challenge the Betrayed?

The crowd cheered on. Alaric had been the star of the arena that day. They would not soon forget him.

Alaric had seen enough. He could do no good. He was better off oblivious. He let himself shatter again, and the darkness bled through the cracks to consume him.

* * *

THE PLANET SCARRED with the eight-pointed star fell from the void towards Drakaasi, a losing battle with gravity. This was what Raezazel had seen. He had let the image slip from his mind as it tried to possess Alaric. It had tried to hide it, and that fact made it important.

More: deep blue and gold; a shrine, dozens of shrines, built to imaginary saints; a religion built on lies, its followers oblivious.

Sacrifices: betrayed men and women, pilgrims and fanatics, lured to their doom.

Raezazel had come to Drakaasi. It was no accident that brought him there. The truth of his arrival had been kept from Alaric, but it was still there in the sea of profane knowledge that had flooded into Alaric's mind.

Alaric held on. It would be so easy to give in and lose his mind completely. It would be such a relief. He would never have to confront the things he was doing in his madness, or be confronted with the possibility that his duty would never be fulfilled. It was the simplest thing in the galaxy to let himself slip away and end it.

But he was the Hammer. He fought to keep hold of the prayer's meaning. Without him and men like him, there was no galaxy, there was no light burning at the heart of the Imperium to ward off the darkness. There was only madness and death.

HE WAS AWARE of a great space around him, echoing with the sound of a chisel against stone.

Alaric was standing in a cavernous hall. It looked like it had once been a great meeting place. Its ceiling was of stained glass, missing so many panes that the design was impossible to make out. The place was half-ruined, the sun falling in shafts through holes in the once-ornate walls. A grand staircase led to nowhere, and weeds were breaking through the floor.

Chunks of cut stone and half-finished statues stood everywhere.

In front of Alaric, a scrawny man worked at a slab of marble with a chisel and a hammer. A figure was rising from the stone, broad-shouldered and fearsome.

The figure was of Alaric.

'What armour does my lord desire?' asked the sculptor.

'No armour,' said Venalitor's voice from behind Alaric, 'but capture the scars.'

'I like scars,' snickered the sculptor. 'So many want to be perfect, but what perfection is there in a flawless form? It is the imperfection that makes all beautiful things. Ugliness, that is the truth. The subject is so ugly. Ah, there is the challenge!'

Alaric tried to turn, but his hands were shackled through a ring driven into the floor.

'And the power!' said the sculptor. 'Yes, no armour, nothing to cage him.'

The statue's face was Alaric's, but he did not recognise the expression: arrogance, certainty, cruelty. The sculptor was a genius, but the person he had captured in marble was not one that Alaric knew.

The statue was not of a Grey Knight, it was of Alaric the Betrayed.

Venalitor stepped out from behind Alaric. He was accompanied by his scaephylyd slavers, and they formed a cordon around Alaric. 'You will be remembered,' he said to Alaric. 'No matter what, there will be a place for Alaric in the annals of Drakaasi. Do you even know how many you have killed?'

'Not enough,' said Alaric. He tested his bonds. They held tight. They were unnatural, as fast as the collar around his neck. The scaephylyds recoiled, ready with shock prods.

'Not enough!' said the sculptor, enraptured. 'Oh, that is wonderful. Such violence! I have never seen so much contained in one human form. This will be a masterpiece, my lord.'

Venalitor glanced at the sculptor with disdain. 'I would not accept anything less.'

'He shall be terrifying, my lord. Men's minds will break beneath the stone gaze of the Betrayed!' The sculptor went back to the stone of Alaric's face, bringing out the large expressive eyes, and endowing them with such disdain that Alaric felt a chill as he looked at them.

This was who he was. This is what Drakaasi saw: Alaric the Betrayed, a monster to take its place among the greatest champions of Khorne.

He fought the urge to vomit. The image of himself filled him with disgust. He had sacrificed so much on Drakaasi that he had lost himself.

He could not look on it any more. He felt himself thrashing like an animal against his chains as his mind sank down again, the cold ocean of oblivion seeping up to fill him. He was drowning in it, and the world slithered away into darkness.

THERE WERE OTHER times when the seas parted and Alaric could see through his own eyes.

He fought many times. He remembered men, Gearth's killers, carrying him upon their shoulders as he celebrated some great victory. He was on the *Hecatomb* with them, too, screaming wordless chants, handprints of blood covering his body.

He was chained to a wall, and people were arguing. He was dimly aware that the argument was about him, about rights and honours, about who the blood he had shed belonged to. One of the voices belonged to Venalitor.

He saw cities he did not recognise, glimpses of Drakaasi's monstrous architecture: a pyramid of skulls, heaps of severed limbs, thousands of bodies writhing in a cauldron of gore. He saw altars to Khorne, men screaming as they were dismembered, Lords of Drakaasi. He saw a towering heap of charnel robes, and a two-headed Traitor Marine, a mass of burning red flesh, looking on Alaric the Betrayed with jealous eyes.

He saw champions slain, and victims hurled to the crowds.

Sometimes he tasted blood and flesh in his mouth, and there was just enough of his mind left to pray that it was his own.

He saw a thousand places, a million victims, and horrors beyond his imagining, but mostly there was only darkness and cold.

SEVENTEEN

VENALITOR WATCHED THE skyship land. The desert was rocky and cold, as bleak a place as existed on Drakaasi, and Venalitor hadn't even been certain that Ebondrake would agree to meet him there. It did not do for the Lord of Drakaasi to answer the summons of an underling. Far away from Drakaasi's cities and without even a blood river crossing it, the desert was one of Drakaasi's least sacred places and it was a wonder that Ebondrake would grace it at all.

Lord Ebondrake emerged from the hold of the skyship. The Ophidian Guard who surrounded him were rendered all but invisible beside his majesty. The skyship was one of the small fleet that remained on Drakaasi, relics of an earlier age, and

Ebondrake owned them all. It looked like a galleon loosed from the ocean, sails spreading out horizontally like the wings of a dragonfly.

'You do me a great honour,' said Venalitor, 'to join me here.'

'I trust you have something to show me,' said Ebondrake, a note of danger in his voice. Venalitor had come to the desert meeting alone. He looked completely out of place in that barren landscape in his red and brass armour.

'Of course, my lord,' he said.

'Nothing can take up my time save for the games and the crusade. If this is some irrelevant flattery, Venalitor, the limits of my patience shall be revealed.'

'The crusade is foremost in my mind, too,' said Venalitor. 'This world is too small to contain us all. If we do not grow beyond its boundaries we will wither away, all the while letting potential sacrifices grow old and die away from the Blood God's sight.'

'Well?' asked Ebondrake.

'Observe, my lord, and it will become clear.'

A storm was building up on the horizon. Dark clouds piled on top of one another, heavy and purple with blood. A colder wind whispered across the desert, kicking up plumes of dust from the broken land.

Venalitor drew his two-handed sword. The sky darkened, and the blade shone like a streak of caged lightning. He held the sword high.

Tiny dark shapes emerged from the closest tear in the ground, like ants fleeing a nest. More and more of them emerged. Darkness was staining the land, more scuttling forms in the distance. They were clambering out of every cave and fissure.

The desert was home to something after all: Scaephylyds, thousands of scaephylyds, more than had ever been seen in one place on Drakaasi before. They were still emerging from their underground caves, covering the desert in their beetle-like bodies. They glinted in the lightning flashing in the gathering clouds.

They began to organise themselves into ranks and files. Standards were raised, each one bearing an ancient totem of Drakaasi's oldest tribes: a predatory bird, long extinct, that was once the scourge of the desert skies; a black tree, with heads and hands impaled on its branches; a brass claw, reaching down from a red sky; a rune shaped like a blinded eye; an axe, and a scaephylyd skull wreathed in black fire.

Ranked up, the scaephylyds formed an army bigger than any that fought in Gorgath. In terms of numbers alone it was the greatest force Drakaasi had seen for centuries. There were a million scaephylyds at least, and they were still clambering to the surface.

'So,' said Ebondrake, 'this is what you bring to my crusade.' He peered across the desert, sizing up the force arrayed before him.

'All devoted to me,' said Venalitor, 'sworn to me in their entirety. These native tribes of Drakaasi have waited long to play their part in Khorne's great slaughter.'

'I see,' said Ebondrake. 'It is fascinating to me, duke, that you sought out the lowest of this planet's low, baser even than the filth of Ghaal, and built from them the army that you believe can put you at my side: from the deepest pits of this planet to the heart of its power.' Ebondrake turned to Venalitor and looked at him with narrowed eyes. 'The Liar God would be proud of such a champion.'

Venalitor smiled. 'He would not appreciate me, my lord. I manipulate others to get what I want, but I will not be lied to. We would not get along.'

Ebondrake smiled. 'So, how many of these creatures will be spent in your feud with Arguthrax?'

The question was supposed to catch Venalitor off-guard, but Venalitor had expected it. No amount of subterfuge and misdirection could keep the silent war from Ebondrake's eyes. The old lizard probably had thousands of spies in every corner of Drakaasi. 'History, my lord,' said Venalitor. 'It is done with. We are in a stalemate. Soon we will come to an undeclared truce. I have no wish to waste more of my troops, and Arguthrax will not risk angering the warp by sacrificing its daemons trying to kill me. I would not admit this to anyone else, my lord, but the feud is done with.'

'You expect me to believe that? When one such as you locks horns with one such as Arguthrax, it does not end until one is destroyed. That is, unless a greater power ends it first.'

'That greater power being you?'

'Of course, and I will end it, duke. If you and Arguthrax continue to waste this planet's armies on killing each other then I will finish the job for you. I will kill you both. You are not too proud to be flayed into a banner, Venalitor, and Arguthrax is not too great to avoid a banishment to the coldest wastes of the warp at my behest.'

'None of this surprises me, my lord,' said Venalitor smoothly. 'That is why I have let this war boil down to a few skirmishes between bands of minor cultists who will not be missed. I believe Arguthrax is letting the same thing happen. Neither of us will back down before the other lords, but neither is foolish enough to defy you.'

'Flattery again,' sneered Ebondrake.

'It is also the truth.'

One of the scaephylyds was approaching. It was a truly huge and ancient example of the species, the size of a tank, its carapace swollen and gnarled. It was covered in colonies and hives, like barnacles. As it aged, it had grown more and more eyes, and its head was just a set of chipped mandibles below a nest of dozens of eye sockets. Each eye moved independently, some settling on Venalitor, and some on Ebondrake. Its like had not been seen on the surface of Drakaasi in the current age. It carried a traditional scaephylyd weapon, a pair of hinged blades like an ornate pair of shears, operated by the two forelimbs on one side, to denote its rank.

'General,' said Venalitor, 'the tribes answer my call.'

'Of course, duke,' said the general in an accent so thick it was barely comprehensible. Its mandibles forced themselves into painful configurations to pronounce human speech. 'How else could it be?'

'Explain to Lord Ebondrake,' said Venalitor.

Most of the general's eyes turned to Lord Ebondrake. The ancient creature lowered its thorax to the ground in a bow, laying its shear blade on the ground in front of Ebondrake. 'Oh great dark one,' the general began, 'Duke Venalitor is our deliverance and our glory. He brought the Blood God to us when all others had forsaken our kind. He taught us that even we, the lowest of creatures, can be beloved by Khorne if we serve. He led us in that service, promising us lives and deaths given over to the Blood God's worship.'

'I see,' said Ebondrake, 'and now?'

'Now we have proven our worth,' continued the general, 'and all of us have the chance to serve. This army has lain beneath the earth for centuries, waiting for a Champion of the Blood God to bring us to the surface. Now that has become reality. I rejoice that I have lived to see the scaephylyd nation take its place among Drakaasi's armies.'

Ebondrake regarded the general with curiosity. 'How long, duke, have you been hiding these?'

'I made use of a few of them,' replied Venalitor, 'and they came to me begging for more of them to serve. Is that not true?'

'We begged,' said the general, 'and we grovelled. Scaephylyds are not proud. We seek only our place in the universe.'

'And you are all pledged to my crusade?' said Ebondrake.

'Every scaephylyd that lives,' said the general. 'The infirm have been put to death. All those that remain are fit to fight.'

'And you?'

'No honour could befall me greater than dying for the Blood God,' said the general, raising his shear blade in a salute.

'Very well,' said Ebondrake. 'Go back to your... to your creatures. Make sure they are ready to leave. The crusade will take flight soon, and all must be prepared.'

'This is your will, my duke and my lord?'

'It is,' said Venalitor.

'Then it shall be so.' The general raised itself from the ground and returned to the scaephylyd army.

'Quite devoted,' said Ebondrake.

'They are.'

'To you.'

'To their god, my lord. They are troops to be herded beneath the enemy guns, who will not be missed, and there can always be more. At my command the tribal elders will begin the scaephylyds' breeding cycle, and thousands more will be hatched. They can fight almost as soon as they are born, if all you want are bodies to be thrown forwards.'

'You would have this be your part in the crusade, Venalitor? Lord of the vermin? Most would consider the greater honour to be among the elite warriors, those who win the battle, not the masses who die before the battle truly begins.'

'Blood is blood, my lord,' said Venalitor.

Ebondrake smiled. 'So it is, duke, so it is. I have heard much of your Grey Knight, too.'

'His holy work is only just begun,' said Venalitor with a hint of pride. 'Truly, he has become a part of this great engine of worship.'

'After all he has resisted, he has taken quite suddenly to the ways of Khorne. His fame grows, as does the speculation as to just what brought him into our fold. Did you break him, Venalitor? Or did trickery rob him of his wits?'

'I am a persuasive man, my lord.'

'There is more to it than that. A Space Marine would be remarkable enough, but a Grey Knight? Come now, do not tell me some petty torture or temptation could break such a creature.'

'He was introduced to an ally from the warp. His mind did not survive the encounter.'

'I would have heard of this from the warp. Flaying the mind of a daemon hunter would be a matter of great celebration among Khorne's daemons.'

'I called upon the services of an old friend.'

Ebondrake raised a scaly eye ridge in surprise. 'Raezazel? So that story is true?'

'Indeed. It was Raezazel who drove Alaric insane.'

'The liar spawn lives?'

'After a fashion. Life, for a daemon, can be a matter of interpretation.'

'I see. One of the Liar God's own flesh amongst us! I had not thought such a thing possible. Do you have any more secrets to reveal, duke?'

'The scaephylyds and Raezazel were the last of them, my lord. You know all there is to know.'

'I take it that Raezazel will not live on long to trouble us? I do not need the likes of him disrupting the crusade.'

'He has been a prisoner of mine since I defeated him. He is just a shadow of what he was. He will never be free, and he will never oppose the Blood God's will. He serves me now.'

'See that it is dead before the crusade launches,' said Ebondrake.

'I shall see to its execution myself.'

'Good. It will have been well overdue.' Ebondrake looked out again across the scaephylyd nation, still assembling on the desert plain. The desert was dark with their teeming bodies, and the sky above had turned a grim purple-grey in response. 'After Vel'Skan, duke, make sure that the crusade is your only concern.'

'Of course, my lord,' said Venalitor.

Ebondrake stomped back towards his sky-ship with his Ophidian Guard. Venalitor watched the great dragon go.

Perhaps Ebondrake believed him. Most of what he said had been true, after all. Or perhaps the creature would never trust him. It didn't matter either

way. Once the crusade got underway, everything
would change. Venalitor was rather looking forward
to it.

ALARIC WAS THERE, in Raezazel's place. The faces of
his congregation were looking up at him, hypno-
tised by his beauty. He had to fight to keep
Raezazel's alien personality from taking over his
own. This flesh was foul, these believers doomed.
Raezazel was revolting. Alaric's disgust propelled
him out of Raezazel's body.

He was outside Raezazel, looking on. He saw a
man of such beauty that he lit up the walls around
him. Alaric looked away. He could see the daemon
underneath.

He looked around: deep blue inlaid with gold,
sirens, panic. Something had gone wrong. Alaric
tasted Raezazel's anger at the intrusion. The place
became dim, and the image of the planet with the
eight-pointed star shone down suddenly from overhead. Raezazel raged, almost knocking out Alaric
with the force of the emotion.

Alaric knew where he was. This was how Raezazel
had come to Drakaasi.

The lie unravelled. Alaric, finally saw everything
that Raezazel had tried to hide from him.

In attempting to possess Alaric, Raezazel had let his
mind touch Alaric's. In that mind was locked the
secret of Raezazel himself, of Drakaasi and of the
Hammer of Daemons. Alaric saw it now, shining in
front of him, unrolling like a chronicle of years.

It was appalling. It was terrifying, but it was the truth.

Finally, Alaric understood.

EIGHTEEN

THIS TIME IT was pain.

Consciousness rushed back to Alaric so fast that it almost knocked him out in the volley of sensations. Raw, screaming pain coursed up his spine, strangling his brain so that sensible thoughts refused to form. There was coldness against his back, and a sense of being trapped, locked down, crushed.

The smell was of blood and sweat.

Alaric gasped and forced his eyes open. White light pounded against his retinas and he thrashed. Something clattered to the ground, a tinny sound just above the white noise of the pain.

Alaric kept himself from going under again. It was an act of will-power, and he didn't have much of that left.

The memories of the daemon still churned in his mind. He tried to strangle them, choke them down, clean out his mind with faith. His chest heaved, and he nearly blacked out.

Then, he could breathe again.

He knew the truth. He wanted to tell someone, but first, he had to know that his mind was intact.

His eyes adjusted rapidly. The chamber was dimly lit, but it had been almost unbearably bright, so he must have been in darkness for a long time. It was a small, hot, filthy room, in the familiar, life-stained ironwork of the *Hecatomb*. He guessed that he was somewhere below the cell block deck.

Kelhedros stood in front of him, stripped of his green armour to the waist. There was blood on the eldar's pale chest. The alien was not wounded, so Alaric surmised the blood must be his, the same blood that coated the sliver of sharpened metal that Kelhedros was holding.

Alaric looked down at his arm, from which the waves of pain were emanating. His consciousness had kicked off the endorphins in his brain, which were dulling the agony, a typical physiological response for a Space Marine, but the pain was still tremendous. The skin of his forearm had been slit and pulled open from the wrist to the elbow, and several pins were sticking from the exposed muscle, piercing nerve centres with such precision that there was no room for any more pain.

Alaric tried to speak. He gasped dumbly. His nervous system wouldn't respond properly. An unenhanced body would have died of shock, he thought vaguely. One again, he was alive because he was a Space Marine.

Kelhedros plucked a couple of the pins from Alaric's arm. Alaric was able to think again, and he exhaled raggedly, chest heaving. He realised that he was chained to the wall of the room with his arm strapped down more firmly than the rest of him, so that Kelhedros could work without Alaric's thrashing disturbing his precision.

'There you are,' said Kelhedros.

'What… why am I here?'

'You were delirious. You have been for some time. I was attempting to bring you back to a level of consciousness where you could be dealt with. Have I succeeded?'

'Yes,' said Alaric, hoping it was true. 'Where am I?'

'The *Hecatomb*.'

'I know. Where on Drakaasi?'

'A week or so out of the *Scourge*,' said Kelhedros.

Alaric looked down at his arm again. For all the work that had been done on it, there was very little blood. 'Did they teach you this in the Scorpion Temple?' he asked.

Kelhedros regarded Alaric with curiosity in his liquid alien eyes. 'We walk many paths,' he said simply.

'Are you going to release me?'

'When the wound is closed,' said Kelhedros. 'Premature activity could render the damage permanent.'

'And you wouldn't want that.'

Again, the strange look; Kelhedros had evidently not had enough experience of human mannerisms to recognise sarcasm. 'I would not. It does us no good for you to be incapacitated.'

'Why did you wake me up?'

'Soon we will be at Vel'Skan. Many believe that our survival at the games depends on you being able to lead us. There was some debate, I believe. Gearth wanted you left as you are. Many of his men have come to idolise you, Alaric. They have followed you on the first steps.'

'Steps to where?'

'Oblivion, Grey Knight. They see you as an example of how a man may lose his mind, and with it all the impediments to becoming a true killer. I believe they speak of this with the same fervour with which Erkhar speaks of his Promised Land. Gearth did not get his way this time, and so I offered to bring you back to your senses.' Kelhedros removed the remaining pins from Alaric's arm. 'I understand you heal quickly.'

'That's right.'

'Then the stitches need not be small.' Kelhedros produced a needle, threaded with cord, and began to sew Alaric's arm closed. Alaric was almost glad of the pain. It was something real, something he could experience honestly without wondering if it was another stage in his becoming something terrible.

'What have I done?' he asked. 'While I was... when I was not myself?'

'You have killed many,' said Kelhedros, 'including Lucetia the Envenomed, the Void Hound of Tremulon, and Deinas, son of Kianon. Some of them were quite the spectacle, and then there were many lesser slaves, of course.'

'That wasn't me,' said Alaric. 'I wasn't there.' He winced as Kelhedros drew his stitches closed.

'That is good to know. You were unlikely to seek escape in such a state.'

'That's why you agreed to being me back.'

'Of course. I wish to escape this world, Grey Knight. You are the most likely among the prisoners to seek freedom, and certainly the most able to achieve it. I dare say that Vel'Skan will be our last chance.'

Kelhedros finished sewing up Alaric's arm. Considering how the eldar must have had to improvise his medical implements, it was a good job. Alaric wondered just what paths the alien had walked, before one of them had led to Drakaasi.

'How long until Vel'Skan?' asked Alaric.

'Some days,' said Kelhedros. 'The games will be great. Many of the best gladiators will compete for the title of Drakaasi's champion.'

'I see.'

'You will be one of them.'

Alaric smiled. 'Of course I will. The crowd loves me.'

'Oh, they do, Justicar. To them I am just Kelhedros the Outsider. Or the Green Phantom, sometimes, but that did not really catch on. You, though, are Alaric the Betrayed, the Crimson Justicar, the Corpse-God's Bloodied Hand. When you are gone there will be statues of you. They will tell stories of how the Emperor sent his best to defeat the warp, and how one of those best became a legend in the arenas. You will inspire champions of the future. Scum of Ghaal will kill their way into the ranks of the elite gladiators because once a Grey Knight did the same thing. You will never be forgotten here, Justicar.'

'You sound like an enthusiast of mine, alien,' said Alaric bleakly.

'Fame is one of the routes to survival on Drakaasi,' replied Kelhedros, unfastening Alaric's restraints. 'It is not the one I would choose to follow, for becoming something I am not is inimical to the path I walk. That is not to say, however, that it is an inefficient or futile way to stay alive. Truly, you are the only slave who has a meaningful life expectancy. You may even one day be more than a slave. That freedom would be earned at the expense of your personality, but it would be freedom of a sort.'

'I would rather die than become a champion of the warp,' said Alaric.

'So I understand, but perhaps you will not have that choice.'

'We will know for sure after Vel'Skan.' Alaric's restraints were free, and he struggled to keep from slumping to his knees. Every muscle was sore. He must have been tied there at Kelhedros's mercy for a long time. He looked down at himself. He was stripped to the waist, and there were countless new scars on his chest and arms. He had a brand, too, a deep angry welt in the shape of Khorne's stylised skull burned into his pectoral.

'When did I get this?' he asked.

'After the sacrifices,' replied Kelhedros matter-of-factly. 'You were rewarded.'

The hateful symbol seemed to stare out at Alaric. 'So I am marked,' he said to himself.

'You took it as a great honour. Gearth and his men now aspire to receive the same mark.'

Alaric touched the brand. It was still healing, and it still hurt. He felt unclean to have the symbol on him. When he got back to Titan, he would have it cut out of his skin.

Titan had never felt so far away.

'The winds are low,' said Kelhedros, who was placing his improvised scalpels and nerve pins neatly into a roll of cloth. It looked like he took great care of his implements of torture. Alaric was impressed that Kelhedros had hidden them from the scaephylyds for so long. The alien had far more freedom than any other slave on the *Hecatomb*, able to operate in secret and go where he pleased. It was the dangers of Drakaasi, not the *Hecatomb's* structure, that kept Kelhedros a prisoner. 'The slavemasters will order us to the oar deck soon. Were you not there, suspicion would be raised.'

Alaric moved his arms, testing his shoulders and back. They hurt. It felt like he had been sparring for hours, as he once had against his friend Tancred. It wasn't just the restraints, he had been fighting constantly for days with few breaks. He must have won great glory for Khorne. He must have taken dozens of skulls for the Skull Throne.

'Then I must be ready to work,' he said. 'It would not do for Alaric the Betrayed to be late.'

VEL'SKAN!

Did some ancient god demand that glory be, and did Vel'Skan spring up in response? Did some titan desire an altar to bloodshed, and did he build Vel'Skan in the image of his madness? Did some battle between the gods of the warp take place there, and scatter their weapons upon Drakaasi, a steel rain that left the mighty heap of war gear to be inhabited?

Vel'Skan's form drives men mad to look at it. Swords and shields, helmets and spear shafts, every thing that one man might use to maim another in titanic proportions heaped up upon the blood shore. Here is a temple in the palm of a gauntlet! There is a dock forged from a broadsword blade. There spins a stirrup, hung with the dead of a hundred executions. Everywhere is Vel'Skan, maddening in its size. And this question burns like a hollow pain in the soul: what manner of slaughter could create these immense instruments of death?

What majesty is in this place, the capital of all Drakaasi, seat of its greatest lords? What glory to the Blood God, what oath to death, what image of slaughter and the hells that follow, is encompassed by the war forged city Vel'Skan?

– 'Mind Journeys of a Heretic Saint,' *by Inquisitor*
Helmandar Oswain
(Suppressed by order of the Ordo Hereticus)

Alaric saw Vel'Skan for the first time from the *Hecatomb's* oar deck. The ship was making a stately approach to the capital, saluted by the ranks of warriors who stood guard on the banks of the blood river.

The slaves around him had their heads bowed, concentrated on keeping the rhythm beaten out by the scaephylyd slave master. Alaric, however, wanted to see what was waiting for them.

'Justicar,' said a voice behind him. Alaric risked a glance around, and saw that Haggard was sitting behind him. The old sawbones had suffered greatly recently. His eyes were hollow and his skin was an unhealthy pale. He had fought, too, for he sported several fresh scars and wounds that he must have dressed himself. Venalitor was sparing none of his slaves in the run-up to the Vel'Skan games. 'It is good to have you back.'

'Thank you, Haggard.'

'You… are back, aren't you?'

Alaric smiled. 'I was not myself for a while. Venalitor tried to have one of his pet daemons take control of me. I did not cooperate, but resisting cost me my mind for a while.'

'You did some terrible things,' said Haggard.

'I know, but then that was true before I ever came to Drakaasi.'

'They are talking about you as a challenger for the title.'

'Who is?'

'Gearth's men. They are… not really with us any more. Venalitor has promised them something if they fight well, and the scaephylyds, too. We… Erkhar and I, and some of others… we talked about killing you. The scaephylyds found out, and they were pretty descriptive about what would happen to us if Venalitor's best prospect got hurt.'

'Then I am grateful that reason prevailed.'

Haggard smiled weakly. 'I suppose I already betrayed you once. Twice would just be rude.'

'No, Haggard. You did what you had to do to survive. I cannot begrudge anyone that, not after what I have done on this planet. At least it will end here.'

Alaric glanced again at the city passing by. He saw the palace of Lord Ebondrake, built into a vast human skull with a corroded dagger thrust through one eye. The skull was from the remains of one of the titanic warriors that had fought over Drakaasi, and it grinned monstrously down over the city.

'We break out here,' said Alaric.

'Why here?' asked Haggard warily. 'What is here in Vel'Skan?'

'The Hammer of Daemons,' answered Alaric.

NINETEEN

TEN THOUSAND SOLDIERS of Vel'Skan fell on their swords in the city's greatest parade ground. The bowl of the upturned shield began to fill with blood as the armoured bodies slid down their blades, grimacing as they refused to cry out in pain. Not one of them did, and in perfect disciplined silence, they died to anoint the Vel'Skan spectacle with blood.

The final body stopped spasming. The priests of Khorne wet the hems of their bronze-threaded robes as they wandered among the sacrifices. They scraped through the pooling blood with their ceremonial blades, and pored over loops of entrails. They examined the angles at which the soldiers' swords had pierced their bodies. They lifted the visors of their helmets, taking careful note of the final expressions on their mutated faces. For several hours, they pursued their divinations, until swarms of insects descended on the fresh corpses, and the blood began to congeal in fascinating patterns on the surface of the bronze shield.

Finally the priests convened at the shield's rim. They discussed the matter for a long time, sometimes arguing, and sometimes letting the more venerable of them address the others. They licked blood idly from their blades as they debated.

Finally, they came to an agreement. One of them, the most ancient, was sent to deliver their pronouncement to the palace of Lord Ebondrake, the giant skull with the dagger through its eye grinning down at them from its place atop the city.

The divinations had proven encouraging. Blood had flowed in such a way that promised more blood would soon follow, that Lord Ebondrake and all the armies of Drakaasi could not have stemmed its tide had they wanted to. Every torn sinew suggested blood and carnage on a grand scale.

Khorne had smiled upon the battle-forged city. The Vel'Skan games could begin.

THEY HAD VERY little time. In less than an hour, they guessed, they would be herded out towards the arena of Drakaasi's capital, and then it would be too late. So they had gathered in an empty cell on the *Hecatomb*, with men posted to give the warning in case the scaephylyds came to search them out and administer lashes. That so many of them were together at once was enough for them to be broken up and thrown into isolation cells.

'You,' said Corporal Dorvas.

'Yes,' said Alaric, 'me.'

The corporal was the highest-ranked survivor among the Hathran Armoured Cavalry who had been brought to Drakaasi. The Hathran Guardsmen had found themselves moved between arenas, brutalised and murdered, until they had been boiled down to just the kind of hard-bitten survivors that Lord Ebondrake needed for Vel'Skan's arena slaves. Dorvas was thin, his cheeks were hollow, and his remaining eye was sunken and dark. He still wore the remains of his Hathran fatigues, which contrasted with the makeshift knives he wore in a belt across his chest.

'You killed us,' he said, 'a lot of us, at the *Scourge*.'

'I did,' said Alaric. 'I almost fell to Khorne, but I did not fall all the way, and I was brought back.'

'Some of us finally lost the will when they realised that a Space Marine had turned to the enemy. First you abandon the line at Pale Ridge, and then you were the executioner in the arena.' Dorvas's voice was level, but there was so much hate in him that he was almost quivering with it.

'You can hate me, corporal, and refuse to have anything to do with me. Or you can put that aside for a few hours and cooperate with us. If you do the latter you will have a chance of getting off this planet.'

Dorvas sat back and looked at the other people gathered in the chamber. Erkhar, the evangelical ex-Naval captain stood on one side of Alaric. On his other side was Gearth, who even to an outsider's eyes was obviously a psychopath, and a killer of impressive pedigree. Haggard the surgeon and the alien Kelhedros completed the ragged escape committee of the *Hecatomb's* slaves. Alaric couldn't quite imagine what it must be like seeing them for the first time. The Space Marine and the eldar in one place without trying to kill each other was remarkable enough.

'What are our chances?' asked Dorvas, sounding unimpressed.

'I wouldn't have smuggled you in here,' said Kelhedros, 'if there were no point in doing so.'

'You're lucky I didn't kill you the moment you put your xenos hands on me,' said Dorvas to the alien.

'Then you understand why I had to use uncultured methods,' said Kelhedros smoothly. Alaric trusted only Kelhedros to make it off the *Hecatomb* and back on again without detection, and at Alaric's order he had brought the blindfolded Dorvas onto the lower decks.

'Then what's the plan?' asked Dorvas.

'Kill 'em all,' said Gearth with a smirk.

'That's it?' asked Dorvas.

'It's a bit more subtle than that,' said Alaric, 'but, essentially, yes. With the help of Vel'Skan's arena slaves we can force an uprising in the arena. If it happens during the contests the confusion will be great. Believe me, the crowd can be a weapon for us if we know how to use it.'

'So I hear,' said Dorvas. 'They say a Space Marine caused the riot at Gorgath. I'm guessing it was you, since there aren't too many Space Marines around. Except even if you're right, there are some old boys among the arena slaves who remember the last revolt. Every single one of the runners died. Even if we break out, we can't hold the arena, or anywhere else, against the Ophidian Guard.'

'The big guy here says he has a plan for that,' said Gearth. 'He isn't being too open with it, though.'

'The fear of any revolt being crushed is what really keeps us here,' said Erkhar, 'us and all the other slaves on Drakaasi. If we are to overcome that, Alaric, we need to know that there is at least a chance that we can survive the aftermath of any escape.'

'That's right,' said Gearth. 'Golden boy here might be willing to go out with a bang for his Emperor, but the rest of us would like a couple more years to enjoy that freedom.'

All eyes were on Alaric. It was true. His word had got him this far. It was time for him to be honest.

'Who among you,' he began, 'has heard of Raezazel the Cunning?'

RAEZAZEL WAS ANCIENT indeed when Tzeentch's web of fate snared him.

The daemon had spent thousands of years in service to Tzeentch, but of course he had not truly served the Liar God, since Tzeentch did nothing so mundane as dispense orders. He manipulated, he bled half-truths into the minds of foes and followers so that they converged at a point in space and time that Tzeentch had conceived in ages past.

Very rarely, he spoke to the souls of his servants. It was a great honour, and yet a thing to be greatly feared, for he still lied. It also meant that Tzeentch was displeased enough to commit the great mediocrity of speaking to his servants as a god.

Tzeentch required souls, new servants, perhaps, or fodder, or maybe playthings to be caged in a maddening labyrinth in the warp, so that Tzeentch could observe their torment with a smile on his thousand mouths. He required souls nonetheless, and the holier the better. The more they believed in the corpse-emperor, the false god entombed on Terra, the sweeter the terror and madness would be.

Raezazel the Cunning was tasked with finding such souls and delivering them to Tzeentch. Why they were needed did not matter to Raezazel. Quite possibly, Tzeentch needed none of them, and it was merely the act of their abduction that would set in motion some impossibly complicated sequence of events that Tzeentch wished to come to pass. It was of no consequence. Tzeentch came to Raezazel in dreams and portents, and spoke to him in a thousands voices that innocents were required, and that was all that mattered.

Raezazel had taken many forms in the past. It was inimical for one such as him to appear as any one creature for long, but for Tzeentch, he was willing to take on a face of mediocrity. He became a human. He made this human magnificently handsome, glowing with charisma. With the irony of which the Liar God was fondest, he made every word of this human seem the truth. He came to a belt of isolated worlds and proclaimed himself a prophet, flitting between these childlike worlds and beguiling their people. It was not easy. Many of them were hard-bitten missionaries of the Imperial Cult, who denounced Raezazel the prophet as a heretic, and implored the people to take up arms and burn him at the stake. A few even claimed he was a daemon from the warp come to tempt them towards some horrible fate, and it was a perverse pleasure to Raezazel that some of them should have stumbled across the truth in their anger.

Raezazel was too brilliant to fall to the torches and pitchforks that the mobs raised against him. For every Emperor-fearing citizen who wanted him dead, there were two or three more who looked upon the bleakness of their universe and sought to find something more in Raezazel's promises. His cult grew, and soon, without any further prompting from him, preachers spread his word. Nobles and governors fell under the spell, for they knew more than anyone how tiny and insignificant any one person was, and they yearned for something more in their lives.

That was when Raezazel invented the Promised Land. He would take them somewhere free of suffering and hatred. There would be no more tithe takers forcing them into poverty, no preachers turning every innocent thought into sin, no law to keep them in fear. They would be free.

They found a spacecraft and used all the cult's resources making it warp-worthy, and making it home to thousands of followers. An altar to Raezazel was built inside it, along with countless shrines to saints and holy spirits that had sprung up in the cult's minds without any suggestion from Raezazel. The spacecraft was holy ground, a mighty ark that was both the symbol and the means of the cult's salvation.

On the day when the craft was to be consecrated and launched, Raezazel appeared to them and told them how they were going to get to the Promised Land. The great warp storm of the Eye of Terror, the weeping sore in the night sky, was their destination. There, hidden among the Eye's corrupted worlds, was a rent in this cruel universe through which the faithful could reach the Promised Land. The Eye of Terror was a test, an icon of fear through which the faithful had to pass to prove that their souls were resolute enough to deserve entry into the Promised Land. There, the true Emperor would receive them, and they would live in bliss for eternity.

The ship was launched. Raezazel was on board, basking in the glory of an altar built to him, mocking the congregation with every word and blessing. The ship reached the Eye of Terror, and the wayward tides of the warp there were calmed, perhaps by chance, perhaps by the impossible will of Tzeentch. The ship surfaced from the warp to be confronted with a bright slash in space, the tear in reality beyond which Tzeentch waited to consume or torment the thousands of pilgrims singing Raezazel's praises.

The pilgrims, though, were only human, and they were fallible. Their navigation had failed to take into account one of the many worlds that drifted across the Eye of Terror on the echoes of the warp's haphazard tides. One such planet was in their path as the ship exited the warp, and the ship was caught in its gravity well, its course spiralling down towards the surface.

The pilgrims screamed. Raezazel raged in frustration. He had come so close to fulfilling Tzeentch's will. He would surely have been elevated to something higher in gratitude for delivering the pilgrims, granted a sliver of insight into the great mystery of the universe. Now some mundane technical matter had forced his plan awry. Raezazel stayed on the ship, using sorcery to force it back onto its course, but Raezazel's powers were not enough to compete with the gravity of a planet.

Through the ship's viewscreen, the pilgrims saw the immense eight-pointed star scored into the planet's surface, formed by canals and rivers filled with blood, and a few of them realised what fate their prophet had truly led them into.

The ship crashed into a city, and its structure was sound enough to keep it intact, but the minds of its inhabitants were not so sound. The madness and murder that followed were so terrible that the whole planet heard the echo of it. Raezazel slipped out of the ship and hid among the planet's terrible, blood-soaked cities, and eventually would be challenged and defeated by the young champion Venalitor.

This was the truth that Alaric had unravelled from Raezazel's fevered memories.

The name of the planet was Drakaasi.

The name of the ship was the *Hammer of Daemons*.

SOME TIME AFTER the conference between the escape committee, Alaric found Lieutenant Erkhar in the faithful's hidden shrine. Erkhar was there alone. His faithful were elsewhere, silently praying for deliverance from the cruelty of Vel'Skan's games. Erkhar was sitting with his head bowed in front of the severed statue head that served the faithful as their altar.

'I know how you feel,' said Alaric after a while. 'You try to hear the Emperor, and filter out His words from the mess of your own thoughts. He's in there somewhere, but it's the warp's own job to find Him.'

Erkhar looked around. It seemed he hadn't heard Alaric approaching.

'I suppose you have to speak with me, Justicar.'

Alaric came closer. He saw that Erkhar' face was long and pale, like a man in shock. 'You don't believe me.'

'I do not know what to believe. I have my faith, but that is something different.'

'You know that what I told the others is true, Erkhar. The book on which you based your preaching was found on this planet, was it not? I believe it is the writings of a follower of Raezazel's. When Raezazel's mind touched mine I saw everything. I saw what the Hammer of Daemons really was. It is not a magical weapon after all. It's not a metaphor for your suffering. It is a spaceship, and it is still here.'

'So everything we believe is just the product of corruption and lies,' said Erkhar, 'woven by a daemon.' He took his prayer book from inside his uniform jacket. It was tattered and torn by the years. He handed it to Alaric.

Alaric read for a while. Erkhar sat looking at him, and Alaric could not fathom what he must have been thinking with everything he believed in shaken so profoundly.

It was the ship's log, written by a captain whose mind was taken up with religious visions. The daily entries read like parables. The ship was described as a metaphor for faith, its journey as a voyage for the soul. The captain's thoughts were written down as sermons or hymns. Without knowing that there was a real ship it would have been easy to believe that the *Hammer of Daemons* was just one more metaphor among many.

'The faith is not a lie,' said Alaric. 'How many of your faithful would have survived without it? How many would have become corrupted?'

'What do you care?' snarled Erkhar. 'Never did you believe, never. We were a resource to be exploited, and now this daemon claims to have brought the Hammer here.'

'I saw into its mind,' said Alaric. 'It was as clear as day.'

'How do you know this is not just more lies?' Erkhar got to his feet. Alaric had told him that everything he believed was a fiction, and his disbelief was turning to anger. 'This could be the daemon's last curse to break us apart, to take away the only thing we have left. Or just another part of some plot to do the Liar God's bidding.'

'I doubt Raezazel's plan included failing to possess me,' said Alaric.

'As one who claims to fight the daemon, you trust them very easily. What proof do you have that the Hammer is even here?'

'None!' barked Alaric in frustration. 'Of course there is none! But it is all we have. I believe I know what the *Hammer* is and where it is, and how it can get us off this planet. How much closer have you ever been to escape? Maybe this is all a lie, maybe the *Hammer* was never here. Maybe the damn thing won't fly any more, but it is still the best chance you will ever get. How long are you going to wait for the Promised Land, Erkhar? Until the last of you are dead or mad?'

Erkhar shook his head. 'You're using us even now,' he said. 'You need a spaceship crew. My faithful and I are the closest thing to it. Otherwise you'd leave us here.'

'No,' said Alaric. 'We're all going. I need you to fly the *Hammer*, that's true, but more than that, I need to hurt Drakaasi. Think about it, lieutenant. If the planet's best slaves disappear from under the lords' noses, at the height of their greatest games, what will the consequences be? Think of the insult to their god. Think of the recriminations. If nothing else, imagine the looks on their faces when they realise we have fled. Sooner or later you will die here and your skull will be a part of Khorne's throne. If you had a chance to avoid giving them that much, is your duty not to take it?'

'Survival is not enough.'

'You will defeat Khorne, is that not enough?'

Erkhar slumped back down against the makeshift altar. He looked up at Alaric, and there were tears brimming in his eyes. 'I want to leave this place… I want that so much… and now that chance is here, but what if it is just another lie? There have been so many, Justicar, about the Imperium, about the Emperor. Now the lies of daemons and the desperation of condemned men have brought us here. Where can the truth be in that?'

'Think of it this way,' said Alaric, kneeling down so that his full height didn't tower so much over Erkhar. 'If we fail, we die. I believe that when we die, we join the Emperor at the end of time, to fight by his side against all the darkness of the universe. That is not such a bad thing. To die trying to wound the pride of the Blood God… well, that is quite a story to tell all the other ghosts.'

'Emperor forgive me, I want to leave here. I want to… I want to die. I cannot see my faithful suffer any more. I am just a man. The saint would stay here. The saint would suffer, and become a martyr, to show the galaxy what will-power and the Emperor's word can do.'

'The saint would lead his followers off Drakaasi and back to the Imperium so he can preach to the rest of the galaxy what he has learned,' said Alaric. 'You might be just a man, Erkhar, but that is all any of us are. If we survive this, you will be something more. If we don't then we die a good death, which is more than most citizens will ever get.'

'It will hurt them,' said Erkhar, 'you promise that?'

'I promise, lieutenant. Fly the *Hammer of Daemons* off this planet, and they will never forget the shame.'

'All of us will leave. Everyone you can get.'

'Everyone.'

'Then we will be with you.'

TWENTY

THE HECATOMB WAS loosed from its moorings on the broadsword docks, and hauled by teams of scaephylyds through the gorget of a massive breast-plate lying on its back. Inside was darkness, broken by the blinking red eyes of thousands of flying dae-mons roosting in the underside of the breastplate. The ship was hauled through the sump of gore lying under Vel'Skan, the detritus of endless sacri-fices on the altars of the city above. During particularly holy times, so many were sacrificed that the sump of blood rose and the most ancient parts of the city were drowned in it. It was a good omen for the blood to reach the high tide marks etched onto the city's weaponry. In anticipation of the closest fought battle for Drakaasi's title, the blood rose very high indeed.

The *Hecatomb* reached the prison complex, based in a huge and elaborate nest of brass struts and steel blades that had once been a titanic piece of torture equipment. The complex was beneath Vel'Skan's arena, and housed the city's arena slaves, among whom were the remnants of the Hathran Armoured Cavalry.

The *Hecatomb* was moored at the prison docks, to keep Venalitor's slaves from mixing with the arena slaves. Venalitor left, accompanied by an honour guard of scaephylyds in dramatic tribal armour, hand-picked from the scaephylyd nation, which Drakaasi was only just learning existed beneath its deserts.

Many of Venalitor's slaves went through final training sessions to keep them sharp, carefully selecting which weapons and armour they would take into the games. Many of them prayed. A few of them wept, convinced that their end had come at last, and that they would die under the eyes of Vel'Skan's citizens. The orks were unusually quiet, with One-ear growling to them in the crude orkish language for hours. Not all of them knew that Alaric had planned an escape. Fewer still knew the sheer insanity of what they would have to do after they got out of the arena, but all of them knew that it would suit Venalitor for them all to die, as long as it was before the eyes of the audience.

* * *

'I AM READY, Justicar,' said Haggard. 'I'll fight.'

'I know you will,' said Alaric. 'I couldn't stop you if I wanted, could I?'

'And would you want to?'

'It would help us if you were alive at the end,' replied Alaric. 'None of us can say what will happen, but I'd be willing to bet that we'll need a sawbones at the end of it.'

'None of that will matter if we don't make it at all,' replied Haggard. 'I was a soldier. I can fight. It would help if you got me a gun at some point, though. I only just scraped through bayonet drill.'

'I'll see what I can do.'

Haggard had chosen his weapons already, a sword and a shield, laid out on the slab he usually used for operating.

'I'm not going to be sewing anyone back together on this slab again,' he said. 'It's as if I've been chained to the damn thing. It's hard to imagine no one ever bleeding on it again.'

'The *Hammer of Daemons* had a medical suite,' said Alaric, recalling the images of the ship from Raezazel's memories, 'autosurgeons, synthi-flesh weavers, maybe even medical servitors.'

Haggard smiled. 'Don't tempt me, Justicar. We have to get there first.'

'And we will. I just have one thing to ask of you. The blade you pulled out of me, do you still have it?'

'The sword? Yes, I have it.'

'I need it.'

'It won't be much of a weapon for you, Justicar. It's no bigger than a dagger.'

'I don't need it for that.'

'Very well.' Haggard reached into one of the pouches in his stained apron, and took out a bundle, carefully wrapped in strips of cloth that Haggard used as bandages. He handed it to Alaric.

'I think it's poisoned,' said Haggard. 'I guess you can filter that out. I don't have that luxury, though.'

Alaric unwrapped the bundle. Inside was the shard that Haggard had pulled out of his chest. He thought about the wound it had inflicted. It still hadn't healed completely, and when it did he would still have a scar to remind him. The shard was an ugly green-black colour, and its dark metal sweated beads of venom. Haggard was right, without a Space Marine's enhanced metabolism, the poison would have killed him. Alaric had died a dozen times over on Drakaasi, but being a Space Marine meant that none of them had quite counted yet.

'What do you plan to use it for?' asked Haggard.

'I'll keep that to myself,' said Alaric, 'if it's all the same to you.'

'Then it's your business.' Haggard tested the weight of the sword he had chosen. It was a good choice for a relatively unskilled fighter, short with a broad blade, made for thrusting. It wouldn't save him if he faced someone competent one-on-one, but it was perfect for stabbing into a surprised opponent's stomach. 'When it happens, Alaric, will you look out for me?'

'I don't know,' replied Alaric simply. 'I will if I can, but it will be too chaotic in the arena to make any promises.'

'Then at least, don't leave without me.'

'Everyone's going, Haggard. If anyone thinks you're not among them then they answer to me.'

'I know, it's just… I got left behind once on Agrippina. If it happens again, that's the end. Salvation be damned, I'll just fall on this sword and get it over with.'

'It will not come to that. I can promise that, at least. Now, I need to find a weapon, too. I left my axe buried in an Ophidian Guard at Gorgath.'

'Choose well, Alaric. They'll make you fight the best. You're famous and they want a show.'

'We'll give them a show,' said Alaric, 'just not the one they came here to see.'

WITH THEIR BURNING eyes and smouldering skin, the possessed guards were the terror of the prison. They were not so much cruel as calculating, treating the prisoners as subjects to be moulded into suitable arena fodder through fear and brutalisation. Their leader, a hulking thing named Kruulskan, who had a face crushed into a grunting pig-like snout, gave the order for the slaves to be herded from their cells into the preparation chambers.

Above them, the sound of the audience echoed down. Hundreds of thousands of voices were raised in a hymn to blood and violence. Blood began to seep down the walls as it soaked through the arena sands, freshly let from the throats of the first sacrifices. The cries of the priests cut through the crowd's roar. They were reading Khorne's words from the patterns of blood on the sand, and crying the resulting praises into the stands. It was a familiar sound to Vel'Skan's arena fodder, but never had it rumbled so loudly above them, never had the blood run so thickly down the prison's brass walls and steel blades.

The preparation chambers held the prison's collection of weapons. Whips and cruel hooked blades were preferred. The Hathran Guardsmen took the swords that most resembled the cavalry blades with which their forefathers had fought, the horse tribes of their home world that had never seemed so far away. Other slaves, many of them Imperial citizens taken in raids throughout the embattled Eye of Terror, armed themselves with whatever looked like it would keep them alive the longest.

A few of them knew they would never be herded through those preparation chambers again, never suffer again under Kruulskan's whip. They were getting out, or they were dying. They would have to trust a Space Marine, and many of the Hathrans blamed the Space Marines for the disaster at Sarthis Majoris. However, Alaric was as good an ally as they could expect to find on Drakaasi. This was their only chance.

'Now you die!' bellowed Kruulskan, cracking his whip. 'Now you die, you lucky ones! Rejoice! Death is your servant! Welcome him! Welcome Khorne!

Khorne is your lord! Die for him!' Kruulskan snorted jubilantly. To see the doomed men and women huddled beneath him, arming themselves ready to entertain the great and powerful of Drakaasi, seemed to give the possessed creature great pleasure.

A few of them, those who knew what was to come, simply waited for the real spectacle to begin.

ONE OF THE scaephylyds had come to Alaric and ordered him below decks. Alaric had gone with the creature, knowing that now was not the time to bring suspicion on himself by disobeying. He was herded into an arming chamber beneath the prison decks and told to make ready.

Alaric was famous. It was fitting for someone of his notoriety to look the part. He lad lost his previous war gear at Gorgath, but he would not be replacing it with the piecemeal armour of a slave. Instead, he would be wearing the armour of the Betrayed.

'I have a great many questions,' said Alaric.

'And so little time,' replied the smith.

Just as when Alaric had encountered him at Karnikhal, the smith was working at an anvil, pinching the last few chainmail links into place with a pair of glowing red tongs. His forge had been set up in one of the many chambers hidden in the Hecatomb's hull, and the smith was silhouetted against its ruddy glow. A stand of armour stood beside him, magnificent and intricate, with hundreds of interlocking plates like the shell of a massive insect. It was obvious from its sheer size that it could only have been made for Alaric.

'Who are you?'

'I am you,' said the smith, 'if you ever give up.'

The smith turned around. Alaric instantly recognised the surgical scars and the black carapace just beneath the skin of his chest.

'You are Astartes.'

'No,' said the smith, and his teeth gleamed as he smiled. 'I have not been a Space Marine for so long that time does not mean anything to me. I am like you, captured a long time ago by a lord of this world. That lord is dead, but I still serve.' He looked down at his hands, scarred from a lifetime at the anvil. 'These hands forged the weapons that killed your comrades on Sarthis Majoris. I am your enemy. I am kept alive and sane because of the skills I still recall, so I serve Chaos as surely as Khorne's own priests. I am not Astartes.'

'What was your Chapter?'

The smith looked up at Alaric. He had room for compassion in his old scorched face, but it had not seen anything but desperation for a very long time. Its humanity had been eroded away until only the eyes were left.

'I don't remember,' he said, 'but the Hammer, is it real?'

'Yes, the message you sent me at Gorgath was correct, the Hammer is where you said it was. It is a spaceship.'

The smith's face cracked, as if it was unused to showing genuine relief. 'A spaceship! Of course! Not some magical trinket, but a spaceship! Of all the weapons that might be hidden on Drakaasi, that is the most valuable. That could do them the most harm.' The smith's eyes were alight. 'I had heard only legends, but this is so much more. Do you still have the weapon I left for you at Gorgath?'

'No. I was recaptured and it was taken from me.'

'A shame. I was proud of it.'

'I killed a few men with it.'

'Then at least its forging was not wasted.' The smith turned to the armour set up beside him. 'I am to fit you for this.'

'A lot of people will be wagering on whether I live or die, so I suppose I have to be easy to pick out from the crowd.'

'My finest work,' said the smith. 'I have waited a very long time for a warrior like you. It is not merely a matter of protecting the wearer from harm, any piece of rusting iron will do that. The true craft is in bringing the soldier out of the form, to give him a metal skin like a projection of himself, a face to show to the world. It becomes an art, Grey Knight. It is all that stands between me and oblivion, this art.'

'Venalitor ordered you to make this?' asked Alaric, examining the intricate plates of the armour and the way they slid over one another like scales on a snake.

'No,' said the smith. 'He ordered me to make you a suit of armour. This is not merely armour.'

'You can come with us.'

'No, Grey Knight, I cannot. I am compelled to serve. I do not even remember what it must be like to resist. It is only by serving that I have been able to help you, by forging weapons and armour for you as my lords decree.'

'You understand what may happen to this world once I have the *Hammer*.'

'Oh yes,' said the smith. 'I am rather looking forward to it.'

Alaric began to put on the armour. It fitted him as perfectly as one of the many enhanced organs of a Space Marine, as if the armour was a part of him that he was being reunited with.

'Then this is the last time I shall see you,' said Alaric as he buckled the armour's flexible breastplate around his chest.

'It is.'

'You have helped me a great deal.'

'I have done nothing, Grey Knight. You are the Hammer after all, not I.'

Alaric finished fastening the armour around him. It felt as light as his own skin. When he looked up from fixing the greaves around his legs, he saw Venalitor's scaephylyds waiting in the chamber's doorway to escort him back to the prisoner decks.

'Will it suffice?' gurgled one of the creatures.

'It will,' said Alaric.

'Then it is time.'

Alaric glanced back once, but the smith was already bent back over his anvil hammering at a half-finished sword.

Then the scaephylyds took Alaric away, and he was gone.

'IT'S STARTED,' SAID Alaric. Venalitor's slaves were in a staging area beneath the main stands, watched over by scaephylyds and warriors of the Ophidian Guard, presumably sent to make sure that Alaric did not start another riot.

'It has,' said Kelhedros. The eldar was in his familiar green armour, and had a couple of swords scabbarded on his back to supplement his chainsword.

'Then it is time for you to go.'

The slaves were being loaded directly off the top deck of the *Hecatomb* into the belly of the arena. The arena structure, embedded in Vel'Skan's forest of blades and spear shafts, was like a massive, gnarled sphere festooned with blades. A passageway into the arena's underside was lined with armed scaephylyds herding the prisoners along.

'I shall still be alone?'

'You have a talent for getting into places you're not supposed to be,' said Alaric. 'You're the only one who can do it.'

'Very well, said Kelhedros. 'I can offer you no promises, human.'

'I expect none, eldar. There's one other thing.'

'Make it quick.'

'Use this.' Alaric handed Kelhedros the shard of the sword that had nearly killed him.

'This?' asked Kelhedros, looking with some disdain at the dagger-sized shard. 'I think my chainsword would make sure enough work.'

'This is poisoned,' said Alaric. 'Believe me, you'll need it, and leave it in the wound to make sure it stays dead.'

Kelhedros didn't answer. He glanced around, gauging the movements of the multitude of scaephylyd eyes. With a grace that no human could match, the eldar picked his monument and vaulted over the side of the ship. None of the scaephylyds saw him go. The eldar had chosen the precise moment when their primary eyes were elsewhere. Whatever they taught the eldar on the path of the Scorpion, they told them how to go unseen. Alaric didn't hear Kelhedros hit the blood below. As far as Alaric knew, the eldar had become completely silent and invisible.

Alaric went with the flow of the slaves as they were forced through the dark passages below the arena. The sound of the crowd grew louder. They were chanting, striking up hymns to Khorne or bellowing insults at opposing factions, cheering in salute to their planet's lords and keening their bloodlust impatiently. Alaric gripped the haft of the broadsword he had chosen to fight with. He didn't know what was waiting for him on the arena floor, but he knew that if any of the slaves were to get off Drakaasi, he would have to survive it.

There was light ahead. After the darkness of the *Hecatomb* it seemed impossibly bright. Slaves ahead were stumbling, blinking, onto the arena floor.

Alaric followed them. He heard the voices rise as he emerged into the light of Vel'Skan's arena.

The crowd cheered insanely. This was what they had been waiting for. They had come to see Alaric the Betrayed, and now, at last, they could watch him die.

TWENTY-ONE

Lord Ebondrake's palace was connected directly to the arena by a magnificent gallery of marble and frozen blood. Enormous chandeliers, hung with skulls, cast their light on statues and portraits of Drakaasi's past champions. General Sarcathoth glowered down, a slab of muscle and hatred, who had once ruled half of Drakaasi, rendered in marble, inlaid with red and black. A huge portrait of Lady Malice, the master torturess who had served the planet's lords for centuries, was barely large enough to contain her merciless beauty and the gallery of torture implements hanging behind her. Kerberian the Three-Headed, the Daemon Rajah of Aelazadne, and Morken Kruul, Khorne's own herald, all of them were a reminder of what any lord of

Drakaasi had to live up to. There was a plinth ready for Lord Ebondrake's statue, and when his crusade hit the wounded Imperium he would finally have earned the right to place his own image there.

'I believe,' said Ebondrake as he padded regally along the gallery, 'in keeping you close.'

'It is an honour,' said Venalitor, walking beside him. For once there were no Ophidian Guard or scaephylyds around.

'It also makes it easier for me to recognise betrayal,' continued Ebondrake, 'and to eat you at the first sign of it.'

'Eat me? I had heard you had consumed your enemies in the past, but I did not know if the stories were true.'

'Oh yes, I have eaten many enemies. It hardly does to possess a form like this and not indulge its appetites. Spies and enemies, and a few sycophants, go straight down this royal gullet. The inconsequential, I chew before I swallow. Those who truly anger me I force down in one go. I can feel them wriggle as they dissolve, most pleasing.'

'As threats go, Lord Ebondrake, that was one of the more civilly delivered.'

'And necessary. You have potential, Venalitor. Nothing more, but a great deal of it. You are ambitious. No doubt it would suit you to see me dead in my crusade, and then divide my world up with a few other conspirators.' Ebondrake looked up at the portraits and statues marching by. 'All of these rose to power during such a period of stasis, and each of them ended his reign in the same way. It is the way of Chaos, and the way of Drakaasi. It is my duty to ensure that I stave that fate off for as long as possible. Perhaps the Charnel Lord has approached you, or Scathach, proposing an alliance during the crusade to see me fall and take my world. I would urge you not to listen, Duke Venalitor. I did not reach my position without foiling conspirators more cunning and powerful than you.'

Venalitor thought about this for a moment. 'It has crossed my mind, my lord. I covet your power, certainly, no sane follower of Khorne would not, but I go where the power is, which means I am by your side. I am more likely to take your place with your blessing than with your opposition. I am young, and there are ways I can outlive you. I am ambitious, yes, but I can be patient.'

Ebondrake smiled his most dangerous smile. 'Exactly what I wanted to hear. You could go far, Venalitor.'

Ebondrake and Venalitor continued along the gallery. At the far end it opened into the great crimson hung balcony reserved for the greatest of the planet's lords.

'I hear,' said Ebondrake, his tone suddenly hardening, 'that Arguthrax's ambassador to the warp was murdered, and his body used to defile the altar at Ghaal. I trust you would know nothing more of this?'

'I know only what you know,' replied Venalitor.

'This war of yours is over, Venalitor. That is what I decreed.'

'There is no war, my lord,' replied Venalitor smoothly. 'Arguthrax and I despise one another, but we will not waste more blood on it.'

Like much of what Venalitor had found himself saying in the run-up to the Vel'Skan games, this was a lie. Venalitor had chosen the most vicious of the scaephylyd nation's hunters, and had set them hunting the emissaries and heralds who formed Arguthrax's link to his court in the warp. Arguthrax might even be forced to retreat there or be cut off from his fellow daemons, and then Venalitor could claim victory.

'Should I discover otherwise, my duke, it may cause me to become suddenly hungry.'

'I do not think that Arguthrax will taste very pleasant, my lord.'

'Then I will save you to cleanse my palate afterwards,' replied Ebondrake. 'Enough of this! This is not the time for politics. See, the arena awaits!'

Ebondrake and Venalitor emerged onto a balcony formed from the jagged steel jaw of a formidable grimacing war mask set into the wall of the arena. The Ophidian Guard who waited there saluted as Ebondrake appeared at the fanged battlements to the ecstatic roar of the crowd. Venalitor roared in reply, and breathed a plume of black fire into the air to acknowledge them. Venalitor raised a sword in salute, too, but there was no doubt that the people of Vel'Skan adored their ruler, and that these games could not begin without him.

Vel'Skan's arena was held up from the mass of weapons and armour by dozens of gauntlets, supporting the arena's bowl like a great chalice. The bowl was formed by the hilt of an enormous rapier embedded point-down in the rock beneath the city, and the hilt's complex guard spiralled above the arena in a magnificent steel swirl.

Inside, the arena was lavish, and death met opulence everywhere. The audience cheered from galleries carved from marble and obsidian. Blades of gold and brass reached over from the edge of the arena bowl, hung with the corpses of those more recently killed, and, from time to time, chunks of rotting meat would fall from the swinging bodies to be fought over by the spectators below.

Daemons were as welcome as mortals in Vel'Skan's arena. One segment of the arena was given over to them, the galleries replaced by terraced, blood-filled pools, where the city's daemons could bathe in the gore of the opening sacrifices. Every shape of daemon was there: bloodletters, snarling fleshhounds, blood-drinking skinless things, and stranger beasts that gibbered and feuded in the gore. Arguthrax was there, too, surrounded by a guard of slaves, ceremonially possessed for the occasion, along with other daemonic lords of Drakaasi: the hulking shrouded form of the Charnel Lord, the enormous dog-like monster Harrowfoul the Magnificent, the red shadow of the Crimson Mist coalesced into a writhing mass with three glowing eyes.

The rest of the audience had come out in all their finery. Many were priests, resplendent in the vestments of Khorne's various priesthoods. Others were soldiers, proud in armour or uniforms. More were simply wealthy or powerful and wore that influence in the lavishness of their dress and their coteries of slaves.

Among them were Drakaasi's mortal lords, from Ebondrake on his perch in the palace pavilion, to Scathach down by the arena edge, a wizened old scribe sitting beside him to note down all the subtleties of strike and parry that he would witness. The Vermilion Knight stood in enormous crimson armour surrounded by silver-masked warriors, and Golgur the Packmaster threw scraps of disobedient slaves to the mutated hounds fighting around his feet. Even Tiresia the Huntress was there, soaring over the arena on the back of a sky whale.

Every lord of Drakaasi was in attendance, some of whom had barely been glimpsed for decades. All of them wished to pay fealty to Lord Ebondrake and to the Blood God, as well as bask in the bloodshed created for their pleasure.

The arena floor was covered in black sand, shining with the blood of that morning's sacrifices. In the centre, where the sword's grip had originally joined the hilt, rose a marble stepped pyramid that dominated the arena. Each level of the structure was its own duelling ground, stained with generations of blood, and scored with hundreds of errant sword strokes.

A few chunks of bone were still embedded in the marble from particularly brutal executions. At the pinnacle of the pyramid was a plinth with a massive brass chalice. The gladiator who drank the blood of his final opponent from that chalice would be crowned the champion of Drakaasi. Many of the planet's lords had heard the ecstasy of the crowds as they drank from that chalice, and had been set upon the path towards earning the mantle of Champion of Chaos. Other past champions still fought, devolved into subhuman monsters by the endless brutality.

'Many would dearly love to see your Grey Knight on that pyramid,' said Ebondrake, his low growl carrying over the increasing sound of the crowd. 'More than half of those have wagered many skulls on him to die. It would be the perfect blessing to have this spectacle sanctified by his blood.'

'He has learned much since he came to Drakaasi,' said Venalitor. 'I cannot guarantee he will die on cue. Believe me, whatever he meets up there, he will put up a hell of a fight.'

'Again,' said Ebondrake, 'just what I want to hear.'

The gates leading to the prison complex opened. The crowd roared their approval as slaves streamed out into the arena, blinking and confused. The crowd loved their fear, loved their innocence, for even the most sinful of them did not know what was about to happen to them. Greenskins among the slaves roared back at the crowd, daring them to throw the worst they had into the arena. One-ear the Brute was a particular favourite, and eagerly howled orkish insults up at the revellers, who leaned over the barrier to curse him. Another cheer met the enormous man who stepped past the threshold behind the crowd. Alaric the Betrayed, the hunter of daemons, turned into a plaything for the Blood God. Many had seen him fight recently, and rejoiced that he had lost his mind to Khorne's rage, but he was calmer now, his jaw set, waiting for bloodshed instead or charging across the floor to seek it out.

They started to chant his name. He did not acknowledge them.

Other doors were opening. Many lords had supplied their very best to these games. Even the finest gladiators had to earn their place on the first step of the pyramid, though, because the best were accompanied by many others, hungry and desperate, who knew that only by fighting their own way into contention could they get out of Vel'Skan alive.

Lord Ebondrake reared up over the battlements. He held out a claw to gain the attention of the crowd. He clenched it into a scaly fist and banged it down on the battlements in front of him.

Slave masters lashed down at the slaves beneath them, driving them away from the doors. The greatest gladiators saluted the crowd, gripped their swords and charged. The others spat a few syllables of prayer, and followed.

* * *

'JUST SURVIVE,' SAID Alaric as Venalitor's slaves gathered on the arena floor, craning their necks as they tried to take in the sheer size and spectacle of the arena.

'They'll kill us if we don't wade in,' said Gearth. 'That's all there is to it.' The prisoner had covered himself in war paint, and he looked like he had more in common with One-ear's orks than with the rest of the human prisoners.

'No they won't,' said Alaric. 'All eyes will be on me. That'll buy you some time. Concentrate on not dying. By the time they're done with me the Hathrans will be here.'

'They'd better be,' said Erkhar. The other doors were opening and the slaves of the other lords were emerging. Among the brutalised humans and mutants were a few who looked as dangerous as Alaric. 'This will not be an easy place to survive for long.'

'Trust me,' said Alaric, 'and trust the Hathrans.' He glanced at Erkhar. 'You and Gearth will be leading the slaves.'

'You won't be with us?'

'I'll be up there,' said Alaric, indicating the pyramid towering over them. 'That's what they want. The slavers will ignore you, as long as I can give them a show.'

The other slaves were running across the arena floor towards the pyramid. Some of them were making for Venalitor's slaves, eager to kill off as many of the opposition as possible in the battle's early stages.

Someone grabbed Alaric's arm just as he was about to sprint for the pyramid. Alaric looked down at Haggard's face.

'I know what you're trying to do,' said Haggard.

'Then you know why I have to do it.'

'Stay with us. Don't die for this.'

'Stick close to Erkhar if I fall,' said Alaric. 'You all know the plan. Stick with him and help lead them.'

Alaric left Haggard behind and ran for the pyramid. A few swift mutants galloped to intercept him, but the greatsword he had chosen as his weapon was surprisingly quick, and he cut one in two before driving the point through the throat of the other, ripping it free without breaking stride.

Killers were swarming all over the lower steps of the pyramid. Men and daemons were dying there already. Alaric was aware of someone running beside him. It was Gearth, his painted face grinning. He loved it. There was nowhere else he would rather be.

'I'm not missing out, golden boy!' he yelled.

Alaric didn't reply. He vaulted onto the top step of the pyramid. The marble was head-height for a normal man, but Alaric jumped onto it in one motion.

The crowd cheered. Alaric the Betrayed would die, and a lot of bets would be won. Alaric prepared to disappoint them.

KELHEDROS SLIPPED THROUGH the wall of blades into the main spur of the prison block. The prison was maddeningly complex, the torture device from which it was built a truly fiendish piece of work, with blades fine and numerous enough to tease out every nerve ending on a victim. There was something admirable about the purity of its purpose. It had been born of a love of pain, some ancient torturer of titans pouring every drop of genius into it.

Kelhedros risked a glance down the cell block. Cells were suspended from blades protruding from the high walls, a web of cranes and catwalks above making the place look like a machine for processing its occupants, which, of course, it was.

The eldar stole across the steel canyon of the cell block, writhing through the spidery shadows that hung across everything. The prison guards were easy to spot; their eyes burned in their ruined faces, for they were just hollow shells of bones and meat to house the daemons controlling them.

Kelhedros ignored them. Killing them would also use up time he didn't have. He passed right under one of them, who was keeping watch from an upper walkway. Neither the daemon, nor the human trapped somewhere inside, had any idea that Kelhedros was there. It was as if the eldar could just opt out of reality and ghost past the perception of anyone he didn't want to see him.

Beyond the cell block were the torture chambers. The smell was the worst thing about them. The air seemed to get thicker with their stink. Then there were the implements themselves, complicated machines mounted on the walls, all blades and restraints in an

echo of the prison structure. Thumbscrews and hot
pokers were far too crude for Khorne's torturers. Lords
from across Drakaasi sent captives to be strapped in
down here where the precision machines would peel
spiral strips from their skin until they broke. A person
could be almost completely dissected, and still
remain alive and conscious. Some of the arena's own
slaves, the troublemakers and would-be escapees, had
suffered just that fate.

A slab stood in the middle of the room, hung
with leather restraining straps. In front of the slab,
with his back to Kelhedros as he entered, was
Kruulskan. The human whose body he had taken
had been huge, his massive chest supporting barrel
biceps and a neck like a battering ram of muscle.
His bald head was scorched with the flames that
spat from his eyes sockets, silhouetting his bulk as
Kelhedros approached from behind. He was clean-
ing a selection of blades, pliers and other strange
implements laid out on the slab before him.

'What are you?' asked Kruulskan in his slavering
grind of a voice.

Kelhedros froze and melted further into the darkness, willing the shadows to congeal around him.

'To delve so deep and reach the heart of this place,
you must be skilled. A daemon? No, you don't
smell right. An assassin! Ha! I lived an aeon in the
warp and a century in flesh. You're not the first to
come to kill me.'

Kruulskan turned towards Kelhedros. The balls of
flame set into his piggy face roved across the room,

but they couldn't focus on Kelhedros. The darkness helped. The waves of pain and misery helped even more. The torture chamber had such a history of suffering that it was like a shroud in which Kelhedros could wrap himself.

Kruulskan picked up a military pick from his side. He stalked slowly towards the centre of the room.

'I can see things no human can see,' growled Kruulskan. 'You can't hide from me. There's a daemon in this head! Hungry and mean, and he wants blood! He ain't had it for so long, just lickings from a slave vintage. You're different. You'll taste good. Aliens always do. Yes, I can smell the void on you. You're very far from home, little bug-eyes.'

Kelhedros slid silently across the chamber, weaving his way between the shadows of the room and the flickering light of Kruulskan's eyes.

'I know,' said Kruulskan, 'you're made of shadow.'

Kelhedros slipped out of the darkness and leapt up onto the slab, behind Kruulskan. Kruulskan whirled around, pick held high ready to bring it down through Kelhedros's skull.

Kelhedros snatched up a blade from the slab, a wickedly curved thing, like a miniature sickle, and threw it at Kruulskan. The blade ripped through Kruulskan's eye and flame sprayed like blood from an artery. Kruulskan stumbled back, roaring.

Kelhedros grabbed a steel spike and threw it after the sickle, and it buried itself in the meat of Kruulskan's shoulder. Another speared the possessed creature's wrist, and sheared through the nerves controlling his hand, forcing him to drop the pick. A fourth got him in the throat.

With his free hand, Kruulskan pulled the blade from his eye. Half of what remained of his face was gone, consumed by the burst of flame, and inside the charred hollow of his skull, Kelhedros could just see the unholy features of the daemon in the fire.

Kruulskan charged, head down, to bowl Kelhedros to the floor and crush him to death. Kelhedros jumped, flipping over Kruulskan with such ease that it was as if he was taking flight. Kruulskan slammed into the slab, spilling torture implements everywhere, and Kelhedros landed behind him. Kruulskan turned around, took a deep breath and vomited flaming bile at Kelhedros. The eldar leapt again, this time flipping up onto one of the torture frames mounted on the wall. He balanced carefully between the machine's blades and spines as liquid fire washed across the floor below him.

Kruulskan grabbed the slab with his remaining good hand and ripped it from its moorings. He spun once, like a hammer thrower, and hurled the slab at Kelhedros. Kelhedros dived out of the way as the metal slab crashed into the wall, crunching through the torture device. The flame was still covering the floor, and Kelhedros angled himself upwards. His hand caught the corroded metal of the ceiling, and his many-jointed fingers wormed their way into a handhold. Kruulskan stumbled forwards under his own momentum, directly under where Kelhedros was clinging to the ceiling.

Kelhedros's free hand drew the black dagger from its scabbard. He was glad that Alaric had given it to him. Clearly, an old-fashioned length of steel wouldn't be enough to kill the possessed Kruulskan, but the venom just might.

Kelhedros dropped from the ceiling and landed on Kruulskan's back. He punched the dagger between Kruulskan's ribs. He felt the blade pierce the tough flesh of the heart. Kruulskan roared and swung around, trying to throw the alien off him. Instead, Kelhedros pivoted and dropped down in front of Kruulskan, planting a foot on the possessed monster's prodigious gut as he drove the blade into his chest.

Kruulskan's heart was pierced from both sides. Green flame drooled from his tusked mouth and spurted from the wound around the dagger blade. Kelhedros twisted it for good measure, and more fire spurted out. The eldar flipped away as Kruulskan's human body began to come apart at the seams. The dagger stayed in Kruulskan's flesh, fire fountaining around it.

'I'll find you!' hissed Kruulskan, his words almost lost in the torrent of flame. 'I'll come back from the warp, shadow-skin, and I will find you!'

Kelhedros paused for long enough to rip the heavy brass key from around Kruulskan's neck. Then he fled from the room just before the possessed gaoler's earthly body exploded.

* * *

Regimaiah the Iron-Hearted killed the twin swordswomen known together as the Blood Serenade. Aethalian Swifthammer, a cudgel held in each of his three hands, cracked open the skull of the disgraced Commander Thaall, once a member of Scathach's army, now cursed and thrown down to fight in the arenas. His curse was lifted at last as his brains spilled down over the lowest step of the pyramid.

Beside him died Sokramanthios the Scholar, the fire-breathing witch mutant, slain by an unlikely and very temporary alliance between Thurgull's champion Murkrellos the Venomous and the skeletal Skin Haunter. Xian'thal, in his intricate segmented armour, wielding a pair of blades connected by a chain, found himself surrounded by clamouring mutants trying to drag him down and butcher him. He killed six of them in a few seconds, but was himself killed when the mutant warlord Crukellen impaled him on spines of bone.

Gearth killed Furanka the Red Dog by stabbing the bestial mutant in the back with his pair of short swords. The crowd didn't know his name, but they loved the savage joy on his face.

Alaric killed a scrawny human slave, who scrabbled towards him with a dagger in his hand. Alaric kicked him off the first step hard enough to shatter the side of his skull, and he was dead before he hit the ground. Alaric hesitated, staring down at the body while the other champions eagerly killed one another. Some watching thought that Alaric the

Betrayed was gone, his spirit broken, but then Leth-los son of Khouros leapt on him, and Alaric rammed the beastman's head into the marble, until Lethlos went limp and three of its eyes popped out of their sockets.

Dozens of feuds were settled and arena careers begun and ended in the first couple of minutes. Some died with a flourish, others had bad deaths laid low by a mistake or a sucker punch. Some killed with raw power and others with a moment of skill, or just with pure luck.

The lesser slaves fought around the pyramid for the right to follow the real killers onto its first step. Venalitor's slaves were surrounded and besieged by half-naked tribal warriors with the brand of a six-fingered hand on their chests. Erkhar and One-ear led Venalitor's slaves in a bizarre alliance. They were fighting for time, and their struggle formed a curi-ous sideshow to the main event.

The crowd was only just finding its true voice, and ancient hymns roared around the arena. Already there had been enough stories and enough blood to satisfy the altars of Khorne. The bloodshed today would be good.

TWENTY-TWO

'You AGAIN,' SAID Dorvas.

The door banged open to reveal Kelhedros coalescing from the shadows, Kruulskan's key in his hand. 'Of course.'

The prison beneath the arena was a dark and foul place. Its cells were each home to two or three Hathrans, with the possessed gaolers patrolling constantly.

'You killed pig-face?'

'It is dead.'

Dorvas banged a fist into his hand. The other Hathrans in the cell behind him hissed their delight. Kruulskan was dead. They had often dreamed of hearing those words.

'Move fast,' said Dorvas.

Kelhedros headed down the cells, opening them one by one. The corpse of a possessed guard still smouldered on the walkway outside the cell where Kelhedros had killed it. Dorvas and the Hathrans rummaged through the body, grabbing whatever they could use as a weapon. More freed Hathrans gathered outside the cells. The feeling of elation was mixed with fear, and the men crouched in the darkness, knowing that they would be found out soon enough.

'You know the plan,' said Dorvas. 'Get to the arming cages, and then to the branding chamber. If you get hurt, you'll get left behind.'

The sound of shouting echoed from down the cell block. The light of blazing eyes glinted off the blades that made up the prison's structure.

'Now!' shouted Dorvas.

The prisoners rushed the oncoming guards. There were fifty of them in the throng by the time the guards reached them.

The possessed were figures of fear, the daemons inside them unfathomably cruel, but the Hathrans were driven by something more than fear now, something more, even than the hope of freedom.

They could bring the fight to their foes at last. They could seek revenge instead of cowering, hoping to be spared. The Hathran Armoured Cavalry charged again.

ALARIC WRAPPED THE chain around the throat of Vladamasca Wrathbringer and crushed the life out of her. The fleshy dreadlocks adorning her head writhed as she fought to breathe. Alaric stamped down on the back of her leg, forcing her to her knees, and she stiffened and died as the chain cut off the blood to her brain.

Alaric wondered for a split second how much had been wagered on her, and what the odds had been. By the Emperor, he hated this place.

Alaric threw the mutant's body off the pyramid. Her corpse slithered down the blood-covered marble. He caught a glimpse of Venalitor's slaves, back to back as they fought. One-ear and the orks were taking the chance to put on their own sideshow, leaping and hacking at the slaves attacking them. Gearth was somewhere lower on the pyramid, fighting his way up. Alaric didn't know if he would make it. He hoped not.

He also saw the crowd. They were chanting the names of their favourite champions. Alaric heard his own name: the Betrayed, the Fallen Knight, the Emperor's Disobedient Gundog. Others howled their dismay that Vladamasca was dead. The lords were as enthusiastic as the crowds, because those were their slaves and their champions dying. Ebondrake's balcony was wreathed in black fire, and Alaric was sure he could make out the red armour and gleaming blades of Duke Venalitor.

The sight of Venalitor filled him with hate. He had never thought he could despise a place like he despised Drakaasi in that moment. Hatred was holy to a Grey Knight and, yet he had never felt it as he did for the vermin who populated the stands. He let it roar through his veins and silently hoped that it would not turn him into one of them.

Alaric forced his way onto the penultimate step of the pyramid. A cloven-hoofed creature lay on the step holding its guts in. Alaric barely paused to break its neck. The beastman had been carrying a spear with a barbed head. It was a more practical weapon than the spiked chain that Alaric had taken off the third fighter he had killed, a red-skinned daemon which had tried to vomit caustic blood over him. Alaric picked up the spear and made it to the top step.

Half the crowd cheered to see Alaric the Betrayed make it to the square of marble at the pinnacle. Alaric was exhausted. He fought to remember how many champions of the Dark Gods he had killed, but their faces and mutations swam in his mind, and he couldn't focus.

He could have let the noise of the crowd in and taken strength from it, but that was not who he was. He was not a gladiator fighting for glory, but a servant of the Emperor fighting first for survival, and then for justice. The crowd would not keep him going.

He had a weapon in his hand and an enemy to kill. That was all a citizen of the Imperium ever needed, that and the hate.

The crowd was roaring in anticipation. The bloodletting had been to get them worked up. The real event was here. The champion would be crowned.

Alaric knew, before he ever saw it, what would come slithering up onto the pinnacle; the tiny glinting red eyes and the fork-tongued smirking mouth, the massive four-armed torso, the kill tallies, and the obscenity of its oversized snakelike body. The sound of reptilian scales on marble was a confirmation that Alaric didn't need.

'I am so glad it is you,' said Skarhaddoth, gladiator champion of Lord Ebondrake, slithering onto the pinnacle. 'I have developed a taste for your kind.'

Skarhaddoth was even bigger up close. He had new kill marks branded into his scaly chest, and one of the hands hanging around his neck must have belonged to Haulvarn. Skarhaddoth had abandoned his shields, and each of his four hands held a well-bloodied scimitar.

'I tend to stick in the throat,' said Alaric.

The two circled slowly. No doubt Alaric didn't look like much of an opponent. His steps were heavy and his breathing laboured, and his magnificent armour was ragged and battered. Skarhaddoth looked as if the blooding on the pyramid had been no more than a pre-match ritual for him. He was sheened with foul-smelling sweat, and he grinned with malice. He had been looking forward to this. Ever since he killed Haulvarn, he had been waiting to finish the job.

'Two Grey Knights,' said Alaric, letting his muscles slide into a familiar combat stance. 'Quite a tally. What will that get you? Freedom?'

'Who needs freedom?' hissed Skarhaddoth. 'What is this fiction that devours your human mind? What more is there in the universe than this? Blood and death and metal through flesh? More of everything, that is what I will be given. More blood!'

'In the crusade,' said Alaric. 'Ebondrake will give you everything you want there. If you kill me.'

'The first wave,' sneered Skarhaddoth. 'First through the breach. First onto land. Blood upon virgin earth. The warp will hear my blades, betrayed one! Khorne will smell the blood I let!'

Alaric smiled. It was a strange thing to feel, some humour, some joy, up there amid the blasphemy and death, but it was there, because Alaric was human, and being human meant dragging hope out of hell. 'There will be no crusade,' said Alaric. 'I know what Ebondrake wants. I know what you want. Neither of you will have it. I want you to know that before...'

'Before what, betrayed one?'

The pause lasted a fraction of a second, but in that time so much went through Alaric's mind that he couldn't see anything beyond Skarhaddoth. The arena, the crowd, the fighting, the menagerie of Drakaasi's lords and daemons, they all became a crimson blur. Angles of attack and best guesses about Skarhaddoth's anatomy, the weight of the spear in his hands and the blood slicking the marble beneath his feet were all coursing through his head. Then it was enough. There were no more guesses to make.

Alaric lunged. He had a long reach, long enough for the point of his spear to punch through Skarhaddoth's chest and out through his back.

Skarhaddoth gasped. For the first time, the smirk was wiped off his face. He looked down at the spear in his chest, and then up at Alaric.

'Your guard is too low,' said Alaric. Skarhaddoth slumped forwards, pushing the shaft further through him as he tried to take a ragged breath. His face was close to Alaric's, and Alaric only had to whisper. 'I noticed it when you murdered my friend. Such a thing tends to focus the mind.'

Skarhaddoth slumped to the floor, still with a look of surprise on his face.

The crowd was quiet for a moment. Alaric had done what no other man on Drakaasi could have done. He had shut them all up.

Lord Ebondrake leaned over the battlements of his pavilion high up in the huge mask mounted on the arena wall. His eyes were slits of yellow fire and his nostrils flared. His wings spread out behind him, and for a moment Alaric was sure the old lizard would swoop down to devour Alaric himself.

The relative silence was broken by the explosion that blew a crater in the arena floor. Alaric was battered back by the force of it, and bloodstained sand rained down.

Uproar filled the silence after the blast. Angry spectators clambered over barricades towards the arena floor. Ophidian Guard stormed from their posts to keep order. The lords began demanding to

know who among them had dared to defile
Khorne's spectacle.

Then, a figure emerged from the cloud of dust
and dirt, tall, lean, armed with a sword and moving
faster than a man. It was Kelhedros.

Behind him were four thousand arena slaves in
the uniforms of the Hathran Armoured Cavalry.

EVERYTHING THAT ALARIC had learned about the
Vel'Skan arena told him that the only way out was
across the arena floor.

From the arena, the slaves and the Hathrans could
make it to the seating areas, hopefully assisted by the
chaos caused by Alaric's victory and the breakout
itself. Many gates led out of the arena, but only one of
them interested Alaric, since it would point the escaping slaves towards their ultimate objective.

As a plan, it was flawed. The brother-captains and
grand masters of the Grey Knights would have
admonished him for suggesting such a mess, but it
was the only chance Alaric would ever have to take
the *Hammer of Daemons*. It was also the only chance
the slaves would have of escaping the planet, but if
Alaric was honest with himself, truly honest, he
had to accept that their escape was a secondary
objective for him.

Many of them would die. Alaric knew he was sacrificing them for his own ends, but that was the way
the galaxy worked. It was a cruel place, and that
meant that, sometimes, he had to be crueller.

* * *

'WHAT ARE YOUR orders, my lord?' asked the captain of the Ophidian Guard.

'What do you bloody think?' snarled Lord Ebondrake through coils of black fire. 'Kill them all.'

'Yes, my lord,' said the captain. He raised his sword, and as one the Ophidian Guard clanked out of the pavilion to join the other soldiers gathering among the spectators below.

Ebondrake turned to Venalitor. 'More blasphemy, and your boy is at the heart of it all, Venalitor. You will answer for this.'

'I have no doubt of that,' said Venalitor rapidly, 'but this may not be the catastrophe it seems. Here is an opportunity to–'

'Less talk!' yelled Ebondrake. 'More death! By the brass gates of hell, Venalitor, take your pretty sword and kill something down there!'

In reply, Venalitor drew the two-handed blade from his back, and vaulted over the battlements of the pavilion, dropping deftly to the seating below.

The audience was in chaos. Alaric's victory, and the manner of it, was enough to send them into a frenzy on its own. Skarhaddoth had died at the first blow. Ebondrake's champion had died, without a fight! A bad death indeed, and nothing stirred up hatred more than a poor death. Then the explosion, and the torrent of slaves suddenly swarming across the arena had forced any remaining sense out of their heads. The spectators were biting and kicking at everyone around them, blaming one another for the obscenity that had blighted this celebration of Khorne.

One of them ran at Venalitor, a bloodied cultist in a torn robe with ritual brass claws implanted in his forearms. Venalitor animated the blood around the man's feet, tripped him up, and cut through his spine with a swipe of his blade. It was barely worth a flick of the wrist to kill such a lowly creature.

'My duke,' said the slurred voice of a scaephylyd. Venalitor's slavemaster picked his way across the wounded and unconscious around the upper seats, 'the scaephylyds have been gathered and await your orders. Should we descend to the arena floor?'

Venalitor looked down at the arena. The Vel'Skan arena slaves were making a break for the northern side of the arena, scrambling up onto the seating, and killing the spectators who tried to resist. Many of the slaves of other lords had joined the breakout, and Alaric was up on the arena wall directing the fight.

'No,' said Venalitor, 'they're heading for the northern gates. Have the scaephylyds gather to the north of the arena. The Ophidian Guard will pursue them. If we can slow the slaves down, they will be crushed between the two.'

'And the Grey Knight?'

Venalitor thought for a moment. 'I was rather hoping I could kill him, but do not pass up the opportunity should it arise.'

'Where will you be, my duke?'

'Lord Ebondrake will need me,' said Venalitor, 'whether he acknowledges it or not.'

'Very well. What were his orders?'

'Kill them. Get to it.'

The slavemaster raised a mandible in salute and turned to the scaephylyds gathering on the upper seating, chittering to them in their insect tongue. They scurried off towards the northern gates, ignoring the riot that was spreading around them.

Alaric was not stupid. He should know full well that a breakout in Vel'Skan would, at most, lead to a day of freedom, and several years of torture. The Grey Knight had an objective in mind, something beyond just running for his life. Venalitor wondered what it might be. There was nothing in Vel'Skan that would benefit the slaves, nothing so defensible that the Ophidian Guard could not besiege and break it.

There was, of course, one possibility, one chance for a dramatic gesture that, while it would surely cost the life of every slave who escaped, would nevertheless appeal to a servant of the corpse-emperor as a dramatic final gesture before death. It was insane, of course, but just because Alaric wasn't stupid that didn't mean he wasn't insane. After all, Venalitor had put a great deal of effort into driving him mad.

That was where Venalitor would confront Alaric and kill him. After all, even if Ebondrake considered him at fault for Alaric's actions, Venalitor was sure that few sights would gain him more respect among Drakaasi's lords than him standing on the battlements holding a Grey Knight's severed head.

Some good would still come of this, Venalitor decided. Idly cutting his way through the few rioting idiots who got in his way, he headed north.

'I SEE,' SAID Arguthrax. 'It started here.'

The daemon's brass cauldron had been dragged through the narrow confines of the prison on chains hauled by his burliest slaves, since many of the ceilings were too low for him to be carried. Hound-like retriever daemons snarled ahead of him, snapping at one another as they tried to find a scent. There was nothing. Considering how the prison stank, that in itself was a sign.

The arena slaves had broken out. Many of them were dead, killed by the gaolers as they fought. The arming cages had been ransacked, and the branding room had been blown up, leaving a crater in the arena floor above. It had been swift and violent. Something had given them enough hope to stage the breakout, and they must have had help from outside to even get out of their cells.

In front of Arguthrax was the wrecked torture chamber. Torment cages had been torn from the walls. Blades and spikes were scattered across the floor, and everything was burned. A charred body lay in the centre of the floor, hollowed out by flame. It had been the body of a large human, but the retrievers shied away from it.

'Daemon,' said the handler, one of the few of his slaves that Arguthrax permitted to speak. The handler was a particularly cruel soul, and probably would have worked for Arguthrax whether he was a slave or not. 'Shell of a possessed.'

'Yes, they guarded this place. Someone knew how to start this. I desire to know why.'

The sounds of battle reached down from the arena. The other lords were fighting up there, some with each other, most to quell the rioting. Arguthrax would have liked to join them, but he had other priorities.

'If we can demonstrate that one of Venalitor's slaves was down here,' he said, 'then he will be suspected of treachery. I can think up a few reasons why he might have done it: to create dissent among the lords, where he might gain Ebondrake's confidence; to postpone the crusade because he is a coward; or to bring the freed slaves into his fold for use as fodder against me. It does not matter. So long as the link is there it will bring him down.' Arguthrax looked around the chamber. Aside from the heady tang of suffering, there was little of interest. 'Bring me the corpse,' he said.

The handler grabbed an intact-looking limb and hauled the body over to Arguthrax's cauldron. Arguthrax reached down and picked up the body. Chunks of burned flesh fell off it. The body was just a shell, the eyes and mouth burned into gaping holes by the force of the flame.

'Possessed,' sneered Arguthrax. 'Such a waste, a cloak of flesh to hide their beauty. This thing probably couldn't remember either of the beings it once was.' Arguthrax paused as he spotted something glinting in the caul of burned meat. He pushed his paw into the disintegrating body and pulled out a jet-black shard, glossy with corrupted blood.

It was the tip of a sword, broken off in the possessed creature's body.

'The Guard,' hissed Arguthrax. 'The Ophidian Guard did this.'

The slaves knew when Arguthrax was angry. They had seen it often enough, and they had seen their fellow slaves die as a result. Even the brutalised cauldron slaves tried to shrink away from their master.

'Ebondrake!' growled Arguthrax. 'Curses upon your scaly hide! Deceitful lizard! Scales and claws and lies! All this to save your damned crusade!' Arguthrax shuddered with anger, slopping blood over the edge of his cauldron. 'To betray us! To betray me, the Despoiler of Kolchadon, the End of Empires, the Bloody Hand of Skerentis Minor!' The blood overflowed, sloshing from the pits of the warp through the bridge formed by Arguthrax's rage. It poured in a torrent, swirling around the torture chamber. 'Take me to the surface! Take me to the lords! Ebondrake will pay!'

GEARTH, WHO HAD somehow contrived to survive, plunged both his knives into the thorax of the scaephylyd who charged at him. The insectoid creature writhed on the twin blades, and collapsed. Gearth's blades went with it, but the killer picked up the scaephylyd's spear. A blade, after all, was a blade.

'They're trying to block the way!' called Erkhar. He and his faithful were on one side of the slave army, safely away from Gearth's murderers and the greenskins who took up the other flank. Alaric was somewhere in the middle, the mass of Hathrans behind him.

Alaric realised that Erkhar was right. The slaves had made it out of the arena, and already many of their number had been lost to the enraged spectators who fought back. Now the way in front of them, along an uneven avenue of blades lined with titanic shields and segments of plate armour, was darkening with the scuttling forms of hundreds of scaephylyds.

Beyond them, up a flight of steps formed from a stack of axe heads, was the palace of Lord Ebondrake. Its half-blinded skull grinned down on the battlefield as if it was anticipating the slaughter.

That was Alaric's objective. He was going to take the palace. If it cost the life of every slave, he would take it.

Alaric turned to the Hathrans behind him. Few of them really understood what was happening, only that they had broken out of the arena, and they were at a loss to know what to do next.

'The Emperor sees us even here!' shouted Alaric. 'For His glory, sons of Hathran! For your lost brothers and sisters, for the man at your side! For the Emperor!'

'For the Emperor!' echoed Corporal Dorvas, raising the axe he had taken from a dead arena slave.

The Hathrans yelled and charged. Alaric went with them, because he was their figurehead now, and if he faltered, they would too.

The scaephylyd line was not yet fully formed, but there were plenty of the creatures to spare. Alaric had not known that Venalitor commanded so many of them, but it did not matter. He had always known that the slaves would not do this without a fight.

The two lines collided. Gearth whooped as he leapt into the air and landed directly on top of the largest scaephylyd he could see. The greenskins followed him, One-ear bowling the closest alien over and pulling its legs off. The other side of the line hit a moment later, Erkhar's faithful charging, in as disciplined a line as they could muster. They had swords, and the scaephylyd had spears, and several of them died in a few moments to the aliens' longer reach, but they had faith and the weight of the charge behind them, and the aliens were forced back.

It was bedlam in the centre. There was no room for skill. A massive press of men heaved down on the scaephylyds. Alaric was face-to-face with one of them, its mad asymmetrical eyes rolling in hatred. His spear was useless in the crush, so he let it go and rammed a fist into the scaephylyd's mandibles, feeling chitin crunch under his fingers. He pulled, and the thing's mandibles came away. It reared and screeched, spraying foul blood everywhere. Alaric drove an elbow into the top of its head, clambered onto its armoured abdomen, and ripped off a limb that stabbed at him. He grabbed a spear that another alien tried to transfix him with, stood up on the body of the creature he had knocked out and stabbed all around him at the sea of insect bodies.

The Hathrans were scrambling all over the scaephylyds. Alaric could see them dying, torn apart or trampled to the ground, but they were also winning. Scaephylyds were weighed down with men and stamped to death in the throng. Others were stabbed dozens of times, their carapaces pierced and broken, spilling blackish organs onto the ground.

Alaric led the way. All the slaves looked up to him. Without him, they were just a crowd of dead men. With him, they were a fighting force.

'Forward! Arm yourselves and leave the wounded!' Alaric tore a malformed alien blade from the claw of a dead scaephylyd, and held it up so that the Hathrans and other slaves could see him. He pointed it towards the palace. 'For your Emperor! For freedom!'

The slave army heaved forwards, and the scaephylyds were pushed back. Scaephylyds were breaking and trying to regroup away from the crush. One-ear and his greenskins, along with many of Gearth's killers, howled war cries as they ran the broken aliens down.

There was no time to pause and finish the job. Alaric led the way right through the middle of the scaephylyds, cutting them down or battering them to the ground. He was covered in their viscous blood and had to wipe it from his eyes to see.

'Leave them! Forward! All of you!'

The slave army rolled over the scaephylyds. Alaric broke into a run, the few knots of scaephylyds still in his way struggling to get away from him. Ahead of him was the short run to the palace of Lord Ebondrake. Vel'Skan rose in sinister bladed shapes on either side, fantastic buildings constructed around the core of a sword hilt or along the blade of an axe. How much of the city was dedicated to hunting down Alaric and the escaping slaves? At least most of the inhabitants would be assuming that they were headed out of the city. If the slaves reached the palace quickly enough, and everything went to plan, there was a chance that they might actually succeed.

There was hope, then, but Alaric could not let it dull his senses. Many more of them would die before they escaped Drakaasi. Alaric knew full well that he could be one of them.

'With me! Bring the fight to them! For freedom!' Alaric charged towards the palace steps, and the army charged with him.

TIRESIA THE HUNTRESS, who had taken the heads of all seven Brothers of the Nethermost Darkness in her youth, loved nothing more than a bow in her hand and a cunning quarry to hunt. The slaves escaping Vel'Skan's arena were ideal.

Her mount, one of her flying creatures akin to a spiny stingray, swooped low at her mental command, weaving between the giant sword tips and spear shafts of Vel'Skan's skyline. She spied one of the arena slaves cowering among the ragged banners of a forgotten lord, clinging to the crossbar of a giant spearhead.

Tiresia drew her bow from her back, and shot the slave through the neck with an arrow tipped with snake venom. She circled as the slave, a skinny pale thing no more than arena fodder, seemed to dance with joy at being shot. It was the toxin sending his muscles into spasm, the same toxin filling his lungs with foam. He lost his balance and fell from the spear, breaking his body against the marble battlements of a fortress mansion below.

Tiresia added another head to the trophy room in her mind.

Arguthrax the bloated daemon and his train of mutilated slaves were making their way, in the direction of the arena, across a plateau formed by a discarded shield. This surprised Tiresia. Arguthrax wasn't a hunter of her prowess, but he still enjoyed killing for sport as much as the next daemon. Throughout Vel'Skan, stray slaves were being chased down and dismembered, or handed over to Khorne's priests to serve as future sacrifices. It was not like something as venal as Arguthrax to miss out on the fun. She swooped low over him, yanking the head of her beast up so that it hung in the air over him.

'Frog-beast!' she called down. 'No hunt for you? Does the warp scorn even sporting death now?'

Arguthrax looked up at her. Like many of Drakaasi's lords, he was spectacularly ugly. Tiresia fancied that the other lords, even the daemons, were on some level jealous of her attractive near-human form. Few could become as corrupt as her and yet stay relatively unblemished by the touch of the warp.

'Faugh! Pretty child. What do you know of death? What do you know of anything? To you, this is just a game!'

'As is all death,' replied Tiresia, 'for the Blood God plays dice with our souls. Blessed are those who play by the same rules as him!'

Arguthrax spat on the ground. 'The game? What game is this?' He brandished the obsidian shard in his paw.

Tiresia guided her mount down and hopped off it to the ground, shouldering her bow. She walked closer to Arguthrax to get a look at the shard.

'The blade of an Ophidian Guard,' sneered Arguthrax, 'used to kill the chief gaoler of the arena.'

'The Ophidian Guard? This cannot be, hideous one.'

'Why not? Are you as dense as you are decorative, hunter of worms? I have prosecuted a war against the deceitful cur Venalitor for months. Surely even you are aware of this?'

'Of course,' said Tiresia. A few of her attendant hunters had seen that she had alighted, and were guiding their own mounts to the ground. They flew blunt nosed skysharks, less impressive than her flying ray, but dramatic nonetheless. 'You defied Lord Ebondrake. There were few who did not see a reckoning for both of you.'

'And this is it! Think on it, girl. Ebondrake wants us united for his crusade, and what better way to unite enemies beneath him?'

'Give them a common enemy,' said Tiresia.

'So you are worthy of your lordship after all. Of course! A common enemy! Something that even dukes and daemons can indulge in destroying together! This! The escape!'

Tiresia's hunters gathered around her. They were not accustomed to seeing their mistress surprised by anything, but she was definitely taken aback by Arguthrax's words. 'Can this be true? With as much honesty as you can muster, daemon. Is this thing possible?'

'It is not only possible, it is inevitable. What more proof do you need?' Arguthrax held out the shard again. 'Dying proof, huntress! The truest thing on this planet! Lord Ebondrake wants his crusade and he profaned the very games of its celebration to ensure that we were of one sword! This blasphemy is his doing! This abomination unto Khorne will be revisited on him! The warp will have its justice!'

'We cannot make such an accusation,' said Tiresia. 'No matter how certain we may be, we are but two lords among many.'

'Then find others!' retorted Arguthrax angrily. 'They will unite behind us! Bring them together, the Traitor Marine and the thing from the deep, the walker of dogs and all the rest of them! Together, we will make Ebondrake pay! Mark my words, I will dine on lizard before the sun sets!'

Tiresia shouted orders to her followers in clipped hunter cant. The hunt was forgotten and they took to the air to seek out their fellow lords and spread the news. Arguthrax's cauldron was borne aloft again, and the slaves continued their procession towards the fortresses and parade grounds of Vel'Skan.

Ebondrake had tried to manipulate them towards unity, but if there was one thing that could truly unite the lords of Vel'Skan, it was news of treachery.

TWENTY-THREE

THE SKULL THAT formed the pinnacle of Lord Ebondrake's palace grinned down as if anticipating the bloodshed. The slope of axe blades leading up to the entrance in its throat was still stained brownblack with the blood of recent sacrifices. Nothing in Vel'Skan, it seemed, could be considered holy or worthwhile if it was not regularly covered in blood. The dagger through the skull's eye cast a long, jagged shadow over the palace approach.

It was silent. The skull's remaining eye socket was dark. The balcony in front of it, from which Lord Ebondrake presumably took flight, was empty. The entrance, a tall narrow archway built to accommodate Ebondrake's wings, was also deserted.

'Looks undefended,' said Corporal Dorvas.

345

'Maybe,' said Alaric. 'The riots at the arena are buying us time. Ebondrake won't be back until the slaves are captured or dead.'

'You know of Ebondrake well?'

Alaric shrugged. 'I tried to kill him once.'

'You tried to kill that? Throne alive.'

'It was not part of the plan at the time.'

The slaves were up ahead, nervously approaching the palace's great brass doors.

'What do you think it was?' asked Dorvas, nodding up at the giant skull.

'A prince of daemons, perhaps,' said Alaric. 'Or something we've never heard of. I feel Drakaasi has a complicated past.'

'Ebondrake likes maintaining an image.'

'That he does, corporal, and if I may say so, that was an impressive move with the explosives at the arena. I had my doubts as to whether it would succeed.'

Dorvas opened his uniform shirt. On his chest was burned a mark in the shape of a serpent, denoting him as Ebondrake's property. 'They branded us with something caustic they kept in barrels underneath the torture block. Turns out it was flammable.'

Alaric smiled. 'I admire the improvisation.'

'Simple field craft, Justicar.' Dorvas looked up again at the palace. 'And it's here? The *Hammer of Daemons*?'

'If it's real, corporal, it is here, and it is real.'

Hathrans were working around the great brass doors, piling up barrels of the caustic gunk they had liberated from the prison's armoury.

'Move!' shouted one of them. 'Away from the doors!' The slaves broke from cover and followed Alaric away from the archway. A few moments later the brass doors glowed, blistered and burst, spraying molten metal as a large sagging hole was torn in the doors.

Gearth was the first through. Alaric wasn't surprised, but even Gearth's step faltered when he saw the inside of the palace for the first time.

It was dark and cool inside. The wind breathed through the dark red silks that billowed from the walls of the entrance gallery. Overhead, shafts of light fell between the skull's teeth, the ceiling vaulted beneath the cranium.

The wind was not coming from outside. It was sighing from the throats of Lord Ebondrake's enemies. They were fused with the walls and ceiling, or with blocks of stone in the centre of the room like sculptures in a gallery. They were still alive. Alaric saw daemons among them, the brutal shapes of bloodletters reaching from the stones. The hanging silks waved around the corpulent form of a mutated human with goat legs and a second lolling mouth in its stomach, pallid flesh veined with granite where its skin met the stone. There was a treacherous Ophidian Guard, its helmet removed to reveal a face without skin, its mouth locked open and a stone tongue hanging down in front of its chest, and a carapaced creature from the seas half-petrified as if trying to swim out of the wall that encased it. One of the victims in the centre of the room was almost the shape of a woman, with a noseless face and claws for hands, her body displayed wantonly as it was consumed by the stone. There were hundreds of bodies, each a thing of Chaos: the many foes despatched by Ebondrake as he closed his claws around Drakaasi.

Haggard jogged up to Alaric. He was breathing heavily; he wasn't a young man any more. 'Flesh of the Saint, look at this,' he said.

'They're alive,' said Alaric.

'Of course. It's no fun for him if they're dead.' Haggard spat on the ground. 'That's Gruumthalak Ironclad,' he said, indicating a creature like an armoured centaur with a scorpion's tail and huge segmented eyes like a fly, trapped in the entrance chamber's ceiling. 'I always wondered what happened to him.'

Gearth was standing by the female daemon trapped in the centre of the room. He was running the blade of a knife along the stone, testing how it felt when it got to flesh.

'Gearth!' shouted Alaric. 'Get your men up front. We need to head up.'

'C'mon then, ladies, let's move!' called Gearth, and his slaves went with him, up the grand sweeping staircase that dominated the far end of the chamber.

'Where is it?' demanded Erkhar behind Alaric. 'The *Hammer*?'

'It's here. Head up. It's in the cranium.'

'Then where...?' Erkhar paused. 'Of course. All this time.'

'There will be more Ophidian Guard close behind,' said Alaric. 'We have to move. There isn't much time.'

The eyes of Ebondrake's defeated foes followed Alaric as he led the slaves into the palace of their captor.

'What does this mean?' demanded Lord Ebondrake.

'As I said, it is still uncertain, but they are moving against you,' said Scathach.

From Lord Ebondrake's vantage point among the daemon eyries at the top of one of Vel'Skan's spears, it was easy to see the enemy assembling. Night was falling, and countless lights of torches and possessed daemons' eyes glittered in a shining host. It was gathering around a complex of barracks and parade grounds a short flight away, an excellent staging post for the thrust forwards.

'Who leads them?'

'I am not sure, my lord, though some candidates seem likely,' said Scathach. His more reasonable head was talking, since the other one was much given to battle-cries and statements of blunt intent. 'Arguthrax, certainly. I believe the Charnel Prince is with them, too.'

'That heap of rags? I gave him every corpse he ever consumed. Base traitor. Who do we know is with us?'

'Thurgull, for sure.'

'Ha! He will be of limited use unless we need some fish spoken with. Who else?'

'Golgur, I wager, and I can bring Ilgrandos Brazenspear in, too. If the treachery becomes open, we can count on many more for certain. You are their lord, after all.'

'We will see about that,' said Ebondrake. 'What of Venalitor? He should be at my side. He would not miss this chance to win my favour.'

'I have not seen him.'

'Perhaps it was him,' mused Ebondrake. 'It was his champion that killed my Skarhaddoth. Maybe that was the signal for the breakout, to create the confusion necessary for the lords to ally against me. I would not put it past the duke to have arranged all this. If he has betrayed me, I shall make a point of eating him. He is too sly an opponent to consign to the walls of my palace.'

'What are your orders, my lord?'

Ebondrake pondered this. The daemons roosting in the eyrie around him were starting to stir as night fell. They were nocturnal creatures, and soon they would be out hunting, plucking the unwary from Vel'Skan's rooftops.

'Gather an army,' said Ebondrake, 'and bring in as many lords as you can. Spread the word. Traitors have defiled the games and spat upon my crusade. For this, they will be given battle, defeated and punished. Make it fast, for the traitors cannot keep their forces in check for long.'

'Yes, my lord,' said Scathach, and headed for the sky chariot stationed beside the eyrie. It was a relic of an earlier age, a piece of grav-technology that the

Imperium, in its bloated weakness, could no longer replicate.

Scathach piloted the craft down towards the sprawl of Vel'Skan. He gunned the engines, for it would not do to be late reporting his findings back to Arguthrax.

THE HAMMER OF DAEMONS was old. It was concealed within a sheath of corrosion so deep it was a wonder there had ever been a spaceship beneath there at all. Now that Alaric knew the truth he could see the flare of its engine cowling, the blunted underside of the prow, the ridges of sensor towers and the indentations of torpedo tubes. It just needed a little imagination.

'This is it?' asked Corporal Dorvas.

'Of course,' replied Erkhar, 'can you not see it?'

Alaric had led the slaves up into the cranium of the palace's giant skull. The great dome of the skull was divided into audience halls and ritual chambers, along with many rooms that defied explanation. This chamber was one of them. Alaric guessed that it was some kind of interrogation room, what with the restraints hanging from every surface and the indentations in the floor just the right shape for a human to be strapped down. However, that did not explain the richness of the decoration: torture implements inlaid with gold, and gorgeous tapestries of battle ruined with dried blood.

The dagger that impaled the skull through the eye socket passed through this chamber, dominating the room with a massive shaft of corrupted metal, from which hung the remnants of dozens of mutant skeletons. It was not, however, a dagger.

'Lieutenant, if you will?' said Alaric.

Erkhar stepped forward and took out the captain's log of the *Hammer of Daemons*. He opened the book and began to read from it.

'Will this thing still work?' asked Haggard, standing beside Alaric, since that was probably the safest place to be.

'It's an old ship,' said Alaric. 'All the best ones are old.'

'My brothers and sisters,' Erkhar was reading, 'this is not just a journey. This creation will not deliver us to the Promised Land on its own. It is just steel and glass. The truth is harder for you to hear, but it is the Emperor's own word as brought to us by the prophet. We, as pilgrims, make our journey not to arrive, but to undergo. '

The faithful were speaking along with him, the murmuring voices like a prayer underlining Erkhar's words. It was the speech read out by the captain of the pilgrim ship before the *Hammer of Daemons* set sail for the Promised Land. The religion of Erkhar's faithful had been based on those words, not as a statement by a captain, but as a metaphor for everything they had suffered. The ship was Drakaasi, and the pilgrims were the slaves, their journey the ordeal of slavery under the planet's lords, but the truth was more mundane.

'It is not enough to trust the Emperor to fend off all the perils of the void for us. On this journey we must change, we must become one with the Emperor's truth. We must abandon the lies that bind us, cast out the vices and doubts that rule us, and throw aside the despairs of this dark millennium. Survival is not enough. The *Hammer of Daemons* must change us into something more than we are. Only then will we deserve our places in the Promised Land.'

Something rumbled within the body of the dagger. Slabs of corrosion cracked and fell from the shaft, smashing to reddish dust on the chamber floor. The faithful took a step back.

'Emperor's teeth,' whispered Haggard.

'It's real,' said Gearth.

A door opened in the body of the dagger, swinging downwards. A shaft of light bled from it. The whirr of life support systems and plasma conduits thrummed through the palace. The *Hammer of Daemons*, responding to the code woven into the captain's speech, came to life.

Every eye was on the door and the glimpse of bright pearlescence inside, except for Alaric's. A Space Marine's peripheral vision was razor sharp, and he recognised the shift in the shadows, the shape that budded off from the gloom at the back of the room to flit through an archway. It was heading towards the front of the skull. Alaric knew it well. It surprised him that it had taken this long for it to show up.

'Stand guard,' said Alaric to Gearth. 'Keep any enemy off us until Erkhar's men can get this thing started.'

'And you?'

'I need to secure this place.'

'Then I'll send–'

'Just me.'

'You know, glory boy, if you're not back by the time we take off, we're leaving without you.'

'If it comes to that, good luck up there,' said Alaric as he left the chamber. Few of the slaves watched him go. They were fascinated by the light bleeding from the *Hammer of Daemons*, or clambering up onto the entrance ramp that had folded down from the corroded body. Chunks of rust were still falling from the body of the ship and revealing the ancient surface of the hull, painted deep blue with the remnants of stencilled designs in gold.

Erkhar was still reading prayers from the book as Alaric passed through the archway.

In front of him was the room, triangular in cross-section, formed by the skull's nasal cavity. It was a room for divinations or strategic planning, judging by the orrery that stood on one side of the room and the table inscribed with astrological designs taking up the other side. Plans of the stars above Drakaasi were etched on the walls.

Alaric paused and held his breath. The hum of the engines warming up behind him reverberated through the palace, but he was searching for something else: footsteps, or breathing.

A shadow was sliding along one wall, barely perceptible as it moved across the illustration of a star system.

'Kelhedros,' said Alaric, 'you can't hide any more.'

The shape stopped, but Alaric had it now, a faint wrongness in the way the light slid off the silver web of the star chart.

'I know what you are, Kelhedros. I've known for a while, and you have served your purpose well enough, but it's over now.'

The shape of the eldar solidified from the caul of shadow.

'Alaric. I am glad I found you. I became separated on the arena floor. I knew this was your objective so…'

'You came to stow away.'

'Stow away, Justicar? Why would I need to stow–'

'Because I would have killed you before we left. The lies end now, alien, if you can even speak the truth any more.'

'Have you evidence of treachery, human? I would like to hear it before I submit to any threats.' Kelhedros's voice was thick with his customary arrogance. Alaric wondered if any eldar had ever paused to wonder if a human being had a soul, or the capacity to suffer. It was more likely not one of them had ever given a human any more thought than a human might give to a virus beneath a lens.

'Thorganel Quintus,' said Alaric. Kelhedros let his sneer fall, just a fraction. 'I was never there. It was an Imperial Guard action I read about. I never claimed to be there, either, except to you.'

Kelhedros would not have seemed to move to an unaugmented human eye, but to Alaric it was clear that his muscles were bunching up ready for action. Kelhedros's way of fighting relied on being the first in with the swiftest strike. Alaric would not give him that.

'Venalitor had heard of it too,' continued Alaric. 'He thought I had been there. The only person who had heard me tell that lie was you, Kelhedros.'

Kelhedros licked his lips. 'You cling to the truth as if it means something here, human.'

'Did you betray the last slave revolt, too? The one they were celebrating when my friend died. Were those games possible because you handed Venalitor and Ebondrake their victory?'

'One does what one must,' said Kelhedros, 'to survive.'

'For a human,' replied Alaric smoothly, 'survival is not enough.'

'What does your kind know?' hissed Kelhedros, drawing his chainblade. The weapon's teeth were clotted with blood. The eldar's cultured exterior was gone, and he looked almost feral, like something born to kill. 'Why do you think I did not tell Venalitor of the *Hammer of Daemons*? Because I believe, Justicar! I believe in escaping this damned world. Nothing on this planet desires escape as much as I do. You can never understand what can happen to a naked soul that dies in a place like this! You will never look upon the face of She Who Thirsts!'

'I understand everything, alien!' said Alaric. 'I know what you are. You never walked this Scorpion path. I have faced your kind before. You are things of darkness, with skin made of shadow, wrapped in silence. Mandrakes, the Guardsmen called you, assassins and spies. How else could you have free run of the *Hecatomb*, and leave it at will? Did you think I would believe this was some trick of the Scorpion path? You are much worse than an alien, and I will not let one such as you escape this world.'

'I will be gone from Drakaasi!' shrieked Kelhedros. His face was bestial, his eyes pure black, weeping tears as thick and dark as oil. He had given up on his disguise. His skin swam with shadows, shifting in and out of reality. 'I will return to the embrace of Commorragh! She will never take me!' Kelhedros was circling around, trying to get closer to the archway leading upwards towards the skull's remaining eye.

'You will die here,' said Alaric, 'and she will most definitely take you.'

Alaric had his spear in his hand. It felt like the thousandth weapon he had picked up since he had come to Drakaasi. He very much wished he had his Nemesis halberd, or one of the smith's marvellous weapons, but the spear would do.

Kelhedros was quick, but he wasn't quite good enough. If there was one thing Alaric could do better than any sentient creature on Drakaasi, it was perform an execution. Alaric drew back his arm to strike.

A sudden sliver of light blazed from the archway behind Kelhedros. It reached from the shadows and sliced through Kelhedros, biting down through his shoulder, and carving down through his back. A good third of his torso flopped to the floor, sliced organs tumbling out of the massive wound.

Kelhedros tried to step away from Alaric, but his body wouldn't obey, and his eyes widened as he realised that he was dead. He stumbled and fell onto his back. Blood had just caught up with the wound and was pumping from his sundered body.

'You have an inflated opinion of your own importance, alien,' said a deep voice dripping with arrogance and authority. 'The flaw of all your race. Do you think that I would ever honour our agreement? Freedom, safety, for a few words of treachery? And now you dare to seek escape from here, so that you can bring what you know of our world to the rest of your breed. You were nothing more than a pet, and you are to be put down.'

'She...' gasped Kelhedros, writhing on the floor like a landed fish. 'She... who... thirsts...' His eyes went dull, and he died as Alaric watched. Alaric thought he could hear Kelhedros screaming in the far distance, howling as his soul was devoured, but the sound was carried away by the wind blowing through the skull.

'A poor spy,' said Duke Venalitor. 'He really thought he was buying some kind of victory with his lies.'

Alaric couldn't speak. Venalitor had found them. Everything would end here.

'It seems that I have stolen your thunder,' said Venalitor, advancing into the room. The segments of his crimson armour gleamed in the dying daylight glinting over Vel'Skan's weaponscape. The sword in his hands shone as it drank the drops of Kelhedros's blood running down its blade. 'When one of my slaves is to be executed, it is I who serve as executioner.'

'What now?' breathed Alaric.

'What do you think, Grey Knight?'

'One of us kills the other.'

'I think you could be more specific,' said Venalitor with an ice-cold smile. 'I have to admit that you are one of those rare breeds of enemies who are more dangerous the closer you get.'

Venalitor was circling Alaric, and Alaric tried to weigh up Venalitor's avenues of attack: a slice low to take out Alaric's legs, a high cut to his head or throat, any one of a million thrusts or slices that would take Alaric's life with a single blow.

'It would amuse me to keep you alive and use you to further the work of Khorne,' said Venalitor dryly, 'but I have grown tired of being amused.'

Venalitor lunged. Alaric was ready. He brought up the spear to block the blow, and the blade cut clean through the haft. The blade was deflected enough to keep it from slicing through Alaric, but the spear was useless. Alaric threw the haft of the spear aside and held the tip away from his body, ready to parry or stab.

'I have learned a lot here,' said Alaric, forcing calmness into his voice. 'I am not the man you defeated on Sarthis Majoris.'

'No, Justicar, you are something less.'

Alaric could have stabbed and blocked and thrust until he died, but that was not the way to win this fight. A Grey Knight might not have seen that. Alaric was not a Grey Knight any more.

Alaric dropped the spear and charged.

TWENTY-FOUR

'I KNEW,' ROARED Lord Ebondrake, 'that it would come to this.'

His voice carried down the Antediluvian Valley. Its slopes were built from stone axe heads and rough hewn spear shafts, the most ancient and primal weapons of Vel'Skan. The valley was a rift through the heart of the city, its depth cutting through aeons of war. The enemy army was strong across the valley, formed from the private forces of several of Drakaasi's lords. Arguthrax's slaves were tethered to posts driven into the ground, and painted with runes of summoning. Tiresia had called forth whole tribes. Scathach's contingent was the largest, with rank after rank of solemn warriors, from uniformed men with guns, to armoured cavalry. These forces had been called forth quickly, their plan to march on Ebondrake, and kill him before he could respond.

Ebondrake lived on a permanent war footing. He was ready.

'Perhaps it would take a million years,' he boomed, his words punctuated by plumes of black fire, 'perhaps a few moments, but you would turn on me. This is the way it has always been. I am as old as these mountains and the stars above us, and I have seen it so many times that I remember only an endless circle of betrayal. I told myself that when my time came, I would defy it. Nothing you have done has been anything but inevitable, and every move you make is one I have foreseen.'

A great host of beetle-black bodies came scuttling from the cracks between the weapons of the Antediluvian Valley. Thousands of scaephylyds scuttled into formation behind Lord Ebondrake, carrying the banners of their tribes. The ancient general, his carapace dulled by centuries, lumbered to the fore.

'You are our master's master,' slurred the general through his mandibles.

'Then you are my servant's servant,' said Ebondrake.

The general waved a forelimb in a signal to the scaephylyds. They all drew their weapons. They were still forming up down the throat of the valley, and there must have been a hundred thousand of them.

'The will of Khorne is with us!' yelled Arguthrax in reply. 'You have created this revolt in the heart of our city, in the midst of Khorne's celebrations, all to force us to unite under your rule! This is no longer a struggle for power, black lizard! This is an excommunication! Khorne despises you, and his wrath turns upon you! We true lords of Drakaasi are the instruments of that wrath!'

'You accuse me of treachery?' Ebondrake rose up off his haunches and spat black sparks in anger. 'The blasphemy in the arena was naught but a distraction created to force my attention away from your betrayal! What fools, what infants, to think such a ruse would tear victory from me!'

Thurgull, an ancient from Drakaasi's deeps, oozed through the valley wall, all gelatinous flesh and tentacles. Others of his kind were with him, smaller and less foul, but still deadly, snapping hooked beaks set into the mass of their mollusc-like flesh. Corpses began writhing up from the ground, and the Charnel Lord, who had against the odds thrown his lot in with Ebondrake, shambled through their midst allowing them to lick the corpse liquor from his funereal robes.

Ebondrake's army was huge. It was the equal of the conspirators', even as Golgur the Packmaster's hounds bounded in to join them. Arguthrax gave the signal, and the slaves pinned to the ground began to writhe, shafts of red light bleeding from their eyes and mouths as his allies from the warp sent their foot soldiers to possess the slaves.

'Enough words!' shouted Tireseia, nocking a flaming arrow to her bow.

'On that alone we can agree,' said Ebondrake. With a mighty blast of flame, he signalled the charge.

A FLASH OF savage satisfaction burst through Alaric as his forehead crunched into Venalitor's nose.

Venalitor stumbled backwards into the table, knocking the orrery onto the floor. The delicate device shattered, scattering tiny brass planets and orbits everywhere.

Venalitor tried to bring his blade around, but Alaric was on top of him. Alaric did not remember the time when he lost his mind, but his muscles did. It was the most natural thing in the galaxy to grab Venalitor by the throat and slam him over and over again into the solid table. Venalitor snarled and tried to struggle free. The table split in two, and Venalitor fell through to the floor with Alaric trying to gouge at his eyes and claw at his throat.

Venalitor jammed his knee up into Alaric's midriff and threw the Grey Knight over his head. Alaric sprawled through the half-wrecked divination chamber through the archway, skidding through Kelhedros's blood as he went.

He was in Lord Ebondrake's trophy chamber.

Bodies and weapons were everywhere, displayed obscenely. A gutted corpse was laid out, plated in gold with rubies studding its wounds. It was a human in uniform, perhaps a Guard general or a planetary noble, laid out on a black marble slab like a sculpture. Alaric saw the soft features warped in anguish, and wondered for a moment if it had been a woman.

Claws and blades torn from the arms of aliens were racked up on the wall beside Alaric. Skulls and ribs that Alaric recognised as being from tyranid creatures formed a display in front of him. A captured siege engine, its black metal wrought into screaming faces, loomed in the middle of the room.

The chamber took up a full third of the palace's cranium, and weapons and body parts taken from defeated foes filled it to the ceiling: enormous totem poles of giant creatures' skulls; chandeliers of severed hands; statues of half-melted swords clad in skins cut from tattooed bodies; whole enemies plated in bronze, or frozen in blocks of ice kept intact by humming cryo-units; spears and swords by the hundred, displayed in fearsome walls of blades; lifetimes upon lifetimes of battles and duels, of treacheries avenged and would-be assassins uncovered: a terrible illustration of what Lord Ebondrake truly was.

Alaric pulled himself into the shadows between a pair of mummified corpses, still impaled on the spikes used to execute them.

He weighed up his situation in a split second, as only a Space Marine's mind could. Alaric wasn't unarmed any more. He could have his pick from any one of a thousand wicked-looking weapons on display in the trophy room, but Venalitor was still the best swordsman Alaric had ever faced.

He was too good.

'Face me, Space Marine!' called Venalitor as he stalked into the trophy chamber. 'Truly, your Emperor must be a weakling god if even his very finest cower as you do.'

'You add too many flourishes to your sword work,' replied Alaric. 'I noticed it when you beat me on Sarthis Majoris. Such a thing focuses the mind.' Alaric took a blade from the closest mummified corpse, a bronze scimitar, inscribed with runes, that he drew silently from the corpse's chest. 'If there's one thing I have learned here, it's that bloodshed is an ugly thing.'

'Bloodshed is an art!' snapped Venalitor, 'and you are my canvas!'

Venalitor swept over the display of mummified bodies, the skirts of his armour billowing behind him like wings. Alaric deflected the arc of his sword with his scimitar and the bronze weapon was sliced in two. Alaric spun, pulled a spike from the skull of a second body and parried again. Venalitor's sword was knocked a centimetre away from gutting Alaric, and the spike was split in two, lengthways.

Alaric lunged forwards and kneed Venalitor in the groin. Venalitor stumbled backwards, bent double, and Alaric sent an uppercut into his chest so hard that Venalitor plunged backwards through the bodies, scattering dried-out limbs and fragments of age stiffened funeral shrouds.

'Too many flourishes,' said Alaric, shaking out his hand.

Venalitor got to his feet. He snarled, and for a moment his consciousness, the true nature beneath the cultured swordsman exterior, flashed across him. A yawning maw hissed through a ring of fangs, and black eyes narrowed into reptilian slits.

There was, however, no one to see it. Venalitor braced himself for the next charge, but it did not come. He looked around, but Justicar Alaric was gone.

It was not like a Space Marine at all, but that did not matter. Alaric was ultimately like any other quarry, a puzzle to be solved, a life to be ended. Venalitor prayed a few syllables to Khorne to keep his sword keen, and began the hunt.

'NAVIGATION'S STILL UP,' said Erkhar breathlessly. 'Praise the Emperor! Praise the saints!' He swung into the command pulpit and read from the age clouded information panel in front of him. 'It's working. There's plasma in the conduits! The reactors are warming up!'

The smiles on the faces of the faithful were reason enough to have made it this far. It was like a rapture, as if the image of the Emperor was hovering on the bridge of the *Hammer of Daemons*, bestowing His blessing upon them.

The ship worked. The Promised Land was real.

'Take-off vectors are pre-loaded,' said one of the faithful from the navigations helm, surrounded by slab-like banks of memm-crystal. 'They're all up. Once the thrusters are on-line and the main engines are primed we can take off.'

'Wait,' said Erkhar. 'Raezazel's followers pro-grammed this ship to fly into a warp rift. Those must be the coordinates in the navigation helm. Use it to take off and then switch to helm control, otherwise we'll pitch straight into the warp.'

'Then... that's it? It's ready to fly?' asked Brother Hoygens. The man looked dazed, the events of the last few minutes almost too much for him to understand. It seemed like only a breath ago that the slaves had been about to die in Vel'Skan's games. Now they had a spaceship.

'It is,' said Erkhar. 'This is a miracle, an honest miracle. To those who denied that the Emperor's light could ever shine on this world, I give you the *Hammer of Daemons*!'

The *Hammer* was a vessel worthy of the Emperor's intervention. Exposure to Drakaasi's elements had covered it in a sheath of corrosion, but the ship inside was magnificent. Raezazel's followers had spared no expense. The corridors and bays shone in deep blue and gold, with a saint's portrait looking over every doorway and porthole. Shrines to the Emperor could be found everywhere, from the sim-ple niches with devotional candles and texts to the great three-faced altar in the ship's main assembly area, with the triptych wrought in gold depicting the Emperor as deliverer, protector and avenger. The bridge was a reliquary with sacred bones and vials of saintly blood hovering in miniature grav-units, bathed in shafts of light in a ring around the helms and command pulpit. Erkhar had never seen anything so beautiful, not even in the days before his enslavement. The *Pax Deinotatos* had been an ugly ship, a base thing of rusting steel and leaking conduits. The *Hammer* was a mighty flying altar to Imperial glory.

'We should... pray, then,' said Hoygens uncertainly.

'We can pray when we're off the ground,' replied Erkhar. He flicked a switch and accessed the ship's vox-caster network. 'Engines?'

'Here, lieutenant,' came the reply. It was Gearth. Erkhar flinched at the thought of Gearth having a place on their holy ship, but he would be judged like the rest of them when the Promised Land was in sight.

'Reactor status?'

'Looks like they're working. Twenty-five per cent, if that means anything.'

'It does,' said Erkhar. 'Keep me updated.'

'Yes, lieutenant.'

'Lieutenant,' said the faithful at the navigation helm. 'You need to see this.'

Erkhar hurried to the navigation helm. Over the faithful's shoulder he saw the cartographic readout that he had pulled up.

'That's Drakaasi,' said the faithful, pointing to a planet marker on the screen, 'and this is the route still loaded into the navigation cogitators. It looks like the route the ship was on when it crashed here.'

Erkhar followed the arc of the ship's path. Its destination was only a short distance from Drakaasi. With a good, fast ship such as the *Hammer* undoubtedly was, it could be reached in less than an hour.

'They were so close,' said Erkhar. 'It must have been the Emperor's will that brought the *Hammer* down to Drakaasi before they reached it. Whatever happened to this ship's pilgrims on Drakaasi, it was surely no worse than what lay past the rift.'

'We'll steer well clear,' said the faithful, 'but what then?'

'Get clear of Drakaasi, and clear of the Eye if we can,' replied Erkhar. His eyes shone. 'Then we find the Promised Land.'

EVERY SINGLE LIVING thing in Vel'Skan had chosen its side.

The power of treachery flowed through the streets of the city like pure molten hatred. Smiths turned their hammers on one another. Drill daemons on the parade grounds ordered one rank to attack another. Strangers in the street called out who was with them and who was against, and knives came out in the alleyways. Half pledged themselves to Ebondrake and the correct order of Drakaasi's monarchy. Half devoted themselves to toppling him, to disorder, ruination and chaos.

The two armies collided all across the city, not just in the Antediluvian Valley, but across Vel'Skan, in every temple and forge, every place one human could murder another.

In the valley, Lord Ebondrake himself led the charge. His great wings pounded once, and he hauled himself up into the air, crashing down on Tiresia the Huntress. He dug her crushed body from beneath him, flipped her into the air and snapped his jaws shut on her, swallowing her in one gulp. Thousands of arrows and spears rained against him, but he breathed a sheet of black fire over Tiresia's tribespeople, and a hundred of them died, gutted to charred skeletons by the force of Ebondrake's anger.

Thousands of Scathach's men slammed into the scaephylyd tide. Scathach himself drew the ancient bolt gun from his back, a relic of his days in the Traitor Legions, and put bolter shells through a score of scaephylyd bodies as his ranks of warriors struggled to hold back the living wave.

The slaves staked to the ground exploded, gore showering down, as daemons fresh and raw from the warp emerged from their possessed bodies. Wet muscle glistened all over them, new limbs withering and reforming as they vomited scalding blood, and ripped into the slimy host led by Thurgull. The Charnel Lord's dead horde clambered over the bodies as they mounted up, dragging soldiers and daemons into caves of the newly dead to devour them.

The battle spilled out of the valley. Daemonic spawn and tentacled horrors from the sea wrestled through the temple galleries and sacred precincts, scattering statues and relics of Khorne. Tiresia's surviving hunters took the battle to the air, flying their aerial beasts of prey into a swirling melee with winged daemons streaming from Vel'Skan's eyries.

After a few minutes, no one remembered why they were fighting. There was a sense of betrayal on both sides, but the details were lost in the blood. Arguthrax, thrashing with a huge mace as his cauldron was hauled forwards through the heaps of dead, did not care to remember just why he had ordered his battered army forwards into the heart of the scaephylyd mass. The Charnel Lord let the events leading up to the battle sink down into the fevered pit of his mind, and concentrated instead on the holy work of bringing the battle dead back to half-life and setting them on the men they had been fighting alongside.

Ebondrake alone remembered. Part of him stayed calm enough through the carnage to remind him that if he lost, he lost Drakaasi. He would rather die as king than live on as someone's slave. As was right and proper for a servant of the Blood God, Lord Ebondrake sought death as eagerly as he sought victory, and there was no shortage of it choking every avenue of Vel'Skan.

THE ECHOES OF the battle rippled through Drakaasi like an earthquake reaching right through the planet's core. Every one of the planet's great cities felt it and they, too, were suddenly divided. The madmen of the *Scourge* stopped ranting and put their divinations aside to bludgeon one another with anything they could find, or hurl one another into the sea. Crested daemonfish rose from the depths to bask in the blood that foamed beneath the abattoir temples of the *Scourge*.

The singing of Aelazadne turned dark and clashing as its voices were replaced by the gurgle of blood in slit throats. Gorgath's battle lines were suddenly redrawn, one army under the banner of the dragon, and the other preaching revolution as they died. Ghaal seethed with murder, its gutters overflowing with blood and its night alive with the sound of knives through flesh.

Karnikhal began to slowly devour itself.

Drakaasi quaked. The day turned blood red, while on the other side of the planet the stars grew into burning rubies like eyes gorged with bloodshed. Howling winds ripped across the plains, rousing every living thing into a frenzy, turning hidden cabals of cultists against one another or forcing the jungles into bouts of continent-wide cannibalism, predators and prey turning on their own. Even in the depths of the sea, bizarre creatures, unknown on the surface, ripped one another to shreds with needle-like teeth.

There was a sound on the wind that carried further than the clashing of blades and the screams of the dying.

It was laughter.

Khorne was enjoying this particular spectacle.

TWENTY-FIVE

DUKE VENALITOR LEFT behind footprints of Kelhedros's blood as he stalked through the trophy
chamber.

He had never been here. Very few, save Ebondrake, ever had. He did not know his way around.
He had not expected it to be this huge, or for there
to be so many places for Alaric to hide.

Somewhere in the sea of corruption that Venalitor had for a mind, frustration surfaced.

'The men you killed in your madness,' said Venalitor, 'they were the ones I took from the cities of
Sarthis Majoris, some of your Guardsmen, too. Did
you recognise them as you killed them?'

There was no answer from the darkness. Night
had fallen, and the only light bled from a few

glowing orbs scattered around the trophy collection, apparently placed there to make the bladed shadows longer.

'What about Skarhaddoth? I saw you kill him. You are the champion of Drakaasi. How does it feel to be proclaimed the planet's most dedicated servant of Khorne?'

A footstep reached Venalitor's ears. He froze, his blade held low, ready to cut the legs out from under the charging Grey Knight.

Venalitor pivoted, and sliced through the dark shape looming towards him. His blade cut clean through the body, the hanging body, strung by a noose from the ceiling, an executed enemy of Ebondrake's left to dangle and rot in the trophy room.

He was jumping at nothing.

Alaric smashed through a bank of blades and shields, scattering ancient weapons everywhere. A blade hammered down and caught Venalitor's sword, snapping the star-forged metal, and sending half the blade spinning off into the shadows.

Venalitor threw himself backwards. He barely escaped being bowled to the ground by Alaric's impact.

Alaric landed heavily, but on his feet, cracking the tiles underneath him. He carried a halberd in his hand: the Nemesis weapon of a Grey Knight.

In his other hand was the gauntlet-mounted storm bolter.

'I hope Ebondrake enjoyed your little gift,' said Alaric, noticing the moment of shock passing over

Venalitor's face as he saw Alaric's weapons. 'It cost you more than you realise.'

Venalitor's eyes flickered down to the haft in his hand and the broken stump of its blade.

'That was my favourite sword,' he growled. He gave up all pretence that he was a normal man, and his features melted away, his nose and mouth joining into one circular fanged orifice and his eyes becoming liquid slits. With a practised motion, Venalitor drew a pair of short swords from his back.

'Now,' said Alaric, 'we're almost even.'

'Almost,' hissed the thing that called itself Duke Venalitor.

The ring of their blades clashing was so rapid and relentless that it sounded like the trophy chamber was filled with driving rain. Venalitor slashed too fast to see, but his blades rang off Alaric's halberd. Alaric knocked Venalitor back with raw strength, his greater reach letting him hack out in arcing strikes, too artless to wound, but enough to force Venalitor back across the chamber, step by step.

Alaric fired a burst from his storm bolter. Venalitor swatted the bolter shells away like insects. Venalitor ducked low and cut down at Alaric's legs. Alaric blocked one strike with the butt of his halberd, swung the blade down to turn the second, and kicked out to catch Venalitor in the chin. A deep cut was opened up in Venalitor's monstrous face, and from the wound reached tendrils of blood, snaking towards Alaric's limbs to entangle them and leave the Grey Knight defenceless.

Alaric grabbed a handful of the tendrils with his bolter hand, and forced them up to his mouth. He bit into them, tearing at them, like he had torn at the raw meat of the Hathran sacrifice in his half-remembered madness. The tendrils fell limp, and Alaric spat out the blood.

He had learned a lot. He could fight like an animal when he had to. He could give up everything he had ever been taught in the duelling vaults of Titan and revert to the brutality written into his blood. He could go further than his enemy, be more relentless, more devoted to bloodshed. That was what Drakaasi had taught him.

Alaric shattered one of Venalitor's swords, knocked the other one aside, and grabbed the swordsman's wrist. He picked Venalitor up, and threw him through the great siege engine in the centre of the chamber. The machine came apart and collapsed, scattering blood-blackened timbers and chunks of iron everywhere.

Venalitor rolled onto his front and got to his knees. Alaric didn't give him the chance to regain his feet. He picked up a length of wood, and smacked Venalitor around the side of the head, hard enough to throw him back again, crashing through a stand of ornamental armour.

Venalitor's hand closed on nothing. He was on the edge of a sudden drop.

He had come to rest on the edge of the opening formed by the skull's eye socket. To one side, through the other eye, stabbed the corroded form

of the *Hammer of Daemons*, shards of rust flaking off
it as it shuddered with the force of its engines.

Beneath was Vel'Skan.

The sight of Vel'Skan at war was enough to strike
the voice from Venalitor's throat. Armies clashed in
the streets. Banners of a dozen lords waved as their
followers clashed. A gout of black flame showed
that Ebondrake himself was fighting. The outskirts
of Vel'Skan were already aflame, tinting Drakaasi's
night a dull orange.

Daemons danced through the carnage. Killers
competed to die first.

'Survival,' said Alaric, 'was never enough.'

'This… this was you,' said Venalitor. His monstrous face was bleeding away as the rage was
replaced with wonder. 'Arguthrax and I, Raezazel,
Gorgath, your madness, this was all you. It was all
your plan.'

'Of course. I am a Grey Knight. I could hardly
come to a world like Drakaasi and leave it intact.'

'You turned us against one another. Our hatred
was our strength and our weakness. Our pride, our
wrath, our devotion, all these were just a weapon
for you.' Venalitor smiled. 'The Dark Gods would be
proud of you, Justicar.'

Alaric had never heard anything so hateful,
because he knew that it was true.

He fired his storm bolter point-blank into Venalitor's chest. Venalitor's armour held, but the force of
the exploding bolter shell was enough to knock
him off his feet.

There was no floor behind him to break his fall. He dropped his sword as he flailed at nothing.

Venalitor fell from the eye socket of Lord Ebondrake's castle. Tendrils of blood lashed out for something to grab onto, but they found nothing. His eyes met Alaric's as he fell, and there was something like horror in them.

Alaric watched Venalitor fall, following him down into the darkness of Vel'Skan.

Haulvarn had been avenged. Alaric sought some elation at that fact, but it was as elusive as Raezazel's truth. There could be no triumph on this tainted world.

Alaric turned away from the eye socket, away from the sight of Vel'Skan at war, and headed for the *Hammer of Daemons*.

THE HAMMER WAS shuddering as its plasma reactors filled up with superheated fuel. Most of the corrosion had been shaken off it, revealing the deep blue of its hull and the gold painted decoration. It must have been a truly magnificent craft when it was launched. It still was extraordinary, and it was ready to take off.

Alaric hurried up the steps towards the torture chamber, dragging his armour behind him. He saw that the boarding ramp of the *Hammer* was still down, but judging by the roar of the engines it wouldn't stay that way for long. It was time to leave Drakaasi.

He heard footsteps behind him. He turned to see One-ear and his surviving orks, still slathered in scaephylyd blood.

One-ear looked at Alaric, and then up at the *Hammer of Daemons*, and in his alien mind he must have known that this was the only chance he and his fellow greenskins had to get off Drakaasi.

One-ear spat on the ground, snarled at Alaric, and led his orks back down the steps towards the war-torn streets of Vel'Skan.

'Justicar!' shouted Corporal Dorvas from the ship's boarding ramp. 'We're on autopilot! We'll leave you behind if we have to!'

Alaric hurried up the ramp just as it began to close and the engines rose in pitch. Plasma was coursing through the ship's conduits, swirling from the reactors through the engines. Inside, the Hathrans were finding whatever they could to hold on to as the ship began to shudder even more, throwing aside anything that wasn't fixed. Candles rolled across the tilting floor and sacred texts fluttered from the walls.

'I see you've found your gear,' said Dorvas, looking down at the power armour that Alaric was hauling along. 'If you get us off this planet you'll have earned it back.'

'Where are we going?' asked Alaric.

'We're worrying about that once we're off Drakaasi,' replied Dorvas.

The *Hammer's* engines flared, and all sound was drowned out as the plasma generators came on-line.

The whole ship lurched, and the sound of breaking bone signalled that the ship, after centuries

embedded in the palace of Vel'Skan, was finally taking off.

LORD EBONDRAKE'S PALACE split in two. Shards of
bone fell and impaled battling cultists on the
palace approach below. The engines flared and
blew out the back of the cranium, incinerating
dozens as plasma fire spewed from the exhaust
housings. The cranium collapsed, burying the torture chamber and trophy hall in a rockslide of
fragmented bone. The *Hammer of Daemons* was
finally free. The last of the corrosion was thrown off
it, and, lit by the fires of the burning city, the ship
rose on vertical thrusters to look out over Vel'Skan.

Very few saw it. Most were too busy killing and
being killed. A few did notice it, and assumed it was
a weapon called forth by Ebondrake or the conspirators. Perhaps Ebondrake's enemies had sent it to
destroy the palace, or perhaps Ebondrake had
finally chosen to reveal it, sacrificing his palace to
bring some ancient wrath down on Arguthrax and
his fellow traitors.

Very few, even of those who saw it, particularly
cared. It was just a distraction from the killing.

ALARIC FOUGHT TO keep his footing as he pushed his
bulk through the door in the bulkhead designed for
a man a metre shorter. The *Hammer* shuddered
again, and Alaric nearly fell. He had to hurry. By the
time the *Hammer* escaped Drakaasi's atmosphere it
might be too late.

The flight deck of the *Hammer of Daemons* was as lavishly decorated as the rest of the ship. The blue walls were inlaid with long ribbons of gold, forged into images from the life of the prophet Raezazel.

The ship's shuttle craft had survived the years intact, sealed inside the flight deck away from the ravages of Drakaasi. It was deep blue and chased in gold like the rest of the ship, and decorated with multiple stylised mouths, which Alaric realised, with a lurch, must be the symbol of Raezazel. A dozen mouths had spoken from the daemon's flesh as it taunted him. Alaric opened the access hatch in the body of the shuttle and threw his war gear inside. He could wear it again when it had been purified.

'Good idea,' said Gearth. Alaric turned to see the killer, still smeared with blood and war paint. 'This thing's full of mental cases. They think they're flying right up the Emperor's arse. If they're wrong, we could end up anywhere, and if they're right, then… well, me an' the Emperor ain't seen eye to eye since I was born.'

'Why are you here?' asked Alaric.

'Same reason as you,' replied Gearth. 'To get off this thing, and take my chances on my own. You're tough, Justicar, but you don't know the nethers of the Imperium like me. Fighting's all very well, but me, I could hitchhike my way out of the Eye. You could use someone like me around.'

'You said once,' said Alaric, 'that you didn't know why you committed your crimes, why you killed those women.'

Gearth glanced around as if afraid that someone was listening. 'I guess. What does it matter?'

'You never will.'

Alaric shot Gearth once in the stomach. The bolter shell exploded in his abdomen and blew a length of spine out of his back. Gearth flopped to the ground.

'The Blood...' he gasped. 'The Blood God... promised...'

Alaric started to clamber into the shuttle.

'You're gonna... leave 'em...' said Gearth, his pained whisper barely audible over the ship's engines. 'Gonna... leave 'em all... the Guard boys, everyone... just... to die out here...'

Alaric ignored the dying man, and hauled the shuttle's hatch closed behind him.

The cockpit was barely big enough for Alaric to fit. He thumbed a command stud, and the flight deck doors ground open. The air in the deck boomed out into the thin atmosphere and took Gearth's body with it, the flimsy corpse trailing blood as it tumbled out into Drakaasi's night. Alaric gunned the shuttle's engines and flew it out of the flight deck, feeling the waves of superheated air from the *Hammer's* engines buffeting it as if it was a falling leaf.

He wrestled for control. He cleared the *Hammer's* wake and had it back.

Now, it really was time to get away from this planet.

* * *

'THE FLIGHT DECK just opened,' said Haggard, clinging to a guard rail around a floating relic as he stumbled onto the bridge. 'Someone took a shuttle out.'

'Then they have forsaken their life's reward,' replied Erkhar calmly. The streams of the upper atmosphere were hammering against the hull, and anything loose was being thrown about, but Erkhar was as calm as if he was sailing on a glassy sea. The rift in space shone in front of him, filling the bridge with crimson light, opening to swallow the *Hammer of Daemons*.

'What's that?' asked Haggard.

'The rift,' replied Erkhar. 'Switch off the autopilot. We'll take her away from Drakaasi on manual.'

'Yes, lieutenant,' said the faithful at the navigation helm.

'The Emperor will show us the way,' said Erkhar as the ship swung away from the rift, towards the billowing nebulae of the Eye of Terror. 'We have but to listen. In our prayers, in our dreams, there is the way to the Promised Land.'

TWENTY-SIX

DUKE VENALITOR'S BODY was impaled on one of the many swords making up the web of steel into which were built the thousands of homes where Vel'Skan's poorest dwelt. The point went in through his back and out through his chest, just below the scar on his armour left by Alaric's bolter shot.

He was alive when he hit. With his spine cut, Venalitor couldn't even writhe, just lie there as the pain racked through him and his body slowly slid down the blade blunted by time.

No one noticed him die. Below him was a battle with no lines, a swirling melee where all sense of order and alignment had broken down and everyone was out killing for himself. It was a riot, a massacre, and a scene being repeated throughout

Vel'Skan, but more than that, it was infecting the whole of Drakaasi.

Venalitor's head lolled to one side. He could see something burning on a blood river snaking out of Vel'Skan's outskirts. It was a ship, his ship, the *Hecatomb*, cut loose from its moorings beneath the city. It blazed from stem to stern.

The wards would have been breached. What was held prisoner there would escape. Venalitor knew then that he should have killed it when he had the chance.

For someone who had not been human for so long, the last thing Venalitor felt was a very human emotion.

He felt despair.

ALARIC SAW THE army falling back through the city, beetle-black swarms of scaephylyds pouring in from every side.

He saw Arguthrax, carried aloft by a tide of daemons, blazing a path of fire and ruination towards Ebondrake's palace. Arguthrax would take the palace, but, once there, he would find that its greatest prize was already gone.

He saw Lord Ebondrake on the pinnacle of a mighty temple, holding its brass dome against a horde of Vel'Skan's citizens who had gathered in a spontaneous army to bring him down. He incinerated them by the dozen, but there were too many of them, and they had set the temple alight, and were working at its columns with picks and hammers.

Soon it would collapse, and even Lord Ebondrake would be gone.

Similar scenes were playing out all across the city. Streets were like cities of fire, buildings like sacrificial candles, battle like a disease gradually claiming everything.

Alaric looked away from the city. There was nothing he could do now to make it worse. He aimed the shuttle's controls upwards, accelerating to orbital speed. He glanced down at the fuel gauge. Much of the fuel had evaporated in the shuttle's tanks in its years lying idle, but there was just enough to get him out of orbit once he was beyond the atmosphere, and perhaps to somewhere the Inquisition would find him. That was why he had left the *Hammer of Daemons*. Even if Erkhar's Promised Land was real, there was no place in it for Alaric, not yet.

The swirls of Drakaasi's atmosphere gave way to the diseased void of the Eye of Terror. It wasn't a good place to be cut adrift, but it was safer than Drakaasi. Alaric could survive for years if he had to in half-sleep, his brain shut down until only the most basic of life processes were continued. After Drakaasi, he could do with a few good years to think it all over.

As Alaric let the main engines kick in, a plume of orange flame licked up from Vel'Skan. It was Ebondrake's temple, finally collapsing in a ball of fire. Ebondrake was probably dead.

Alaric took no satisfaction at all from that knowledge.

The rumble of the planet's atmosphere ceased, and Alaric left Drakaasi behind forever.

RAEZAZEL THE CUNNING licked the blood from Dorvas's face.

Around him, hundreds of Hathrans lay torn and bloody on the deck of the *Hammer of Daemons*. He had come to them as swift as a whirlwind, their tiny determined minds reduced to fear, and then silence, by Raezazel's touch.

He slid through the corridors and decks of the ship. It was as familiar as one of his own forms, like a cloak of flesh that fit him perfectly: the shrines and inscriptions put up by pilgrims who never understood that they were doing the work of Chaos; the ship's own structure, in itself a subtle prayer to the Liar God; the smell and the feel of it.

The *Hecatomb* had burned, the wards about his prison had crumbled, and Raezazel had been free. His punishment at Venalitor's hands had been severe, but Raezazel was still a daemon, still a thing of the warp, and he was still dangerous. He had bled through Vel'Skan, revelling in the war overtaking it, and had found the *Hammer of Daemons* as he had left it in the half-blinded skull. Boarding it had been simple. Scything through the Hathrans had been more taxing than Raezazel had anticipated, for he was out of practice, but it felt so good to be free, so good to kill. He would soon get the hang of it again.

Raezazel slipped up the decks towards the bridge. As he went, the Hathrans tried to fight him, but their eyes went blind with shock as he punched tentacles through their stomachs or extruded golden sickle blades to slice them apart. Some he sucked dry, leaving them husks like the cast-off skins of lizards. A few, he melted into the sacred walls of the *Hammer* or turned inside-out.

He was powerful now. He was free of his bonds. One form had been crippled, but a hundred more emerged into existence. He was glorious. He was the Lie given form.

The bridge was ahead. Raezazel melted the blast doors into a pool of molten gold.

Inside was the most beautiful collection of minds that Raezazel had seen for many centuries.

They believed.

He could taste their faith. They believed in a religion that had sprung up from the detritus of Raezazel's own flock: snatches of sacred writings, half-formed memories of the pilgrimage. From nothing had sprung yet more believers in the lie.

Raezazel laughed. What a wondrous thing. Without willing it, his deception of his pilgrim flock had given rise to a whole new breed of deluded faithful.

Raezazel swept onto the bridge, taking on the form of a nightmare.

ERKHAR GRABBED THE autopistol holstered beneath the command pulpit. He didn't bother to aim, since the daemon boiling onto the bridge was large enough for any shot to hit it.

He loosed off half the weapon's magazine, ears full of screams and rushing blood. Hoygens disappeared into the daemon's churning blue-gold mass.

They had come so close. They had left Drakaasi and its horrors behind, and now this.

At least they had got a taste of what it meant to be free. This was what Erkhar told himself as bladed tendrils wrapped around his waist and sliced his stomach open.

He was lifted off the pulpit. He dropped his pistol, and his hand with it, a golden scythe having sliced through his arm at the wrist. He looked into the scores of eyes and mouths looming in front of him and knew instinctively that he was in the clutches of Raezazel the Cunning.

Erkhar screamed in defiance, and a hundred mouths devoured him.

RAEZAZEL REACHED OUT and plucked the soul from the faithful at the navigation helm, rending the insubstantial stuff of the spirit from the fleshy frame. Other pilgrims were trying to flee or to fight back. Those who fought amused Raezazel greatly, stabbing at him with whatever came to hand. A couple had guns from the ship's armoury. Raezazel turned the floor beneath them to liquid, and they sank to their thighs in molten gold, spasming in shock as they were incinerated.

The *Hammer of Daemons* was a fine ship. Once the bridge was clear, Raezazel could take it over and fly it to a new world. There, he would begin again. He would find himself a planet of the ignorant and the desperate, and give them a prophet. Tzeentch would finally have his due.

Raezazel absorbed a man named Hoygens, and devoured his memories, glimpsing scenes of a life of fear and horror, and the final delicious denial of his faith.

He was so enraptured with eating Hoygens's ignorant mind that for a moment Raezazel did not notice the last survivor grabbing the autopistol on the floor.

HAGGARD KICKED ERKHAR'S severed hand aside and picked up the pistol. He stumbled back against the navigation helm as the full horror of Raezazel oozed finally onto the bridge. The last few faithful were disappearing into its mass. Haggard knew that the others on the ship were dead. There would be no freedom from Drakaasi. None of them would survive.

Finally, Haggard understood that survival was not enough.

Hundreds of eyes turned to look at him. Haggard didn't know if he could move. It was the most horrible thing he had ever seen, glowing blue flesh and golden blades, rippling with silver.

'Where…' he stuttered, 'where are my friends? Are they dead?'

'Of course,' replied Raezazel in a hundred voices at once.

'Good,' said Haggard. He slammed the butt of the pistol down on the navigation helm.

The command stud rescinded the last coordinates input into the cogitator. The *Hammer of Daemons* reverted back to its previous course: the way to the Promised Land.

Haggard emptied the rest of the gun's ammunition into the navigation helm. The controls exploded in sparks and blue flames. Haggard fell to the deck, slick with the blood of the faithful.

Raezazel the Cunning looked up at the viewscreen. The *Hammer of Daemons* swung around, the stars marching past until the view centred on a glowing red slash in space. It was the warp rift, the gateway to the warp into which Raezazel had promised to deliver souls for Tzeentch.

The daemon's eyes widened in something like fear.

Raezazel threw Haggard aside, but the controls were ruined. Raezazel's realm was the human mind. Machines were just tools, just pieces of metal. He had no way of rewriting the ship's cogitators as he might rewrite the memories of a victim.

Deep inside the warp rift, a great golden eye opened.

The *Hammer of Daemons's* main engines kicked in, propelling the ship towards the rift. It grew larger and larger in the viewscreen, the eye unblinking, transfixing Raezazel where he stood.

'RAEZAZEL,' said a voice that boiled up from the warp. *'YOU PROMISED ME SOULS. YOU PROMISED ME THE FAITHFUL. YOU HAVE FAILED ME.'*

For those last few moments, Raezazel screamed, and Haggard laughed.

ALARIC WATCHED FROM the cockpit of the shuttle as the *Hammer of Daemons* suddenly veered off course, main engines flaring. The ship rocketed towards the red slash that Alaric had guessed was the warp rift, the intended destination of Raezazel's flock.

There could be little doubt that everyone on the ship was doomed: Dorvas and the brave men of the Hathran Armoured Cavalry, who had been failed once more by Alaric; Erkhar, whose faith had kept him sane while men like Gearth were losing their souls; and Haggard, the only friend Alaric had really had on Drakaasi.

He tried to grieve for them. He tried to feel the weight of their deaths on him, but he was tired, and he could feel nothing.

Alaric lay back in the grav-seat of the shuttle. The constellations of the Eye of Terror whirled around him in their endless pattern, unconquerable and infinite.

Alaric wanted very much to sleep. He surrendered his mind to the suspended animation membrane that covered his brain, and the stars went dark.

* * *

ALARIC STAYED IN suspended animation for seven months.

The catalepsean node in his brain shut down everything except for his breathing and heartbeats. He woke once every several weeks to deplete the shuttle's meagre food and water stash and keep his muscles from atrophying. He was glad when he went back into suspension, because in deep, total sleep he did not dream.

A salvage team trailing an Imperial battlefleet found the distress beacon on Alaric's shuttle. Thinking it was a saviour pod from a larger ship, and that they could ransom the crew inside to the Imperial Navy, they eagerly boarded the shuttle among visions of retiring on the armfuls of credits the Navy was sure to give them for the officers inside. By the time they breached the hull they had become convinced that the occupants were officers, rapidly rising in rank until they expected to see a rear admiral or fleet commissar weeping with joy to see them.

Instead, they got their first look at a real live Space Marine.

Since they had no idea how valuable a Space Marine might be, but were very aware of how dangerous he was, the salvage crew debated whether to cast off and leave the shuttle to drift. The Space Marine's great size suggested that he would eat too much for the salvage ship to be able to make it back to port without running out of supplies. Other crew members were in favour of killing him, since he was no doubt a devout warrior monk hell bent on exterminating evildoers, and none of the crew had particularly spotless records. Alaric put a stop to all this by kicking down the airlock door and telling them that if they did not take him to a location of his choosing, he would kill them. The crew believed him.

His chosen location was the Inquisitorial fortress on Belsimar.

THE GENERAL LUMBERED up onto the peak of the ridge. He had lost many limbs in the past few months, but he still had just enough to drag his insect bulk around. His abdomen was covered in scars, and his mandibles were blunted by enemy armour and bone, but he was alive, and that was more than could be said for any of Drakaasi's lords. They had burned brightly, charging at the head of their armies, and duelling one another in week-long conflicts, but they had burned out first as well.

The old scaephylyd took in the scene around him. Aelazadne stood in the distance, its crystal towers shattered and blackened like the stumps of decaying teeth. In the valleys formed by the undulations of the plain, he could see bands of humans, near-feral, armed with teeth and fingers and the odd stone spear, scrapping with one another.

New champions would be born from this, new heroes of the Dark Gods. They would look upon the collapsed heap of ancient weapons in Vel'Skan and the corpse-mountains of Gorgath, and they would seek to emulate those who had created them. The general, and the scaephylyd nation, had seen it happen before.

For now, there was nothing: no order, no structure, and no power save that which a man could wrench from the bodies of his enemies.

More scaephylyds clambered up the ridge. Many of them were scarred by war too, and all of them had become veterans. It had been a long time since the scaephylyds had marched to war, and before long, when the predatory war bands began to organise themselves again, they would retreat below the earth and take up waiting once more.

Among the scaephylyds were newcomers. Green-skinned and hulking, most of them were brute animals, barely able to hold an axe the right way, but a few of them had enough cunning to lead their fellow creatures, and one, the grizzled one-eared greenskin, had a light in his eyes that suggested he might still understand.

The scaephylyds and greenskins assembled around the general, lowering their weapons in deference. The general waved a forelimb, encompassing the shattered city and the landscape still torn by desperate, endless war.

'Do you see now?' he asked, his intonation of the scaephylyd tongue a momentous rumble. 'Chaos.'

'THIS PLACE,' SAID Inquisitor Nyxos, 'used to be a pleasure world.'

Nyxos leaned his old body against the railing of the balcony. He looked out on a rampant forest dappled with dead browns and greys. Colonies of swooping predators fought for scraps in the treetops. The sky was stained, and the rivers flowing down from the distant mountains were the colour of mud.

'You could win a place here with a lifetime of service and a few medals. Lord generals, admirals, that sort of thing. Good hunting, plenty of imported lads and lasses, all very willing. Hot and cold running narcotics. Well worth a couple of centuries in the trenches.' Nyxos turned away from the sight with a smile. 'I suppose the planet didn't like it.'

Alaric did not return his smile. There wasn't anything particularly funny about Belsimar.

The stately pile, half-reclaimed by the forest, had apparently once been the Inquisitorial fortress. All the equipment had been stripped out when the planet decided to turn on its inhabitants, but the mansion still had warrens of cells and storage vaults beneath the handsome exterior. Alaric fancied it looked better now than it had ever done, its garish mosaics fragmented and its overwrought architecture split and dragged down by the forest. Belsimar had been worth watching over once, no doubt because of the temptations of pleasure cults and the dangerous nature of knowledge being brought together by noteworthy people from across the Imperium.

'You picked a hell of a place to turn up, you know,' said Nyxos.

'It was the only place I could think of in the Eye that wasn't under siege,' replied Alaric. 'I'm surprised I remembered anything was here.' Alaric had heard that there was an Inquisitorial facility on Belsimar from an inquisitor he had been assigned to before he had attained the rank of justicar. That same inquisitor was probably elsewhere in the Eye, trying to fend off the tide of Chaos that was flowing out of the Eye.

'And I'm surprised you're alive.'

'Haulvarn is dead.'

'So is Thane. Dvorn and Visical made it.'

'They're alive?' For the first time in a very long time Alaric felt something like elation. He had thought he was the only one left.

'They made it to a refinery and got out on the last fuel container. Dvorn is assigned to Brother-Captain Stern's Terminator retinue. Visical's under Inquisitor Deskanel around Agripinna. I don't know how they are faring, I'm afraid. Things are rather confused around the Eye.'

'Not so confused that you couldn't find me.'

'Ah, Justicar, what are friends for?' Nyxos sat on the stone bench beside Alaric. The room had once been a ballroom, with grand windows opening onto the balcony and its once stunning view. Now chunks of fallen decor and an orchestra pit full of dead leaves were all that remained of its opulence. 'I have read your preliminary report.'

'The full one will be a lot longer.'

'So it will, so it will.' Nyxos looked up at the sound of footsteps on the stairs. 'Ah, Hawkespur.'

The last time Alaric had seen Interrogator Hawkespur, he hadn't been able to tell if she was dying or not. It had evidently been a close thing. The lower half of her face was ruined by pockmarks and chemical burns from the pollution she had inhaled on Chaeroneia, and the front of her throat was taken up by a bulky rebreather unit. She still wore her naval uniform, stripped of its insignia. She was carrying a heavy piece of machinery that looked like it was designed to punch holes in metal.

'It's primed, sir,' she said, her voice stiff and metallic.

'It'll work?' asked Nyxos.

'There were good results with prisoners at Subiaco,' replied Hawkespur.

'Then proceed, interrogator.'

Hawkespur stood behind Alaric. Even with him seated, she had to hold the device at eye level to reach. Clamps fastened around the Collar of Khorne around Alaric's neck. A flash of heat hit the back of Alaric's neck, and the clamps banged shut. Alaric felt pain, and a great pressure on his neck. Metal complained, and then barked as it was sheared through.

The two halves of the Collar of Khorne clanged to the floor.

Alaric gasped. He saw the ghost of Belsimar, the image of a beautiful planet flickering over the dreary landscape. Then it was gone, replaced with a new hyper-awareness. Alaric could feel the echo of

Belsimar's sorrow, and the pain of the war in the stars overhead.

'Did it work?' asked Nyxos.

'Yes,' said Alaric, a slight shudder in his voice. 'I am whole again.'

'You will be back to normal in a few days,' said Nyxos. 'Disorientation is normal.' He prodded the remains of the collar with his toe. 'Dispose of this thing,' he said. Hawkespur obliged, picking the halves of the collar up with sanctified tongs and carrying them away.

'I'm glad she's alive,' said Alaric when she was gone. He fingered the callous around his neck where the collar had rubbed away at his skin.

'She would say the same about you,' said Nyxos, 'if she felt that such a thing was appropriate. We had written you off, Alaric, I am sorry to say. When we found out who had raided Sarthis Majoris we feared the worst. I hoped that you had died on that battlefield, Emperor forgive me.'

'Perhaps...' said Alaric faltering, still coping with the return of his psychic awareness, 'perhaps it would not have been such a bad thing.'

'What makes you say that?' asked Nyxos. He did not sound surprised to hear it. 'There are few enough Grey Knights in the galaxy. Why would it benefit from one less?'

'To survive,' said Alaric, 'I did some terrible things. I turned Drakaasi's lords on one another, just like a cultist would to foment rebellion. I consorted with heretics, and aliens. I left a great many people to die to escape, and to get revenge. A Grey Knight would not have done those things. Many times, I wondered if the right thing to do would be to just die, but I… could not. I had to survive. I had to go that far, and even survival was not enough.'

'You fear corruption,' said Nyxos.

'I do. More than anything. I know what fear is now.'

Nyxos smiled again. He was a very old man, probably centuries old, and even by Inquisitorial standards he had done a sterling job of avoiding death. He had probably seen just about every strange and terrible form corruption could take, but a Grey Knight who had fallen was beyond any of that. 'Alaric, there are ways you can be purified. It is not easy, or painless, but it can be done. We have ways.'

'Can I fight as a Grey Knight again?'

'Ah, what an interesting question. There is more than one way for a Grey Knight to serve, and many more for you. You have an imagination, Alaric, dedication, yes, but creativity too. How many Grey Knights could have survived on Drakaasi? Ignoring whether it was right or not, how many could have thought it up in the first place?'

'Not many,' admitted Alaric.

'That is something to be proud of. It is another blade in the Emperor's hand. I dare say my word would get you back into the training halls of Titan, if that is where you can best serve, but matters at the Eye are reaching a dire state and we need more than

Ben Counter

just soldiers, even Grey Knights.' Nyxos dusted his hands on his long dark robes and stood up. 'Our shuttle leaves in two hours. Say some prayers and forgive yourself for a while. Think about what you can do for your Emperor, instead of what sins you committed in the past. I have some very particular plans for you, Justicar Alaric. You might be surprised just what a man of your skills can achieve. Although no one on Drakaasi would be in any doubt.' Nyxos followed Hawkespur down to the lower floors of the mansion and the shuttle hangar.

Alaric hung his head, feeling the psychic eye inside him blinking in the sudden light. He was glad that it had been shut while he was on Drakaasi. The underlying ugliness of the place might have been too much.

He thought about Haulvarn and Erkhar, and the Hathrans on the *Hammer of Daemons*. He thought about Raezazel, Ebondrake and Arguthrax. He saw Venalitor's face as he fell, the expression turning to horror as he realised he had failed. Thinking about it, reliving it, would not change it.

He clasped his hands in front of him and began to pray.

'I am the Hammer,' he whispered. 'I am the point of His spear, the mail about His fist…'

and framed her severe, angular face. A scarf of black silk covered the Navigator's high forehead, concealing the pineal eye that was the source of her psychic talents. Gabriella turned her head slightly as Ragnar's gaze fell upon her and nodded a curt greeting. Then she rested her hands in her lap and turned her attention back to the Great Wolf.

Ragnar stepped forward and knelt before the Grimnar. 'Lady Gabriella said a ship has come from Charys bearing news,' he said without preamble. 'What has happened? Why didn't the astropaths–'

'According to the Lady Gabriella, you encountered the Chaos sorcerer Madox on Hyades,' the Great Wolf said, cutting Ragnar off. 'What did he say to you?'

The question took the young Space Wolf aback. 'We did not meet face to face,' he replied. 'He only revealed himself through one of his minions, just as we were about to leave the planet.'

'And?' Logan growled.

'He said his men were going to kill us,' Ragnar said with a shrug.

Grimnar turned, fixing the young Space Wolf with an icy gaze. 'What of the Spear of Russ? Did he say anything about it?'

Ragnar frowned. 'No, lord, he didn't. The traitor Cadmus, however, claimed that Madox was seeking a relic that was a crucial component of a ritual he sought to perform, a ritual that also depended upon Space Marine geneseed.' A chill raced down Ragnar's spine. 'This was all in my earlier report. What is all this about?'

'Madox has been sighted on Charys, lad,' spoke a voice beside the council table. Ragnar turned to meet the gaze of Ranek, the great Wolf Priest. 'He has the Spear of Russ with him.'

Ragnar leapt to his feet, startled by the news. 'The Spear!' he said, forgetting himself. Russ be praised, he thought, perhaps all is not lost.

'This is hardly a cause for celebration, lad!' Ranek snapped. 'Now the full scope of the Chaos incursion becomes clear.'

'How so?' Ragnar asked.

Ranek reached down and touched a rune at the edge of the council table. A hololith mounted in the tabletop glowed to life, creating a detailed star map of the sector. Fenris lay near the centre of the map. Systems currently under attack or in revolt shone brighter than the rest. Minor attacks or incursions were coloured yellow, while major attacks were red. Ragnar was shocked to see that more than thirty systems were affected.

'We have been studying the pattern of the Chaos incursion since it began,' the Wolf Priest said, 'trying to ascertain their ultimate objective. Many of the initial uprisings made sense from a military standpoint: forge worlds, industrialised hive worlds and trade centres, attacks designed to sow confusion and cripple our ability to respond. But many others confounded us.' He pointed to a pulsing red system. 'Ceta Pavonis, an airless rock occupied by gangs of pirates and slavers. Or here: Grendel IV, an old world all but abandoned three centuries ago when the last of its radium mines played out. Even Charys is nothing more than a minor agri-world, with little strategic value other than its proximity to Fenris. Yet, in each of these places there are major uprisings and reported sightings of Chaos Marines.'

Ragnar considered this. 'Diversions,' he concluded, 'meant to draw our attention from the true objective. What else could they be?'

Ranek gave the young Space Wolf an appraising look. 'What, indeed? We wondered much the same thing.' The Wolf Priest shrugged. 'If they were meant as diversions, then our foes chose poorly. There are far more important systems that require our protection. But we know that our enemies are not fools, however much we would like to believe otherwise. There was a plan at work here, but we could not see it at first.' Ranek gestured at the collection of Rune Priests standing quietly around the table. 'The runes were consulted, and they suggested we seek a new point of view on the problem.'

The young Space Wolf turned, pensive. 'Well, I'm not sure how much help I will be, but if you think I can be of use–'

A melodious laugh rose from the far side of the table, and in moments the assembled Space Wolves joined in, breaking the tension in the room. Gabriella covered her mouth with one pale hand, her human eyes twinkling with mirth. 'Ranek was referring to me,' she said, not unkindly. 'He and the Great Wolf thought I might see a pattern where a warrior might not.'

Ragnar fought to control the flush rising to his cheeks. 'Ah, of course,' he said quickly, 'and were you successful?'

Gabriella's angular features turned sober once more. 'Unfortunately, yes,' she said. She turned to Ranek. 'If you will permit me…'

'Of course, my lady,' the Wolf Priest said, stepping away from the table.

Gabriella rose from her chair and stepped over to the hololith controls. 'The problem was that everyone was viewing the incursion as a military campaign, not unlike a Black Crusade,' she said. 'As Ranek said, nearly all of the minor targets had military value, but if we just focus on the areas with a major Chaos presence, we are left with this.' She touched a rune and the yellow indicators faded from view, leaving thirteen systems scattered in a roughly spherical arrangement around Fenris.

Ragnar studied each of the systems in turn. 'None of these are major military or industrial targets,' he said, a puzzled look on their face.

'Indeed,' she said, 'but, being a Navigator, another prospect suggested itself to me: what if the systems weren't important because of what they were, but rather, *where* they were?'

Gabriella touched another rune. The hololith drew blinking red lines connecting each of the systems together. Ragnar watched them converge, and his eyes went wide. 'It's a symbol of some kind.'

'Not a symbol per se,' Gabriella replied. 'It's a sorcerous sigil, and Charys lies at its centre.' She glanced up at Ragnar. 'Do you remember what the city of Lethe looked like when we left for the *Fist of Russ*?'

Ragnar nodded. 'Fire from the burning promethium lines stretched all across the city. It looked like… well, I remember thinking it looked like a ritual symbol of some kind.'

She nodded. 'That was the ritual symbol establishing Hyades as an anchor point for this larger sigil,' she said, pointing to the blasphemous sign hanging before them. 'Madox has laid the foundation for a sorcerous ritual of enormous proportions. If what you learned from Cadmus is correct, he now has all the elements he needs for the ritual to begin.'

The scope of the sorcerer's plans staggered Ragnar. He looked to the Great Wolf. 'A ship arrived from Charys, bearing news. What has Berek found?'

The Old Wolf's expression turned grim. 'Berek has been gravely wounded,' he said, 'and the Rune Priest Aldrek is believed to be dead.' Logan turned away from the window and stepped heavily to the table.

'When Gabriella revealed the importance of Charys I sent Berek's great company there to bring an end to this monstrous scheme. It appears that Madox was waiting for him. Berek and his men were lured into a trap.'

The Old Wolf leaned forward, resting his scarred knuckles on the table's glass surface. His lined face was grim. 'Mikal Sternmark commands the great company for the moment, and he and the Guard regiments continue to fight against the rebels, but warp storms are growing in the region. Soon the system will be isolated altogether, and the Chaos uprisings have scattered our forces across the sector.' The Old Wolf banged his fist on the tabletop. 'Madox and his one-eyed master must have been planning this for decades. They've outmanoeuvred us, and their teeth are at our throats.'

A low growl began to build in Ragnar's throat. Suddenly he was very aware of the blood rushing through his veins and the pounding of his hearts. Every Space Wolf in the room sensed the change. Hands clenched and heads lowered as they caught the scent of the Wulfen.

'Master yourself, young one,' Ranek said in a low, commanding voice. 'Save the wolf's rage for our foes.'

Ragnar struggled to control his rising fury. 'What of your company, Great Wolf?' he said in a choked voice. 'Surely they can turn the tide at Charys.'

'My company is scattered across our domains, bolstering the efforts of the other Wolf lords who are hard-pressed,' Grimnar replied. 'Berek's company was our reserve force.'

'Send the Wolfblade to Charys, then,' Ragnar snarled, unable to contain himself.

The Old Wolf's fists clenched. 'What, the three of you?' he thundered. 'Do you imagine you'll turn the tide all by yourselves?'

'I'll die in the attempt, if I must!' Ragnar shot back. 'I'd rather lie on a field at Charys than live another day here.'

'Arrogant pup!' Grimnar roared. He straightened to his full height, his fierce presence seeming to fill the entire chamber. He crossed the space between him and Ragnar with a single step, and lashed out with his open hand, cuffing Ragnar on the side of the head. 'I couldn't have said it better myself!'

The Wolves roared with laughter. After a moment, Ragnar joined in as well. Gabriella studied the giants' bloody-minded mirth with an expression of startled bemusement.

'You will have your wish, young Space Wolf,' Grimnar said, clapping Ragnar on the shoulder. 'We are sending every warrior we have left to add their swords to the fight, and Lady Gabriella has pledged her skills to guide our reinforcements safely to Charys,' the Old Wolf said, nodding respectfully to the Navigator.

'Report to Sternmark when you arrive. I'm sure he'll be glad for every stout arm he can get.'

In a flash, Ragnar's anger turned to a fierce, blood-thirsty joy. Death might wait for him on Charys, but so be it, he would face it as a Space Wolf, fighting alongside his battle-brothers. 'The Spear of Russ will be ours once again, lord. On my life and on my honour, I swear it!'

'I hear you, Ragnar Blackmane,' the Old Wolf answered solemnly, 'and Russ hears your oath as well. Spill the blood of our foes and return to us what was lost, and try to set a good example for the lads when you're getting yourself hacked to pieces, eh?'

The action continues in Wolf's Honour, coming soon from the Black Library. *www.blacklibrary.com*